Second Chances

by

Rita M. Reali

Little Elm Press

Copyright 2021, Rita M. Reali
Cover by Al Esper Graphic Design
Author photo by J Addeo, November 1991

Reali, Rita M.
Second Chances

ISBNs:
Paperback: 978-0-9966800-6-6
Ebook: 978-0-9966800-7-3

Printed in the U.S.A.
First American edition, August 2021

Acknowledgments

Many thanks to my dear friend (and fellow award-winning author) Dee Lynk, who has encouraged me throughout the writing and revision process, and been supportive of my literary efforts amid countless lunches and laugh fests.

Thanks, too, to my adopted sister, Monica Hackett, for her periodic "Get to work and write something" exhortations.

Thanks to Christina M. Eder of GuestStarCoaching.com, for her persistent joyfulness and enthusiasm for my deeply flawed characters – and her unflagging confidence in their ability to prevail (and her joyful exclamations when they do so).

Copious thanks to:
– My husband, Frank, who after all these years still has not made good on his threat to put me out in the garage to fuss over my fictional characters.

– My team of beta readers: Joe Clarizio, Tim Claflin, Kim Dwelley and Patti Pensanti. I don't know what I would've done without you!

– Members of the Write Away! writing group at the Art Circle Public Library, for their support and encouragement along the way.

And endless thanks to you, my dear reader, for being the reason I wrote this in the first place.

Dedication

**For Aunt Jo Gleba, to mark
the occasion of her 90th birthday**

You were the best little sister Mom could have asked for. Some of my earliest childhood memories were of the two of you on the phone, sharing "delicious" reads you'd just devoured and giving each other recommendations for new books to look for at the local library. Mom was constantly amazed that your small-town library always seemed to get the best new releases first. Thanks for generously sharing your love of reading with her over the years.

For my friend and literary cohort, George Lillenstein

Thanks for being the one I could always turn to with new scenes or snippets of dialogue – and feel secure you'd give them proper dignity and respect. I miss your wisdom on so many topics, your wicked sense of humor, generous spirit and willingness to help rework scenes to make them shine. Without your assistance and your brilliant sense of creative tension, the therapy sessions and courtroom scenes would have fallen flat. I miss our banter, our regular exchanges during Fabulous Fictional Five writers group meetings, our giggling tendency to defenestrate pesky fictional characters and our shared fondness for (and appreciation of) a clever and finely crafted obituary. :)

Second Chances

Part I

Chapter 1

(May 31, 1991 – Friday)

Gary climbed the porch stairs and poked at the doorbell. How strange to be at the front door of this house, instead of the more friendly back entrance! He'd been family here once.

Inside, footsteps crossed the hardwood floor. The sturdy oak door swung open. His daughter's grandmother looked far older than Gary expected for the nine years since he'd last seen her.

She peered at the young man on her porch. "Yes?"

"Hi, Mrs. Farricelli."

The woman inspected the visitor, as if trying to place him in her memory. Her hand flew to her mouth. "Gary! What are you doing here?"

His heart raced. "I've come to see Erin."

"I don't think that's such a good idea." She began closing the door.

"Please. I'm not here to cause any trouble. I just want to get to know my daughter."

Christina Farricelli's mouth tightened into a grim line. "*You're* not someone she needs to know."

This woman used to welcome him into her home as if he'd been her own son. "Mrs. Farricelli, please – don't do this." Gary faltered. "I know you're angry about how things ended between Ellen and me, but don't take it out on Erin. She deserves to know her father."

"Some father *you* are! You don't even show up in her life 'til there's a chance you can get your miserable hands on her inheritance!"

"I never even knew about her 'til four months ago!"

"You knew my Ellen was pregnant! How can you say you didn't know about Erin?"

Gary shifted from one foot to the other. Naturally, Ellen wouldn't have told them the truth. This would take a world of explaining. But it would be futile to divulge Ellen's lie. "May I come in?"

"No and you've got some colossal nerve coming here."

He laid a hand against the door. "Erin is my daughter. You have no right to keep her from me."

"I have every right," she retorted. "Anyway, she doesn't get off the bus 'til three thirty."

Gary checked his watch: 3:12. He leaned against the porch rail. "No problem. I'll wait."

"Not here you won't."

He met her gaze and held it. She wouldn't back down. He shrugged. "Fine. I'll wait in the car."

As she watched him go, Christina thought back nearly a dozen years to when Ellen first brought this boy home. How taken, how impressed she and Robert had been with his courtesy and respect. It made her sick to think how he'd ditched Ellen when she was six months pregnant – with *his* baby! Dumped her, just like that. Said he didn't want to see her again. *I ought to call the cops… teach him a lesson!*

Reaching for the phone, she jabbed at the numbers.

On the third ring, someone answered.

"I think you'd better get over here."

"Why?"

"Just get over here," she snapped, fidgeting with the coils of the phone cord. "And hurry!"

Seven minutes later, a blue Dodge Dart pulled to a sputtering stop. A young woman in dark glasses emerged and sprinted toward the porch.

Mrs. Farricelli conferred with her daughter, then pointed at the red convertible across the street.

Ellen's head swiveled toward the street. Her short-bobbed hair followed.

From the car, Gary watched her hand fly to her mouth. Separated by thirty-two feet of asphalt, the former lovers eyed each other: her with suspicion, him with questioning.

Minutes later, with a hiss of hydraulics, a school bus lumbered to a stop in front of the house, its red lights flashing. The door clunked and folded open. Out darted a little girl. Her long dark hair flew loose, like a banner streaming behind her, as she ran up the front walk. She was small for eight and a half.

"Momma, Momma!"

The young woman stooped down and swept the little girl into her arms. "Hi, baby. How was school?" She kissed Erin and pushed a wisp of hair out of her daughter's face.

"I'm so glad to see you! I didn't think you would be here. Does that mean you're having a good day?"

Erin still lived with her grandparents. She had since March, when Ellen went into the hospital for emergency surgery. Afterward, she was committed to the psychiatric ward for a week – her doctor feared she might be suicidal, given the nature of her surgery.

When she was released, Robert and Christina Farricelli insisted their daughter wasn't well enough to be on her own and brought her back to their home. Ellen had finally returned to her apartment last week. But, still battling depression, she couldn't care for Erin alone. Nor had she returned to work in the reference department of the Toms River Public Library.

The thump of a car door startled the women. Three sets of deep-brown eyes turned toward the man crossing the street.

The young woman straightened up. "Gary." Her voice wavered. "What're you doing here?"

So as not to worry the child, he kept his voice calm – even managed a smile. "I think you know why I'm here, Ellen."

For the first time, Gary stood face to face with his daughter. It scarcely seemed real. Dizzied, he grasped at the newel post to steady himself. His eyes lit up as he smiled at her. "Hi."

Erin took a wary step backward. "Who are you?"

Ellen stooped to speak to the girl. "Honey, this is" – she fired a warning glance at her daughter's father – "this is Gary. He's a friend of Mommy's from school."

"If he's a friend, why don't you look happy to see him?"

"I-I'm just surprised to see him, is all." She caressed her daughter's cheek. "It's been a long time since I've seen Gary."

Liar. Gary watched her carefully avoid eye contact. *So much sadness about her. I wonder why…*

Grabbing the railing with both hands, Erin picked up her feet and swung from it. Peering at the visitor, she squinted into the afternoon sunlight, addressing him matter-of-factly. "If you're a friend from school, I bet you knew my daddy. Grandma says he's a big jerk and Momma's better off without him."

"Erin." Ellen's cheeks flushed at her daughter's candor. "You know that's not a nice thing to say."

Gary could almost hear Mrs. Farricelli thinking, *Even if it <u>is</u> true.*

The girl stopped swinging and planted both feet on the porch again, hands poised on her hips, as Gary had seen her mother do countless times. "Well, it's true! That's what she says. She said he's a snake in the grass and" – now she turned to Gary – "Mister? What's a snake in the grass?"

"W-well, I" – he glared at Mrs. Farricelli, whose expression he could only describe as victorious. *I don't think that's a very nice thing for a little girl to be saying,* he wanted to say; but it wasn't his place. Not yet. He looked at the child watching him expectantly – "well, a snake in the grass is not a very nice person."

Erin nodded. "Okay," she said, accepting that definition. "That sounds like him. Thanks, mister."

Mrs. Farricelli brushed her hands against her jeans. "Well,

we'd best get inside. I'm sure Miss Erin has homework to finish. Thank you for stopping by, Gary," she said crisply. Despite her smile, daggers glinted in her eyes. "Do come again when you can't stay so long."

Ellen gazed backward at Gary as her mother propelled her toward the door.

Chapter 2

(June 2 – Sunday)

"Michael, I need your advice." The two men stepped onto the porch, goblets in hand. It was high tide. Gary's wife, Michaela, was upstairs, lying down. Doctor's orders.

State's Attorney Michael Conwaye turned toward his son-in-law. "At two hundred bucks an hour, you can ask me anything you want," he kidded, swirling the ruby liquid in his glass.

"Glad those rates weren't in effect while Micki and I were dating. I never could've afforded to marry her!"

They laughed easily, like old friends.

The older man took a sip of his wine. "Seriously, Gar' – what's up?"

"I need a referral." He paused. "Child custody."

Michael's eyebrows darted upward. "Oh?"

"Remember that high-school girlfriend I told you about?"

"Mm-hmm."

Not long after he started dating Michaela, Gary confided that he and Ellen were expelled from St. Joseph Academy after he got her pregnant. He'd worried aloud Michael would think less of him and would make him stop seeing Michaela. "I told you she aborted our baby…"

"I remember."

"She lied. I've got an eight-year-old daughter I found out about earlier this year."

"And you're seeking joint custody, or full?"

"Whatever's best for Erin. Ideally, a loving, stable two-parent family, which she *doesn't* have now."

"How's Kayla feel about this?"

"She's the one who suggested I seek full custody. And do whatever it takes to get it."

Michael smiled at his daughter's tenacity. "So you want to take a more aggressive tack…"

"As aggressive as necessary."

"Then there's only one way to go: Julia Ashwell. But I gotta warn you: She doesn't come cheap."

"I didn't expect she would. But money's no problem." When his father-in-law looked like he was about to protest, Gary repeated, "Money's no problem. Honest."

Gary called Julia the next morning. He explained his situation and she agreed to meet with him.

In her office later that day, when he said his father-in-law – Michael Conwaye – recommended her, Julia agreed on the spot to take the case.

Michael was a trusted colleague. Had been for years. They'd known each other since first year at UConn Law. She knew Michael wouldn't have recommended her unless it was a must-win situation. And if this guy was his son-in-law, Michael wouldn't want anything but the best.

And Julia Ashwell was the best. Her expertise in child-custody cases was unparalleled, her won-lost courtroom ratio staggering. If anyone could win Gary full custody of his daughter, it was Julia.

First thing she did was file a motion to have Gary granted immediate visitation.

***

(10:35 a.m., June 8 – Saturday)

The last religion class for the year had just ended. Gary knelt at a bookcase, shelving a stack of the first-graders' Bibles. A hesitant voice called his name.

He looked backward. "Hey, Ryan. C'mon in," he invited, getting to his feet.

Ryan Campbell had been in his first CCD class, back in '82. "Can I talk to you?" He needn't have asked. Gary always listened when his students needed to talk.

Handing Ryan a stack of Bibles, Gary motioned for the teen to follow. "Everything okay?"

"Oh – yeah. I just… wanted to ask you something." Ryan was finishing his freshman year at Pomperaug High. And his first-year confirmation class; he'd be confirmed next spring. "It's kind of important."

Moving to a circle of low seats, Gary pulled one back and perched on it.

"These looked so much bigger nine years ago," the teen observed, settling into the armless chair.

"Time's got a way of changing your perspective," Gary replied. "I used to think thirty was *ancient*. Now it's just a few years off, doesn't seem so old anymore. But you didn't come to hear me philosophize about aging. You wanted to talk to me about something."

Ryan tugged at the sleeve of his jacket. "Y-yeah. And if you don't want to, that's fine – but I was wondering… Would you be my confirmation sponsor?"

The question struck with a force Gary couldn't have imagined. In a way, it galvanized his spiritual mentor role in his former students' lives.

"It's okay if you don't want to," Ryan stammered in anxious haste. "Really."

"Ryan, I'm—" Gary began at the same moment. "I'm honored you think that highly of me."

"But?" the boy prompted, his eyes reflecting his growing worry.

"No 'but,'" he assured the teen. "I'd be honored."

"You *will?*" Quickly squelching his enthusiasm, Ryan tried to seem indifferent. "That's great. Thanks, Gar'."

"Just curious, Ryan: Why'd you want me? No living male relatives?"

Gary's gentle ribbing made Ryan grin. "Nah, I got plenty of *those*; two older brothers and four uncles. But, you've been such a good role model… you were my first choice."

"You're giving me an awful lot to live up to here."

"I hope the pressure's not too much for you," Ryan teased, at ease again. "Hey, how's Michaela?"

"Pretty good. Still some morning sickness now and again, but otherwise okay."

"She's pregnant?"

"Yeah; she's due early October. She's had some issues; doctor wants her to take it easy." He felt a twinge of unease, discussing this with a student. "She needs me at home more."

"Well…" Ryan mused, "I'm s'posed to do a hundred hours' community service before I'm confirmed. Helping a pregnant lady could probably count for something…"

"I'm sure your time would be better spent helping someone who coul—"

"Could what? Use help? Sounds to me like a pregnant lady could use some help."

Just be gracious. Smile, nod and say, 'Thanks, Ry, we appreciate that.' "You've got a point. Thanks, Ryan."

"Now I just hafta get permission from Father Dave." He smirked. "*That* won't be easy. I sure miss Deacon Greg. What happened to him, Gary? Why'd he leave?"

Gary opted for just enough truth. "He got reassigned." He hoped the tension in his voice wasn't evident. "Deacons get reassigned, like priests do. They move 'em around to different parishes, where they can, uh – be of greater service."

"My dad said he was sleeping with one of the confirmation students. Is that true?"

His "No!" was almost too emphatic.

"If it wasn't sex with a student, what was it? Embezzling funds?"

Gary stood. "I doubt your dad would appreciate our having this discussion. Michaela's waiting for me. I'll tell her about your offer." He scrawled his number on the back of a business card and handed it to the boy. "Let me know what Father Dave says."

"That's awfully sweet," Micki remarked, raising herself on an elbow when Gary explained Ryan's offer. "What a good kid."

He didn't say the boy had ruminated about Greg's sudden departure three months earlier. *What good would it do? What purpose would it serve – other than to make her feel guilty all over again?* Ryan didn't need to know Gary had gotten Greg transferred. And Micki *certainly* didn't need to be reminded why.

***

(June 17 – Monday)

Judge Mary McCarthy reviewed the papers before her. "Says here, Dad hadn't paid a dime in child support the past eight years. And I'm supposed to be impressed by his wanting to be involved in his daughter's life now?"

"He was deceived, Your Honor, into believing the child had been aborted," Julia responded.

Gary scrawled on a pad of paper and pushed it across the table. Julia read it quickly.

"Furthermore, Your Honor, my client has consulted with his accountant and determined what those payments would've amounted to. Plus interest. He's sent the child's mother a certified check for" – she glanced again at what Gary had written – "forty-seven thousand, five hundred eighty-six dollars."

The judge's eyebrows leapt upward. "Is that true?"

Gary stood. "Yes, Your Honor. I searched through journals at the UConn and Yale law libraries and found no legal precedent involving lump-sum payments of back child support; so my accountant and I determined what we believed to be a fair amount – taking into account my annual salary over those years and average costs of caring for a child during that same period. Plus interest."

"That's kind of a lot of money for a young man to come up with all at once, wouldn't you say?"

"Yes, ma'am."

"So, Mr. Sheldon, tell me: How *does* a young fellow" – she glanced at the paperwork – "a radio announcer... amass that kind of money? Surely radio doesn't pay *that* well." She paused. "And please don't address me as *ma'am*."

"Sorry, Your Honor." Gary was sure he'd blown it. "I got

10

a rather, um… sizeable inheritance when my grandfather died."

"Ah, yes" – she flipped through papers – "that would be… Edward Sheldon. The architect. But he died several years ago, did he not?"

"He did, Your Honor. The money was held in trust 'til I turned twenty-five."

"I see." Judge McCarthy addressed Julia. "I'll take this matter under advisement and render a decision by the end of the week."

(11:30 a.m., June 21 – Friday)
"Congratulations, Gary," Julia said. "You get visitation – first and third weekends. Starting next month. You need to work out pick-up and drop-off times with Ellen. But you've got your visitation."

His hand holding the receiver shook. This was better than he'd expected.

"I know it's not exactly what you'd been hoping for," she assured Gary, mistaking his silence for disappointment. "But it's a start. We'll take it a step at a time. One victory at a time. You'll get your daughter. I'll have the paperwork over to your office by the end of the day."

Four hours later, visitation was off Gary's radar as he and his boss raced toward New Haven.

He'd barely begun his show when he got the call telling him Micki – now six months pregnant – had been admitted. Her water had broken and she was having the baby.

By the time he arrived at St. Raphael's Hospital, their baby had been rushed to neonatal intensive care. Then complications arose and Michaela slipped into a coma.

In the anxious days and nights that followed, Gary divided his time between ICU and the NICU: sitting at his unresponsive wife's bedside, holding her hand, or suited head to foot in surgical garb to visit his preemie daughter from the other side of her Plexiglas incubator. Because the infant was hooked to all kinds of monitors, plus oxygen and IV feeding tubes, he could only reach a latex-gloved hand through the side of her Isolette to stroke her cheek or a tiny arm.

He'd kept up a running conversation, telling her Mommy couldn't visit yet, but she couldn't wait to meet her; and she needed to rest so she could get strong enough to come home with them.

When the baby's eyelids fluttered in response to his voice, Gary, overwhelmed by love, wept. "You know my voice, don'cha, little one?" he whispered, his voice choked with emotion. *I spent enough time reading to her these last three months. I knew it wasn't a waste of time. She knows me — my little girl knows me!*

That recognition buoyed Gary's spirit; it gave him hope through long hours when there was little optimism to be had upstairs. When he wasn't in either intensive-care unit, he was in the chapel. Praying. Or crying. Sometimes both.

Through it all, when she wasn't tending to Michaela or her other patients, ICU nurse Amanda Petersen sat in the chapel with the new father. Praying with him. Holding his hand. Offering hope when the news seemed bleakest; that's when their prayers grew even more fervent.

At last, Gary received encouraging news: Both mother and baby would live.

Summer was over before Amanda Josephine — named after the nurse and Gary's grandmother — came home from the hospital.

By then, Gary, Ellen and their lawyers had hammered out visitation. He would pick Erin up at home after school on Friday. She'd spend the weekend in Connecticut with her father, stepmother and half-sister; on Sunday, he'd drive her home to New Jersey — by 7 p.m.

"You were supposed to be here twenty minutes ago!" Ellen snarled from her porch the first time he was late. During her rant, she threatened to negate the visitation arrangements.

Not wanting to engage her in an argument, Gary reached into the trunk to retrieve Erin's bag. "I'm sorry. There was a big accident; traffic was backed up for miles. I'll leave a little earlier next time."

Erin stood on the porch, smirking, as Momma tore into him. She was already plotting to dawdle when it was time to leave next month – just so he'd get in trouble again.

"If you can't get her back on time, you won't see her at all," Ellen continued. "I mean it, Gary: I'll haul your ass back into court and we'll see what they have to say about it!"

Ellen's attorney managed to dissuade her from threatening Gary further.

After that, she'd just mutter and grumble about how she "never *could* depend on you."

Gary knew she was only saying it to be hurtful. Trouble is, it was working.

Chapter 3

(September 21 – Saturday)

"He turned me down," the teen grumbled. "I can't believe he did that!"

Yeah, 'cause I asked him to. "I'm sure he had his reasons."

"I bet Deacon Greg woulda said yes."

Gary's jaw clenched. He tried to keep his tone light. "Sometimes, Ry, things don't work out how we want. Guess this is one of those times."

(September 23 – Monday)

"I've decided to stop doing New Music Monday."

The program director looked surprised. "You can't do that; you've got sponsors. And why would you want to? I thought you loved that feature."

"I used to," Gary admitted. "But the music's gone from techno-synth to screaming grunge. I won't subject my listeners to it. I know we've got sponsors, Pete. But I wanted to run something by you – something else."

His boss nodded, looking hesitant but receptive. "I'm listening."

"I still have to work out the details," Gary prefaced.

"Understood. What do you propose?"

"Since the eighties stuff was so well received, I'd like to do a daily all-eighties music feature – the Retro Ride Home – from, say, four thirty 'til six ten."

"Why such a screwy time slot?"

"Stick with me here, Pete. We've got plenty of New Music Monday sponsors; if five of 'em buy into the idea, they can each sponsor a show. Or ten on a two-week rotating basis. We give them two sixty-second spots – or four thirties – and seven six-second drop-ins: 'The Retro Ride Home, brought to you today by Moroni's Chevy Emporium, Route 188, Middlebury.' And mathematically, it works. Out of a hundred minutes, we've got two-point-seven minutes of ads. That's 97.3 percent commercial free."

Pete nodded. "Let's run it by Charlie, make sure we can do this. It's a prime advertising period – right in the middle of afternoon drive."

"And precisely when people don't want a lot of yammering commercials. They'd prefer music to drive home by. Wouldn't you?"

Pete considered that. Then something else. "What about traffic sponsorships? And weather?"

"Package 'em into the programming; or extend it to two hours: four thirty to six thirty, and plug in commercials proportionally. Each tag line's what? Ten seconds? Traffic's sponsored four times an hour and weather twice? That's another minute. We may need to fudge actual percentages, but I doubt anyone will time it and take us to court over it."

"While we're at it, why don't we change our broadcast frequency to 94.3? That way we can stuff in more commercials and still be well within the percentage, music-wise."

Gary laughed. "That could work. Just be thankful we're not 106.7. That'd give the ad execs fits!"

Pete shook his head. "Have you discussed this Retro Ride Home idea with the music director? You know how protective he is of that eighties library."

"I've tried. Whenever I call, his line's busy. And if I knock on his office door, he's never in there."

"Maybe you should just barge in."

"I could, but you know how I hate talking to myself."

"Right. Makes people think you're crazy." Returning the grin, Pete motioned toward the door. "Get outta here."

At the door, Gary turned back to his boss. "So, what about the Retro Ride Home?"

Pete gave a pensive nod. "Let me think about it. Let's talk again in a few days."

(11:37 a.m., October 4 – Friday)

Gary had spent the week filling in for the morning team, which meant getting up at 2:15 every morning. If they'd been in Southbury, he could have slept until three; but being at the cottage added forty minutes to his drive. Each way. At least he got to blow out of there when his shift was over. And if traffic was light, he was back at the beach by eleven. Anyway, they were going home today. He poured himself some more coffee, then refilled Micki's mug.

"Why'd *you* have to do the morning show, anyway?" she complained as Gary replaced the coffee pot. "Couldn't Rob or Pete or someone else do it?"

Sighing resignedly, he sank back into his seat. It seemed like they went through this every time he filled in for Ken and Barb. "That's just how it's done. Morning drive's the most crucial time slot; when there's a vacancy, they go to the next-highest-rated shift to cover."

Micki pouted. "Why couldn't Steffi do it?"

"Steffi? Do mornings? That dolt couldn't pull off ten minutes of topical programming if her life depended on it – let alone four hours a day for a whole week! Not to mention, she's about as entertaining as dryer lint."

"A little stuck on yourself, are you?"

Gary bristled at her dig. "No. I just know there's no way she could hack it, that's all. Besides, they wouldn't ask her. I already explained that to you."

Micki didn't want to fight. She put down her coffee mug, looked across the table at her husband and changed the subject. "You going to get Erin today?"

"It's first Friday of the month, isn't it?" he shot back testily.

Gonna be one of those weekends. She suddenly felt sorry for Erin, who'd have to endure her dad's cross disposition the whole way home. Micki laid a hand atop his. "Hey," she whispered. He looked up in silent reply. "I love you," she told him, hoping to defuse his vile mood.

The corners of his mouth twitched. "I love you, too." He paused. "I'm sorry I snapped at you."

Grinning roguishly, Michaela patted his hand. "That's okay. I know how crabby you get when you aren't getting enough sleep."

Gary's face relaxed into the easy smile she knew so well. One eyebrow arched. "It's not lack of *sleep* making me grouchy." He winked, took her hand and kissed his way up her arm.

"Is that a fact?" Micki giggled. "Well, let's see if we can do something about that." She chased her husband upstairs to remedy his grouchiness.

An hour later, Micki dropped Gary at Tweed-New Haven Airport, wished him a safe flight and kissed him goodbye.

After paying the pilot, he waited while the ground crew fueled the single-engine Cessna. Last month he'd realized it made more sense to charter a flight to Toms River, rent a car for the weekend and fly home Sunday night than fight New York metro traffic four times in three days.

An hour later, Gary stared out the window as the plane made its approach over Ocean County Air Park. Landing made him jittery. Gripping the armrests, he tried to focus on something other than the roar of the engine. Erin would be nine on Tuesday. He still had no idea what to get her. *What's a nine-year-old girl like, anyway? What does she want?*

What she wanted was him out of her life. This was worse than contemplating landing.

When the plane touched down, Gary hurried to retrieve his rental car.

He consulted his watch as he neared Ellen's street. He was early, but that might give them time to hash out visitation for the holidays.

***

"Do you *have to* take her this weekend?" Arms folded, Ellen's hands gripped her elbows.

Something about her tone sounded strange – *desperate* – Gary noted. "Let's not get into this again." He leaned against the porch rail. "We've been through it half a dozen times. You always have some excuse why I shouldn't take her. It's getting old real quick."

"But it's the weekend before her *birthday*…"

"I only see her two weekends a month as it is; you expect me to miss one of those visits so you can have her for her birthday weekend?"

He raked a hand through his hair. "You've been with her every damn birthday she's had!"

"I promised her we'd go roller skating this weekend, and to a movie; then out for pizza – just us," she wheedled.

"Now you have something to look forward to for next weekend."

"Don't be like that, honey. Please?" Reaching out a beseeching hand, Ellen touched Gary on his hand, his arm, his chest. "Please, Gary, don't do this. Or" – she brightened – "why don't you stay? We'll have a little family birthday party. Just the three of us: You, me and Erin. This way you get to have your weekend and I don't have to be without her on her—"

"Stop!" Gary moved her hand away. "Quit trying to make us a family. We're *not* a family. We're never going to *be* one. You had your chance – and you pushed me away. I loved you once, but that was a long time ago, El. A *long time.*"

"Gary, *please!*"

"No. Accept it, Ellen. I'm married. I moved on. It's time for you to do the same."

She shook her head emphatically. "Don't say that. Please, honey…"

He pulled free of the hand she'd laid on his arm a second time. "For the last time, no! I'm not going to let you con me into jeopardizing my marriage" – *again,* he added silently – "Get it through your head, Ellen: I'm in love with Michaela.

How many different ways do you need me to say it? I almost lost her once. I don't intend to make that mistake again."

"But" – she sounded frantic – "I'm so lonely without you. Please, honey; if you don't come back to me, I – I don't know what I'll do…"

He folded his arms. "Guess you're gonna find out, then."

"I swear, Gary, if you don't stay, I'll – I'll… I'll kill myself."

"Don't even kid about that." He wasn't about to give in to threats, but he couldn't assume she was bluffing. Not about suicide. She probably was, but he couldn't risk it. After all, this was his daughter's mother. Seeing her tears, panic grabbed at his heart. "Ellen, if you're considering suicide, you need to get help." When she balked, he added, "At the very least, we need to talk about this."

"What's to talk about? You said you don't want me. So just go. What d'you care if I kill myself? You don't care about me. You never did!" Her lower lip quivered.

Suddenly Gary realized why she was behaving this way. He'd seen this belligerence from his dad; and he recognized it in himself.

His voice was kind. "El, how much have you had to drink?"

"I dunno what you're talking about," she blustered, looking away.

Gary turned her face toward him and held it steady while he searched her eyes. "I think you do, Ellen. C'mon, this isn't like you. You're not being rational. How much have you had to drink?"

"I'm not a drunk!"

"I didn't say you were. But, honey" – the word slipped out unbidden – "it's not good for you to drink so much." Gary bit back his next question, knowing how she hated it when anyone asked about her blood-sugar levels. Instead he asked, "Have you eaten at all today?"

"I don't – I…" She paused, her hands shaking. "I don't remember."

"Crap," he muttered. He had to get some food into her — quick! It was still an hour 'til Erin got home. "C'mon." Gary herded her toward the rental car, a late-model Audi. "Let's get you something to eat. You can't do this to yourself, Ellen."

"Gary, no. I don't want to go." She pulled back, resisting the arm Gary slid around her.

"Ellen… shh – c'mon. Don't fight me." He pulled her close to subdue her.

Ellen stopped resisting, snuggled against his chest; she felt his heart beating. Oh, how she needed the comfort of his embrace! Especially now. She felt so safe, so secure. So loved. Ellen stretched upward and kissed Gary, her open mouth seeking his.

Pulling away, he grabbed her by both wrists and shook her. "Stop it! I'm not playing with you, Ellen. Now get in the car."

As Gary drove, Ellen's left hand crept across the divide between the seats and rested on his thigh. He pushed it away. She tried again – a little higher.

Again he pushed it away. "Cut it out," he ordered.

The third time, her fingers crept toward his crotch. This time he pinched her arm, just above the wrist. Hard.

"Oww!" she yelped, recoiling. She slapped at his shoulder, then rubbed at the pinched spot with her other hand. "You hurt me!"

"Then don't be putting your hand where it doesn't belong."

She pouted fiercely and wouldn't speak to him for the rest of the ride.

Gary drove to the diner nearest her apartment, where they used to hang out. *Great. Just what I need: to stir up her old memories.* The next-closest one was fifteen minutes out and he doubted they'd get back in time to meet Erin's bus.

Sipping coffee, he watched as Ellen wolfed down a bacon cheeseburger and onion rings. She always craved burgers and o-rings after they'd been out drinking. Her choice of food was completely wrong for her diabetes. But mentioning it would be like pogo sticking through a mine field.

How long has it been since we've done this? After learning she was pregnant, Ellen pushed him further and further away. By the time they got expelled, their relationship was pretty well shattered. *Must've been before Christmas in '81.* Ten years ago.

Most times, they'd sat in that booth in the corner – where an old couple now sat, sharing a slice of apple pie. Gary recalled his early coffee-and-pie pseudo-dates with Micki.

Ellen was too busy licking onion-ring grease from her fingers to notice his smile.

Now that she'd eaten, he figured she might respond to reason. "Listen to me," Gary commanded in an undertone. "You weren't serious back there when you talked about killing yourself, were you?"

She sneered. "Don't flatter yourself, Gary. The world doesn't revolve around you."

Twenty minutes ago, she was begging me not to go. "I just don't want you to do anything stupid." He felt stupid himself now for having been concerned.

"Don't worry," she snapped. "I'm over you, alright? Like I said: Don't flatter yourself."

"It's not *me* I'm concerned about," he hissed, leaning across the table. "It's our daughter!"

She leaned back against the booth. Wadding up her napkin, she shot it at him; it bounced off his nose. "She hates you, you know," she said nonchalantly – or what she must have hoped was nonchalantly. Ellen uncrumpled the napkin and started tearing it into strips.

"I know. She tells me that all the time." Gary paused. "I wonder who instilled *that* in her."

She blew into the pile of tattered paper, sending the shreds scuttling toward Gary. "Well, how was I to explain she didn't have a daddy?"

Lie to her. You're good at that. He gathered up the bits that hadn't blown onto the floor.

When he didn't reply, she continued. "I told her you'd left. It was the truth."

"Half of it."

"Okay, so I made a mistake," she blurted, slapping a hand on the table. Gary's coffee cup rattled. "I couldn't let her see me as a failure, alright? I didn't want her to know how weak and stupid her mother was for pushing her father away."

Gary shook his head. "So instead, you make me out to be the bad guy. Thanks a lot, Ellen!"

"That's not what I intended; but by then, my family had the wrong idea about you and—"

"Who *gave* them that idea? Did you ever bother to set them straight? Or did you just perpetuate the lie?"

It was her turn to not answer.

"I thought so," he huffed. "Well, let me tell you something, El: Your family may put up with your manipulation, but I'm not playing into it. I'm not gonna let you mind-fuck me anymore. You hear me?"

She pretended not to.

"When we go back, I'm picking up Erin and she and I are going to Connecticut." He plucked stray napkin shreds from his sweater, then suggested a compromise. "Tell you what: I'll bring her home tomorrow, so you can have part of the weekend with her. I don't want to be a jerk about this, El. I know how hard it is. But we need to do what's best for Erin." He covered her hand with his. "Okay?"

When Ellen nodded, Gary could tell she wasn't exactly receptive. *What's she want? I'm cutting short my visitation so she can spend part of the weekend with Erin.*

The ride back was uncomfortably silent.

Erin's bus showed up a few minutes after her parents did. The child ran up the driveway and into her mother's arms, ignoring her father. Chattering excitedly about her day, Erin handed Ellen a fistful of papers. She reached into her backpack and brought out an art project; she explained what the assignment was, and how she came up with the idea, and built it all by herself.

When Gary asked to see it, she scowled, then turned away. The rest of the time, she acted like he wasn't even there.

When it came time for them to leave, Erin kissed Mom goodbye, gave her an extra-big hug and told her she loved her and couldn't wait to see her again. Then she climbed grudgingly into the car. And the long, ugly silence was on.

Every time Gary came to get her, Erin was either hostile or ignored him outright. This time, he planned to fill the silence with his favorite music. He slid *Dream Into Action* into the tape player. Howard Jones was cheerily singing, "Things Can Only Get Better." Gary exhaled quietly. *That's for sure!*

Although futile, he asked the requisite questions: "How are you feeling?" "Did you do anything interesting in school today?" "Is there something special you'd like to do this weekend?" "Would you like to stop for something to eat?" And a new one today: "What do you want for your birthday?"

"I wanna go home, you big dumb jerk!" the little girl muttered. Other than that, she gave him withering stares, sighed aloud and looked out the window.

Erin rummaged through her backpack until she found a book. Pulling it out, she plopped the satchel onto her lap and propped the book on top of it. Minutes later, she dug through the bag again. This time she brought forth a Walkman. Donning the headphones, she pressed PLAY, giving her father a petulant glare.

After a few minutes, Gary tapped his daughter on the shoulder.

Turning to him in annoyance, she pulled the headset away from her left ear. "What?"

"I have other music if there's something else you'd rather listen to," he offered, indicating a stack of cassettes in the space between the bucket seats.

In ill-tempered silence, she examined the tapes, one by one, then flung them over her shoulder into the back seat.

The last one Erin threw out the window, watching with evil delight as Yaz's *You and Me Both* hit the asphalt at sixty miles an hour and was pulverized by a tractor trailer.

Gary bit back an angry "Hey!" and a lecture on respecting other people's belongings. He knew she was trying to get a rise out of him; he wasn't about to let her think she had.

***

By the time they reached their exit, Gary felt so weary of grasping for things to talk about with Erin – and so hungry for real conversation – he could hardly wait to hear his wife's voice. *Any* voice, for that matter!

"Anyone call?" he asked after Erin grunted a hello and stomped up to her room with her things.

"No – wait, yeah. There was one call. I was feeding Mandy so I let the machine get it. I'll go see who it was."

Gary touched her on the arm. "That's alright, hon. I'll go."

"By the time you hear this, it'll be too late." Her voice sounded frightened. "I always loved you, Gary. Always. You might as well know that now. I'm sorry I ever hurt you… and sorry I sent you away. I never shoulda done that. I shoulda said yes when you proposed. I always regretted not marrying you." She sniffled. "Make sure Erin knows I loved her. Please tell her that. Tell her I loved her." A long pause followed, then desperate weeping. "Goodbye, Gary. I love you. Please forgive me."

The timestamp at the end said 6:18.

A cold ache swept through Gary as he stared at the answering machine, then at his watch. 7:22.

Fingers trembling, he punched in the number he'd called hundreds of times as a teenager.

"Mrs. Farricelli, you've got to get to Ellen," he pleaded. "Right away! She's trying to kill herself."

"What? Who is this?"

"It's Gary; please, Mrs. Farricelli – you've got to hurry!"

"What're you talking about? Why would you think sh—"

"*Please!*" he interrupted frantically. "If you hurry, it might not be too late." He was near tears. "Please, you've got to stop her…"

Gary paced the bedroom until he regained his composure; then he went downstairs and, in low tones, told Michaela about Ellen's message.

Christina and Robert Farricelli rushed to their daughter's apartment; the door was ajar – as if she'd been expecting them.

They found Ellen on the bathroom floor, in a crimson puddle. Blood dribbled from the jagged vertical gash along her right wrist. She was barely breathing. Her left hand clutched a chunk of glass. On the floor, splashed with blood, lay fragments of a shattered jar. Two empty prescription bottles lay by the sink. Percocet and sleeping pills, dating from mid-March and early May.

Mrs. Farricelli screamed. Dropping to her knees in the sticky pool, she gathered her unresponsive daughter into her arms.

Her husband dashed to the phone. But Gary had already called 911 – just before calling Ellen's mom. The ambulance arrived a minute later. By then, Ellen's pulse was extremely faint.

The EMTs hurried her to the hospital. Covered in her eldest child's blood, Christina Farricelli watched – numb and helpless – from her seat in the ambulance as the crew worked on Ellen.

Robert followed, equally numb, equally helpless, in the car.

When the ambulance arrived at the emergency room, the paramedics – still performing artificial respiration – rushed her limp body in on a gurney so an ER physician could call the time of death.

They were terribly sorry, the EMTs told Ellen's traumatized parents. She'd lost too much blood. Not to mention the effects of the drugs. If they'd gotten the call ten minutes sooner, they might have been able to save her. Again they expressed sorrow at the couple's loss, then began filing the necessary reports.

The Farricellis clung to each other in the hallway, paralyzed by shock and grief. Christina tried to claw her way back into the room to wail and grieve over Ellen's lifeless body. The EMTs subdued her and brought her instead into another room in the emergency department, to be seen by a trauma nurse. Her husband stood by, holding her hand, at a loss for anything to say to give her comfort.

They would have to tell their other children.

They'd also have to call Gary. That would wait until morning.

***

Gary decided until they heard back from the Farricellis, there was no sense telling Erin anything. For her sake, they had to pretend everything was fine. Or if not fine, at least normal. That meant gritting their teeth and dealing with her hostility as they always did; otherwise, she'd suspect something was up.

"What would you like to do today?" Gary asked. Perhaps a benign topic could give rise to pleasant breakfast conversation.

Ignoring her father, Erin turned instead to Michaela. "Tell him I wanna go home."

Kept awake half the night by the baby, Micki was in no mood for this. "Tell him yourself."

Gary and Erin's heads both spun around; two jaws dropped in surprise at her sharp tone.

Gary tore himself away from his hazy fog of guilt and regret long enough to marvel at his wife's nerve. *Attaway to show some backbone!* He instantly regretted his insensitivity. And hers.

"Bitch," Erin muttered at the same time, staring at Micki.

"Honestly, Erin" – she was on a roll – "I'm not going to spend the next nine years playing this game with you. So just suck it up and start talking to him."

Erin stared at her. Then she glared at her father. "I want to go home," she said, slowly, distinctly.

"Yeah? And I want a polite, respectful daughter. Let's see who gets their wish first."

Erin shoved her pancakes away and stalked out of the room.

Chapter 4

(1 p.m.)

"Mrs. Sheldon" – it still seemed strange to Michaela, being called that – "this is Bob Farricelli, Erin's grandfather. Is Gary there?"

"How's Ellen?" she asked, concerned more for this nice-sounding man with the tremor in his voice than about her husband's ex-girlfriend.

"It's not good news."

"I'm sorry," she murmured, meaning it. "Just a moment. I'll get Gary."

"Mr. Farricelli – is Ellen…?"

An awkward pause followed.

"She uh… it was too late," he whispered. "She didn't make it."

Gary felt as though he'd just taken a length of rebar to the teeth. "I'm so sorry. How – I mean, what did she…?"

"Slashed her wrist."

The phone nearly slid from his hand. A month before Gary turned seventeen, Ellen's Christmas-morning phone call had kept him from slitting his wrists. He still recalled the sweetness of her voice that cold, sad morning. It had warmed the icy despair in his heart and made him reconsider his tragic plan. It was as if she'd given him another chance: a second chance to turn things around, a new chance to live. *I couldn't do the same for her! And now she's dead.*

"…and OD'd on painkillers and sleeping pills," Robert was saying.

Gary scarcely heard. Ellen was dead. *Dead.* The news tried to worm its way in. But he wouldn't let it. This seemed less real than when she'd told him all those years ago she aborted their baby.

He knew her dad was waiting for him to say something. Anything.

"I'm so sorry, Mr. Farricelli." Gary's throat constricted. Something lodged in his windpipe. It felt like a whole potato. "She was agitated when I got there, but she seemed fine when I lef—"

"If you knew she would do this, why didn't you stop her?"

"I *didn't* know," Gary countered. "She left a message on my machine when she knew it'd be an hour 'til—" he paused. "I called 911 as soon as I heard it," he finished quietly.

Guilt's voice clamored in his head: *He should blame you! If you hadn't left, she'd still be alive. It's all your fault.*

Silence lingered between them. "I wanted to let you know what the, uh… arrangements are," Mr. Farricelli said. "The wake is Monday, from six to nine. The Mass is Tuesday, ten o'clock, at Holy Family."

Gripping the phone, Gary tried to steady his voice. "We'll be there." He could envision the other man mopping away tears with a damp handkerchief clenched in one hand.

"How are you going to tell Erin?"

Gary's voice snagged in his throat. "I don't know." He desperately wanted not to be the one to tell her. "We should bring her home now, let her be with her – with her family when she finds out." He faltered. "I mean, let's face it, this is hardly the kind of news you want to hear from someone you hate."

Robert hesitated. "If you think that's best. Still, I'd like you to be there when we tell her."

Gary shut his eyes against the unwelcome tears, his "Whatever you think is best" scarcely audible.

When the bedroom door creaked, Michaela looked up from folding laundry. Gary stood in the doorway, trembling and teary eyed.

She approached on hesitant feet. "Honey? Are you okay?" Pulling him inside, she shut the door.

He slumped onto the bed and related his conversation with Mr. Farricelli, choking back emotion. As he did, Micki retrieved a suitcase from the closet and started packing. Gary hated being watched as he talked; he'd once described that awkward, conspicuous sensation as "feeling like a goldfish in a bowl."

In the long, uncomfortable quiet, Micki held up two suits. "Black or grey?"

"I don't care," he replied miserably, raking a hand through his hair.

Putting away the black suit, she pulled out Gary's dress shoes, her navy-blue dress – the one with the white lace collar and tiny buttons down the front – shoes to go with it, and pearl earrings. She packed Gary's black-onyx cufflinks and the monogrammed gold ones she'd given him for his birthday last year. In case he felt like deciding.

Then, when Michaela could think of nothing else to busy herself with, she sat with him.

At the touch of her hand on his, Gary's composure fled. Leaning his elbows on his knees, he drooped forward and covered his face with his hands. Deep, painful sobs tore out of him.

Micki drew him into her arms, glad she'd closed the door; she would have hated for Erin to catch her father in this vulnerable moment.

While Michaela took the cats to the kennel, Gary threw their suitcase into the trunk of the rental car; he hung the garment bag containing his suit and her dress on a hook in the back seat.

"C'mon, Erin; we're going home." He reached for the girl's bags that slouched in the corner.

Erin wouldn't let on he'd said anything she wanted to hear. "I can carry 'em!" she snapped, snatching the bags away. "I don't want your help." Elbowing past her father, she stomped down the hall.

The ride to Pine Cove felt interminable. Traffic through New York was horrendous. Erin demanded frequent bathroom stops. Plus, they needed to stop midway for Micki to nurse the baby.

Typically quiet, Erin spoke only when she had to use the bathroom; and then, only to Micki.

Gary was too steeped in guilt to notice – or care. He fretted, too, about how his reunion with the Farricelli clan would go. While Ellen's mom made no pretense of hiding her revulsion, Mr. Farricelli had acted almost nice. Gary knew he had no right to expect warmth, but maybe they would at least be welcoming.

He could only imagine how her sisters and brother would treat him. No doubt they'd been fed the same line: that *he* was the one who'd left *her*.

***

"Hey," Erin called out mistrustfully. "Why're we at Grandma's house? I wanna go home. I wanna see Momma!"

Gary hesitated. It was a struggle to keep his voice even. "Your grandpa asked us to come here."

"But I wanna go *home!* I wanna see Mommy!"

Michaela gave Gary's hand a reassuring squeeze.

Walking to the front door seemed to take as long as the whole drive from Connecticut.

The instant the door opened, Erin pushed past her grandmother and tore into the house.

"Hello," Christina Farricelli greeted them as the child darted by.

She looks so frail – almost brittle, like she'd shatter if a sudden wind blew past.

Gary clasped her hand; his voice wavered. "I am *so* sorry." Before she could pull away, he released her hand. "Mrs.

Farricelli, this is my wife, Michaela, and our daughter Amanda."

Tears filled Mrs. Farricelli's eyes as she stared, unseeing, at the little family: Gary, a young woman and an infant in her dad's arms who had wisps of dark hair and the same pretty blue eyes as her mother.

Micki took the limp and trembling hand the woman extended. "I'm so sorry for your loss," she murmured, laying her other hand soothingly atop Mrs. Farricelli's.

The woman began to sob, drawing in huge, noisy breaths as anguish consumed her.

Michaela turned her gaze toward her husband, her eyes seemingly imploring, *Do something!*

Gary handed the baby to his wife and drew the weeping woman to himself. Suddenly, he didn't care she'd spent the past nine years hating him and treated him like an outcast these past four months. All that mattered was she'd loved him once. She'd been his surrogate mother, offering care and love when he needed it most. And now Ellen was dead and *she* needed comfort, he wouldn't deny her that.

Her shoulders shook violently as grief poured forth. She opened her mouth and let out a deep and terrible moan.

Gary remembered his anguish after Ellen said their baby was dead. An unbearable, stabbing pain ripped through him, leaving a raw, throbbing gash that festered, oozed and bled. It got far worse before it ever got better. For years afterward, the lingering ache made his insides crumble to dust at the mere sight of other people's babies.

He vividly recalled sobbing and beating his fists against the sand at the beach after the long-ago news. Breathing was torture – as if his lungs were being squeezed by iron bands. And once, gasping for air, he'd inhaled a mouthful of sand. Even the gritty, awful feeling of it rasping against his throat didn't compare with the agony he'd felt at the loss of his child.

Of course, the child – Erin – turned out not to have been aborted; but not even the eventual truth could erase the anguish he'd endured. All those years. All that suffering. Losing a child was a pain he wouldn't wish on anyone… not even someone who hated him.

The excruciating memory made Gary draw Mrs. Farricelli closer, made him want to hug away the hurt – and shield her from its return.

At first she resisted. When she finally gave in, he consoled her as best he could. And when she'd quieted some, Gary led her inside and helped her to the couch, where she collapsed. As soon as he left her side, hurrying toward the kitchen, Mrs. Farricelli's wails bubbled up and spilled from her lips again, building to a crescendo.

Micki stood at the entryway, wondering how familiar Gary had been with this family that he'd presume to waltz in here uninvited and go wandering through their home.

When he returned with a glass of water for the hysterical woman, Micki retreated from her initial criticism; she watched as he tenderly ministered to her – *like she was his own mother.*

He smoothed the hair back from her forehead. "Shh," he murmured, stroking her flushed cheek. "Shh. Here" – he took her hand, helped her sit up. Holding the glass to her lips, he tipped it so she could take a sip – "drink. That's it."

***

Mr. Farricelli entered the room, approaching the young woman and her baby. "Hello. Who might you be?"

Beside him, Erin tugged at his arm and pointed. "Grandpa, what's wrong with Grandma?"

Micki shifted Amanda to a different position. "Hello," she replied. "I uh" – she motioned toward the couch, where Gary still knelt beside Christina – "I'm Michaela, Gary's wife." She offered her hand and lowered her voice. "I'm so sorry about Ellen, Mr. Farricelli."

"Thank you," he said, meeting her gaze as his hand closed around hers. He appreciated her use of his daughter's name. Trying to put her at ease, he asked conversationally, "And who is this?"

33

"This is Amanda. She's our baby," Michaela blathered, as if he couldn't have figured it out.

"She's lovely." Mr. Farricelli managed a trace of a smile. *She looks like Erin… in a Gary kind of way.* "Won't you come in and sit down, dear?"

Erin stamped her foot. "Grandpa!"

He looked down at the dark-haired girl still tugging his arm and pointing at the couch.

"What's wrong with Grandma? And where's Momma?"

By now, Gary had propped pillows behind Mrs. Farricelli and sat beside her, holding her hand.

"Grandpa, why's everyone but Momma here?" Erin asked, tugging more insistently at his sweater. When he didn't reply, she queried her aunts, who had just entered the room. "Auntie Roma? Auntie Kat? Where's Momma?"

Neither sister answered. Their eyes were riveted on Gary.

Rosemary bent down and put an arm around her niece. "Shh, calm down, honey," she soothed. In deference to her now-dead sister — *whom he dumped,* she reminded herself bitterly — she eyed Gary with icy contempt, replying with polite coolness when he greeted them. She quickly excused herself and brought Erin out to the kitchen to get some juice.

When introductions were made, everyone genuinely seemed to like Micki. And they adored the baby. As they cooed and awwed over Amanda, making funny faces and googly noises for her amusement, the front door opened. In walked Tommy, the youngest Farricelli.

At eighteen, the 6'2" Johns Hopkins freshman was nearly as tall as his father.

His eyes swept the room. Mom sat on the couch, crying. As he made his way to her, he saw Dad, Katrina and some lady he couldn't identify, with a baby. And someone else. When he recognized Gary, Tommy's fists clenched and his expression changed from sadness to contempt.

Rosemary returned to the living room with Erin; the child stood just inside the doorway, weeping.

"Hey, Funny Face, why don'cha come sit down?" Tommy tried to sound inviting.

"What're you doing here, Uncle Tommy?" she asked, suspicious. "You're only s'posed to be here in summer."

When he couldn't come up with a reply, Erin again demanded to know where Momma was. No one would say, which agitated her further. Trembling with sobs, she ran to Grandpa, who did his best to quiet the distraught child.

Tommy parked himself in a wingback chair opposite the couch. Arms folded hard across his chest, he glowered at Gary, daring him to speak.

Robert seated Erin next to Grandma on the couch; he settled beside his wife. Gary and Michaela sat on Erin's other side. Roma and Katrina perched over the back of their brother's chair.

Grandma took Erin's hand. "Sweetheart—" her voice cracked. "There's something we need to tell you, honey. It's about your mom."

Eyes wide, she gaped at her grandparents. "Is she alright? She's not in the hospital again, is she?"

Grandma swallowed hard, trying to keep her composure.

Alarmed, Erin looked around the room – at the somber faces of everyone she loved and the one person she hated.

She flung herself onto Grandma's lap and wailed – huge, sorrowful moans; tearless at the moment… but not for long. She wasn't sure what was wrong, but *something* was going on – and it couldn't be good. Not with everyone here like this. *If Momma was okay, they woulda told me!*

"There was a terrible accident." Grandpa stroked her hair. "Mommy… fell and hurt herself. The ambulance took her to the hospital. But there wasn't anything they could do to help her."

Erin drew back from her grandfather's touch. "Is – is she… *dead?*" She spoke the word warily, trying hard to be brave. Her bottom lip quivered and her eyes welled with tears as Gary reached out and took her hand.

Erin glared at him, but didn't pull away. "Is she dead?" she repeated dully. *Don't say yes, please don't say yes!*

"I'm sorry, honey," Gary whispered, his eyes filling with tears, too. His mouth twitched. "I'm so sorry." One tear slid down his cheek and dropped onto his jeans; a second one followed. Then a third.

It took a moment for the news to register. When it did, the child balled up her little fists and struck him repeatedly. After several punches, words accompanied her blows. "I hate you! You made me leave – and now Mommy's dead! It's all your fault! I hate you!" she screeched, landing three solid whacks to his chest and left shoulder. "I hate you – and I never wanna see you ever again!"

Grandma tried to pull Erin out of striking distance, but she hurled herself even more violently toward her father, and resumed pummeling and kicking at him.

Grandpa wrapped his arms around Erin, restraining her. Thwarted, she continued screaming. She struggled mightily for nearly a full minute. Finally, she wilted into Grandpa's arms and sobbed.

Despite her grandfather and her aunts' efforts, Erin could not be comforted. She tore free of her grandfather's embrace and ran to her bedroom, still shrieking. Rosemary, who – at twenty-three – was closest in age to Ellen, raced upstairs after her.

Mrs. Farricelli jammed the heel of her hand against her mouth and fled to the familiar safety of her kitchen. Her son and husband followed.

Katrina remained behind. She watched as Gary crumpled forward in silent agony, and his wife tried to comfort him. Making brief eye contact with Michaela, Katrina gestured toward the couch, as if asking permission to sit.

Having observed the Farricelli sisters during the ordeal, Micki got the feeling this one was at least sympathetic to

Gary. She stood and busied herself checking to see if Mandy's diaper needed changing.

With a grateful glance in Michaela's direction, the nineteen-year-old sat beside the man who used to tug her pigtails when she was eight. "This must be so hard for you, Gary," she whispered, hugging him. "I know Ellen hurt you; but I also remember how close you two were." Her last words caught in her throat and she stifled a cry.

She knew the others still believed her sister's twisted version of the truth, but she'd always loved Gary – even before Ellen confided in her about what really happened. Her folks were acting nice because they were in shock. But Katrina knew they retained none of their affection toward him – affection they'd *all* felt, even Tommy – all those years ago. She was the only one here who still loved him.

His steadfast exterior shattered; he clung to the teen and wept. When he could form words, they were an admission of guilt. "Erin's right: It *is* my fault!" He sobbed against her shoulder as his wife looked on in helpless worry, cuddling their baby.

Katrina did her best to console him. "It's not your fault, Gary." *Of course it's not: It's __my fault__.* "What would make you say a thing like that?"

Little by little, he pieced together the story for Ellen's sister. "I didn't think she'd really *do* it," he sobbed. "I'm so sorry, Kat! I never should have left her without getting her some help."

"Please don't cry," Katrina begged. "You had no way to know she'd do this. You did what you could. You did more for her yesterday than *I* did."

Gary gaped at the teen.

"I knew she was depressed. She tried to kill herself a few months back. But I didn't reach out to her. I couldn't. Not after how she lied to you. I know what really happened. Ellen told me. I told her she wrecked Erin's life when she sent you away. She threw away her chance for happiness with the one guy who really loved her – and who woulda been a terrific daddy – 'cause you were such a great big brother." Now she was crying. "El called me yesterday, after you and Erin left. I guess it was about six. She told me you refused to let her 'have' Erin for her birthday weekend. She said if you 'wanted her so bad' for this birthday, you 'might as well have her for all of them.'

"She always tried to make me feel sorry for her. I told her to quit trying to punish you for getting on with your life. El threatened to kill herself and I said, 'You've said that before; you're all talk.' She kept saying life wasn't worth living without you, and she wanted to die" – Katrina took a shuddering breath – "so I told her, 'If you're so miserable, go ahead and do it.' And I hung up on her." She put a hand to her mouth to stifle her guilty sobs. She rocked back and forth on the couch in distress. "I'm sorry all of this had to happen, Gary," she wailed, "so sorry. If it hadn't been for me, she'd still be alive!"

It was Gary's turn to offer comfort. "It's not your fault, Kitten," he said, using the nickname only he had ever called her. "Nothing you said made her do this – and nothing you could have said would've stopped her." Gary and Katrina hugged as they tried to internalize his words.

At last, Katrina pulled away. *This is kinda awkward – especially with his wife right there.*

Long minutes later, Rosemary returned downstairs, leading Erin – red eyed and still crying – by the hand. Seeing her sister sitting with Gary, she hurried her niece toward the kitchen. As their eyes met, Katrina interpreted her sister's glare: *Traitor! How dare you take his side over your own family?*

Not long afterward, Rosemary returned – with the curt announcement dinner was ready.

Gary knew the Farricellis were only being polite in inviting them to stay for supper; they needed family time to grieve. Amid Robert's gracious protests, they gathered up Mandy and made their way out.

Robert and Christina bade Gary and Michaela farewell at the door. Roma called a disinterested, "See ya," from across the living room, accompanied by a halfhearted wave. Erin, leaning over the back of the couch, stuck out her tongue at Gary.

"Good riddance," muttered Tommy.

Only Katrina hugged the Sheldons.

Chapter 5

(10:23 a.m., October 7 – Monday)

"Good morning," the young receptionist chirped. "Can I help you?"

"Is Paul Ramsey in?"

"Was he expecting you?"

"No. But I—"

She wore an efficient I'm-trying-to-look-helpful-while-I-stonewall-you expression. "I'm sorry; Mr. Ramsey's very busy today and I don't think he's—"

"Please" – he handed her his business card – "I'm only in town for the day. I'm sure he'll see me. Could you let him know I'm here?"

Studying the card briefly, she stood. "I'll tell him, Mr. Sheldon; please have a seat." She motioned to the small seating area off to her right, then headed toward the program director's office.

Gary paced the lobby. Not much had changed. What had it been – nine years since he'd roamed these halls? Being back felt strange. At the same time, it felt like coming home.

He'd asked Micki to join him; but she declined. "You go ahead. I won't know anyone. Besides, it's hard to catch up with someone while having to explain everything to a third party. Go on."

He had to admit, she was right. It would have taken forever to bring her up to speed on – well… everything.

The receptionist returned. Right behind her bounded a smiling Paul Ramsey. "Johnny Mayhem!" he exclaimed. "How the hell are you?"

Gary grinned at the air name he hadn't been called in years. "Hey, chief!"

"My God, I haven't seen you in ages!" He shook Gary's hand, clasping his arm just below the elbow. "Look at you, all grown up! Last time I saw you, you were a kid." Paul patted him on the shoulder. "C'mon, let's not stand around out here. Let's go talk in my office."

Gary started to protest, not wanting to keep him from his work; but Paul would have none of it.

"How're things at the mighty Z97-3 these days?" he asked, once they were settled. He turned down the radio on the shelf behind his desk that blared a classic seventies rock anthem from The Who.

"Not bad. I'm happy there. It's been a good run."

"But?"

He shook his head. "No 'but.' I've got no complaints."

Paul waved the card Gary had given to the receptionist. "Music director, eh?"

Gary gave a self-conscious shrug. "Yeah…"

"Actually, I knew about that," Paul admitted. Noting Gary's questioning look, he added, "From the trades. You've done well since you left here. I knew you would."

"What about you? Stations get sold all the time – this place included. How'd you manage to stay PD through all that, after all this time? We almost lost ours in a buyout a few years back."

"What can I say? I'm the best there is" – Paul grinned – "I'm kidding. I'm not just PD. I'm a VP of the corporation that owns the station. Actually, it's funny, your coming here today. I've been thinking about you. I'm kind of sorry to hear you're so happy at 'ZBX."

"Why's that?"

"There's an acquisition looming. I was hoping we could lure you away, to take over as PD there."

It was one of those mind-numbing moments. Gary did his best to *not* sound like a dolt. "Really?"

"Interested?"

"Depends." His eyebrows rose. "Where?"

Paul met his gaze and held it. "Beantown."

Boston! Gary'd been accepted to college there; but after Dad kicked him out, there went his chances of attending BU. He had no way to pay for it on his own, either. Then, at Paul's urging, he met with Steve Reynolds, a New York based media mogul whose assets included WZBX-AM & -FM. Steve referred him to Pete Donovan. Offered the afternoon-drive shift at Z97-3, Gary had jumped at it.

His grandfather insisted Gary continue his education. So, ignoring the teen's protests, Edward Sheldon had funded his grandson's education. "Just because your dad refuses to pay, doesn't mean you should go without," he'd insisted. It was pointless to argue; Grandpa never accepted opposition.

UConn was no BU; and Waterbury couldn't begin to compare to Boston. But it was near home and work. And the education was more than adequate. He had no regrets. Truthfully, he'd probably had better opportunities, on air at a commercial station while attending college, than if he'd had to compete with a thousand other students for a weekly three-hour air-shift on BU's campus radio station.

Now he was practically being handed a plum job. *In Boston, of all places!* he thought longingly. *But it'd mean uprooting my family… and leaving* 'ZBX. Gary couldn't fathom doing that. *But it's* <u>Boston</u>, *for goodness' sake. Boston!*

"Thinking about it?" Paul asked, hopeful.

Gary sighed. "If you'd offered two years ago, maybe. There's too much keeping me where I am. It's tempting; but I" – he shook his head – "I just couldn't; it wouldn't be fair for me to consider it now."

The other man cocked his head. "Fair to whom?"

"To my wife… our folks… the kids."

Paul leaned forward, elbows on his desk. "Wait a minute: You're saying *No* to a PD position – in the number-seven market in the nation – because you don't want to move your family? I don't think you understand what a choice opportunity this is."

"I understand, Paul. Believe me; I do. And the answer's still *No.*"

"You're turning it down – just like that?"

"I'm three hours away from my daughter as it is. I have no intention of doubling that. My wife's dad is nearby; plus she's got a job she loves. I can't tell her my job's more important and she has to give hers up."

"Don't you make more money than her?"

Gary shook his head. "Money's not the issue. Home and family, *that's* what matters. Besides, what I said before is the truth: I'm happy where I am."

"I've never had someone refuse a job so eloquently before. And for such noble reasons. Nicely stated, kid. I knew there was something I liked about you." After a brief silence, Paul stood. "C'mon, I don't want to keep you all to myself; there's other folks around here who'll be glad to see you."

Dave Stanton thumped the onetime production whiz on the back as Paul retreated to his office. "Mayhem! Good to see you!" The morning guy's hair was grayer at the temples, and he sported more forehead than Gary remembered; otherwise, he looked the same. "What brings you back to this neck of the woods? Bored with Connecticut?"

"Hardly. And even if I was, Toms River's not exactly a hotbed of excitement." His smile faded. "We're here for a family funeral."

"Not one of your parents?"

"Nah. Mom's fine; Dad died last January." When his former colleague paled, Gary's lip curled in a sneer. "*That* was no great loss."

Dave nudged his arm. "So, while you're in town, you gonna look up that little hottie you used to date? If I remember correctly, you two were goin' at it pretty good for awhile."

He shook his head. Sadly.

"Why the hell not?"

" 'Cause it's *her* funeral I'm here for."

Dave gasped. "Oh my God! Hey, wait – I thought you said it was a *family* funeral."

"We've got a daughter." Saying that still felt so strange! "She's nine. Or, will be tomorrow."

(7:55 p.m., October 7 – Monday)

The door to the ladies' room lounge flew open. A young woman burst in, nearly careening into the woman adjusting her stockings near the sitting area.

"Sorry!" the human missile gasped. She seized the other lady's hand to help her regain her balance. "Are you alright?"

"I'm fine." She straightened up. Their eyes met.

"Oh!" the younger one exclaimed, still flustered. "Hi."

"Hi," came the guarded reply.

"I was hoping I'd run into you—" Her cheeks reddened. She giggled nervously. "Not literally, I mean; but I – oh, you know what I meant…"

"Of course." Micki smiled. "Why'd you want to see *me?*"

Katrina motioned to the couch at one end of the lounge. "Um, why don't we sit down?"

Michaela sat. The teen was tall, with dark hair that fell to her waist and eyes the color of the ocean sky after an early-August storm.

"I know Gary feels guilty about Ellen." Katrina's words tumbled out like gravel from a dump truck. She twisted her hands in her lap.

Micki listened in polite silence as the teen prattled on about why Gary oughtn't feel guilty over his ex-girlfriend's suicide.

"Ellen was pretty unstable these past few years. But she really went downhill after she lost the baby. She jus—"

Micki's head snapped up so fast she thought it would break off. "After she what?"

"Lost the baby," Katrina repeated, then – maddeningly, Micki thought – went back to what she'd been saying. "El was never the same after Gary left. She never told anyone the truth, either. At least, not 'til earlier this year. She said she told him she had an abortion and never wanted to see him again. But she was miserable. And they'd always been so happy. I know you probably don't want to hear this, and I'm so sorry to throw it in your face. But it shows how different El was after Gary lef—" she stopped, corrected herself. "After she sent him away."

She was right. Michaela *didn't* want to hear this. What she *did* want to hear more about was this baby. She had to know about the pregnancy loss. That, to her, was significant.

"And she only told me the truth after she left the hospital," Katrina continued. "She spent almost a week in the psychiatric ward – 'cause she kept saying she wanted to kill herself."

"Why?"

"Because of the pregnancy loss."

Michaela felt her heart rate quicken; she forced herself to remain calm. "When was that?"

Katrina put a finger to her lips. "Mid-March? Yeah, that sounds about right. The thirteenth. It was a tubal pregnancy – which is why she was rushed to the ER. Severe abdominal pain. Almost ruptured her tube; she coulda died right then."

She went on, but Micki scarcely heard. *Mid-March. A tubal pregnancy. She couldn't've been more than eight weeks along... That'd put it at— No!* Her heart plunged into her ankles; she felt ill. Even as the idea occurred to her, she prayed for it to be wrong. *No, no please, it can't be! Dear God, it's not possible... Is it?*

"She was devastated! Mom and Dad hadn't known Ellen was pregnant and" – Katrina whispered confidentially – "she hadn't been seeing anyone at the time. She never told *them* who the father was."

Repressing the impulse to flee, Micki forced herself to remain on that divan beside Ellen's sister and listen to her as though her world weren't crashing to pieces.

"*I* only knew 'cause she called me a couple weeks before and said she might be pregnant. I mean, she kinda *suspected*, but she wasn't sure" – she paused – "then when she told me who the father was, I was thrilled 'cause I thought it meant they got back together… and how wonderful that'd be for Erin! I knew how much El loved Gary and I – I mean" – she stammered – "my God, I never knew he was *married*—" Katrina clamped a hand over her mouth. She reached toward the stricken woman. "I'm so sorry. Breaking it to you like this… you must think I'm horrible!"

Michaela wanted to scream. She wanted to cry. And she wanted to kick this wide-eyed teen who'd just reminded her – again – of Gary's infidelity. She wanted to throttle her husband. She wanted to kill Ellen. She— no, wait: Ellen was already dead. She wanted to punch holes in the walls and shatter the full-length mirror on the opposite wall. She really wanted to scream.

But Michaela did none of these things. She merely sat – as composed as she could – and focused on breathing: In and out. In and out.

"I'm so sorry," Katrina repeated, her hands flapping ineffectually, like a newly hatched bird. "I didn't know you um… I mean – oh, I don't know *what* I mean!" she exclaimed in a frenzy.

Numb, Micki felt tears prick at her eyes. She patted the teen's arm. *Strange, I'm the one comforting her.* "It's okay, Katrina. I knew. I mean, I knew she and Gary" – her lips felt thick and immobile; she gestured clumsily – "but I had no idea she got pregnant." Shaking her head, Michaela stifled a cry. Her final words were a whisper. "Neither did Gary." Palpable silence filled the air. And lingered.

"How long have you and Gary been married?"

"A little over a year – in August."

Katrina nodded. Part of her desperately hoped they had only been married for a few months, so he wouldn't necessarily have been unfaithful to Micki by having sex with Ellen in January.

She felt a rush of disappointment, as if Gary had let *her* down, by betraying her memory of him.

The teen ached to restore her former image of Gary; she wasn't comfortable with this new one at all. Thinking back to how things used to be with him and El made her feel better. She was uncertain whether to say this – but she was anxious to assuage the awkwardness that had seeped between her and Michaela. She liked Gary's wife, and she really wanted this woman not to hate her. So Katrina forced a smile and hoped Michaela would think it looked natural.

"Gary's such a nice guy. I mean, I don't have to tell *you* that… he was like a big brother to me. He used to pull my pigtails all the time. I would act mad, but I kinda liked the attention." Katrina blushed at the memory of the crush she'd had on him. "I'm sorry Roma's being so mean to him. Tommy, too. They used to love Gary as much as me. Guess they're still angry. Like my folks… because they don't know the truth. Ellen never told 'em." Her voice grew wistful; her eyes filled with tears. "I wish she *had,* 'cause that woulda made this so much easier to take, if they still treated him like one of us."

***

They're being almost civil; maybe this won't be so horrid after all, Gary mused during a lull in the stream of mourners.

The approach of Ellen's father interrupted his hopeful outlook.

Sitting in an empty seat, Mr. Farricelli leaned in close. "When this is over, Gary, I want you to leave. And don't come back. It's too destructive, having you in the picture."

It felt like Robert Farricelli had punched him in the throat. "You can't be serious. How is it destructive for Erin to have contact with her father?"

Pain flickered in his eyes. "I've made my decision, Gary. I want you out of Erin's life."

"*You* want!" Gary sputtered. "You can't do that. I've got court-ordered visitation."

"Don't count on it. We've filed a motion to get it overturned. We're petitioning for full custody." He paused. "It's better this way."

"Better for whom?" He was about to say something more, but Mr. Farricelli stopped him.

"Let's not drag this out, Gary. Don't make it more unpleasant than it already is. After the funeral, just leave. You walked out on Erin before. If you know what's good for you, you'll do it again."

Christina Farricelli peered over as her husband stalked back to his seat. She studied Gary's stoic countenance, as if searching for anything that would give away his emotions.

Gary had learned long ago how to mask his facial expressions. He did so expertly now; he wouldn't give her the satisfaction of seeing him crumble.

You walked out once; if you know what's good for you, you'll do it again. Almost verbatim what he'd told Mom nine months earlier, at Dad's wake. He mused whether his hurtful words had torn as painful a hole in her heart as the one he felt now. Regret oozed through him.

Straightening his shoulders, Gary glanced at the open casket. He turned toward Ellen's mom and eyed her intently for fully half a minute – until she looked away, made uneasy beneath his gaze. *Where did Micki run off to?* he wondered as he stared the woman down. *I thought she was just going to use the restroom.*

From the corner of his eye he saw his wife approach, poised and graceful. *I love that woman. And the only way I'll get through this whole mess is if she's on my side.*

Michaela sat. She leaned toward her husband slightly.

He did the same. "I need to talk to you," he said with quiet urgency, just as she said, "We've got to talk."

Confusion flickered between them. There was no time to explain, for just then, in a rustle of brown robes, in whooshed Father Maynard.

Father Justin Maynard was pastor of Holy Family Parish. Years ago, he'd been dean of students at St. Joseph Academy, while Gary and Ellen were there.

Going to the family, he extended condolences, assuring them of his prayers, bidding them peace; he hugged Erin and spent a long time talking with her, sharing her tears and her sorrow at the loss of her mother. Making his way past the Farricellis at last, Father Maynard approached Gary.

The young man stood.

The priest embraced him. "I'm so sorry, Gary. I can't imagine how difficult this is for you."

A cry caught in Gary's throat. *He knows me better than anyone; even Micki.* The Franciscan priest had been his confidant and, over time, his friend. Not to mention, his confessor. *Hell, he knows things about me I never told another living soul.* The thought was simultaneously disturbing and comforting.

Father Maynard felt him tense.

"I should've done something," Gary whispered. "I was *here!* I was with her three hours before she did it. I should've been able to *stop* her!"

The priest pulled back, his eyes reflecting concern. "That's not always possible, Gary. I can see how badly this has upset you. Would you like to talk about it?" he offered in an undertone, laying a hand on the younger man's arm.

Gary considered this. There was so much to say, both about Ellen's suicide and the threat from Mr. Farricelli. Guilt and anger, fear, pain and sadness swirled through him. It felt as if each emotion were attached to a cord that wrapped – tighter and tighter – around his heart. He took a deep breath, let it out slowly. "I don't know," he replied truthfully. "Maybe later?"

Father Maynard nodded, patting Gary's arm. "I'll be home. You know where to find me."

After the wake, promising to talk with her as soon as he got back, Gary left Micki and the baby at the hotel, then drove to the friary.

"I hope it's not too late," he fretted when Justin came to the door, looking decidedly un-priestly in faded jeans, St. Bonaventure sweatshirt and grey wool socks.

"Not at all. Come on in. Can I get you something? Beer? Wine? I've got a great Merlot in the fridge. Care for a glass?"

"I could do with a glass of wine. Thanks."

Father Justin indicated a room across the hall. A single lamp cast a soft glow from one corner. "Make yourself comfortable. I'll be along in a sec."

The room felt cozy, with shelves of books and a fire crackling in the hearth. Gary inhaled deeply; the welcoming scent of hickory filled his nostrils as he settled onto the couch. A minute later, soft footfalls approached and the priest reappeared. *He looks so at home here. Stupid! He is at home!* Gary, still in his suit, suddenly felt out of place – at least overdressed.

Handing him a goblet, Justin sat at the other end of the couch, beneath the lamp's glow. Setting his glass on a low table, the priest tucked his feet beneath him, then reached for his wine again.

On the table lay a Tom Clancy novel. *I shouldn't have come; he was enjoying a quiet evening by the fire, and I ruined that.* "I'm sorry, I – I'm intruding." Gary shifted his glass nervously from one hand to the other.

"Nonsense." Leaning back, Justin swirled his wine gently, then held the glass up to the firelight. "I was waiting for you. I'm happy to see you, Gary; I'm glad you came by."

Gary looked down. *God, I hope you really mean that.* "So am I," he said awkwardly, then stammered, "happy to see you, I mean."

Smiling, Justin lifted his glass. "To old friends… and delight at seeing them."

The two friends clinked glasses.

"Mmm." The priest savored his first sip. "Looks like fatherhood agrees with you. That baby of yours is adorable!"

Gary smiled, glad Justin had chosen to open the conversation with something easy to talk about. "She's got her mother's everything."

"How old is she?"

"Three and a half months; she was three months early; her due date was this past Wednesday."

"Wow – and she's okay?"

"So far, yeah. But it was a long road. She was in the hospital for months. It was a scary time," he admitted. "I almost lost them both. Micki was in a coma and nearly died; and Amanda was so early, for a while they thought she wouldn't make it."

He paused. "They're fine now, thank God. It's amazing what a crisis can do to your prayer life. I must've harassed every saint there was. And this sounds silly, but lately I've developed a really close bond with St. Joseph."

Justin shook his head. "Not silly at all. Excellent choice. Patron saint of home and family. And fathers. Frankly, at this point in your life, Gary, I can't think of a better saint for you to align yourself with." He cocked his head. "Wasn't Joseph your confirmation name?"

"How do you remember these things?"

The priest shrugged. "It's a gift."

Sipping his wine, Gary watched the flames dance and crackle.

Justin took a sip of wine. "I'm glad you came. I can tell you're having a hard time. It's not easy," he acknowledged, gesturing with his free hand, "having a relationship end this way… through suicide."

Gary's eyes locked on the other man's; he swallowed hard, waited for him to go on.

"No matter what that relationship might have been," Justin clarified. "And no matter how contentious or upsetting it may have been. It's devastating to have it come to such a sudden – permanent – conclusion. With no opportunity for real closure."

Gary nodded. *That's _exactly_ how I feel.* Fearing he'd spill the wine because of how badly his hand was shaking, he set his glass on the table.

Justin put his down, too. His kind eyes fixed on Gary again. "Were there unresolved issues?"

Gary looked away. Hurt bubbled up within him. For a long time, he said nothing. He took a deep breath. "It's all my fault," he whispered.

Justin inclined his head toward Gary — a kind of unspoken encouragement to continue.

"It's my fault she killed herself."

The Franciscan planted both feet on the floor. Resting his elbows on his knees, he reached one hand toward Gary. "Why do you say that?"

"Now they want me out of Erin's life altogether," he continued, his voice choked with pain.

"Gary, hold on. Back up. You said you blame yourself for Ellen's death. Why?"

Gary explained how they'd argued over who should have their daughter that weekend; that Ellen was drunk and irrational, and had left what amounted to an audio suicide note on his answering machine.

The priest nodded as the story unraveled painfully, piece by piece.

"I just know if I hadn't done that — if I hadn't left her alone — she'd still be alive!"

Justin caught the hand Gary flailed about; he held it between his hands and offered words of comfort. "You couldn't have predicted this, Gary," he reassured him. "Ellen was a deeply troubled young woman. Even if you'd stayed, she'd have waited for the right moment, when she was alone. Please: Don't beat yourself up over this."

His head bowed, Gary nodded. "That's what Michaela told me, too." He looked up at the priest, his eyes filled with desperation. "But I still feel so" — he shook his head — "so *responsible!*"

A pitcher of water stood in the center of the table. Justin poured some for him.

Gary tried to hold the glass steady as he took sip after calming sip, then set it down on the table.

"You did your best," the priest assured him. "You reached out to her and tried to help — without getting sucked back into an improper relationship."

"If what I did was so right, why is she dead? And how come I still feel like shit?"

Now it was Justin's turn to look away uncomfortably. "I don't have an answer for you. Not one that'll help. We may never know in this lifetime why she did it. I know it doesn't offer much comfort right now, but someday we *will* know. Someday all these questions will have answers.

"But, what I need you to know is you're not to blame." The priest laid a compassionate hand on Gary's suit-jacketed arm. "It might not seem like it now, but in time you'll realize your intervention was a blessing for Ellen – a *blessing*. But she was so mired in hopelessness she couldn't see it for what it was. She couldn't recognize you were reaching out in a true spirit of love." He clasped Gary's hand. "I believe she knows that now, and knows the peace that eluded her in this life. Ellen suffered. She suffered terribly. But now that suffering is over. And she's with Christ."

His words spurred Gary's tears. He tried to wipe them away. "But, I thought – I mean, she – she killed herself… and… and isn't that…?" Gary floundered, unable to finish his question.

Justin's voice was as comforting as the words he spoke. "If you listen to the prayer at the end of the funeral Mass, you'll hear me say, 'Forgive whatever sins she may have committed in human weakness and grant her your pardon and salvation.' If Ellen was distraught enough to kill herself, she wasn't in her right mind and can't be held responsible for her actions.

"We believe in a loving and compassionate God, a Savior who loves us, warts and all – in spite of what we do. I truly believe He wouldn't hold a single act of desperation against Ellen. This won't condemn her, Gary. Please believe that." The priest laid a hand on Gary's shoulder. "I know you loved Ellen – you had a long history – and it'll hurt to say goodbye tomorrow. But if it makes it any easier, please know she's at peace. Okay?"

Snuffling, Gary wiped at his eyes. "I can't imagine what Erin's gotta be going through right now. But, thanks for listening, Justin – for letting me talk, letting me get this all out."

Justin put an arm around Gary, offering quiet reassurance, then poured him some more water.

Accepting it gratefully, Gary felt a sense of peace flow through him. When he set the glass back on the table, his hand didn't tremble.

For a moment, Justin said nothing.

Gary wondered where the priest would lead the conversation now. He braced for the worst.

"What you said before," Justin began, broaching the subject gently, "about them wanting you out of Erin's life – what did you mean by that?"

Gary felt a twinge of hurt at the memory of Robert Farricelli's words. *Was that just tonight? Seems like forever ago!* Giving a quiet sigh, he related what Ellen's dad had demanded.

The priest nodded in silent acknowledgement.

"I can see how it'd be upsetting for Erin now – right after her mom's death – being shuttled back and forth every other weekend," Gary postulated. "But how can he say having me in her life is *destructive?* Erin's my daughter – and I love her! Can't they see that? Don't they know what this is doing to me, too?"

"Maybe there's something I can do," Justin offered. "Would you like me to talk to them?"

A glimmer of hope crossed Gary's face; just as quickly, it faded. His shoulders drooped. "I don't know what good it'd do, Father; but if you think it'll help, sure." For an instant, Gary seemed once again a helpless youth, at the mercy of grownups who wielded all the power, his angst assuaged only by the presence of the one adult he could still trust.

The priest offered a compassionate smile. "Couldn't hurt to try… right?"

"I suppose."

"Then consider it done. But I'll work on them in quiet little baby steps."

Gary recalled something Father Maynard used to say when he'd sought counsel as a teen. "Like eating an elephant, right?" He leaned against the couch cushions again.

Justin handed Gary his goblet, then reached for his own. Leaning back, he rested his feet on the table. Taking a sip of his wine, he looked over at Gary and smiled. "Yep. One bite at a time."

Gary checked his watch: It was after 10:30. He hadn't meant to stay so long! Father Justin had to celebrate early Mass tomorrow… then the funeral. He sat up, set down his wine. "I didn't realize how late it was. I'd better go. I'm sorry, I shouldn't ha—"

"Don't be silly," the priest chided gently. "I'm glad we had this chance to talk."

"Me too. I really do feel a lot better. Thanks, Justin."

"What're friends for?" He tilted his head. "How long you in town?"

"We're leaving tomorrow, right after the funeral." His grin was almost playful. "I'm not welcome here, remember?"

"Right. I forgot." Justin nodded. "Let me take you and Michaela to lunch. Wait for me after the graveside service."

(October 8 – Tuesday)

Erin could not be comforted. Today was her birthday and, instead of getting to spend the day with Momma, they were going to put her underground!

Momma always let her take her birthday off from school; they'd go to the movies and then out to lunch, just the two of them. They were all that mattered, Momma always said. The two of them were all the family either of them needed. They didn't need a daddy, she'd said. Were better off without one.

Then that guy showed up. Claimed he was her daddy. Took her away all the time – and pretended to be nice to her, pretended to love her.

But still, Momma's words came back all the more strongly. We don't need a daddy. Don't need a daddy. Don't need a daddy.

Erin had never agreed more. She didn't need a daddy – certainly not *this* one. So she fought him when he tried to console her. Fought him when he said it was okay to be sad.

She knew it was okay. *You're s'posed to cry when the only person in the world who means anything to you goes away; and fake people try to come into your life and take over and mess everything up!*

"I hate you," the little girl hissed when he stooped to comfort her. "Go away!" She scratched at his face with her fingernails.

The awful man put a hand to his cheek. It came away streaked with blood.

Erin smiled. It felt good to do that. It felt good to see him hurt.

Then Auntie Roma came over and led her away by the hand. It was time to go to that big old house with that room with all the flowers; the one where they left Momma last night. Left her all by herself. In the dark. Erin wondered whether Momma had been afraid, lying there in the unfamiliar dark all night in that strange box with all those flowers around her.

"It's always difficult to say goodbye to someone we love," said Father Maynard during Ellen's funeral. "It's especially hard under such tragic circumstances. Yet as we bid farewell to Ellen Farricelli this morning amid wrenching sadness, we do so in a spirit of great trust – trust that the Lord who loved her so dearly in life will now embrace her in the promise of Eternal Life…"

Micki entwined her slender fingers with her husband's. Yesterday, his face had been a mask of anguish; now he looked tranquil. His eyes were red, but he had a look of peace about him.

Glancing past him down the length of the pew, she noted wounded expressions on the faces of Ellen's family: grim mouths contorted in pain; pallid skin; dull, staring eyes.

As much as she resented who this woman had been in Gary's life – and what she stood for – Michaela couldn't halt the wave of sympathy she felt toward Ellen's family. As an only child, she had no inkling what it must be like to mourn a sister. But she did have a daughter, and one thing was certain:

If she ever lost Mandy, she'd probably look just like these poor people did now.

Gary turned to look at his wife as tears spilled down her cheeks. He slid an arm around her, drew her close and wiped them away.

Michaela turned in to the comfort of his embrace and wept.

Chapter 6

(10:23 a.m., October 28 – Monday)
Gary looked skeptical. "I don't know about this."

Waiting by the bank of elevators, Julia looked him dead in the eye. "Do you trust me?"

"*Yes*... but—"

" 'Yes' or 'Yes, but,' Gary? And let me tell you, 'Yes, but' sounds an awful lot like 'No' to me. So let me ask you again: Do you trust me?"

He sighed. "Yes."

The door slid open. Julia stepped in, turned and faced Gary. "Good. Then let's go fight for your daughter."

He followed the attorney into the elevator. It sped to the 27th floor. He felt as if his stomach had boarded the freight elevator instead. When it caught up, he felt ill.

It would be difficult, facing Christina and Robert Farricelli again. Because now he'd face them as adversaries. He hated fighting them for custody of their grandchild. But Erin was his daughter – about whom *their* daughter had lied to him. And to them.

In an unconventional move – ill advised by his lawyer – Gary went to talk with the Farricellis. As he approached, Christina Farricelli wept.

"Can we talk?" he asked reservedly.

Exchanging glances, they nodded. Their eyes reflected curiosity.

Pulling back a chair, he sat, facing them with compassionate eyes. "Mr. and Mrs. Farricelli" – *It's so strange, calling them that!* But 'Mom and Dad' was no longer appropriate – "I know how hard it is to lose a child; and I can understand how difficult this must be for you—"

"So why are you trying to make it *worse?* Why are you *doing* this to us, Gary?" Christina implored. "Why are you trying to take our baby away?"

Gary wanted to hug her. But, again, where to draw the line of propriety? A hug would have been so wrong. He laid a hand on her shoulder. "I'm sorry, Mom— I mean, *Mrs. Farricelli.* I'm not trying to hurt anybody – least of all, *you.*" He tried a different approach. "Look, I'm not a monster. I'm not trying to snatch your granddaughter away when you've just lost Ellen. I'm *not.* But I'm her *father.* I have rights, too."

"So, where *were* you all this time?" Mr. Farricelli blurted. "All of a sudden, you want to be the hero: swoop in and take off with the child you could never be bothered with, not once in eight years!"

Gary's insides felt ready to explode. But he remained calm. "I wasn't involved in her life because Ellen told me she aborted the baby."

Christina gasped. "Our Ellen would never have done such a thing! You're lying."

"When did she say that?" Robert demanded.

"The day I asked her to marry me – the day we should've graduated. She said she never loved me and she didn't want me. Or the baby." It'd just be hurtful to tell them Ellen had expressed doubt the baby was his. "She threatened to have me arrested if I contacted her again. *That's* why you never heard from me. *That's* why I left. I only found out the truth after my dad died."

Mr. Farricelli clenched his fists and his teeth. "Ellen *never* would've done something so deceitful!"

"You're lying," Mrs. Farricelli insisted again.

"Why would I lie? I *loved* Ellen. More than anything. I wanted us to be a family. I wanted our baby. And I wanted her. But she said she never wanted to see me again – and aborted the baby."

"She wouldn't have done that. Our Ellen would never have lied to you. She loved you – and you left her when she needed you. You walked out and *destroyed* her!"

"Think about what you're saying, sir," Gary said softly. "If I'd intended to abandon Ellen when she was pregnant, would I have waited so long? For that matter, you think I'd have gone to Monsignor Streng's office voluntarily to tell him the baby was mine?"

"Voluntarily?"

"That's right. I didn't have to get expelled. Or get the crap kicked out of me when we got home. I could've kept my mouth shut and let her get thrown out." Gary winced at the memory of the beating from his father.

"I could have graduated and gone to BU like I'd planned. But I didn't. I loved Ellen – and the baby we'd created. And I owed it to *both* of them to take responsibility. If I wanted to run out, I'd have done it long before she started showing. Sure, I was scared: I was a kid, for God's sake! But Ellen was gonna have *my* baby. I wouldn't have left her. I *loved* her!"

Robert glared at his grandchild's father. "So why'd you just disappear? Doesn't sound much like love to me!"

"What would *you* do if your world was destroyed? And your drunk, abusive father beat you up – *again* – and threw you out of the house?! I'll tell you what you'd do: You'd do the same thing I did. You'd try to bury" – Gary slapped the tabletop – "the pain and make a new start. And if you want to condemn me for that, then God damn you!" He turned away abruptly.

Grim faced, Julia eyed Gary as he stalked toward her, his eyes glistening with fury. As she shook her head, her dark hair skimmed her shoulders. "I warned you not to do that; but you had to go and antagonize them. That temper of yours is going to cost you big time."

"They accused me of abandoning my daughter – they're trying to paint me as an unfit parent!"

"That's what they're *supposed* to do. What *you're* supposed to do is control yourself – and your temper! We tried it your way. Now sit down and let me do what it is you've hired me to do."

(9:15 a.m., November 7 – Thursday)
"I've given this a lot of thought," Gary told Julia at their next meeting. "I don't want to go ahead with it. Not now."

The attorney shoved a glossy curtain of hair behind her ear. "Why not?"

"Erin's just lost her mom. I won't rip her away from the only family she knows. Especially not in the middle of a school year."

"Are you sure about this?"

"Positive."

"Okay. But it can take months to reach an agreement. If you wait 'til the end of the school year, by the time a judge rules on it, the new term may have begun. You'll be right back where you are now."

Gary shrugged. "So how long can it take? Three months? Four? Longer?"

"Could be as much as six."

"So let's start again after the first of the year."

"If that's what you want to do." It sounded to Gary like she was questioning his sanity.

"I can't take my daughter away from her grandparents now. I won't."

"If that's what you want."

"You keep saying that – but I get the feeling it's not what *you* want, and you're waiting for me to change my mind."

"I don't want you to be without your daughter any longer than necessary."

"I don't either; but now is *not* the time to pursue this."

(December 23 – Monday)
Gary was feeding the cats when Hurricane Erin blew in. Apparently, just being in this house was enough to set her off.

"Why are you trying to keep me from my family?" she demanded, stamping her foot a little too close to Attila's tail.

"I hate you! You can't make me stay here. I wanna go home!" She kicked at the little tabby, then fled the room.

'Good morning' to you, too. Gary figured they'd gotten past all the unpleasantness last night; but a good night's sleep had only restored his daughter's depleted hostility. He sighed as the child careened into Micki, coming into the room with the baby.

"Whoa there, little one." Michaela smoothed Erin's hair, then stooped to draw her close. "Why so upset, sweetie?"

Still pouting, Erin eyed the infant in her stepmother's arms, but the tears in her eyes stayed put.

Micki stood and took her by the hand. "C'mon," she invited. "Let's go see if Amanda needs changing. Then after breakfast, we can put on your snowsuit and go out and play. How's that sound?"

It snowed last night, so the whole yard was white. "Alright," the little girl agreed, wiping at tears with the back of her free hand.

Gary watched Erin skip toward the stairs with Micki. *She turns that charm on and off like a faucet!* He was glad Erin had taken so readily to her stepmother. Since her first visit here, in mid July, Erin had been almost magnetically drawn to Michaela.

Purring wildly, Ginger swirled around Gary's calves. Attila stood on his back paws, stretching against Gary's denim-clad leg and batting affectionately upward at his hand.

Patting his cat's head absently, Gary bent to put their food dishes on the floor.

Michaela had told him all along not to let Erin get to him. *After all, she's just a child,* she'd said. But, after last night, maybe ignoring the little monster's behavior wasn't at all the right thing to do.

That night, Erin had won the battle.

(December 22 – Sunday)
It had been four days since Gary picked Erin up for a ten-day visit, and she hadn't uttered a civil word to him yet.

Mostly, Erin refused to acknowledge her father at all. She never addressed him as Dad, and, when speaking to Michaela, referred to Gary as "him," in the nastiest tone she could muster.

From the nursery, where he was rocking Mandy to sleep, Gary heard Erin talking to Micki in the hallway. "I dunno why *he* had to go and *ruin* my life! Everything was perfectly fine before him. We were just great – 'til *he* showed up and ruined everything! I *hate* him!"

Accustomed to love and acceptance from the kids in his first-grade religion class, he struggled to contend with a child who not only spurned every attempt at affection, but was plain vicious. Instead of getting up and closing the door, shutting out Erin's venom, Gary just sat and rocked the baby.

Micki's soft voice intervened. "Don't say that, honey. Your daddy *loves* you. How do you think he must feel, hearing you talk that way?"

Gary could envision his wife's slender fingers caressing his daughter's cherubic cheek.

An instant later, he wanted nothing more than to slap that little face.

"I don't *care* how he feels!" Erin blurted. "And don't call him that. He's *not* my daddy! A daddy is someone who *loves* you – and if he loved me so much, why did he leave me? All I had was my mommy and Grandpa Sheldon – and they died!"

Erin appeared at the nursery door. "My Gramma was right – you're horrible! You're a snake in the grass and I hate you!" She slammed the door and ran to her room. With a wild shriek of juvenile fury, she slammed that door, too.

Michaela stood in the hallway, helpless. Two wounded hearts needed comfort. One was a little girl's; the other belonged to the man she loved. Following her own heart, she swept into the nursery and lifted the now-squalling infant from her husband's arms. Cradling Mandy in the crook of one arm, Micki kissed Gary's forehead. "She didn't mean it, sweetheart. I'm sure she didn't."

At the sound of her mother's voice, the baby stopped crying.

"Why don't you go check on supper? I'll be right down." She laid Amanda in her crib and gave Gary a proper hug. "I know it's difficult right now, honey, but Erin'll come around. Give her time."

Looking disheartened, Gary slipped free of his wife's embrace and trudged downstairs.

Laying a blanket over the baby, Michaela shut the light on her way out. She went down the hall to Erin's room and rapped at the door. "Erin. Open the door." When the child obeyed, Michaela had to bite her tongue to keep from yelling. "That was a very naughty thing you did," she scolded. "It was hurtful and mean. And I want you to apologize to your father."

Erin flopped down on her bed. "No."

"What do you mean, *No?* You listen to me, little girl. I don't know what you're allowed to get away with at your grandparents' house, but that behavior doesn't fly here. Now, you go downstairs and apologize. And don't you give me that *He's not my daddy* garbage. He *is* your daddy and he loves you — and what you said to him was horrible. I want you to go say you're sorry."

Erin pouted. "I'm not telling him nothin' — 'cause I'm *not* sorry." Her brow furrowed intensely as she stared at Micki and spilled her litany of repugnance. "I hate him! I hate being here! I hate this house, I hate this room — and I hate you!"

They both knew that last part wasn't true.

"I really don't care *what* you hate." Her stepmother's stern tone warned the child she was treading on dangerous ground. "But you'd better go down there right now and apologize for those awful things you said to your father." Erin's intent to protest was met by a firm, "I mean it!"

Sighing excessively, she rolled her eyes. "Oh, al*right!*" She tromped downstairs, Micki at her heels.

They found Gary in the kitchen, peeling carrots.

"Honey?" Michaela called tentatively.

Gary turned. As his eyes met his wife's, some of the hurt melted away. When he saw Erin, however, he grew wary.

"Erin has something she wants to say to you." Laying her hands on the girl's shoulders, Michaela steered her toward him. "Don't you, sweetie?"

The child glowered. Gary felt the acid sting of her hatred.

The silence grew thick and palpable. And ugly.

Still glaring, Erin spat out the nastiest thing she could think of. "I'm sorry you're my father! I wish I never met you! I wish *you* died instead of Momma – I hate you!"

She ran back up the stairs, stomping her Keds as hard as possible on each step. Just for spite, she pounded at the door to the nursery and screeched, "Wake up! Wake up! Your father's a big jerk and I hate him! I wish he was dead! I wish you were dead, too!" She ran down the hall to her room – shrieking out her anger the whole way there – and slammed the door as hard as she could.

Awakened again, the baby wailed.

Michaela gaped at Gary, horrified. He looked back in disbelief. And withering pain.

"I'm going up there to give that little brat a piec—"

The hand he laid on her arm was gentle, his voice filled with weary resignation. "No. Let her go."

"Gary… you can't let her get away with talking to you like that."

Gary remembered how it felt to be abandoned, to feel lost and unloved. Especially at Christmas. He couldn't explain that to Micki, didn't even want to try. He gathered her into his arms. "It's okay, baby," he murmured against her chestnut hair. "She's got every reason to be angry."

"But she doesn't have to take it out on you."

"She has to take it out on someone. If it has to be me" – he shrugged – "at least she's not bottling it up inside."

"Still, it's not right."

"I said, Let her go," he repeated. "If I want her in my life, it has to be on her terms. And right now, she doesn't want any part of me. So I just have to accept that."

"But *Gary…*"

"No, Michaela. Don't argue with me. Not about *this.*"

"Doesn't it bother you that—"

"Of *course* it does, Mick." He pulled away. "But I'm the grownup; she's a little girl. A little girl who's lost her mom and her grandfather in less than a year; and now some stranger's yanked her away from the only family she knows. She's angry, she's sad… she's frightened. How do you expect her to react?"

Michaela looked unconvinced.

Gary took her hands. "Trust me," he murmured. "Okay? Just trust me."

"I do," she whispered back, squeezing his hands. "I *do* trust you, honey."

"Then let me handle this." It sounded more like a question than a directive. He headed upstairs.

Amanda was still wailing, so Gary settled her back to sleep, then went to Erin's room. He stood outside her door, trying to assemble coherent thoughts. He didn't know how to talk to her. And his heart was racing so fast he thought he'd pass out. *It'll have to wait.* With a morose backward glance, he plodded toward his bedroom.

During dinner, Michaela tried repeatedly to make lighthearted conversation. Neither Gary nor Erin was receptive.

Afterward, Erin asked to use the phone to call her grandparents. Then she retreated to her room.

At bedtime, she put on her pajamas and brushed her teeth without being told.

When it was time for prayers, she asked God to bless Grandma and Grandpa and her aunts and uncle and to watch over Momma and Grandpa, "and *please* let me go back to my real family, 'cause I hate it here."

As he tucked Erin in, Gary leaned to kiss her cheek. "Goodnight. Sweet dreams, little one. I love you."

She turned her face away from his kiss and muttered a terse, "Go away," into her pillow.

He sighed. At least she didn't say she hated him – as she had the past two nights.

***

Gary shuddered at the memory. *Was that only last night?* He was ladling more pancake batter onto the griddle when Michaela and Erin returned.

"Those smell great." Micki gave him an appreciative kiss before disappearing into the family room to feed the baby.

Erin leaned against the refrigerator. Sidling over to where the cats were eating, she kicked at their water bowl. A small wave cascaded onto the floor. Attila skittered away. Ginger leapt a foot in the air, her tail puffing in alarm. When the big red cat landed, she watched the child through wary green eyes, and swished her tail disapprovingly, slogging it through the puddle of water.

Gary looked up when he heard the bowl tip; he tried to convince himself it was an accident, until he saw his daughter's smirk of cruel satisfaction.

"Erin, leave the cats alone," he reproved halfheartedly, flipping a pancake.

In reply, the child slapped at the spilled water with a sneakered foot, splattering it everywhere and intentionally splashing Ginger. Erin stared her father down, daring him to stop her.

"Erin." Now his voice held a warning. "What did I just tell you?"

"I'm not touchin' the stupid cats!"

Gary took a deep breath and let it out slowly, counting silently to twenty. He'd promised himself he wouldn't spoil the holidays by blowing up at Erin. Still agitated, he continued on to thirty-five.

"Breakfast is almost ready," he said, his voice gentle. "Please go wash your hands and sit down."

Instead of obeying, Erin grabbed Ginger's tail and yanked her off her feet. Yowling in protest, the cat swung around and scratched her. Erin screamed and clutched her arm, which was now bleeding.

Gary thumped the pancake turner down on the stovetop. "Dammit, Erin!"

Erin's lips curled in a sneer of triumph.

So much for that promise… Still, he caught himself before he lost it completely.

Abandoning the pancakes, Gary rushed to his daughter's side. Stooping, he dabbed at the trickle of blood with a damp paper towel. After examining the scratches, he smoothed back her hair and wiped the tears wending their way down her face. He marveled at how much she resembled her mother. *Not just in her looks, either.* As he daubed at the blood again, Gary made a mental note to check the cats' rabies vaccinations. "There… that's better," he cooed, leaning in to kiss Erin's cheek. "Does it hurt?"

She shoved him away. "What do *you* care? You care more about those damn cats than you do about me!"

As Gary stood, he noticed the burning smell. Smoke spewed from the scorched, blackened mess and billowed about the room. The smoke alarm, mounted almost directly overhead, screeched.

Snatching the griddle from the stove, he scraped the smoldering lot into the trash. Tossing the pan into the sink, he reached for the smoke detector. He tugged off its cover and yanked out the battery. The shrieking stopped. But the pounding in his head continued.

"That's *not* very *safe*, ya know," Erin remarked, crossing her arms in apparent disgust. "Or *smart*, for that matter."

He bit back an *Oh, shut up!* He opted instead for: "Ya know what, Erin? Go to your room. Just go. I don't wanna deal with you right now."

"Fine! I don't wanna see *your* face either!" She flounced toward the door.

Then she turned. Standing with her hands on her hips, she yelled at him. "Look – you don't want me here; and *I* don't wanna *be* here. So just do what we both want: Take me back home!"

Gary stared after his daughter in numbed dismay. Shutting off the burner where the griddle had sat, he slid the platter of non-ruined pancakes into the oven to keep warm.

After dispersing what he could of the choking black smoke by fanning it out the back door with yesterday's newspaper, he slumped into a seat at the table. Reaching into his pocket, he felt for his rosary. His fingertips brushed against the smooth onyx beads and the sterling-silver crucifix. It was the rosary Grandma Jo had given Grandpa on their wedding day nearly sixty years ago, the set Grandpa used daily as he trod the beach… the ones he'd been holding when he died. Gary pulled the treasured rosary from his pocket. Making the sign of the cross and touching the crucifix to his lips, he began to pray.

Micki thought it best not to get involved in the father-daughter fracas. Besides, it was comforting, sitting here with Mandy, who periodically made little yummy noises. Suddenly, it grew too quiet. But she couldn't exactly get up to see what was going on – not with an infant suckling at her breast.

She leaned back against the pillows. They were a family of four now. Like it or not.

That's not fair. Family was family. And it was mean to think evil thoughts about a child who was having such a rough time adjusting. She was Gary's daughter. And her stepdaughter. Erin was just fifteen years her junior. In years to come, the closeness in their ages might work in their favor: She could be a confidante during the girl's teen years. And when she was grown… gosh, they'd be more like sisters than mother and daughter!

For now, she'd have to be content being Mama to the little peanut at her breast and stepmother to Erin. Micki shuddered. *Stepmother! Never thought <u>that</u> would happen. Let alone at 24! Yet here I am: the wicked stepmother. No, that's not quite right.* She cuddled Mandy. *Erin actually likes me; it's Gary she hates.* Sighing, she prayed Erin would get past her anger or hatred, or whatever it was, and realize Gary was doing his best to reach out to her in love.

Meanwhile, in the kitchen, Gary silently prayed his way through the Joyful Mysteries, all the while thinking there must be *some* joy in having Erin here.

That's not fair, he rebuked himself. *She's your daughter…* Somewhere in his heart he felt Erin might come to love him some day. Pocketing the beads, he spent a few minutes praying to St. Joseph. As he did, his prayer for guidance turned to one of remorse.

For all his trying to live up to the saint's impossibly high standards, Gary felt – no, *knew* – he was failing. "I'm sorry," he murmured, his head bowed. "She's just a little girl. I shouldn't get so upset; but I don't know how to reach her. Please, St. Joseph… what do I do? Please help me."

Listening closely, he heard the answer enter his heart: *Keep reaching out in love. Be loving and gentle and kind. When she lashes out in anger, respond with love. When she's hurtful, be loving in return. Whatever she does, however she acts, respond with love. Eventually, she'll get the message. The key to good parenting is an abundance of love.*

Gary didn't know if he'd imagined the answer, but it seemed plausible. Gathering his courage for what he hoped wouldn't be too awful a confrontation, he went to the family room for a hug from Micki and a snuggle with Amanda. Then, bolstered by their comforting touch, he was ready to face Erin.

Standing outside her door, he prayed. *God, please help me. Help me say the right thing. There's so much at stake here. Please, God, don't let me screw this up!*

He had no doubt God would answer that prayer. But Grandpa's words came back to him: *Sometimes, Gary, the answer is 'No.' Or 'Not now.' You have to be prepared to accept that answer.*

Grandpa was good at dispensing sound advice. Gary missed that. He loved how Grandpa always seemed to have the right words. He envied him that. Gary made a living at being good with words, but they seemed to come so much easier – so much more wisely – from Grandpa. With a final, *Please, God, let her be receptive,* he knocked.

And waited.

The knob turned and Erin opened the door. "What do *you* want?" She looked like she wanted to shut the door.

His mouth felt dry and he could feel his heart racing. "Okay if I come in?"

"I suppose," she muttered grudgingly, going back to lie down. She pouted and stared at the wall. But before long, curiosity won and she turned to look at her father.

Gary took the chair from in front of her desk. Placing it beside the bed, he sat.

She cringed a little, as though he was going to yell at her.

"Ya know," he began conversationally, leaning his elbows on his knees, "it's okay to be angry."

"What?"

"It's okay to be angry." His next words were as much a surprise to him as they were to her. "And I want you to know I'm not mad at you about what you said."

Her interest piqued, Erin sat up. "You're *not?*"

"No. It's been a lousy time for you, and I know how upset and angry you must be."

"No you don't. You don't know *anything.*" She flopped back down. "You don't know how it feels when your momma dies!" The little girl buried her face in the pillow.

"No," Gary acquiesced. "I *don't* know how *that* feels. But I *do* know what it's like to lose someone you love; I know how much that hurts. I remember how sad I felt when my grandpa died."

Erin turned her head; her eyes locked on his.

"*I* was really close to *my* grandpa – just like you were to yours – because *I* didn't like *my* daddy very much, either."

"Why not?"

How'm I gonna say this? I don't see 'He used to beat the crap outta me' going over real well. "We didn't exactly get along. He was angry a lot of the time. And he" – dare he say it? – "well, he used to hit me a lot."

There was no real malice in her tone, just childlike speculation. "Maybe you were a horrible kid, and that's why you grew up to be such a crummy father."

Ouch! He'd been about to say something about Jeremy having a big job with a lot of pressure. "Maybe you're right," he heard himself tell her instead. "But I didn't get a chance to be a good daddy."

Suspicion brewed in Erin's eyes. "Why not?"

"Because I didn't know your mommy was going to have you."

The little girl sighed aloud in disgust. "You'd hafta be pretty *stupid* not to know *that*. Didn't you see her getting all big?"

"Of course." It all seemed so simple to her. But how could he explain Ellen's lie? *God, help me.* "It's kind of hard to explain, but I'll try: I knew your mommy was pregnant, but she told me she, uh… stopped being pregnant. She said something happened – and she wasn't going to have a baby after all."

Erin looked at him like he was an idiot. "But – duh! I'm *here*. What were you *thinking?*"

"I thought you had died. Then my daddy and I got into a really big fight and he sent me away. So I came to Connecticut, to stay with my grandpa. I wasn't around when you were born. I never knew your mommy *wasn't* telling me the truth. If I had known that, Erin" – he stroked her hair – "I would never have left. I would've married your mommy; and I would have been your daddy, all that time. I'm sorry, honey. I'm so sorry I missed out on all those years with you."

She sat up, cocking her head. "So… you *wanted* to be with Momma and me?"

"Yes!" Gary's voice crackled with emotion. "Of course I did. I *loved* you."

Saying nothing, the little girl continued to eye him. He went on.

"When we found out she was going to have you, we were scared… because we were both so young – younger than Uncle Tommy is now. But I loved your mommy; and even though you weren't born yet, I loved *you*. And I wanted us to be a family – a *real* family."

Erin took a deep breath and let it out slowly. "So, how are you related to the rest of my family?"

Relief flooded Gary. *Finally, something* *easy*. "Your Grandpa Sheldon was my daddy. Just like I'm *your* daddy, he was *my* daddy."

She pondered this. "So your last name is Sheldon." When he nodded, she went on. "Is that what *my* last name is gonna be, too?" Plumping her pillow, she leaned back against it again.

"Yeah. I suppose."

"My grandpa was your daddy?"

"That's right." Gary could practically hear the thought process going on in her head.

She frowned. "So you're saying Grandpa Sheldon did all that bad stuff to you?"

He hedged. "Yeah. But that doesn't mean he didn't love me; it just means he didn't know how to show it. And it doesn't mean he didn't love you. He *did*. And he'd never have done anything to hurt you."

The little girl studied her father. "Are you happy he's dead?"

The question was like a slap in the face. "No," Gary replied sadly. It was the truth, he realized.

"Even though you didn't get along?"

"Even though we didn't get along," he echoed with a nod. "I'm sorry we never made up before he died. And I'm sorry we didn't get along" – a sad smile twitched at the corners of his mouth. *And now I'm a dad, sometimes I really do miss him* – "but I'm glad he was so good to you." He caressed Erin's cheek.

"Why did Momma tell you I died?"

"I'm not sure. I'm guessing she probably said it because she was angry with me. And when we're angry, honey, sometimes we say things without thinking – awful things – just to hurt another person's feelings… even someone we really love a whole lot, deep down. We say things we don't mean."

"Why?"

He shrugged. "It's just what people do sometimes."

"Is that what Momma did? Say something she didn't mean?"

"I think so," he said gently.

"But if you knew she didn't mean it, why'd you go away?"

Was nothing easy? "Because I *didn't* know. Not then. I didn't know she was saying it just to be cruel. I thought she was telling me the truth."

"But, not telling the truth… that – that would be lying."

He nodded, then offered a quiet, "That's right."

Erin's lower lip trembled. Rolling onto her tummy, she flattened herself against the bed as much as she could and hugged her pillow. "You mean she *lied* to you? On purpose?"

Gary gestured awkwardly. "I doubt it was on purpose. I think she was just scared."

"Just so you'd go away and she could have me all to her-self?"

"I don't know *why* she did it, sweetheart," he told her truthfully, his voice soft as a caress.

Her pout was back. A long silence ensued. "I bet you're glad *she's* dead, huh?"

The force of her words jarred Gary. A sharp edge found its way into his voice. "Of course not, Erin! Don't say that."

The little girl sat up again. "But if she was so mean to you…?"

He stroked her hair. It was so soft! "Well, like I said, sometimes people say mean stuff to people they love… 'cause lots of times it's easier than saying things you should say. Like sometimes it's easier to say 'I hate you' than 'I'm sorry' or even 'I love you.' "

Erin fidgeted. "Why's that?"

"I dunno. Maybe we're afraid to say what we really feel, 'cause we don't want to be rejected… or made fun of – or risk being hurt by someone we love."

"Oh."

They sat in silence for a long time. Finally, swinging her legs over the side of the bed, Erin got to her feet. To Gary's amazement, she climbed into his lap and reached up to put her arms around his neck. And hugged him.

"Daddy? I'm sorry I was mean to you before." She looked up, seeming surprised to see him crying. Erin gave his tear-streaked cheek a tentative pat. "Don't cry, Daddy. I don't want you to be sad."

"I'm not sad, baby," he assured her. "These are happy tears."

"Oh." Accepting his explanation, she cuddled closer and slid her arms around him again.

***

On Christmas morning, Diane watched expectantly as her granddaughter tore the wrapping off the small flat package.

Erin pulled the last shred of tissue paper away. It was a photo of two people – teenagers – she couldn't identify. Studying it closely, a slow smile of recognition overtook her face as she let out a yelp. "Hey!" she shouted, looking at the grandmother she'd only met a few months earlier. "This is so cool!"

Gary craned his neck to see. No use; Erin was holding it at too odd an angle.

Diane smiled. "It's always been one of my favorites. I thought you might want it."

"What is it?" Gary asked his daughter, trying to sound nonchalant.

When Erin handed the gift to her father, he nearly dropped it. He stared at the photo – then at his mother. Betrayal and hurt nudged aside a nauseating ache. *In a way, it's nice to see those smiling faces again.*

Gary recalled that day. It was a Wednesday in July, summer before junior year. He'd taken the day off from work. He and Ellen packed a picnic lunch and rode their bikes down to the shore.

The brightness of their smiles contrasted with the depth of their tans. Ellen, who'd used baby oil instead of suntan lotion, was a toasty brown. And, blessed with Mom's Mediterranean complexion, he was already a deep bronze. Their hair was mussed from daylong exposure to the salt water, a stiff shore breeze and the half-mile bike ride back home. Marie had captured that image.

The young lovebirds were wheeling their bikes into the garage, before going inside to shower and change for dinner. Gary had one hand on his handlebars, the other around his girlfriend's shoulder. One hand guiding her bike, Ellen had her free arm around his waist. She was smiling, her upturned face aglow with affection and the kiss of summer sun. Gary had just started to lean in to kiss her.

Erin had never seen a picture of them together. Daddy's words – *I* _loved_ *your mommy* – played through her mind. She'd never seen them looking happy together. Mesmerized, she stared at it for a long while. Then she hurtled toward Diane, flinging outstretched arms around her. "Thank you, Grandma! It's just what I've always wanted!"

That night, before bed, she asked Daddy to help her put the picture on the wall in her bedroom.

Chapter 7

(February 1992)

"Your Honor, I don't see why my wife and I should be deprived of our only grandchild because *he* feels guilty about having run away from his responsibility." Robert Farricelli's voice wavered as he pointed across the courtroom.

Gary leapt to his feet. Julia pulled discreetly at his sleeve to restrain him.

"I *didn't* run from my responsibility," he asserted, undeterred. "I was told I no longer *had* a child – that she was aborted. I'm not here to point fingers, Your Honor. I know that wasn't her grandparents' fault. I'm sorry they think I'm trying to hurt them. All I want is for a wrong to be righted – and a chance to be Daddy to my little girl."

"She doesn't want to be with you; she hates you!" Christina Farricelli shrilled.

Gary's eyes flashed. "Not anymore. But she *did,* because you poisoned her against me!"

Judge Mallory O'Neill banged her gavel. "Enough!" She reviewed the paperwork before her, then glanced at the attorneys and their clients. "I've heard from both sides" – she looked disapprovingly from the Farricellis to Gary – "frankly, far more than I wish I had. Still, I don't see why Mr. Sheldon shouldn't be awarded at least partial custody of his daughter."

"Your Honor – that's… why that's insane!" the older man sputtered. "You can't do that!"

"Mr. Farricelli, kindly refrain from telling me what I can and cannot do in my courtroom. And Mr. Williams, please advise your clients of proper decorum in here."

The Farricellis' attorney shifted foot to foot. "Yes, Your Honor."

Julia refocused the judge's attention. "Your Honor, there'd been a visitation arrangement in place since last June; but upon the death of the girl's mother, my client requested it be amended."

Ken Williams glanced at Julia; she gave a slight nod, as if to say, *Consider it a professional courtesy.*

Judge O'Neill's eyebrow arched; she addressed Gary. "What sort of amendment?"

"I didn't think it was right to take Erin from the only family she knew — even two weekends a month, which was what our agreement stipulated. I felt any separation would be damaging so soon after her mother's death."

"Did you advise your client in this matter?"

"Yes, Your Honor. I advised keeping visitation as it was — for sake of continuity for the child."

"Did he follow your advice?"

Julia cast a sidelong glance at Gary. "No, Your Honor; he did not."

"And why was that, Mr. Sheldon?"

"For the reason I stated, Your Honor: I felt it wasn't in Erin's best interest at the time."

"And now it *is* in her best interest — for you to take her away from us?"

Judge O'Neill banged her gavel. "Mr. Williams, please control your client." She turned to Gary. "He raises a valid point, Mr. Sheldon: Why do you feel it's in her best interest now?"

"Your Honor, Erin's had time to begin working through her grief. She came to Connecticut for an extended stay at Christmastime; and she's begun to accept me in her life."

"So, what is it you want?"

"I'm petitioning the Court for full custody."

Christina Farricelli gripped her husband's hand. "No! No! You can't do that." Her eyes wide, she turned to her attorney. "You can't let him do that."

The judge turned compassionate eyes toward the distraught grandmother. "Why?" she prompted kindly. "Why do you protest his getting custody?"

"She's just a little girl! He wants to take her away from everything she knows." She wept into the tissue wadded in her hand. "Please don't let him take her… not now."

"No, not *now*," Gary reassured her. "Not right away" – he addressed the bench – "Your Honor, I meant at the end of the school year. I wouldn't take Erin away now; not when she's just beginning to regain some stability. The Farricellis have done a remarkable job caring for Erin. I don't dispute that. That's not what this is about. *At all.* I appreciate everything they've done for Erin, and will continue to do as loving grandparents. But her day-to-day care is *my* responsibility, Your Honor. Let me take that responsibility."

The judge nodded. "Again, you make a good point, Mr. Sheldon." She waited for Christina to pull herself together. "Mr. and Mrs. Farricelli, I realize it's been difficult, caring for your grandchild after your daughter's death; but I have to ask: Is there any *legal* reason Mr. Sheldon should be denied custody of his daughter?"

Mrs. Farricelli seized her husband's arm. Burying her face against his suited shoulder, she wailed, "Don't let him take away my baby… not my baby."

Consoling his wife as best he could, Mr. Farricelli said, "No, Your Honor. No legitimate reason."

"In that case, I'm going to grant Mr. Sheldon's petition for full custody of the minor child Erin Farricelli Sheldon. Said custody shall be effective July first of this year. Until then, the original visitation agreement remains in effect. But be advised, Mr. Sheldon: I'm granting *temporary* custody, pending further study." She banged her gavel. "This proceeding is adjourned."

Outside the courtroom, Mrs. Farricelli seized Gary by the arm. "Why are you doing this?" she demanded bitterly. "Why do you want to snatch our baby away?"

"I'm not trying to hurt you. I'd never do that. Like I said: You've gone beyond the call, raising Erin; but you've done your job. It's time for you to enjoy being her grandparents."

Her eyes filled with tears. "How can we enjoy being her grandparents if she's not around?"

"I won't keep her from you. I promise. Erin will live in Connecticut, but that's *all* that'll change. We've got a big ol' house with your name on the guest bedroom. You're always welcome" – he handed Mrs. Farricelli his handkerchief; she mopped at her eyes – "and last I knew, there's still train service from Waterbury to Toms River." Instinctively, Gary hugged her; she didn't resist. "It'll be alright; it's just going to take some getting used to. For all of us."

Sniffling, she handed back the damp handkerchief as Robert led her away.

"It's good of you to be so conciliatory toward her; that'll play well with the judge," Julia remarked after they were out of earshot.

"Conciliatory, nothing. I *love* that woman; she was like a mother to me after—" he rephrased what he was about to say, "while I was growing up. Do you think I want to see her hurting?"

(July 10 – Friday)
There was no shortage of tears as Erin hugged her grandparents goodbye. Three of her friends also came to see her off. The little girls hugged their pal, soliciting promises from her to call.

Hoping to stave off the girls' tearful farewell, Gary took them all out for ice cream before loading up the car and bringing Erin home to Connecticut.

"Your dad's pretty cool," he overheard one of them say outside the ice-cream parlor.

Erin smiled. "Yeah, he is. And my stepmom's really great, too." She sighed. "But I sure am gonna miss my grandma and grandpa… an' you guys."

(July 24 – Friday)

The first time Gary brought his daughter in to the radio station, Erin was enthralled with the trappings of her dad's job: music, production studios and microphones, recording equipment and sound-effect CDs. And those five gleaming awards on his office wall.

"What're those?"

He explained how record companies award gold records to artists for record sales.

"Then why do *you* have 'em?"

He handed her the latest *Radio & Records*. "If other radio stations start playing a song because of what we said about it in this magazine, sometimes the record company will send a gold record – like that one – to the station."

"But why's *your* name on 'em?"

"It's my job to help decide what music we play. When record companies call to see how often we play their songs, they talk to me."

"Oh." Erin nodded pensively. A smile broke across her face. "Cool."

(August 27 – Thursday)

"It's been two months," said Judge O'Neill. "I trust everything's going well?"

Nods from Gary and the Farricellis. "Yes, Your Honor."

"Erin's settling in well in her new home?"

"She is, Your Honor," Gary said. "Naturally, she misses her grandparents – and her friends in Jersey; but she's adjusting. And she knows she can call them whenever she wants."

"And you've got adequate access to her?"

The Farricellis nodded. "Yes, Your Honor. Gary's been most accommodating."

She flipped through the paperwork. "I see from the periodic visitation reports there appear to be no problems at home." She looked up again. "The transition went smoothly?"

"Pretty much, Your Honor." Gary didn't elaborate.

The judge studied another page. "I should advise you, Mr. Sheldon, the Farricellis noted an incident surrounding the transfer of custody they wished to have taken into consideration."

Gary's heart thudded to a dead halt. He swallowed hard, tried to breathe normally.

"It says here, knowing they always visit family in Ohio over Fourth of July, you offered to pick up Erin the following weekend, so she could spend time with her great-grandparents. Is that right?"

"Yes, Your Honor. I knew how much it would mean to Erin – and to the rest of her family."

"Well, as you'll hear, it was certainly appreciated." The judge picked up Bob Farricelli's letter dated July 1 and read a line from it. " 'I believe it should weigh heavily in his favor that Gary showed such consideration for Erin's feelings.' Mr. Sheldon, I commend you for your sensitivity toward your daughter and her extended family. And, Mr. Farricelli, as requested, these circumstances are so noted; I thank you for bringing it to my attention. Now, with all the paperwork completed and visitation reports duly filed, I'm pleased to award permanent custody of Erin Farricelli Sheldon to her father."

(September 2, 1992 – Friday night)
While it made sense to schedule Erin's party for the weekend after her birthday, Gary agonized over its timing. "It seems like we're throwing it in their faces, celebrating just after the anniversary of Ellen's death," he said as he and Michaela washed the dinner dishes.

"Honey, no matter when we have it, there'd still be that… *specter* of Ellen's death overshadowing it. And you can't just *not* celebrate Erin's birthday. If we did it the third, that'd be kind of rotten timing. But the tenth falls right after her birthday; plus, it's a long weekend. Her grandparents are more likely to come if they've got a day to rest up afterward. This way, Katrina and Joey can be here, too."

Gary finished drying the last of the dishes. "I guess that makes sense."

The following week, when Gary called to invite the Farricellis to Erin's party, he expected a polite refusal.

"Why, Gary, that'd be wonderful! Of course Bob and I will be there."

"We'd love it if Tommy and Roma came, too."

"I don't know if Tom can get away; it's an awfully long drive from Baltimore. And I'm not sure what Rosemary's got planned. But I'll ask them."

Gary couldn't fault Christina for covering for them. He knew Tommy blamed him for El's suicide, and Rosemary still harbored plenty of bitterness herself.

Katrina bore no such hostility. She'd always loved Gary — and she adored Micki. She visited them regularly; they lived less than an hour's drive from Central Connecticut State in New Britain, where she was a sophomore. Since the party was over the Columbus Day holiday, she accepted their invitation to stay the weekend.

(October 10 – Saturday)
"Look who's getting all cozy with the enemy camp," Rosemary muttered, sneering when her little sister answered the door. "What are you, their personal maid now? Or just a hired flunky?"

Ignoring her sister's remark, Katrina kissed her parents. "Hi Mom, Daddy. C'mon in. Let me take your coats" – she called up the stairs – "Erin! Grandma and Grandpa are here… and Auntie Roma."

Erin flew down the stairs. "Grandma! Grandpa!" she cried out, dashing into their waiting arms. A moment later, she'd wiggled free of their embrace and hugged her aunt. "Auntie Roma – I'm so glad you came! You've never seen my house. C'mon" – she tugged at Rosemary's arm – "I'll show you my room. You're gonna love it! Daddy an' Micki an' I painted it. It's like the ocean!"

Gary came in from the kitchen. "Erin, what's all the yelling, honey? Oh—" Catching sight of the new arrivals, he smiled. "Hi. Good to see you again" – he hugged Christina, then shook Robert's hand – "and Ro, I'm so glad you made it." He went to hug her; she drew away.

"I wouldn't miss my niece's tenth birthday," she told him curtly, folding her arms.

Gary read the venomous look in her eyes: *Not even if it means having to spend the day with you.*

He ushered them into the kitchen. "I think you know my mom, Diane – and my sister, Marie." Crossing the room, he wrapped his arms around Erin from behind, and bent to kiss her forehead.

She squirmed away and skipped over to her aunt. "*C'mon,* Auntie Roma – come see my room. Auntie Marie, you come too." Taking them each by a hand, she tugged them toward the stairs.

Just before cake, Christina approached Gary in the kitchen. "Could I have a word with you?"

Apprehension crept into his eyes. "Sure." He led her to the living room. "What's on your mind?"

"You were always like a son to us, Gary." She reached out her hands to him. "For so long, we felt angry and betrayed at how you" – she stopped – "at how *we were told* you abandoned Ellen. But last week, Katrina confirmed what you'd maintained all along: that Ellen lied to you – and *us*. At first we didn't want to believe it. Then we…" She shook her head. "I'm so sorry – we both are. For how we treated you and the animosity we harbored toward you these last ten years."

Something prickled at Gary's insides. *This is a forgiveness moment,* Grandpa's voice urged, *a real opportunity for healing… for all of you. Don't pass it up.* He held her hands. "I can't hold that against you. Or Ellen." The prickling subsided. "She must've been terrified about having a baby on her own. She may have realized it was a mistake to push me away and, to save face, she said *I* was the one who left *her*" – he glanced at their joined hands. His voice sounded small and faraway – "but by then it was too late."

"Gary, what about *now?* I feel so awful about the things we said, how we behaved. You must despise us for how we treated you."

"It wasn't easy, having you all hate me." Gary grinned, hoping she'd realize he was making a stab at levity. He was relieved when she smiled. "But I don't blame you. What matters is Erin's surrounded by people who love her." He paused. "Although, I must admit I'm relieved you know the truth."

She nodded. "Me too. I wish things had turned out differently: that El hadn't lied to you, and you hadn't left" – she held up her hands – "I don't mean anything against Michaela, because she's a delightful girl, Gary – really a *wonderful* girl. But a little part of me still wishes things could've been different."

"I know," he replied with a wistful smile. "It's only natural to think about the what-ifs." He slid an arm around her and pressed a tender kiss against her temple.

They were silent a few moments.

Reaching out, Christina patted his knee affectionately. Her voice was filled with longing. "I used to love that you called us 'Mom and Dad.' " She paused. "I noticed, the last few times we've talked, you don't quite know what to call us anymore."

Gary hadn't realized his discomfort was so evident. "I guess."

"I know you're not comfortable calling us 'Bob and Christina'; but 'Mr. and Mrs. Farricelli' makes me feel like we're strangers; I'd really like if you would call us Mom and Dad – unless Michaela might feel somehow…" Her uncertain words decayed into even-more-uncertain silence.

"I see," Gary said softly, not sure what else to say. "We can give it a try and see how it goes. Okay, Mom?" The last word tripped off his lips as nimbly as if it had never stopped doing so.

The look in her eyes was one he couldn't immediately pinpoint. Gratitude? Reconciliation? Relief? No, he realized; it was remembrance. Familiarity. Belonging.

***

(November 26 – Thanksgiving)

"I don't hafta do what you say. You're not my mother. You can't tell me what to do!"

"Erin—"

"No! Stop trying to take Momma's place. You can't do that – you're just a lousy substitute!"

Gary appeared in the doorway, arms laden with firewood. "Hey!" The word was at once an admonition and a command to stop.

Erin's head whipped around in Dad's direction. She watched in silence as he carried the logs into the living room and dumped them beside the hearth; then, sitting on the couch, he beckoned her in.

The child approached on hesitant feet.

Gary's initial impulse had been to shout and insist she apologize for her rudeness; but he let years of gentle grandfatherly influence intervene. *How would Grandpa have handled this?*

Listening carefully, he got his answer: *She's just a child, Gary; appeal to her sense of tenderness.*

When she was close enough, he lifted Erin onto his lap. "Erin, honey, no one's trying to replace your mommy. No one could *ever* do that. We – all three of us – know Micki's not your mommy. But it doesn't mean you can disobey her. Or talk back. She's my wife; she's also your elder – which is reason enough for you to obey her. And Micki loves you, Erin. She'd never ask you to do anything that was bad; or something that would hurt you."

Erin's pout was becoming steadily more pronounced – a sure sign her father's words were getting through.

He held her close and cuddled her; when he spoke again, his words were as gentle as a kitten's purr. "You know how it feels when someone says mean things, just to hurt your feelings?"

Erin gave a little nod.

"Kinda makes you feel sad, doesn't it? And maybe a little bit angry inside?"

"Mm-hmm."

"Well," he said, stroking Erin's hair. "I saw Micki's face after you said those things. It looked to me like you hurt her feelings. I bet she's feeling pretty sad right about now, 'cause you said some hurtful stuff." He stopped smoothing her hair for a moment. "But you didn't really mean to upset her… huh?"

Sniffling, Erin shook her head.

"I've got an idea: Why don't you go out there and tell her that? Tell her you didn't mean to hurt her feelings. Okay?"

Now the child nodded. "Mm-hmm."

"You might want to give her a hug, too. I bet that'll help her feel better." Gary kissed his daughter on the forehead. "I'm guessing you'll feel better, too."

"Okay, Daddy." She slipped her arms around him and gave him a squeeze, then slid off his lap and headed purposefully out to the kitchen.

Micki was scrubbing potatoes. With the water on, she didn't hear Erin say her name. But when she felt a tug at the back of her sweatshirt, she gave a start and shut off the faucet. Turning, she expected to see Gary, and wondered why he didn't pull her ponytail or kiss the nape of her neck, like he usually did. "Oh! Erin, you startled me." Micki wiped her hands on her apron. "What is it, honey?"

Erin reached up and put her arms around her stepmother. "I wanted to tell you I'm sorry, Micki. I didn't mean to hurt your feelings… or make you sad. And even though you're not my real momma, I want you to know I love you and I'm so glad you're Daddy's wife."

A swell of emotion swept over Michaela at the little girl's words.

"And I'm ready to set the table now," Erin added contritely, beginning to sniffle. "I'm sorry I said I wouldn't do it before. I'm sorry I made you sad." She rubbed at her teary eyes.

Micki hugged her. "That's okay, honey. Shh… don't cry. It's alright. Thank you for coming back to tell me that, Erin. I accept your apology." She planted a kiss on her stepdaughter's forehead and held the girl close for a long, comforting moment. Then she took her by the hand. "C'mon, I'll get the dishes from the cupboard; you get the silverware. After the table's set, you wanna help me mash the potatoes?"

Erin's face instantly brightened.

(6:42 p.m., November 30 – Monday)

"You made a real big hit with the kids," Gary told Marc, as fond Thanksgiving images tumbled through his mind. "You're welcome to join us for Christmas – if you can stand another holiday with the Sheldon clan."

Marc Lindsay was the nighttime jock at Z97-3; he was also Gary's best friend and Amanda's godfather. A confirmed bachelor, he seldom turned down a holiday invitation from Gary's family – and they loved having "Uncle Marc" around.

"I'd love to, but I'll be with my girlfriend's family."

"What?" Gary's eyebrows shot up. "Why haven't you mentioned this girlfriend before?"

"I kinda wanted to keep it quiet… just 'til I knew where things were going between us. Besides, I knew you'd react like this the minute I said anything," Marc teased. "Anyway, I go through women the way most guys go through" – he paused, laughed – "well…women."

"So… tell me!" Gary urged. "Where'd you meet her? What's her name? What's she do?"

Marc shrugged as he pulled commercials for his first hour. "I met her at a funeral."

Gary laughed aloud. "That's just twisted! You're the only guy I know who can pick up women at funerals! Who was she – the grieving widow?"

"This is why I didn't say anything before. If you're gonna make fun—"

"No, really" – Gary forced back a smile – "go ahead. This I gotta hear."

"If you must know, it was her father's funeral."

"How'd you know the father and manage not to know her?"

"I *didn't* know him," he said. "Her brother and I go way back."

"How's *he* feel about you doin' his sister?"

Marc gave a little shrug, but didn't deny anything. "Poor guy's clueless."

Over mugs of cinnamon-laced coffee, Gary and Michaela watched the girls tear downstairs Christmas morning. Mandy squealed when she saw the shiny red tricycle with its big blue bow; Erin reacted with equal enthusiasm when she saw the metallic-blue bike peeking out from behind the tree.

"Where'd those come from?" Michaela asked as the girls ran to inspect the gleaming vehicles.

"Santa must've brought them." When Gary had said this, Erin glanced over her shoulder, eyeing her dad skeptically. He gave her a slow wink, as if to say, 'Don't rat me out on this, okay? Just play along.'

Erin smiled. "That Santa!" she exclaimed, running a hand lovingly over her new bicycle's frame. "He's so cool! He knew exactly what I wanted – and the right color, too!"

Suddenly, Amanda looked up, as if she'd remembered something important. "Santa cookies?"

Gary was about to say she couldn't have cookies so early in the morning when Micki said, "Let's go see." She dashed into the kitchen. "He did!" she cried out. "He *did* eat the cookies you left!" She held up the plate and the empty milk glass. "All that's left is some crumbs… and a drop of milk."

"Did the reindeer eat the carrot sticks we put out?" Erin called, sharing a private grin with Dad.

"Most of 'em," Micki reported. She came back into the living room holding a partially gnawed carrot stick. "Look – they didn't finish this one."

Amanda's eyes widened as she took the carrot stick and examined it. "Woo-doff?"

"Perhaps." Gary swept his little daughter up in his arms and kissed her loudly on the cheek. "Or it might have been Blitzen."

"Or Dancer," Michaela added, laughing as Gary twirled around the room with the child.

Catching his wife's eye, he raised an eyebrow. "Coulda been Vixen."

She winked as if to say, 'Maybe it was.'

"No," Amanda decided as Daddy set her on her feet again. "It was Woo-doff."

Gary knelt beside her. "Why don't you have Mommy wrap that in plastic and put it in the fridge... You can show it to Auntie Marie when she comes – it's proof Santa was really here."

"So, was it you or Micki who chewed that carrot stick?" Erin asked as she and Dad carried dishes and mugs into the kitchen.

He paused to listen to the sound of Mandy's laughter as Micki whisked her upstairs to get dressed. He tweaked Erin's nose. "Silly girl. You heard Amanda; it was Woo-doff."

"Daddy..." Shaking her head, Erin sighed as she put the dishes on the counter.

Gary rinsed the mugs and set them alongside the dishes. "Would I lie about something like that? If I said reindeer made those teeth marks, then reindeer made those teeth marks."

"Sure, Daddy; whatever you say. Although... I bet your dentist would say different."

"You think so, huh? Maybe I'll just have to get Woo-doff back here to destroy the evidence." He paused. "Thanks, though, for going along with the whole Santa bit..."

She grinned. "I didn't want to spoil the fun. You and Micki seemed to be enjoying yourselves."

Just before eleven, the doorbell rang.

"Merry Christmas, Marie!" Micki exclaimed. She nodded toward the long-coated figure reaching into the trunk. "That's the boyfriend, eh?"

"Nope." Marie tugged off her left glove and held out her hand, wiggling her fingers. "Fiancé."

Michaela's eyes widened in astonishment. "When did that happen?"

Marie smiled broadly. "He asked me last night."

Squealing, the two women hugged each other as the dark-haired man, now laden with presents, shut the trunk and strode toward the house.

Micki gasped, gripped Marie's hand. "Gary didn't tell me—"

Grinning, Marie shook her head. "He doesn't know."

Climbing the porch stairs, he handed Marie one of the bags, then leaned to give Michaela a kiss. "Hey, hon. Merry Christmas. Thanks so much for having us."

Just then Gary came downstairs, carrying Amanda. "Who's down here making all that racket?" he called. "Oh, I mighta known it was *you*," he teased as Marie stepped into the house ahead of her new fiancé. Gary leaned to kiss his sister. "Hey, sis."

"Auntie Ma-wee!" the toddler exclaimed, reaching out her arms toward her.

"Hey, sweetie!" Marie plucked her niece from her brother's arms.

Almost instantly, Amanda screeched with delight. "Unca Mahc!"

"Marc!" Gary exclaimed. "I thought you were spending the holiday with your girlfriend's family."

"Well, there was kind of a change of plans." Grinning, he drew Marie close and kissed her on the temple. "I'm spending it with my *fiancée's* family instead."

Chapter 8

(9:20 p.m., January 21, 1993 – Thursday)

Michaela settled onto the couch beside her husband. "I've been thinking…"

"Uh-oh. That's never a good sign." Laughing, Gary grabbed at the hand she raised to swat him. "What were you thinking, honey?"

"I love what I do at the retreat center, but I miss crisis counseling. And I had an idea that'd let me use the counseling piece. I'd like to approach St. Mary's Hospital about developing an in-house rape-crisis center. A dedicated staff there could ease the burden on Lisa's people."

"Have you talked to anyone about it? Do you even know if Lisa's still at the crisis center?"

"She is. I called yesterday."

"What did she say?"

"I didn't talk to her," Michaela admitted. "When I heard her voice, I chickened out and hung up."

"Doesn't sound like my ever-confident Michaela Divan," Gary teased gently, shaking his head.

Micki smiled at his long-since-abandoned nickname for her.

"Sounds like a great idea. Why don't you give her a call tomorrow? And actually talk to her," he said. "Then you can ask Father Dave who to approach at the hospital; he's pretty well connected. Is that something you'd do instead of working at the retreat center?"

"I don't know. I love what I do there; but if I can reach women who are in crisis now – instead of years down the road – it could prevent a whole lot of suffering." Her eyes looked troubled. "Do you think I could do it?"

Gary hugged his wife, proud of her sense of initiative. "Baby, I think you can do anything you set your mind to. I say you should go for it."

The next morning, Lisa Barrows listened as Micki outlined her idea. "That's definitely got merit. And I applaud you for turning an obstacle into another opportunity. I was sorry to lose you, because you really did great work here; but this sounds like something that could really pan out.

"And don't give another thought to that 'taking clients away from me' notion. Having a facility at St. Mary's would let our staff devote more time to clients at Waterbury Hospital. I think it'll work out on all sides. I'd be happy to help you set up a program," Lisa offered. "Let me know how I can help."

"I pretty much envision it operating along the same lines as yours, but focused more on getting women through the initial crisis of the assault, then providing support in the event of a pregnancy; but because it's a Catholic hospital, we wouldn't promote abortion."

By the end of April, Micki had secured the necessary approval from the hospital, and support from Lisa, to set up and run the rape-crisis center. The administrator at St. Mary's sought and received an allocation of archdiocesan funds. Father Dave helped Micki organize parish-based fundraisers to offset the costs of incidentals.

Meanwhile, Gary quietly wrote checks to cover shortfalls. "What's the point of having money if you don't use it to do good?" he asked Father Dave.

With Lisa's guidance, Micki oversaw the training of a team of volunteers and the center's two paid crisis counselors.

Sister Mary Louise O'Connor, the hospital administrator, praised Michaela's efforts when the center, located near the emergency department, opened. "This is a remarkable thing you're doing," she said, hugging the young woman. "It's something women in crisis have needed – counselors to meet their emotional needs while being sensitive to their regard for life at all its stages. God bless you, child."

Because Micki was working half days now, Gary would leave for work when she got home – or bring Mandy in to the station if his mom couldn't watch her. It helped that Diane had moved from Madison to nearby Oxford last year.

But they both knew that couldn't last.

"I know you're not thrilled with this arrangement, honey," Micki told him one night in early July, after a particularly bad day. "And I promise, I'll cut back my hours as soon as I get my new counselors trained. Or I could bring Amanda to the on-site daycare at the hospital."

Gary frowned. "We've talked about this before, Mick. We're not going to dump our daughter in some stranger's lap. I realize how important this center is to you, and Pete's been really good about my coming in later these last few months; but this can't continue much longer."

"Are you saying you want me to quit?" Michaela's voice wavered.

"Of course not. I don't want to see you abandon your dream. But what happens once we have another baby? There's no way they'll put up with me bringing two kids in to work. It was one thing when you were taking a few classes a semester and Mandy slept while I was on the air; but now she's running around, wreaking havoc. My meeting today was a disaster! Presenting a report to the station manager and sales staff with crayon scribbles all over it is not exactly the way to be taken seriously at work."

"I know, honey… and I'm sorry she ruined your report. When we have another baby, I'll turn the center over to the other counselors."

"I hope so, 'cause if something like this happens again, they won't think it's funny – *or* cute. And there goes my credibility as a department head."

Chapter 9

(February 19, 1994 – Saturday)

Gary looked up to see his daughter waiting outside his classroom. "All set, punkin?"

"Uh-huh."

Grabbing a pile of his students' worksheets off his desk, he tidied them into a bundle. Pulling the door shut, he slipped an arm around Erin as they left the parish center.

The eleven-year-old was oddly quiet on the ride home. Gary glanced over at her. "You okay?"

Erin mumbled something he couldn't quite hear, but assumed was a dismissal of his concern.

By the time they herded the cats into the car for the ride to the cottage, Erin was fighting tears.

Some conversations were best had in moving cars – and Gary had a feeling this would be one of them. "Gonna do any writing this week?" he asked when they were finally underway.

Micki had given Erin a set of blank books for her birthday; she'd begun journaling, and writing poetry and short stories. Four months later, the girl was already on her third book.

"I dunno." Letting out a tremulous sigh, Erin shut her eyes tight against the tears.

Gary didn't like the sound of that sigh. "Honey? What's wrong?"

She sniffled and rubbed at her huge brown eyes. Her head drooped.

"Erin?" he prompted. "Why so sad, baby? Did something upset you in class?"

"I miss Mommy." Tears slid down her cheeks. "And today's her birthday."

Erin's words jolted through Gary's brain. *That's right!* She would have been twenty-nine. "Ohh, sweetie. I know you miss her, honey." He pushed a curtain of hair back behind his daughter's ear.

The girl's deep, sorrowful cries persisted for nearly a mile. "She used to read to me… and help me with my homework. And tuck me in at night," she mumbled amid a series of loud sniffles. "I know you and Micki do all that stuff, but it's not the same" – she rubbed at the tears with her fists – "not like having a real mommy. I mean, I love Micki… but she's not *mine*."

Gary longed to rock his daughter in his arms and ease away the hurt. For now he'd have to settle for holding her hand. "I'm so sorry you're feeling sad, punkin."

In the murky silence that lingered the rest of the way, "she's not mine" echoed in his heart.

A note on the kitchen table told him Michaela had taken Amanda grocery shopping. They'd be back around noon. In the study, Gary sat with Erin, wiping the last traces of her tears and cuddling her.

As Erin told her dad about how empty and sad she felt, an idea came to him. "I bet Grandma and Grandpa would love to see you."

The child brightened a bit. "Yeah?"

"Yeah. Let's give 'em a call." Reaching for the phone, he dialed the number he'd called so many times as a teenager.

"Just for the afternoon?" Michaela asked when Gary told her about the road trip.

"That's what we talked about. Why?"

She nestled into his arms. "It's winter break. Why don't you see if they want her to stay a while. We could pick her up Wednesday or Thursday. Even Saturday, if they want."

Why not? I was eight when I started going to stay with Grandpa every summer. He kissed the top of her head. "That's a terrific idea, honey."

Erin chattered excitedly the whole way there. And when the car pulled to a stop in the Farricellis' driveway, she darted out, skipped across the snow-frosted lawn and up the porch stairs. Turning at the top step, she waved goodbye.

(February 26 – Saturday afternoon)
The Sheldons were out front when the Farricellis' blue Taurus pulled into the driveway. Gary was shoveling the walk; Amanda and Micki played together in the snow.

"Daddy!" Erin galloped into his arms. "I missed you so much!" Then she charged at Michaela. "I missed you, too, Mom!"

Gary watched, astounded, as Erin hugged her, then dropped to her knees to help Amanda fashion a snowball for the top of her miniature snowman.

The Farricellis emerged, watching their granddaughter play with her half-sister. Christina hugged Gary. "We had such a wonderful time, Gary. Thank you for letting her stay with us."

"No need to thank me, Mom. Erin can visit whenever you want."

"Daddy?"

Gary had stooped beside his daughter's bed, about to kiss her goodnight. "Yes, angel?"

"I was thinking… y'know how we were talking last week, about me not havin' a mommy?"

He stroked her cheek. "Yeah…"

"Is it alright if I ask Micki to be my mommy? I mean, for keeps."

"Ohh, honey – of course it's alright. I think it's a wonderful idea!"

Erin sat up. "D'you think she'll say yes?"

Gary nodded. "I do."

The child threw her arms around him. "Oh, Daddy! I hope she says yes… I hope she does."

Next morning, when he came downstairs with the girls, Gary found Michaela making breakfast. Settling Mandy in her high chair, he motioned for Erin to sit, then went to the stove. "Hi." He kissed the side of his wife's neck, then reached for her spatula and prodded the scrambled eggs in the skillet. "Go sit down."

She looked at him strangely.

Slipping an arm around her waist, he kissed her cheek. "Go on. I'll finish up here."

"Wh—?"

He met her gaze, then put a finger to her lips. "Shh. Go sit."

Gary looked at Erin, who was taking anxious sips of orange juice. Crossing his fingers, he winked in her direction. She smiled from behind her glass.

Casting a confused-looking glance at her husband, Michaela set a plastic bowl of Cheerios and a sippy cup before Amanda, then joined her stepdaughter at the table.

Erin crumpled and uncrumpled her napkin. "M-Micki?" she squeaked.

Wiping a dribble of juice from Amanda's chin, Michaela turned partway around. "Hmm?"

"Can I, um – can I ask you something?"

"Sure, honey" – now she turned all the way toward the little girl – "What's on your mind?"

"I asked Daddy, and he said it was okay to ask you." Biting her lower lip for an uneasy moment, Erin faltered; her request spilled out in an awkward jumble.

Micki felt like someone had squeezed all the air out of her lungs. "Of course I'll be your for-real mommy!"

The child flew out of her chair and hugged her. "Oh, Mommy – I'm so happy you said yes!"

The next morning, Gary put in a call to Julia Ashwell, who explained the process and timeline, and advised him which forms they'd need to fill out.

In mid April, Michaela and Erin received official-looking envelopes from the Department of Children and Families. More forms to fill out – and a mention of a court appearance that terrified Erin.

"What if they hate me? What if they say no?" she fretted. "What if they won't let Micki adopt me?"

Gary shushed away her worries. "They'll love you, punkin. Who wouldn't? As for approving the adoption: It's all just formalities. You sign some forms and the judge will stare down his nose at you and Micki" – he mimicked the action he was describing – "and make sure all the paperwork is in order. Then he'll bang his gavel, mutter a bunch of stuff no one'll be able to understand – something about pronouncing you mother and daughter… and bingo-bango-bongo, Micki'll be your Mommy."

She giggled. "Bingo-bango-bongo?"

Gary tweaked her nose. "Yep. Just like that."

(May 10, 1994 – Tuesday)

When they entered the building, Micki bent down to whisper something to her young daughter.

The toddler nodded, then marched up to the receptionist's desk. "Hi," she announced brightly, standing on tiptoe to see over the desk. "I'm Mandy. Is Daddy here?"

Brenda smiled. "Hello there, sweetie-pie! Why, yes, Daddy's in his office."

As she pointed down the hall, she looked at Michaela. "Would you like to go back and see him? Or shall I ask him to come out?"

Without hesitation, the almost-three-year-old answered the question posed to her mother. "We need to talk to him in pwivate."

Both women had to bite back laughter.

"Should I let him know you're here? Or is this a commando raid?"

Michaela grinned at the other woman. "Commando raid, if you don't mind."

Brenda nodded down the hall. "Go ahead in."

Gary was on the phone when the rap came at his door. "Great. I'll see you next week, then," he told the caller. "Thanks for calling." Setting down the phone, he looked up. "Come in."

"Go ahead," he heard Micki's muffled voice say. "Open it."

The knob rattled for a few seconds as little hands fumbled with it; the door slowly lurched open. "Hi, Daddy!" Amanda exclaimed, rushing toward his desk.

"Sweetheart!" Gary stood, a broad smile lighting his face. His eyes caught Michaela's; she looked impish. No, excited. Coming around his desk to greet them, he bent down to pick up the child. "What a nice surprise! How wonderful to see you!" He leaned to kiss Micki. "Hi, Mommy."

"Hi, Daddy," she replied with a grin, reaching up to caress his cheek.

"What brings you here?"

"The cah!" Amanda exclaimed, bursting into gleeful giggles.

Gary tweaked her nose. "Silly goose!" He rephrased the question. "To what do I owe the pleasure of this visit?"

"We went to the doctah," Mandy blurted out, drumming her sneakered toes excitedly against her father's midsection.

He tried not to wince. "And were you a good girl?"

The little girl giggled. "Not *my* doctah, Daddy. Mommy's doctah."

"Oh." Gary slid an arm around his wife and kissed her nose. "So, were *you* a good girl?"

Now it was Michaela's turn to giggle. She nodded. "Mm-hmm." Her eyes shone. "Have you got a few minutes?"

It was Tuesday. There was music to add to the play list;

meetings with Pete and the other jocks; record-company reps to call back… "For you? Of course. What's up?" He set Mandy down. She darted behind his desk to his swivel chair. It rolled away as she tried to clamber up into the seat. Gary moved to the chair and held it steady as she climbed up and got settled. He spun her around and around while the sounds of her giggles resounded through the office.

Micki watched with amusement as the child whirled and whirled…

A moment later, Gary looked up in time to see a fluid swoosh of hair fly past.

"Where'd Mommy go?" Amanda wanted to know.

"I dunno; but she sure left in a big hurry, didn't she?" All of a sudden it made sense: the doctor's appointment; their impromptu visit; that look of playful excitement in her eyes; her hurried departure. *Of course!* Absently, he stopped spinning Amanda.

She tugged at his sleeve. "Daddy," she urged. "Spin me!"

"Please," he prompted, jarred from his rumination.

"Pwease," the little girl repeated dutifully, smiling as her father complied.

A few minutes later, Michaela returned, looking just a smidgen green.

Gary left off twirling the child and went to his wife's side. "Everything come out alright?" he teased gently.

Micki smiled at their longstanding vomit joke. "Just fine."

"Daddy!" Amanda protested. "Spin me – pwease?"

Gary turned back to her. "Not now, sweetie. Daddy needs to talk to Mommy for a minute." Still, he gave her a quick whirl. "So, I guess it's a real good thing we got that five-bedroom house?"

Micki grinned. "Mm-hmm. Congratulations, Daddy," she said quietly, slipping her arms around her husband and kissing him. "You're a daddy again."

He'd suspected as much – he had for a few days; Micki had been crampy and achy and irritable. Filled with love for her, his kiss was warm, tender. "Best news I've heard all day."

He caressed her still-flat tummy, marveling at the miracle of the new life growing within her. "That's our baby in there," he whispered. "Our baby." Gary's eyes shone as he hugged his wife.

(May 23 – Monday)
The paperwork was in order, the home study finished. All that remained was the appearance before the judge. Micki had called Memorial Middle School to excuse Erin. And Gary had taken the day off from work.

Erin had been up and around since dawn; she'd barely slept the night before. Too excited.

"Honey, you almost ready?" Gary called up the stairs to Micki. "Erin's waiting outside."

"Be right down."

Three minutes later, he stood in the doorway to the bedroom. "Michaela?"

"I said, I'll be right down," she snapped, turning in his direction. She'd been sitting at the vanity, staring at the mirror when he startled her.

Looking perplexed, he approached. "You okay?" Picking up her hairbrush, Gary ran it through her long chestnut mane; she always loved it when he did this.

She caught his gaze in the mirror's reflection.

"Are you alright?" he asked again, smoothing Michaela's hair down her back with his other hand.

Micki shook her head and, in the tiniest voice ever, said, "No."

The brushing stopped. "Baby, what's wrong?"

She turned her head away and mumbled something inaudible.

Laying aside the brush, Gary crouched beside her. "Micki?"

Can't he just leave me alone? She turned back to him. "What?" she asked, exasperated.

"What's the matter? Are you queasy? Do you need to throw up?"

Michaela sighed, shook her head.

"Then… are you having second thoughts? You don't want to go through with the adoption?"

She swiped at the mist of tears clouding her vision. "Of course I want to. It's just—" Shaking her head again, Micki broke off. She knew Erin was waiting outside, barely able to contain her excitement, and they'd be late if they didn't leave soon.

Gary took his wife's hands. "Just what? Honey, tell me."

After a long silence, during which she assembled her courage and her thoughts, she raised her eyes a bit – barely enough to look at his face. "Do you know what today is?"

"Of course; it's the twenty-third of May."

"And do you know what that means?"

His voice sounded impatient. "Yeah, it means you're twenty-seven years and one day old."

She shook her head. "No!"

"Then why don't you tell me what it means," he suggested in mild frustration.

"It means" – upset he wasn't acting more compassionate, she swiped away tears and mumbled – "today it's six years since I killed my baby."

"Ohh, honey!" Gary's arms were around her in an instant. "Sweetheart, I'm so sorry."

Two years before they were married, Micki had been assaulted by a serial rapist; Gary never knew she'd gotten pregnant – and had an abortion – until years afterward.

She crumpled forward, burying her face in her hands. Rocking forward and back, she mourned her lost child, just as she had every May 23, as soon as Gary left for work. *It's such a relief not to have to hide this from him anymore!*

"Do you want to postpone the adoption – get it rescheduled for another day?"

Michaela shook her head vigorously. "No. I don't want to disappoint Erin. Besides" – she wiped at her eyes – "I'm glad it's today. Gives me something positive to associate with the day. So I can have good memories of this date."

Gary's hand closed around hers; he drew it to his lips. "It's almost too coincidental to be coincidence. Like it's God's way of equalizing things."

She looked at him, perplexed. "What do you mean?"

"Six years ago you let go of one baby; now you're getting a second chance — a chance to call *another* child your own. And at the same time giving *her* a mommy." He kissed her on the forehead. "It all comes around in a big circle. One great big circle of love, with you at its center."

Smiling at last, Micki hugged him. "Thank you," she murmured. "Thank you for understanding."

"Anyway, you know what they say" – Gary tweaked her nose – "Cast bread upon the water and it comes back soggy crumbs."

Amid her tears, she laughed. *He's so wacky – he always knows how to cheer me up!* "I love your twisted proverbs, Gary. I have no idea what that means… but thank you."

"It's nice to hear you laugh." Wiping the last of her tears away from her upturned face, he stood, then helped his wife to her feet. "C'mon – your daughter's waiting."

Just over an hour later, they were an honest-to-goodness family. With a certificate to prove it.

Gary had worried the Farricellis would take the news badly; but he was surprised at their show of support. They even came to the courthouse, and brought flowers for both Erin and Michaela.

Gary and Michaela watched as their daughter rushed to embrace her aunt and her grandparents.

"It's so good to see you," Gary told the trio when Erin released them. "I'm glad you came."

"We wouldn't have missed it," Christina said. "After all, you're Erin's father" – she turned toward Micki and smiled – "and mother. Congratulations, dear."

Micki hugged her, tears glistening in her eyes. "Thank you, Mrs. Farricelli. That means so much to me. Erin's been so excited. I'm so thrilled you wanted to be here for her."

Christina took Micki's hands. "We're delighted to be here. For *all* of you," she replied graciously. "And the timing was perfect" – she motioned toward her daughter – "Katrina's graduation was yesterday. We were already here."

When her mother released Michaela, the new college graduate was waiting to hug her. "Congratulations, Mommy," Katrina squealed, embracing the woman whom she'd grown to love like a sister.

At lunch, Christina laid a hand on Gary's arm. "Thank you for including us today, even though, legally, we're no longer Erin's grandparents."

"What are you talking about? Of course you are."

"Only biologically. As soon as the adoption was finalized, we lost all legal standing – even our right to see her."

"Where'd you get that idea?"

"Our lawyer told us – in February – when you told us Erin had asked Micki to adopt her."

A pang hit Gary in the midsection. *They knew? All this time? And they did nothing to contest it?* He was filled with a deeper respect for the Farricellis. "As far as I'm concerned, you're Erin's grandparents. You always will be" – he squeezed her hand for emphasis – "Always."

(10:18 p.m., November 30, 1994 – Wednesday)
In her dream, Michaela awakened from a nightmare. Hearing the four-year-old's cries, Daddy dashed into her room, gathered her in his arms and allayed her fears. "It's okay, Kayla. It was only a dream. Daddy's here, precious. I'm here. You know you can't count on Mommy." He held her close and wiped away her tears.

When her terror abated, she settled down enough to go back to sleep. Daddy tucked her in, picked up Cuddles from the floor, handed the toy bear back to his daughter. Then he kissed both child and bear goodnight. As soon as the door closed behind Michael, the stuffed animal turned into a real bear cub and nipped at her fingers until she released him; he loped down the length of the bed. Jumping off, he leapt into the chair in the corner – where Gary sat, rocking. But it wasn't a rocking chair. And he was knitting. But she couldn't figure out what he was knitting. Sitting up, she strained to see in the dark. He was knitting Ginger!

Michaela jolted herself almost awake. In a drowsy semiconscious haze, she tried to analyze her dream. It sure was strange! For starters, most kids would have cried for their mommies. Not her: She was Daddy's angel, but Mommy's little nightmare. *He never woulda said that, about Mom being unreliable.* Even half sleep, she knew it made no sense. *It's simple,* she reasoned. *He's the one who's here for us, not her.*

But why would Cuddles have turned into a live cub? Maybe I'm afraid the baby will reject me. Why was Gary there? Maybe I'm afraid the baby will hate me and only want him.

And why was Gary knitting the cat?

While pondering this, Micki drifted to sleep again, back into her dream. She somehow knew the soft *creak-creak* was Gary rocking in the non-rocking chair, still knitting. Suddenly, she sat up in bed, crying. Gary laid aside needles and yarn and went to her bedside. "What's the matter, sweetie?" he asked, gathering her into his arms.

She clung to him and wept, ashamed to say she'd wet the bed. He held her close and said it was okay. She was a little girl; accidents were bound to happen. He smoothed her hair, dabbing at her tears with the end of Ginger's half-knitted tail. The dream felt so real Micki startled herself awake. She swore it was real! She felt wetness on her legs; she could almost feel the sensation of the sopping bedclothes…

Suddenly she was fully awake. The bedclothes were soaked. She was crying. And Gary was there.

"What's the matter?" he asked in the voice of one startled from a deep sleep.

"I – I had a dream," she sobbed. "And… I – I think I wet the bed," she admitted, ashamed.

Gary noticed the wet sheets. "No, honey. Let's get you to the hospital. I think your water broke."

"Sorry to wake you, Grandpa," Micki said when she heard her dad's sleepy 'Hello,' "but it's time."

Michael arrived within thirty minutes. While they waited, Gary brought Micki's bag downstairs, then he changed the sheets on their bed.

The guest room was already made up, so Micki put on the light and turned down the bedclothes for her dad, so it looked welcoming. Then she found the sheet of paper detailing the kids' schedules.

They'd already talked with both girls in the past few weeks, to prepare them for the possibility they might wake up one day to find Grandpa there, because Mommy and Daddy were at the hospital to have the baby.

Because Erin was old enough to understand, they'd only had that talk with her once; but Mandy needed the information repeated occasionally. Each time they discussed it, she'd ask the same thing: Why do you have to wait? Can't you just have the baby now?

Still, they wanted to leave notes for the girls.

Punkin,

We've gone to the hospital... Mommy's having the baby. I know you wanted a puppy, but you'll just have to settle for a little sister or brother. We'll talk about that puppy some other time. After Mommy has the baby, I'll bring you both to visit them. Be good for Grandpa - please don't give him any more grey hair; he looks distinguished enough already.

We love you both very much.

Hugs and kisses,

Daddy :)

Manda-Panda,

Daddy took me to the hospital to have the baby.

Everything's going to be fine. Grandpa will take care of you and Erin until we get back. Daddy will bring you to see the new baby at the hospital.

*Be a good girl for Grandpa. We'll see you soon -
promise.*
   We miss you, sweetie - and we love you.
   Tons of smooches and cuddles,
   Mommy :)

Thirteen hours later, Michaela cradled her son. "I can't get
over how beautiful he is," she cooed, stroking his tiny brow.
It furrowed at her touch. "Gary, he's *perfect!*"

He bent to kiss her cheek. "I'm glad you think so; I doubt
we can send him back."

She smiled at his gentle teasing.

Gary kissed her again, a more prolonged kiss this time.
"You are so beautiful," he murmured, pushing her sweat-
dampened hair off her face.

She drew away. "Ick – Gary! I'm all sweaty and gross
and—"

"And you just gave birth to our son," he finished.
"You're more radiant than I've ever seen you." He caressed
her cheek and kissed her. "Motherhood looks great on you."

When Erin got out of school, Gary was there to meet her.

Her "Hi, Daddy!" was joined by a chorus of "Hi, Gary"s
and "Hey, Mr. Sheldon"s from her friends, many of them his
former religious-education students.

"Hi there," he greeted them, accepting their hugs and
high fives.

"How's Mom?" Erin asked, hugging her father.

Gary understood she didn't want to call her 'Mommy' in
front of her friends. "She's fine. So is your little brother."

"A brother?" she squeaked. "Cool! When can I see
them?"

"Right after we pick up Mandy." Waving goodbye to the
others, he ushered Erin to the car.

Micki was asleep when they arrived, so Gary put a finger to
his lips to keep the girls from waking her. "Shh… Mommy's

sleeping." He stooped down and put a hand on each of their shoulders. "C'mon, let's go down to the nursery to see the baby."

Taking their hands, he led them down the hall and toward the nurses station.

A nurse there greeted him. "Hi, Mr. Sheldon. Are these your daughters? They're beautiful!" Then she turned toward the girls. "Hi there; are you here to visit Mom and your baby brother?"

"Yeah," Erin replied quietly.

"Uh-huh," Amanda said, nodding. She smiled broadly. "We'ah gonna see Mommy… but she's sweepin' wight now."

"We're hoping to have a look at the little guy; any chance you can point us to him?"

"Sure thing," she said, checking a chart. "In fact, I'll do you one better; he's due in her room for a feeding in a few minutes. Why don't you come with me; you can see him up close – instead of from the other side of the nursery window." She looked at the girls. "Would you like that?"

Amanda clapped her hands excitedly. "Yeah!" She tugged at Gary's pants leg and tilted her head way back to look up at him. "Can we, Daddy?"

He bent down and put an arm around her. "Shh," he shushed her. "Settle down, honey. Yes, we can go see him. But remember what we talked about before: You have to be gentle with the baby; he's not used to loud noises or rough handling. Erin, I think you're old enough to hold him" – he turned to the nurse – "eleven's old enough, right?"

She nodded. "Oh, sure. We'll let kids as young as six hold newborns."

Amanda pouted. "What about me? Can't I hode him, too?"

Gary did his best to explain the baby wasn't like a doll she just pick up any old way; he'd have to be handled really carefully, so his little head wouldn't flop around.

The little girl was insistent. "I can do dat. Why won't you wet me hode him?"

Not relishing the prospect of a meltdown in the hospital corridor, he offered a compromise. "How about this? After Mommy feeds the baby, you can sit on the bed with her and hold him in your lap for a little while. Alright?"

This seemed to placate her.

"Okay, Daddy." Slipping her tiny hand into his, the three-year-old skipped between her daddy and her big sister all the way to the nursery.

Hopping up and down excitedly – in hopes of catching a glimpse of her baby brother in the bassinet, Mandy followed the nurse all the way to Mommy's room. Erin hung back, to walk with her dad.

Gary draped an arm about his older girl's shoulder. Leaning close, he whispered something. She listened, nodded, then stopped in the hallway and hugged him.

While Michaela fed the baby, Erin settled into a bedside chair to talk to her. Gary excused himself, saying he needed to see someone – and asked Amanda to come along.

"Where we goin', Daddy?"

After checking the floor directory, he poked the elevator button. "There's someone I want you to meet."

"Who?"

"You'll find out in a minute."

"Who?" she asked again. He didn't answer. The little girl tugged at his arm. "*Daddy! Who?*"

"What are you, an owl?" Reaching down, he caressed her cheek. "Someone special. Someone who did something really, really nice for Mommy and me once – oh, almost three and a half years ago."

Stepping out of the elevator, Gary led his daughter down the hall to the left. The corridor opened out into an oval nurses station.

"Can I help you?" the woman at the desk asked as they approached.

"Yes." He told her who he was looking for.

The nurse checked the duty roster. "You're in luck. She's still here – she was supposed to be off half an hour ago, but she's checking on a patient. Do you have a family member in ICU?"

"Uh, no… but" – he placed both hands on Amanda's shoulders – "there's someone I'd like her to meet." Glancing down at his daughter, he looked at the nurse again and smiled.

"I don't expect her to be too long; I can page her if you'd like."

"I don't want to interru—"

"Oh – there she is now!" The nurse waved her arm in a broad sweep to catch the other woman's attention. "Amanda, could you come here for a moment, please?"

Gary's daughter whipped around at the sound of the nurse calling her name.

Apparently thinking something was wrong, the nurse sped along the corridor on silent, rubber-soled shoes. "What's the mat—?" Her hand flew to her mouth as she saw Gary. "Oh my goodness!" she breathed. "Mr. Sheldon! Are you—? Is everyth—? I mean… you aren't here with…?"

Smiling, he shook his head, amazed the nurse still remembered his name after all this time. "No. Everything's just fine. Michaela's upstairs" – he motioned toward the bank of elevators – "in maternity. We just had another baby. Little boy. Full term." He rested his hands on the three-year-old's shoulders again. "I wanted you to see what became of your namesake. Amanda, meet Amanda."

The nurse looked at Gary – then at the little girl, and back at Gary – in awe. She took a step backward. "Sweet Jesus," she murmured, "*this* is that tiny little baby from NICU?" She crouched down to her eye level. "Hey there, precious. I remember the day you were born. You were just a wee little bit of a thing. Look at you now – you're so grown up…"

Suddenly shy, Mandy hid her face against Daddy's leg.

The nurse looked up and smiled. "She is just the absolute image of her momma."

Part II

Chapter 10

(March 25, 1997 – Tuesday)

The phone's ringing jarred Gary from sleep. He groped for the receiver. Drawing it beneath the covers, he mumbled a greeting.

"Gary, dear, I'm sorry to disturb you so late… It – it's Sam. He's gone."

The words drilled through him. Instantly alert, he forced his eyes open and sat up. "What do you mean, 'gone'?" He shivered, only in part because of the chill in the room.

Martha's voice wavered. "He's missing. I – I woke up when I heard a noise. He's not anywhere in the house…" she trailed off to uneasy silence.

"You stay right there; I'll go look for him."

This was no time to fumble in the dark for clothing. Gary flipped on the light.

Michaela rolled over and rubbed at her eyes. "Gary? What's the matter? Who was that?"

Hastily pulling on jeans and a shirt, he related what Martha had told him. "I'm gonna go look for him." Slipping his bare feet into loafers, he headed for the door.

"Take a coat."

"I'll be fine."

"Put on a coat, Gary. It's freezing out there. Last thing we need is for both of you to catch your deaths of cold. And bring a sweater for Sam, for when you find him." Micki tried to give her words a positive spin to reassure her husband; she knew how fond he was of the old man.

"Good idea." Grabbing a thick sweater from his bureau drawer, Gary gave his wife a kiss. "I've got my phone," he called over his shoulder. "I'll call as soon as there's news."

Taking a flashlight from the kitchen cupboard, he tore out the door and down the steps. Shivering, he shone the beam across the sand. Nothing. He could almost find his way without it; the late-March moon cast a brilliant glow, turning the sand an eerie white. He dialed 911, telling the dispatcher an 89-year-old Alzheimer's patient was missing and presumed wandering outside.

Gary wanted to check in with Martha, to calm her, but he was heading away from the Johnsons' home – and there was no time to lose. Instead, he punched in her number and re-assured her they'd find Sam soon.

Minutes later, he heard a noise. His heart leapt into his throat; his gaze darted toward the water. Something was there… offshore. Something shadowy. It lurched unsteadily through the water.

"Sam!" he called out, racing across the soft sand. "Sam, don't move – I'm coming."

Suddenly, with a splash, the dark shape disappeared.

"Sam!" Kicking off his shoes, Gary tore off his shirt and dropped both flashlight and phone. He raced toward the water, guided by moonlight, eyes locked on the spot where he'd seen the old man fall.

Sam wasn't too far out, but Gary knew he'd reach him faster by swimming than trying to run. Plunging into the frigid water, he ignored the pleading of every nerve ending to return to dry land. His only thought was saving his elderly friend.

Reaching Sam at last, Gary tried to tow him back to shore.

Frightened and disoriented, the old man fought him. "Who are you? Let me go! Let go. Leave me alone, I say!"

"Sam, please," Gary begged softly, trying not to alarm him. "I'm trying to help you. You're going to be fine. I prom-ise. Just let me help you."

The old man's teeth were chattering. So were Gary's. He had to act fast.

Scrambling to his feet, Gary righted the old man; clasping one gnarled hand, he put a steadying arm around Sam's mid-section and guided him back toward the shore.

A stiff breeze whipped across the water. Stripped to the waist, Gary shivered. It had to be in the mid 30s — and the water couldn't have been more than 45 degrees. Good thing Micki suggested bringing that sweater for Sam; he was only wearing his pajamas. And one slipper.

Gary helped Sam back to where he'd left his things. First order of business was to get him into something dry. He wished he'd thought to bring sweats or something for Sam. Getting him out of his soaked pajama top, he dressed the shivering old man in both his flannel shirt and the sweater, then slipped his shoes onto Sam's feet. So what if it wasn't a perfect fit — at least they were dry!

He dialed 911 again to summon an ambulance. Then he called Michaela, asking her to bring two pairs of sweats and a bunch of blankets.

She showed up within minutes, panic etched into her face. One look told Gary she was upset he hadn't taken a coat; they both knew addressing that wasn't a priority.

Micki bundled Sam in blankets and helped Gary put the sweatpants on him. "You must be freezing," she fretted as she draped a blanket around her husband's shoulders and handed him the second pair of sweatpants.

"I'm fine. It's him I'm worried about." Peeling off his sodden jeans and leaving them in a heap on the sand with the rest of the wet clothing, Gary quickly donned the sweats, grateful for their warmth; the night sand felt like icy pebbles beneath his bare feet.

He called Martha to say he'd found Sam and an ambulance was on its way.

She wanted to come right out, but Gary convinced her to stay inside where it was warm. He promised to come over and fill her in on Sam's condition as soon as possible.

A minute later, the ambulance arrived, disgorging paramedics with heated blankets and a stretcher.

Disoriented, Sam appeared agitated and unresponsive; Gary answered the EMTs' questions as best he could.

They assessed Sam's vital signs and checked for hypothermia, then carried him to the ambulance on the stretcher so they could transport him to the hospital for observation.

Before they took him away, Gary gave the bewildered old man a tender kiss on his chilled forehead. Assuring him he'd be fine, he clasped Sam's hand and promised he and Martha would be there soon.

"Is that your grandfather?" one of the paramedics wanted to know.

Gary shook his head. "No, but he might as well be."

The EMT patted his arm. "Don't worry. We'll take good care of him for you."

As the ambulance roared away up Oakland Avenue, Gary picked up their sopping clothes, then turned toward home. "Go on back," he told Micki wearily, planting a kiss on her forehead. "I'm gonna take Martha to be with Sam."

"Not like that, you're not," she insisted. Huddled beneath that blanket, he wore only a pair of sweats. "Go change; *then* take her." She paused. "And this time… would you please wear a coat?"

***

(May 15 – Thursday)

Father and daughter walked east along the beach.

Four houses up, Sam sat on his back porch. "G'morning, young fella," he called brightly, waving.

"Morning, Sam." Gary bent to whisper to Amanda. "Can you say hello to Mr. Johnson?"

"Hi, Mr. Johnson," the little girl greeted him dutifully.

Sam didn't seem to notice.

"Tell you what, honey," Gary said. "Why don't you go collect some pretty shells while I visit with Mr. Johnson… and we'll decorate your room with 'em later, okay?"

"Okay, Daddy," Amanda agreed.

The almost-six-year-old tilted her head upward for a kiss, then scampered toward the water's edge, swinging her yellow sand pail.

He watched her go, then climbed the stairs. "How're you feeling today, Sam?"

The old man looked at him. His expression grew confused. "Do I know you?"

Gary's heart ached. They went through this nearly every morning now. Sam was slipping fast. It wouldn't be long before Martha couldn't continue caring for him in the home they'd shared for nearly fifty years. *Permanent twilight*, Gary called it. Resting against the porch rail, he leaned to push wisps of snowy hair out of Sam's vacant blue eyes. His hand lingered on the wrinkled forehead a moment; his touch became a caress. "Yeah. I'm Gary. I live a few houses up. We met the other day." He forced a smile. He hated to lie to his grandfather's best friend; but it seemed kinder than reminding him, day after day, they'd been friends for fifteen years.

The old man pointed. "That your little girl?"

Shoving aside the heartache, Gary nodded. "Yeah. That's Amanda."

His brow furrowed. "Hmm… don't think I've ever seen *her* before. You live around here?"

"A few houses up," he repeated.

"Oh." Sam nodded as if he understood. "You lived here long?"

Gary swallowed hard. It always went this way. "Couple months." Sam wouldn't notice the catch in his voice.

The door opened. Martha stepped onto the porch. "Oh — good morning, Gary." She hugged him. "I thought I heard voices out here, but I… well, I'm never sure…"

Gary gave her a compassionate look that said she didn't need to finish her sentence.

She released the brakes on her husband's wheelchair. "C'mon, dear; time to get ready to go to the doctor."

Last month, just three weeks after Gary rescued him from drowning, Sam had taken a tumble down the porch stairs and broken his leg; it had been discouragingly slow in healing.

Sam looked as if he didn't even recognize Martha. "Oh." Then, giving an excited little clap of his weathered hands, his eyes sparkled with the closest thing to recognition Gary had seen there in months. "We're going to go for ice cream after we're done at the doctor's office."

Gary didn't look at Martha. If he did, he'd see the tears in her eyes. And he didn't want the ugly truth to taint his response. Instead, manufacturing a smile, he patted Sam's shoulder and summoned all his enthusiasm. "Won't that be a nice treat!" Leaning, he placed a tender kiss on the old man's craggy forehead and clasped his hand. "Bye, Sam. I'll see you tomorrow."

Straightening again, Gary hugged Martha briefly, offering an assurance of prayers, and quiet words of encouragement. Drawing back, he met her gaze. Acknowledging the tears in her blue eyes, he gently wiped them away.

Sniffling, she clasped his hand. "Thank you, Gary. Thank you for all you've done for him."

He caressed the woman's soft, wrinkly cheek. "You and Sam have been such a treasure to our family. I couldn't have loved you more if you were my own grandparents."

Gary held the screen door as Martha maneuvered Sam's wheelchair into the house. He ached. *It's so hard to lose a friend this way.* He'd lost friends before… but never like this. It was hard enough when it happened all at once, through a falling-out or a betrayal – *like with Greg.* But it was infinitely worse to see a relationship disintegrate little by little, spalling like old concrete, until nothing remained but dry, gritty residue.

Brushing the mist from his eyes, he hurried up the beach to join his young daughter. As he went, he heard his grandfather's voice offering words of comfort. *The heart remembers what the mind forgets.*

Chapter 11

(9:04 a.m., August 8 – Friday)
Pete rounded up all the jocks and department heads and herded them into the conference room. He found Marc slouched in a chair in Gary's office, grousing with his brother-in-law.

"C'mon, guys; time for show and tell," Pete said, leaning in the doorway. "We're already late."

Marc gave a melodramatic sigh. "Geez, Pete, I hate the Rah-Rah Hour. Can't you tell 'em I died? Or the fall semester started early?"

While still doing his seven-to-midnight air shift, Marc studied architecture at Yale part time. He'd taken several classes a semester since spring 1993 and had four semesters left.

"Sorry, bud," Pete said, trying to ignore Gary's smirk. "You know the rules. Mandatory meeting."

Several months ago, Tom had decided monthly staff meetings would improve interdepartmental communication and boost morale. But mostly, the staff stared, glassy eyed, grunting terse replies when pressed for input.

"Level with us, Pete," Gary prodded, "you gotta hate these meetings, too. Right?"

The program director shut the door to the music department and leaned against it. "Honestly? The only good thing about 'em is I can say things once instead of four or five times."

Still, it was what the boss wanted; so on Friday of the first full week of the month, they dutifully (if reluctantly) gathered for the requisite dog-and-pony show.

Today, the primary focus was station promotions, as Pete had announced in a memo shortly after their previous meeting; he'd asked everyone to consider ways to heighten the station's community visibility. He and promotions director Laira Penfield would conduct this meeting together.

"Okay, we've got the after-grad party and the Holiday Bash," Pete began, once everyone had taken seats. "Those are our anchor events. Plus charity softball games. But we need to be more visible the rest of the year. Especially spring and fall." He scanned the room. "Recommendations?"

The staff eyed each other. No one wanted to be the first to speak.

"We could do a family fun day at Quassy," Steffi suggested. Lake Quasapaug was a family-style amusement park in Middlebury.

"Good idea," Laira said, nodding. "Unfortunately, we won't have time to plan it this year. We'd have to coordinate a date with the park, plan the event, promote it, then print tickets and t-shirts. But let's definitely keep it in mind for next summer. That'd be a great family event."

Steffi looked deflated and hurt.

"It's a great idea, Steffi," Pete reassured her. "We've done 'em in the past, and they're always well received." He glanced around the room. "Does anyone else have suggestions?"

Gary spoke up. "I like Steffi's idea. Along those same lines, could we do a Picnic in the Park kind of thing? Take over a local park for a day. Supply hot dogs, hamburgers and soft drinks. Folks can bring their own sides and chips and stuff. We could do softball, volleyball and badminton. Maybe get the police to do bike-safety inspections or child fingerprinting – in advance of the whole back-to-school thing."

Laira was nodding. "Nice idea, Gary," the promotions director said. "Let's brainstorm on that."

"Not so fast," Pete interjected. "Let's hear some other ideas first, see what the rest of you are thinking."

Awkward silence descended again.

Gary nudged his brother-in-law. When Marc turned, Gary mouthed, "Go ahead."

Marc looked uncomfortable.

"Say it," he urged silently.

Still Marc hedged. He shrugged, shook his head.

"I don't know why he's not saying anything," Gary spoke up, "but Marc had an idea I thought was terrific: a listener-appreciation party."

Laira turned toward Marc; her eyebrows arched. "Marc?"

"Well" – shooting Gary a look of death, Marc sat forward in his seat – "I was thinking: We could plan a party for, say, a thousand people. Invitation only. We'd give away passes on air. As the main draw, we could get a name act to perform… like a private station concert."

A murmur of approval circulated through the conference room.

Laira leaned forward. "Great idea, Marc. Tell me more."

"I haven't worked out any details – I mean, it's just an idea we were throwing around; it'd have to be at least in the spring, to give us time to plan, and line up a performer – a singer or comedian, maybe."

Pete nodded. "I like it. This could work. Who were you thinking of for a headliner?"

Marc shrugged, glanced at Gary as if to say, *You got me into this. Any other brilliant ideas?* "Maybe the music director can figure that out."

"Gary?"

"Funny you should ask, Pete. I'm thinking we go after someone who'd offer mass appeal – kind of a broad fan base."

"Okay; like who?"

"The Rolling Stones would be ideal – but I doubt we could get them."

A snicker circulated the room.

Pete smirked. "Alright, wise-ass, who d'you think we *could* get?"

"Realistically, we want someone who's drawn listener interest over a period of years," he mused, "someone who'd appeal to our younger audience members, as well as our mid-demographic."

"Do you have anyone in mind?"

Gary shrugged. "Howard Jones is too narrow a draw for what Marc had in mind; he's touring, but his demographic scope's not wide enough… Depending on when we schedule this event, we could probably get Cyndi Lauper; she'd tie in with the whole eighties retro thing—"

"Yeah, right; like you're gonna be able to get *her*."

He scowled briefly at his longtime adversary, then continued, as if there'd been no dissention. "But we probably couldn't get her 'til spring, anyway; 'cause she's pregnant – and due in November."

"We couldn't draw a top name like her. Not to come *here*."

"Actually, I don't think that'd be a problem," Gary replied coolly.

Pete looked back and forth between them as if watching a tennis match.

"Sure," Steffi scoffed. "Do you have any idea how much that'd cost? I'm telling you: We won't be able to get her."

Gary leaned both elbows on the conference table and stared her down, his words clipped. "And I'm telling you it won't be a problem."

She smirked. "You're crazy, Gary. What it would cost to get her, you don't even *make* in a year."

Irked, Gary ticked items off on his fingers. "First of all, Stef, you don't know shit about what I earn, okay? Second, some things are more important than money; like friendship and loyalty. And third, there's a good reason *I'm* music director." His South Jersey accent surfaced. "So why don'cha put a sock in it 'til you know what you're talking about… and since *that'll* be a while, I plan to enjoy the quiet."

"Oh, you think you're so—"

"Alright, enough!" Pete chided. "Cut out the bickering – both of you! You're acting like a couple of four-year-olds!"

A few people stifled snickers. Pete glared at them.

The two combatants glowered at each other from across the conference table.

"Gary, look into who we can sign for a listener-appreciation party. Target mid- to late-April. See who's appropriate – and available – and get back to me in two weeks. If you can get Cyndi, great; if not, explore other options. Marc: You and Laira check out possible venues." Pete glanced around the table. "Any questions?"

Half a dozen heads shook no.

"Good. One last thing: This fall, we're starting an intern program with Glenmede. Before you start complaining, don't. Most of you started in this biz as teenagers; and you owe a debt of gratitude to the pros who helped you along the way. So think of this as your chance to give back."

The Glenmede School was a private girls' boarding school on the other side of Middlebury.

Pete went on. "It's a pilot program; the school's chosen a few industries the girls expressed interest in, and they'll do internships this fall. If it works out, fine; if not, we tried. Tom and I are excited about this opportunity – and we hope you will be, too. Questions?"

"When will they be starting?"

"Last week of August, when school starts. They'll have selected the departments they want to learn about and come in for an orientation session. I shouldn't have to say it, but I want you all on your best behavior." As he spoke, Pete eyed his midday and afternoon-drive jocks.

Gary looked away; Steffi did likewise.

"Any other questions?"

"Will we know in advance if we'll be getting any interns in our department?" Laira asked.

"I'll know about a week before they come in. I'll tell you as soon as I know who they are."

There were nine interns in all: five in the news department, three in production and one in music.

News director Barbara Kowalski, who went by Barb Dwyer on air, held weekly meetings with her interns; she monitored their progress closely. Production director Paul J. Randonovich met with his interns occasionally. Paul, who used the air name Randy Lear, did overnights. Most of the staff called him Caveman.

Gary'd had an intern once before, several years back: Danny Kramer, a UConn junior, seemed more intent on hitting on Steffi than doing any work. He'd show up on time, but his efficiency ended there. He began cataloguing the music library, but never made it past "L." And the quality of his work was so atrocious, the "somewhat unsatisfactory" Gary wrote in his final assessment was a gift.

Gary didn't expect much from Teresa Abbott – especially since she was a full four years younger than Danny had been. Still, he tried to appear enthusiastic for her benefit; he felt he owed it to the kid to give her a chance.

(August 27 – Wednesday)
"I'll start you out with basic stuff – but it's integral to what goes on here," Gary told Teresa that first morning. "It's what I started out doing in Jersey seventeen years ago. Some of it *is* pretty boring, but it's essential. And I won't ask you to do anything I'm not willing to do – or haven't done – myself."

Teresa nodded. A shy, overweight teen with deep brown eyes, she was too self-conscious about her extreme stammer to speak. And Gary seemed so self-assured, the mere thought of speaking in his presence staggered her. Her heart thumped and she was afraid she'd faint dead away.

"…and of course, you'll feed the rhinoceros and take her to the groomer monthly."

She just nodded.

"Teresa."

No answer.

"Teresa! Are you listening to me?"

Jarred her from her frenzied thought, "Huh?" she squeaked, her face burning. "Wh-what?"

Gary smiled. "I said, Are you listening to me?"

"Uh, I um – I'm s-s-sorry. I" – Teresa heard a whooshing sound in her head. She didn't dare look at him – "gee, I – I guess not. I-I-I'm sorry." She felt her notebook and pen slip from her useless hands. Her eyes flew open wide; the beginnings of a silent *Why?* formed on her lips. Her cheeks blazed.

Gary laid the notebook and pen on his desk. "You don't need to take notes right now," he said softly. "I just want you to listen."

Embarrassed and overwhelmed, Teresa nodded. "Okay," she whispered.

Again he went through the information. After each item, he paused to ask if she understood.

"Y-y-yes, sir," she said, nodding vigorously and crossing and re-crossing her ankles.

"Remember, if you have questions – anything at all – just ask. You're here to learn. I want you to make the most of this internship," Gary told her. "Since it's just us, we don't need to schedule meetings. If you've got a question, Terri, I'm right here. And if I need to see you about something, I know where to find you." His smile set aside her panic.

Terri. She liked that he called her that. She swallowed hard. She nodded. "Oh-oh-okay."

In bed that night, Gary talked with Micki about his new intern. "She's a nice kid," he mused as Micki nestled against him. "Sweet. But she's so quiet. Almost like she's – I dunno – afraid to talk to me or something. I'm not scary, am I?"

"Only first thing in the morning," she teased, sliding her arms around him. "And even then you're kinda cute." Snuggling closer, she gazed up at him, wrinkling her nose.

He flicked the end of her nose with his forefinger. "Very funny. I'm *serious.* It's like she's afraid of me. How do I get her to feel comfortable around me? I never have a problem with my first graders."

"Maybe she's got a crush on you." Micki pinched, then patted, his cheek. "Who wouldn't?"

"Don't be silly; she's just shy."

"It's the quiet ones you gotta watch out for."

"Like *you*, huh?" Gary tweaked her nose. Still, he secretly wondered whether she might be right.

Michaela grinned. "Precisely."

He shook his head. "I honestly don't think that's it. There's real eagerness, but it's buried so far beneath that timidity. I'm not sure how to get past it. I'm supposed to be *teaching* this girl; how can I teach her if I'm not getting through to her…?"

Micki gave a sly smile. "Oh, I think you're getting through… just not how you expected."

(September 22 – Monday)

"I-I'm sorry. Wh-what?" Teresa still hadn't gotten over her shyness, even though she'd seen Gary three times a week for nearly a month.

At least that stammer seems to be diminishing. "How do you think it's going? Do you feel confident in what you're doing?" Gary was careful to assign tasks he knew she'd excel at, things designed as much to foster her self-confidence as to assist him. Terri was a quick study; he constantly had to scramble to come up with new responsibilities for her.

"Y-yeah, I… I mean, I-I *guess* so," she faltered. "But how – how do *y-y-you* think I'm d-doing?"

I'd __kill__ for a full-time assistant like you! How much longer 'til you graduate? "I wasn't sure about giving you so much so quickly," Gary admitted, "but you've caught on great. I think you're ready for something new. Something a little more involved." He smiled. "Would you like that?"

Her eyes widened. "Y-yeah!"

Gary motioned Teresa over to his desk. "Come sit down." He outlined the new tasks, explaining their value to the overall workings of the station. "Here" – he slid a stack of CDs toward her – "give these a listen. The songs I'm considering for airplay are marked on the cases. Tell me what you think: Do we add them or not?"

When he saw her startled expression, he said, "I'm not implying you've got final say. *I* don't even have that." His smile eased her nervousness. "That's Pete's job. But I want your input. Your computer's equipped with CD-ROM… and you can use my headphones. Just plug 'em into the front of the speaker where it says 'phones' and you're all set. Okay?"

"Sure," she murmured, shuffling through the stack of music. "I think I can handle that."

It was the first time he'd seen her smile – or heard her say something without that blasted stammer. "Any questions?"

"You just want me to listen to 'em?"

"And jot down a few notes if there's anything you want to comment on."

Teresa looked perplexed. "Comment on?"

"Yeah" – reaching back, he grabbed a magazine at random from the bookcase behind his desk; flipping to the back, he passed it to the intern – "read these. Music directors submit comments to trade publications on songs they add – or don't add – to their playlists. It gives other stations a push about whether a particular song might be right for their market."

"Oh." She scanned the magazine intently. "Hey!" she exclaimed, shoving it back across the desk and pointing to the top of page 81. "This is you!"

"Yeah, well, they quote me a lot. Guess I never know when to shut up."

Teresa giggled. "*Chiacchierone.*"

Edward had always called him that. Chatterbox. Gary stared at her in surprise, then laughed. "Did you just call me '*chiacchierone*'?"

Terri blushed fiercely. His proper pronunciation of the unwieldy Italian word startled her. "Y-you *know* that word?"

"I should say so! 'Til I was ten, that's what I thought my name was," he kidded. "My grandpa used to call me that."

Her eyes widened. "Me too!"

"My grandfather used to call *you* '*chiacchierone*'?"

Now she laughed. "No! *My* grandfather did!"

"Oh." Gary feigned sudden understanding. "I'm glad we got that cleared up. Anyway, if you'd like to comment on something, feel free. If it's good, I'll submit it. Of course, I'd make sure they credit you for it."

"M-me?" Terri squeaked.

"Why not you? It's how I got *my* first comment printed."

The teen giggled nervously. "Really?"

"Yep. I wasn't much older than you. I was just a snot-nosed kid with a quirky music sense."

A playful smile crossed her face. "Whaddaya mean *was?*" she teased.

Where'd that come from? His voice conveyed mock annoyance. "Don't you have work to do, missy?" When she nodded, he chuckled. "Then get to it." Shaking his head, he grumbled, "Smart-mouth kid."

Grinning, the girl handed back the magazine. She brought the stack of music to her desk, along with the headphones he gave her.

Terri slipped the first disc into her computer. Gary watched as she reacted to the music pulsing through the headphones: watched her expression change from solemnity to delight, from vexation to revulsion, as she removed one CD and inserted another, then another.

Periodically she'd comment aloud on something. Mostly it was just "Yuck!" or "Ooh!" or "Hmm." But once he even heard her mutter, "They call this crap *music?*"

He turned away so she couldn't see his grin. *I knew she was in there somewhere. It just took music to reach her.* Suddenly Gary knew how he would draw her out.

(September 29 – Monday)

"Umm… M-Mr. Sheldon? I um, I'm done with my – with my work, sir. Is there um, anything else y-you want me to do?"

"Already?" Gary glanced at the clock. It had only taken forty minutes. "That's terrific. Uh, I don't have anything else to give you right now."

She twisted her hands together. "Then could I, uh – I mean, if it's okay with you – could I look at some of the – the trade magazines?"

"Sure!" Delighted at her interest, Gary handed her the one in his IN box. "Here's the latest *Radio & Records* – just came in."

"N-no – I don't wanna take a – a *new* one. I'll just look through some of the older ones."

"Teresa. Let's get something straight."

She gulped. Her eyes widened at his serious tone. And he never called her Teresa anymore!

"You're a valued member of this team; you should have access to the new trade rags." He held it out. "All I ask is that you put it back when you're done. Same goes for headphones, music, anything. Use whatever you want. Just put it back where you found it."

"Y-you trust me?"

"Why wouldn't I? Like I tell my kids: I trust you 'til you give me reason not to. *Capisce?*"

A shy smile crossed Terri's lips. She nodded. "Yeah. I understand. Thanks, Mr. Sheldon."

(11:30 a.m., October 6 – Monday)
"Hey."

Gary looked up. "Hey yourself. How was your weekend?"

Terri draped her jacket over her chair. Settling into a seat opposite his desk, she smiled. "Great! My parents and little sister came down for parents' weekend."

"Sounds like fun."

"It was. We went to some on-campus events; then on Sunday, we went to New York City to visit my brother." She paused, then added wistfully, "It was good to see everyone. I missed them."

"It's hard, being apart from people you love," Gary acknowledged. "How far is home?"

"Just outside Worcester."

"Bay State girl, huh? How come no accent?"

"Oh, w-we haven't lived there that long. We came from Ohio a few years back. Near Cleveland." She paused. "How 'bout you? H-how was your weekend?"

"The little ones are sick, so they were cranky. Otherwise, it was fine. We always have fun."

"What'd you do?"

"My brother and his girlfriend came up from New York on Sunday. I keep telling Joey he's too young to date; but he insists now he's twenty-four, he can do what he wants," Gary deadpanned.

Terri snickered. "Yikes! You sound almost as strict as my dad. And he's got an excuse. He's a minister! Let me guess: Your girls won't be allowed to date 'til they're twenty, huh?"

He scowled. "Fifty."

Now she laughed.

"Not just the girls, either; the boy's not quite three and he's already got a roving eye. We'll need to keep him on a leash. He'll have his first girlfriend in kindergarten. And knowing him, it'll be the teacher!"

***

(12:07 p.m., October 13 – Monday)

"Tea?"

Teresa nodded as she settled into the booth. "Sure." She felt grown up, being asked to a lunch meeting with her supervisor. He'd said there was something he wanted to discuss with her. A project.

Jasmine-scented liquid dribbled from the teapot's spout and pooled at the base of Terri's cup.

"You're making a mess," she observed, a teasing grin lighting her face.

The grin was contagious. "It's kind of a law of nature," Gary explained. "Teapots in Chinese restaurants drip – no matter how careful you are about pouring."

"Is that what it is?" The girl's eyebrow arched, punctuating her question.

"Think you can do better?"

She gave a slight shrug. "I could give it a try."

Gary slid the teapot across the table, turning it so the handle faced her. "Be my guest."

Terri filled his cup without spilling a drop. Her eyes glinted playfully. "You were saying?"

A smile danced about his lips. "Nobody likes a showoff. Drink your tea."

The waitress breezed over to deliver hot, almond-scented hand towels. "Hi, Gary. Miss," Ming greeted them cheerfully. "Still having that pouring problem, I see."

She opened her order pad. "What'll it be? The usual?"

'The usual' for Gary was mu shu pork. With extra plum sauce. And hot and sour soup.

"Not today."

Taking a half step back, she studied him. "Let me guess: You're in a… Cantonese shrimp kind of mood."

"I eat here too often – is that what you're trying to tell me?"

"Not at all," Ming replied. "Chopsticks, yes? And hot and sour soup?"

"Of course. But I'll need a spoon for that."

Shaking her head, Ming sighed. "Always a wise guy." She turned toward Terri. "For you, miss?"

Terri chose General Tso's chicken and, at Gary's recommendation, the hot and sour soup.

"Chopsticks for you as well, miss?"

"Uh… sure. Why not?" *I hope he'll teach me how to use 'em… if not, I'll die of embarrassment!*

While they waited for their soup, Gary gave Terri an overview of the listener-appreciation party. He highlighted her role in planning the event.

Her eyes widened in delight at the new responsibilities – and in amazement he'd place such trust in her. The confidence in his voice intimidated her. "Y-you really think I can do this?"

"If I didn't, I wouldn't have asked for your help."

Terri wasn't ready for how hot the soup would be. It felt like someone stuffed a dozen atomic fireballs into her mouth. In her haste to grab her water glass, she knocked it over. It tipped toward Gary and broke, sending a rush of water and ice cascading into his lap.

"Omigod – I'm so sorry!" she gasped, blushing fiercely.

Gary blotted at the spill with his napkin, then moved a file folder out of harm's way. "It's okay, Terri. It's just water."

Still she stammered apologies, grabbing her napkin to help wipe up the spill, too.

Breezing over, Ming discreetly traded their sopping napkins for dry ones. Teresa spluttered an apology, embarrassed that the waitress had witnessed her clumsiness.

The pretty Asian woman smiled. "It's okay; the gravity's real strong in this place whenever Gary's here." She whisked the broken glass away.

A minute later she returned with their lunches and a new water goblet. And the chopsticks.

Gary waited for Teresa to pick up the slender sticks before reaching for his own, but she just stared at them.

"What's wrong? Did she give you left-handed chopsticks?" The corners of his mouth twitched.

"Uh… I – I dunno," Terri stammered. "How do you tell the difference?"

Now his grin prevailed. "There's no such thing. I'm just playing with you. Want me to teach you how to use those? It can be a little tricky, first time."

The teen tried to focus on his words as he described, and then demonstrated, how to hold the bamboo utensils.

"See? Like this." Gary deftly plucked a straw mushroom from his plate and deposited it on the edge of Terri's plate. "Easy."

Terri tried her luck with the mushroom he set there. After a few false starts, she managed to pick it up and get it into her mouth.

"Nicely done!" He gave her a triumphant smile. "Try holding this one a bit farther down and angle your finger more… like this. There. Try that… Good. You're getting it."

Little by little, Teresa gained confidence as she manipulated the chopsticks.

Over lunch, they discussed ideas for the listener-appreciation party. For the first time in her life, the girl felt a sense of self-assurance, bolstered by Gary's confidence in her ability to contribute positively to the project.

The way he spoke in terms of "what *we* need to do to make this happen" validated Terri, making her feel like a real part of the team.

Partway through the meal, as Terri brought a piece of chicken to her mouth, the morsel spun off the chopstick and fell on her. It sat just long enough to leave a stain, then rolled down her front, trailing sauce the whole way. The errant tidbit landed with a little *pfff-lunk* in her teacup. The tea splashed.

Terri felt her face turning several progressively deepening shades of red.

"Hey" – Gary gave her hand a paternal pat – "I've done that myself, a dozen times. Go rinse it off before it sets."

Mortified, she ducked into the ladies room and wiped at the splotches with a damp paper towel. Her effort sullied the blue silk even worse. Terri tried applying soap, but the wall-mounted dispenser spit out too much and it splurted everywhere, then dripped out of her hand before she got it onto the stain. In desperation, she unbuttoned her blouse and took it off to apply more soap. In her frenzy, she slogged the blouse through the water and soap that splashed on the countertop. Now there was sauce *and* a huge wet splotch. "*Now* what'm I gonna do?" she wailed aloud.

Teresa tried to wring and squeeze out the water, but she only succeeded in wrinkling the delicate material, leaving it looking even worse. In her haste to dress and get back to the table, she re-buttoned it wrong. As she was about to leave, the button on her right cuff caught in her hair, pulling it askew. She hadn't brought her purse into the bathroom, so she didn't have a comb. When she tried to realign the topknot by tucking the tugged-loose lock back in and patting it into place with her fingers, that made it worse. The lopsided bun sagged off the back of her head; puckered hair loops stuck out in three places.

Shoulders hunched, hands clutching at the mess on her blouse, Teresa hurried back to the table. Head down, she nearly crashed into a busboy carrying a tray piled with dirty dishes.

When she sat down, Terri was too embarrassed to look at Gary. She laid aside her chopsticks and reached for her fork, hoping he wouldn't notice. She scooped up a small forkful of rice; her hand shook so badly the food spilled into her lap. Her face turned as red as the tassels hanging from the jade carvings on the wall.

Finally, Ming brought the check. Gary signed the credit-card slip and they got up to leave.

Exiting the restaurant, Terri kept her head down, her white sweater clutched tightly about her chubby midsection. As they crossed the parking lot, Charlie arrived with a prospect. Gary acknowledged the sales manager with a perfunctory wave, then hurried the teenager into his car.

"Wasn't that your afternoon guy?" Sam Davies asked Charlie as they were shown to a table. "I thought he looked familiar. I've seen him on that billboard on I-84."

Soon after they were seated, Charlie excused himself to use the restroom; there, he made a call on his cell phone.

When Gary and Teresa returned, Pete instructed Terri to go about her work, then escorted the music director into his office and shut the door. Pete dropped the WZBX employee handbook onto his desk, facing Gary, open to the page about staff interactions with student interns. "Look familiar?"

Gary gave it a cursory glance. "Yeah."

"Any idea why I bring this to your attention?"

He shoved it away. "We weren't *consorting*, Pete. We were discussing business; we just happened to be doing it over lunch. There's a big difference. Geez, Peter! I'm married. I'm not *dating* my intern!"

"Whether you are or not isn't the point. You had *no right* to take that girl off station property."

Gary didn't try to justify his actions. "You're right," he conceded. "I'm sorry. It won't happen again." He wondered how Pete knew.

Then he realized: Charlie!

"It better not. Gary. What were you thinking? It's bad enough a prospective client saw you – never mind the folks at Wong Lee's; they're *already* clients, for crying out loud!"

"And they saw us eating lunch. We ate and discussed the listener-appreciation party. That's it."

"What if that kid goes and tells someone at school you took her out? Or – worse: What if she turns around and accuses you of something?"

"Teresa? Pete, you gotta be kidding! Something like that would never even occur to her!"

"What if it did? What if she *does* accuse you of something improper? What then, Gary? You want us to have a lawsuit on our hands?"

"Of course not." Gary averted his eyes in capitulation. "I'm sorry. I wasn't thinking. But that's the extent of it. I didn't set out to do anything wrong. If you think it'll head off any unpleasantness, I'll write a letter of apology to the head of the intern program."

The PD nodded. "Good idea. Fax it – *and* get it in today's mail. But let me see it before you send it out. And just so you know: A copy will be placed in your personnel file."

Gary nodded. He knew, from Pete's tone, his boss meant for the letter to be entered as part of his official written reprimand – as outlined in the employee handbook.

Pete looked across the desk and shook his head. "Direct and blatant disregard for station policy."

"It wasn't *disregard*," Gary countered weakly.

He stretched out his hands in a gesture of futility. "You're a department head, Gary. You should have known better."

"I know." His shoulders drooped. "I'm sorry."

Pete's tone softened. "Okay, go on. Better get that letter written. And cc the dean."

Gary slunk away, berating himself all the way to his office. *How could you be so stupid? Pete's right: You <u>shoulda</u> known better.*

It was only the second time he'd been in trouble at work. He'd had scrapes with Charlie his first few months, but always managed to fix things or charm his way out of it. *That won't happen this time. This is too big.* Last time, he was verbally reprimanded – and that was thirteen years ago. Pete pulled him off the air for two days after he'd run himself ragged with school and work. Gary vowed never to do something that boneheaded again. *I guess this time I blew right past boneheaded. I could get fired or, like Pete said, the station could get sued or—*

He stopped, not wanting to think about what might happen as a result of his careless, albeit well-intentioned, action.

Uncharacteristically silent when he returned to the office, Gary sat at his computer, staring at the monitor for the longest time, drumming his fingers on the desk. He typed furiously for several minutes, stopped and drummed his fingers some more. Then the cycle of typing and stopping repeated.

Terri wondered if he was angry at her – but she didn't want to risk having him yell, so she didn't ask. He'd never yelled at her. *But why take chances? Maybe he's in trouble with Mr. Donovan. Maybe that's why he got called into his office.*

As much as she hated the thought of it, she kind of hoped that's what it was… just as long as he wasn't mad at her. She really liked working for Gary. He made her feel important; he listened to her ideas and never made fun of her suggestions. She'd be devastated if she'd disappointed him in some way.

Forty minutes later, Gary returned to Pete's office with a draft of the letter.

Rita M. Reali

October 13, 1997

Mrs. Alice J. Curtis
Intern Supervisor
The Glenmede School
Middlebury, Connecticut

Dear Mrs. Curtis:

In an error in judgment on my part this afternoon, I took Teresa Abbott – a Glenmede student intern under my supervision at WZBX-FM – to lunch offsite. While my intent was to discuss her role in an upcoming promotion, I failed to consider the ramifications of escorting a minor off station property.

Unwise as this was, I assure you nothing improper happened between Teresa and me. We had lunch and discussed station business. Nothing more.

I apologize for this lapse in discretion and offer my assurance this breach of station protocol will never be repeated.

As the father of a teenage daughter myself, I admit I should have been more cognizant of my actions – and realized their questionable propriety at the time. I likewise apologize for my lack of foresight in this matter.

I recognize the seriousness of these actions and will, if you deem it necessary, voluntarily withdraw from participation as a mentor in your intern program with WZBX-FM. I further understand this indiscretion will, at the very least, result in an official reprimand from my superiors, if not meriting even more serious repercussions.

The actions taken were mine alone and they should not be construed as "normal operating procedure" at WZBX-FM. Nor should any fault rest upon Miss Abbott. I accept full culpability for this incident and respectfully ask it not reflect poorly on the other department heads or the management of the station.

Very truly yours,

Gary J. Sheldon
Music Director, WZBX-FM

cc: Nancy D. Meyers, Dean of Students, The Glenmede School

Pete handed the letter back. "A little heavy on the *mea culpa*, don'cha think?"

When Gary didn't reply, the program director nodded. "That's fine. Fax it, and get it to the post office now – so it'll show up first thing tomorrow. We want to head off any potential problems at that end."

Gary nodded, then headed toward the door.

"Oh, and Gary?"

He turned back.

"I also want you to cc Tom, Teresa and me – and your file. When you get back from the post office, bring the copies here, would you?"

Pete slid one copy into the personnel files in his desk, dropped another facedown in his IN box and returned the others to Gary. Standing, he asked the music director to join him for a brief meeting.

Terri was already in Tom's office, seated beside the operations manager's desk, looking terrified; she'd fixed her hair, but her blouse was still askew. Tom greeted Gary and Pete and motioned toward the vacant chairs beside the intern. Pete closed the door; he and Gary sat.

"Am I – um… Am I in trouble?"

Tom attempted to quell the girl's fears. "Of course not, Teresa. No one's in trouble" – he shot a meaningful glance at Gary – "well, not really *bad* trouble, anyway."

Gary stared at the photocopies he still held. He looked up when he heard Tom speak his name.

"You want to tell me what this is all about?"

Haltingly, Gary explained about taking Terri to lunch at Wong Lee's – how he hadn't given it a second thought, really, because he was used to conducting lunch meetings with associates, and he simply viewed her as a coworker. "I'm sorry," he concluded. "I didn't mean any harm. I just took a colleague to lunch."

Tom nodded, then turned his attention to the intern. "Teresa, is that what happened?"

"Y-y-yes, sir, M-Mr. Finnegan." Her stammer was back. And worse than ever. "J-just what Mr. Sheldon said. W-we were starting t-t-to work on a n-n-new project… a-and – and he asked me to g-go over some of the – the d-d-details over l-l-lunch." She kicked the toe of one shoe against her chair leg.

"And you didn't think that was unusual?"

"N-no… I – I mean, he – he's always been r r really nice to me and all… I d-d-didn't think there w-would be anything wr-wr- um… anything wrong…"

"Did he make you feel uncomfortable at any time?"

"N-n-no – no, sir! I mean, well, he – he opened d-doors and stuff for me, and I – I'm not used to – to that k-k-kinda thing… but he was just – he was r-r-real nice to me. A… a real gentleman."

She was blushing. Tom looked at Gary again. "Do you have anything to add?"

Gary shook his head. "No, sir. Nothing."

"Did you touch her at any time?"

He looked stricken. "No!" Then, "I helped her in and out of the car. It's kinda low, and pretty awkward if you're not used to it."

"And that's all?"

A beleaguered-sounding "Yes" fell from his lips.

"There was no other contact between the two of you?"

"No."

"N-n-*no*," Teresa echoed, her cheeks blazing as she re-called the single comforting touch of his hand on hers in the restaurant. She cast a guilty glance at Gary, but he wasn't looking in her direction.

"Just checking," Tom said, holding up his hands. His tone sounded calming; Terri needed that. If the look on Gary's face was any indication, so did he. "I just want to be sure what we're looking at."

After an uncomfortable silence, Gary spoke. "May I speak, sir?"

As Tom met his gaze, one eyebrow arched puckishly. "As if I could ever stop you." When Gary didn't react to his attempt at levity, the operations manager grew serious again. "Of course, Gary."

"It was a business lunch," he mumbled. "Nothing more."

"I understand that," Tom replied with a nod. "Pete tells me you've prepared a letter for Mrs. Curtis."

Gary nodded. "I have your copy here" – he handed it over – "and one for Teresa."

Tom looked up when he finished reading. "Well, Gary, I certainly hope this matter ends here."

"Yes, sir. So do I."

"Alright. Pete, I'd like to talk with you some more. Gary, you and Teresa may go now."

"Yes, sir. Thank you, sir." Gary got up to leave.

"Thank you, sir," Teresa echoed.

She followed her supervisor back to their office. "I – I'm r-r-real sorry, Mr. Sheldon. I didn't m-m-mean for you to g-g-get into – into trouble."

"It wasn't your fault, Terri. I should have known better."

"Known what?" She started to close the door.

"Don't." When he said that – a little too sharply – she turned and looked at him in confusion. "We can't have that door shut. Going forward, I can't afford to do anything that even *looks* improper."

"D-do you w-w-wanna talk about it?" He'd occasionally lent an ear when she was having trouble at school or just needed to vent. She was eager to return the favor.

"Thanks, Terri. I appreciate the offer. But it's not the kind of thing I want to burden you with." He held out her copy of the letter. "This is for you. I'm really sorry I got you dragged into this."

Gary did one of his best, most energetic shows ever. And it was all faked. He didn't stick around to chat with Marc when he got off the air; drained from tearing himself to bits over his ill-fated lunch and the dressing-down that followed, he stowed his headphones in the bottom drawer of his desk and slunk out of the station.

At home, when Micki asked what was wrong, Gary insisted he was just tired.

She knew he wasn't being forthright with her. But she wouldn't pursue it now.

While they got ready for bed, he still looked uneasy, like he wanted to talk about something, but felt uncomfortable as to how, or where, to begin.

Micki sat beside him on the bed. *If I'm gonna ask, now's as good a time as any.* She stroked his earlobe with one finger. "Honey? What's the matter?" she cajoled.

It wouldn't do a bit of good to continue denying anything was wrong. He sighed heavily, ran a hand through his hair. "I did something really stupid today."

She found that hard to believe. But he looked so troubled! "What's that?"

"I took Teresa to lunch."

She kissed him on the cheek. "But that's *nice*. Why would you say it's stupid?"

"She's a minor. She's not supposed to be off station grounds. What if something happened to her or – God forbid – what if she accuses me of something? I could get in deep shit over this."

"Teresa wouldn't do that… would she?"

"Probably not, but who can afford to take chances?"

"You won't get in trouble over it," Michaela soothed, smoothing his hair.

"I'm already in trouble. Pete's preparing an official reprimand."

"That doesn't sound too bad…"

"Well, it *is*. It's a heck of a lot worse than getting called on the carpet in the boss' office – which is what *also* happened." He sank his head into his hands. "Not to mention the little closed-door meeting with Tom." Gary stood, crossed the room. "I just gotta hope this all works out – and watch my step around the interns from now on."

Chapter 12

(October 17 – Friday)
A heavy cream-colored envelope arrived for Gary, bearing The Glenmede School's crest. Identical envelopes appeared in Pete and Tom's mail slots. Pete's was especially thick. Gary's stomach lurched and he suddenly wished he hadn't eaten breakfast.

Collecting his mail and his production assignments, he retreated to his office. He slit the envelope and held it for a moment before laying it aside. After reviewing the rest of his mail, Gary picked up the envelope and pulled out Mrs. Curtis' two-page handwritten reply.

October 15, 1997

Mr. Gary J. Sheldon
Music Director, WZBX-FM
Middlebury, Connecticut

My dear Mr. Sheldon:

I am in receipt of your letter dated October 13, 1997. On behalf of The Glenmede School, I appreciate – and gratefully accept – your apologies. I've conferred with Glenmede's trustees, our attorneys and your station manager. We are satisfied with the steps already taken and do not wish to pursue the incident further. I will assume, by my official acceptance of said apology, we may consider the matter closed.

I admire your forthright approach and commend you for your open admission of something that could easily have been swept aside – or ignored by someone of lesser character. You are truly an honorable young man, Gary, with great strength of character. I'm certain you have worked hard to instill those same qualities in your daughter; she is certainly a lucky girl to have a father like you.

Of course, I would neither seek nor expect your withdrawal from the internship program. It would be a shame to lose so dedicated a professional as you. I've also spoken at length with Teresa; she has expressed nothing but praise and admiration for you, as well as your commitment to excellence and devotion to mentoring. At no time did she misconstrue your intentions, or find them less than proper. She further indicated you have behaved well and professionally at all times – in all of your dealings with her.

As to the actions of your superiors regarding this incident, I do hope they won't be too harsh in dealing with you. It clearly was – as you said – an "error in judgment"; as I am sure you realize, we humans are far from perfect. No one was harmed and there have been no lasting ill effects. Dean Nancy Meyers and I have discussed this matter in depth; if our opinions count for anything, we both feel that your prompt and forth-right apology is sufficient.

I anticipate a long, mutually beneficial relationship with you and the rest of the staff at WZBX-FM. During these past fledgling weeks, our girls have blossomed as interns there. And I thought you should know: Early on, I asked the girls about the station staff they found most helpful or accommodating; right after their own mentors, every single one mentioned you – by name. Teresa, naturally, has been most effusive about your kindness and patience from the start; but I wanted you to know how well thought of you are among the other Glenmede interns as well.

Keep up the good work.

Yours truly,

Alice J. Curtis
Intern Supervisor, The Glenmede School

P.S. Perhaps you will allow Teresa and me to return the favor and take <u>you</u> to lunch some day soon.

cc: Nancy D. Meyers, Dean of Students; Teresa Abbott, Music Intern, WZBX-FM; Peter Donovan, Program Director, WZBX-FM; Thomas Finnegan, Operations Manager, WZBX-FM; personnel file of Gary J. Sheldon

When Pete came in to get Gary's signature on the reprimand documentation, he nodded toward the envelope on Gary's desk. "I see you got your reply. She seemed really impressed with you. Have you always had that effect on women?" The boss' grin indicated he didn't wish to belabor the issue.

Gary's return smile was halfhearted. "I guess so."

"Well, you're damn lucky. This could've gone a lot differently. Whoever's the patron saint of saved butts, you'd better say a novena to that one!"

***

Gary's office door was always left open now; his interactions with Teresa were stilted – if they talked at all. Mostly, he'd leave written instructions and either be monumentally busy or out of the office while she was there. And he went out of his way to avoid being alone with any of the other interns.

Lacking direction and interaction, Terri's confidence and enthusiasm plummeted; her work tanked. The last week of October, she didn't come in at all.

The following week, Gary requested a meeting. But he had no phone number for Teresa; and he didn't want to raise any red flags by calling Mrs. Curtis before he knew what was behind his intern's unusual behavior. So he contacted the girl the only way he knew how: via Instant Messenger.

> **EBSpike118 (8:32:20 PM):** Terri?
> **Tabby714 (8:32:42 PM):** *Yeah?*
> **EBSpike118 (8:33:29 PM):** It's Gary. I need to see you tomorrow. Please be in the office by 10.

Minutes passed. No response.

> **EBSpike118 (8:36:20 PM):** Terri?

EBSpike118 (8:38:15 PM): Terri…
EBSpike118 (8:40:14 PM): Teresa? Are you there?
Tabby714 (8:40:24): *What!!!*
EBSpike118 (8:41:37 PM): 10 o'clock tomorrow. Please be there on time. No excuses.
Tabby714 signed off at 8:41:48 PM

Gary scowled. About to delete the message window, he thought better of it. He saved the message first, then shut down his computer.

(November 4 – Tuesday)
Teresa slumped into the chair opposite Gary's desk.

She despised him for ordering her in here. She hated how he sat behind that desk, keeping her at bay. And she hated that he'd made her feel like just another nuisance part of his job. Teresa glowered, toying with something in her lap.

Gary glanced at the clock: 10:46. "What happened?" He tried to sound non-threatening.

Jaw set, the teenager grumbled her reply. "I overslept."

He knew it was a lie. "That happens. But if you're going to be late, Terri, I'd appreciate a call."

Teresa muttered something Gary couldn't understand. He let it go.

For a while, neither spoke. Then, gently, he broke the silence. "Where've you been?"

The girl gritted her teeth. "I *told* you: I overslept."

One eyebrow arched. "For a whole week?"

She shrugged, said nothing.

"Terri…"

"I had other things to do, alright?"

"You should have called." *I was worried about you.*

"What's the point?" Teresa snapped. "We never talk any-more. You leave me notes" – she waved the pad on which he'd jotted his instructions – "I'm not just some servant girl you can order around in writing, and expect things to get done. I'm supposed to be *learning* from you; but there's not a whole lot I can learn from these!" Terri flung the pad at Gary and turned to flee the room.

"Miss Abbott, *sit down!*"

Terri did as she was told; she looked like she was fighting tears. He'd never raised his voice to her. Or called her Miss Abbott.

Gary got up and shut the door. Firmly. He loomed over the shrinking teen for a moment. "I don't tolerate that kind of disrespect from my own children," he scolded. "You think I'm gonna take it from *you?*" His mouth formed a tight line.

The girl stared at a patch of carpeting.

"Teresa."

She didn't respond, didn't move at all.

Gary leaned against his desk, his arms folded. "Look at me when I'm talking to you." His voice was quiet, but his staccato delivery told her he meant business.

Her gaze inched upward.

"We need to have a talk. I'm not sure what's going on with you, but your effort the past two weeks has been second rate – that is, when you've bothered to show up."

Now her eyes flashed with defiance. "Oh, so you finally noticed!"

Noticed? Confusion flickered across Gary's face. "What's that supposed to mean?"

Teresa sat up straight. "You want to know what's going on with me? I *used to* have a mentor, alright? I *used to* have a supervisor who cared about me and wanted to *teach* me stuff. But now *you* can't be bothered. So why should *I?*"

Incongruously, he noticed her stammer was gone. "What do you mean I can't be bothered? That's absur—"

"You haven't spoken to me in weeks! You leave these stupid notes telling me what to do. I haven't learned anything new from you in I dunno how long! I used to *love* coming here. I *enjoyed* working with you – 'cause you treated me like I mattered. Like I was somebody." Teresa swiped away a tear; she looked like she was fighting to keep her composure. "Now you just treat me like your flunky!"

"Terri… I never meant to come across that way. Why didn't you talk to me sooner?"

"How *can* I," she shrilled, "when you go out of your way to avoid me?"

"I'm not avoiding you."

"Well, it sure seems like it!" Teresa howled.

"There's no need to shout," he told her quietly. "If you want to discuss this, fine. Let's talk. You and me. We'll talk this out, okay?"

"Don't bother," Teresa spat out. "I quit!" She headed for the door.

Gary got to it first and held it shut. He wanted to clasp the girl by the shoulder and turn her around to face him, but he didn't dare lay a hand on her. "Teresa."

She didn't move.

"Teresa, turn around." His tone was gentle, but it commanded compliance. "Look at me."

When she obeyed, her eyes were filled with tears. Her bottom lip quivered.

His heart trembled. "Terri…" he beseeched.

At the tenderness in his voice, Teresa's tears spilled over. Turning away again, she hunched against the closed door, put her hands over her face and cried.

Gary hesitated, one hand poised above Terri's shoulder. He couldn't bear to let her remain uncomforted. In his second violation of the station's non-consorting directive, he put an arm around the weeping teen.

Consoling her as best he could, he helped Terri into her chair again, then stooped beside her, his grey eyes dark with concern. "Do you need a tissue?"

Terri shook her head. Digging in her sweater pocket, she found a rumpled tissue. She swiped it across her eyes a few times, then dabbed at her drippy nose. She stuffed it back in her pocket, scrounged for another one and blew her nose.

"I wish you had come to me sooner about this, Terri," Gary murmured. "I had no idea you felt that way. I'm sorry it had to get to this."

It took a while for Teresa to pull herself together. She sniffled, still dabbing at her eyes.

"How 'bout some fresh air?" Gary opened the windows behind his desk, then crouched by her chair again. "Better?"

She nodded, then blew her nose.

"I feel awful that you're so upset over this, Terri. Could we talk about it?"

Another nod.

Instead of sitting behind his desk, Gary pulled a chair over and sat beside her. "I owe you an apology, Terri. I never meant to offend you or demean you. Or take you for granted. And I'm really sorry I did.

"I was so concerned about impropriety, I neglected my obligation to you. I didn't want it to seem like I was getting too close; but in trying to play it safe, I'm afraid I ran too far in the other direction. I'm sorry my skittishness came across as dislike or disregard. Please accept my apology, Teresa. You've been a tremendous asset to this office and I hope you'll reconsider and stay."

Terri gaped at Gary. "Y-y-you mean that?"

He nodded. "Every word."

She sniffled.

"*Will* you stay?"

The intern fidgeted. "I–if you'll let me… I – I mean, I s-said some pretty awful things to you."

"Nothing that wasn't warranted. You were right: It was insensitive of me to leave notes and not be available to you. You've done so well, I guess I forgot you're still learning."

For nearly half a minute, the only sound in the room was Teresa's sniffling.

Gary reached back for the box of tissues on his desk; he held it out to her.

Taking one, she blew her nose. It was another minute or so before she looked up. Impulsively, Terri hugged him. "Thank you," she whispered when she drew away. "For treating me like someone who matters."

He gave her shoulder a fatherly pat. "You *do* matter. And

Terri, thank *you* for setting me straight."

After a brief silence, she asked, "So… what did you w-want to see me about?"

"I was concerned about you… I wanted to be sure everything was okay."

Meeting his gaze, she gave him a cautious smile. "It is now."

Gary watched Teresa, amazed at the sudden change in her demeanor. Despite her tears, her dark-brown eyes were serene. And when she smiled like that, she looked so poised! "I'm glad to hear that."

The silence took over again. Teresa uncrossed her ankles, then crossed them again. "Um, Gary?"

It was the first time she'd called him by his first name. She sounded like she was trying to get a feel for it. He tried not to look astounded. "Yeah?"

"D'you have anything for me to do?"

Now he smiled. "Funny you should ask. There's music to be taped for Pete; and I want to check on your progress with the listener-appreciation party…"

(12:27 p.m., November 7 – Friday)
Gary leaned against the program director's open door. "Guess where I just came from."

Pete looked up; he smirked. "I'm afraid to."

"You kill me," Gary said as he sat opposite his boss' desk, a huge grin on his face. He looked like a kid about to spill a secret. "Well, if you're not even gonna *guess*, I'll just have to tell you: I spent the morning down in New Haven; at 'The Rock.' Their GM's been pestering me for months, trying to get me to jump ship."

Pete's left eye twitched. "Why are you telling me this?"

"Thought I should give you a heads up." He eyed the program director carefully, then grinned. "You won't believe what they offered me. I still don't believe it."

Fear nibbled at Pete. "Gary, as your boss, I gotta tell ya: I'm hoping you turned them down. But as your friend… if they're offering good money, you'd be a fool not to make a move. It's a bigger market, better opportunities. Hell, if the right person hears you… you could be on your way to New York in no time. Besides, we're in no position to compete with them, money-wise. We couldn't possibly match what they offered." When Gary didn't speak, Pete added, "What *did* they offer you?"

"It's not important. I turned 'em down. Anyway, I only went to shut him up."

"So, what'd you turn down?"

He waved away the question. "Ah, you don't wanna know."

"No, really: What'd they offer? Just out of curiosity."

Gary met the repeated query with dismissive silence. But when Pete fixed him with an intense gaze, he caved. "Alright. They offered me morning drive, program director" – he paused, then mumbled the last words – "and six figures."

"And you said no?" Pete couldn't believe his ears. "Are you crazy, Gary? You turned it down?"

Gary shrugged. "They couldn't offer me what I've got here."

"Whaddaya have here that's worth a hundred K?"

"Actually, it was more like one twenty," he admitted. "I've got roots here, Pete. Family. There's a sense of loyalty here I didn't feel there – not for an instant. I don't need to be some high-paid voice at 'The Rock.' You guys – *you're* my rock. I'm happy here. I've got people who care about me. It's not about being on the air and playing music and giving shit away. It's about building relationships with people who matter. People I love. People I'd do anything for… and who'd probably do the same for me."

Chapter 13

(November 12 – Wednesday)

Gary had left work sick yesterday; before he went home, he left a message on Terri's desk. *Sorry 'bout the note J but please see me when you get in.* He had a specific task in mind for her. Something special.

***

"Your bloodwork came back okay; except your iron and potassium both seem low. Try eating more bananas. And spinach."

"Then I can give both Popeye and Magilla Gorilla a run for their money?"

The doctor smiled as he positioned his stethoscope. "I see no reason not to. Deep breath. Good… again. You still running every day?"

Gary shook his head. "Couple times a month – when I can fit it in."

"Family's good?"

"Kids're fine; I think they're finally over their colds. Micki's been a little down, though."

"Why's that?" Dr. Caron produced a tongue depressor. "Don't answer yet. Say 'Ahh.' "

He did.

The doctor reached for a swab to do a throat culture. "Okay, why's Michaela been so down?"

"We've been trying for nearly two years to have another baby. We've done everything right. And still nothing. She's never had a problem before. And she's only twenty-nine."

"Maybe the problem's not with her."

"You mean—?" Gary stared at the doctor. *Impossible! I've fathered four kids.* He shook his head. "You don't think…?"

The doctor's right eyebrow rose a fraction of an inch. "It *is* possible, Gary. Your first child was conceived when you were… what?"

"Seventeen," he replied, a little ashamed. "Then twenty-six; twenty-seven and twenty-nine." He hoped Dr. Caron wouldn't ask about that third child: the one he conceived with Ellen – the one she lost, sending her spiraling into lingering depression and suicide. Gary shifted on the examining table. He shivered. It was cold in here.

Dr. Caron didn't ask. "And now you're…?"

"Thirty-three."

"Well, you're still young, but it *is* possible we're looking at diminished sperm levels… or reduced motility. We could get a sample, run some tests… find out for sure."

"How do we do that?"

The doctor looked at him. "How do you *think*?"

"Oh." Gary colored slightly. "Been a long time since I've done *that*."

Going through a cabinet of medical supplies, Dr. Caron glanced over his shoulder and smiled. "Lucky man." He rummaged around for a moment, then straightened and handed Gary a clear plastic tube with a rubber stopper. "You'll be needing this."

Holding up the tube, Gary gave a nervous laugh. "Gee, Doc, I don't think it'll fit."

"You're right." The doctor produced a Dixie cup. "That's why you get this, too."

"How soon do you need it? Next week okay?"

"Maybe I wasn't clear, Gary. I want the sample before you leave."

"Now?"

"Unless you happen to be out of stock." Seeing Gary's perplexity, he asked, "Have you and Michaela made love in the last twenty-four hours?"

Gary wanted to lie. But he shook his head. It was just a routine test for the physician; but still…

"Good. Go on down the hall to the right. Last door on the left."

"Just like that?" He tried to mask his uneasiness. "You're not gonna buy me dinner first?"

"Sorry. Your insurance won't cover that."

***

The door to the music department creaked open. "You wanted to see me, Mr. Sheldon?"

Gary smiled kindly at Teresa's continued timidity. And formality. "Yeah, Terri, c'mon in."

The teen hovered by his desk. "What'd you wanna talk to me about, sir?" She blanched, biting her lower lip.

"Have a seat. I just" – the ringing of his phone interrupted – "excuse me." He lifted the receiver. "Music Department. This is Gary."

The corners of his mouth dipped downward in concentration. "I see," he said, reaching for his pen and scribbling on a pad of paper. "Yes. I'm about to go into a meeting; I'll have to get back to you. Is there a number where I can reach you in, oh… say, half an hour?" In the silence that followed, Gary jotted a number. "Got it. Great, I'll do that. I appreciate your calling."

Teresa squirmed, still chewing her lip. "Should I go?" she mouthed, gesturing toward the door. She started to get up. Gary shook his head and motioned for her to sit back down.

She looked around the office they'd shared for two and a half months; she recalled the first time she set foot in here, how awestruck she was by this office and the confident young man who occupied it. Five gold records hung on the wall to her right, and several framed photos on the other walls. Her eyes had widened at seeing Gary with Billy Joel, David Bowie, Howard Jones and Cyndi Lauper. She studied photos of Gary's family interspersed with the celebrity shots. *What cute kids!* They all seemed to have inherited their dad's smile. *And his wife is gorgeous – I'd kill for a figure like that!*

152

When he hung up, Gary turned to the young intern. When he spoke, it startled her from her reverie. "I'm sorry, Terri; this'll just take another second." He pressed the intercom button. "Bren? Terri and I are in a meeting; if anyone else calls, could you take a message? – unless it's Micki calling to say one of the critters is in the hospital."

Terri could hear the half smile in the receptionist's voice. "Critters? You mean kids?"

He grinned. "Critters, kids – call 'em what you want."

Involuntarily, Terri smiled. It made her feel almost important that he'd do this so they wouldn't be interrupted. *Then again* – she gulped – *maybe that's __not__ a good thing. Maybe he doesn't wanna be disturbed 'cause he's still so disappointed with my work that chewing me out is gonna take a while…*

"Sure, Gar'. I'm sorry; I didn't know you were in a meeting when I sent that call in."

Gary smiled back at Terri. "That's okay, Bren. I figured your crystal ball was in the shop."

His good mood didn't fit with what she was expecting. *He should be grouchy. After all, he's gonna yell at me about how awful my work's been, isn't he? Why else would he have left me a note saying he wanted to see me first thing?*

Brenda laughed. "You're such a brat. When do you think you'll be through?"

"Dunno yet. Thanks, Bren." He released the button and turned his attention back to the teen. "Sorry to make you wait, Ter'."

Terri waved off the apology. "No problem, Mr. Sheldon." She paused uneasily. "Umm… what'd you wanna see me about? Did I do something wrong?"

Gary remembered being that young and afraid. "No, Terri. You haven't done anything wrong, Terri. And please: You don't have to call me 'Mr. Sheldon.' It makes me feel really old" – he smiled, recalling Pete's having said practically those same words to him fifteen years earlier – "Just 'Gary' is fine. Okay?"

Teresa nodded. The expression of relief on her face was evident. "Okay… Gary."

Her performance lately had more than made up for her lapse a few weeks back – which he could hardly blame on her. After they cleared the air, she'd dug right in and gotten to work, erasing Gary's prior misgivings about student interns.

"I spoke with Mrs. Curtis yesterday; I told her how pleased I am. Your work exceeds everything I'd expected. Bottom line: Your performance thus far has been superior. Your enthusiasm and attitude are terrific. And I know I can count on continued excellence. In fact, I'm so confident in your abilities, Terri, I want you to oversee something for me."

"Me? But… but I'm just – I'm just an intern."

"You're not 'just' anything. You're a valued member of this team. And I'm sure I can trust you to do your usual spectacular job." He leaned back slightly. "I thought about having you help me with this; but frankly, I think you're ready to handle it alone…"

Gary walked Teresa through calling record-company reps to secure promotional copies of CDs and premium giveaways for on-air contests. Once she was taking care of that on a regular basis, it would free him up to concentrate on other projects.

Twenty minutes later, Terri set about her work with a whole new sense of purpose. And Gary was off to a meeting with Pete, Steffi and Laira Penfield, the promotions director.

Meanwhile, down the hall, another intern was working out the details of a new project of her own. Without sanction or approval from her supervisor.

Next morning, she sidled up to her target in the break room. "Gary? Could I ask a favor?"

Still stirring milk into his coffee, Gary turned to the news intern. "Sure; what do you need?"

"Well," she said shyly, fidgeting with the can of Coke in her hand. "I was wondering…"

***

(November 14 – Friday)

"Well, it's not strep," Dr. Caron told Gary on the phone at mid-morning. "Just a nasty sore throat. It's probably something you picked up from one of your kids. Keep the talking to a minimum for a few days. I know, that's not easy for a radio announcer, but do what you can. And drink plenty of warm liquids."

"Got it. And doc, what about…" The cough drop in his mouth rattled against his teeth. "The uh… the other test?"

"You're fine," he said. "Count's good; motility's excellent. Like a million little Mark Spitzes."

"So, what's wrong?" he asked, speaking stiltedly. "Why isn't… why isn't it working?"

"Can't speak openly right now, huh?"

"Uhh… that's right, yes."

"Short of examining Michaela, I can't make a diagnosis; but my best guess is you're trying too hard."

Gary ran a hand through his hair. *Trying too hard?* "Shit," he hissed, lowering his voice at the last moment when he saw Terri's head swivel toward him in alarm. "That's all you can tell me?"

"Gary, I understand the frustration you must be feeling over this – believe me. Becky and I faced the same issue ourselves. We'd tried for over a year and a half; then, when we decided to stop taking things so seriously and just enjoy being together, *that's* when she got pregnant." He paused. "I'm not being flippant or insensitive here. I'm speaking from personal experience."

Gary squeezed the little "tension buster" squishy ball on his desk. "I understand. What do you suggest?"

"Quit trying. Make love when it feels right, not when all the signs point to fertility. Surprise her with a romantic getaway. Or a quiet evening alone: dinner, candlelight, roses — you know what to do."

"I think I can manage that."

"Good. Keep me posted. I want to see you in four months. We'll recheck your potassium and iron levels then.

And if you're still tense and crabby, I might just order another sperm count."

Caught off guard by the doctor's comment, Gary laughed aloud; he felt his cheeks radiating heat. He turned away from Terri, glad she couldn't hear the other end of the conversation. "Maybe by then I'll have a better HMO — and we can have a nurse take care of that."

"Gary — you're awful!" It was Doctor Caron's turn to be caught off guard. "How's late March? My scheduler's out, but it looks like I have Monday the thirtieth open. Nine a.m.?"

"Perfect." Gary jotted the appointment on his desk calendar. He was still chuckling as he hung up the phone.

(9:37 a.m., November 25 – Tuesday)
Brenda looked up when the door swung open. Before her loomed a uniformed police officer.

Removing his cap, the officer tucked it under one arm and nodded. "Morning, ma'am."

"Good morning, officer. How can I help you?"

"I need to see Pete Donovan, please. Tell him it's Officer Friendly. He'll know me." The corners of his mouth twitched into a slight smile.

The name on his tag said KEARNS. She pressed the intercom button. "Pete, Officer Friendly is here to see you."

"Great. Send him in, Bren."

Brenda directed him to the program director's office down the hall on the left.

Although Pete and his old high-school chum lived nearby, they seldom ran into each other. They chatted for a few minutes, catching up; then the policeman got down to the reason for his visit.

Pete felt his throat constrict. "You gotta be kidding! Tell me you're kidding, Bobby."

His mouth a grim line, Officer Kearns shook his head. "Wish I was. This is no joke. It's gonna be nasty stuff. Especially since the girl's a minor."

"Geez!" Pete put his head in his hands. "There's gotta be some mistake…"

Bobby shook his head again. "That's what it says on the warrant." He opened the official-looking paper for his friend to see. "I just hope he's got a good lawyer, 'cause he's gonna need one."

Pete felt like all the air had been sucked out of his lungs. "What happens now?"

***

The intercom buzzed. "Could you come in here a minute, please?"

"Sure. Be right there."

When Pete opened the door to admit him, Gary saw the uniformed officer. But he assumed Pete had sounded agitated because the policeman was there to see him.

Without preamble, the officer outlined the charges and informed Gary he was under arrest.

"Because he's a friend of mine," Pete added, "Officer Kearns is doing me the courtesy of not taking you out of here in handcuffs. Instead, we'll follow you home. You'll be read your rights there. That'll give you a chance to tell Micki in person."

***

The charges were many, each of them devastating – and all in the first degree: two counts of sexual assault; two counts of sexual assault of a child sixteen or under; two counts of sexual coercion; fifteen counts of impairing the morals of minors – even two charges of offering a minor drugs in exchange for sex. Altogether, twenty-three charges.

While Officer Kearns reeled off the list of charges, Gary sat at his kitchen table in stunned dismay. He gripped Micki's hand, but he didn't feel a thing.

The policeman asked him to stand and put his hands behind his back.

Not wanting to add resisting arrest to the list, he did as he was told as the officer read him his rights and fastened the steel cuffs around his wrists. They felt cold and humiliating.

Neighbors peeked from behind curtained windows as Gary was escorted down the sidewalk and placed in the back of the cruiser. The bolder ones stood in open doorways as the police car drove away.

Pete stayed behind to comfort Michaela. Everything would be fine, he assured her. It was just a formality; it'd all get straightened out. They'd probably arraign him that afternoon and he'd be home in time for supper.

But she could not be consoled. Her brain kept replaying the image of Gary being led to the squad car to be taken to the police station. And charged with unspeakable crimes against a minor!

Gary was processed, fingerprinted and interrogated at length. The incessant hum of fluorescent lights in the interrogation room gave him a headache. He denied everything. The cops kept pressing him to confess, telling him it'd go easier if he came clean.

But Gary maintained his innocence.

After two and a half hours in the dismal little room with uncomfortable chairs and two-way mirrors, the two detectives gave up trying to wrest a confession from Gary and led him to a cell in the windowless lower level. No one had said a word about arraignment. Gary figured he'd be here awhile.

It was after three the day before the start of a long holiday weekend. No one would be at the courthouse until Monday. Instead of enjoying Thanksgiving with his family, he'd spend it alone. In a jail cell. There had to be a law against holding someone without arraignment so long – but in a small town, who would enforce that? He used his one call to phone Michaela, to give her the bad news – and to ask her to get him a lawyer.

At first she cried; then she railed at the injustice. She even called her father. But not even State's Attorney Michael Conwaye could persuade a judge to schedule an arraignment or set bail before the holiday. Gary had no choice. He was stuck in jail until Monday at nine. At the earliest.

***

By noon, Marc and Barbara had gone to Pete; they'd heard reports on other stations' news, and read disturbing items about Gary on the local AP wire.

Pete knew he had to address this before it mushroomed. And that wouldn't be long. He asked them not to tell anyone what they'd heard; then he went to the on-air studio to tell Steffi Gary had to leave unexpectedly and wouldn't be on the air today.

Early that afternoon, Pete and Tom called an emergency meeting.

Pete addressed the staff in a somber tone. "As I'm sure by now some of you are aware, this morning Gary was arrested and—"

A gasp tore through the room. A murmur of disbelief circulated the room as the staff absorbed the unsettling news. Barbara and Marc stared at each other.

Pete looked at Tom, then at the numb, disbelieving expressions on his employees' faces. He took an unsteady breath and continued, hoping to allay their fears without citing details. "In the coming days, you're going to hear his name crop up in the news. It won't be pretty. Bottom line: This stuff will be hard to hear. That's all I'm prepared to say about it."

Now the room buzzed with questions. Pete held up his hands and called for quiet. Gradually, the staff fell silent.

"Gary's requested an indefinite leave of absence. Effective immediately, I'm enacting these lineup changes: Morning drive and midday slots remain unchanged. Marc, you'll do afternoon drive; Rob, you take over the seven-to-midnight shift. Caveman, go back to sleep; you're still on overnights."

"Whoa – no can do," Marc countered, shaking his head. "I've got classes through December."

Pete frowned. "Crap, that's right. Okay, the only change for now is Rob takes over afternoon drive. You can swap after the first of the year."

Nods and murmurs of acknowledgement came from all the announcers.

"And let me just add this." This was Tom. "WZBX is a family. And as family, we don't go airing our business in public. That said, I want no mention of this. Any discussion of it on air is grounds for *immediate* dismissal. Is that understood?"

Nods and "Yes, Tom"s filled the conference room.

"Same goes for phone calls. If anyone asks, the official answer is: *Gary has taken a leave of absence.* Period. Anyone discussing the matter further – or making unwarranted or unnecessary comments – will likewise be terminated. Jocks and office staff alike. Is *that* clear?"

Another round of "Yes, Tom"s circulated the room.

"Good. And so you can't say you weren't warned" – he distributed sheets of paper – "each of you will sign a statement acknowledging these directives. They'll be kept in your personnel files. Understand: I've got no qualms about making an example of anyone." Tom's eyes swept the room, meeting each person's gaze. "This is family business and it stays here!"

Pete glanced around the room, first at the thunderstruck expressions on the staff's faces, then at Tom's grim visage. Tom was a good boss. He demanded unswerving compliance, but he was fair. He was also fiercely loyal – and he expected loyalty in return.

"What about news coverage?"

"Good question, Barbara. Report actual news, and only when there's something legitimate: like if the jury's reached a verdict, or the parties settle out of court. Salacious details have no place in our news coverage." Tom eyed the news director. "Does that help?"

Barbara nodded. "Yes, Tom. Thank you."

"Two things need seeing to right away. One is the Holiday Bash. The kickoff is set for Monday. Marc, Laira, Charlie and Pete, see me after this meeting. The other is the internship program. As of now, it's suspended. I'll contact the school." Tom glanced at his team's shocked, saddened faces. "Questions?"

Eighteen heads shook *No.*

"Good. Okay, that's it, people. Marc, Pete, Laira, Charlie, I'll meet with you now in my office."

A little after two, Pete went into the on-air studio to talk with Steffi, outlining the directives given at the general staff meeting.

The midday announcer stared at the program director. "Are they sure? Gary?"

Pete nodded. "That's what the warrant said. I know you two have had issues, Stef, but this is a time for unity. Tom wants no disparaging remarks. In fact, he wants no talk about this at all. Anyone mentioning it will be fired. Period."

Steffi started to complain that Pete was singling her out unnecessarily.

He held up his hands. "No. I'm not coming down on *you*, Stef. I'm reiterating what Tom told us all. He made it clear he intends to enforce this. I know things have never been rosy between you and Gary. But you're a good announcer, Steffi; I'd hate to see you lose your job over some careless comment."

Just before three, the program director called Marc into his office.

"I realize this is especially hard for *you*," Pete acknowledged as Gary's brother-in-law and closest friend slumped into a chair. "I won't pretend it'll be easy on any of us, but, as awful as things seem – and as bad as we all feel – we've still got jobs to do." He watched the other man's jaw set resolutely. "I'd like you to pinch hit as music director until Gary comes back."

Ignoring Pete's request, Marc shook his head. "Who would've done this?" he asked, numb. "Who would have said something like this about Gary? *About Gary!*" – he pounded the arm of the chair – "I heard what they charged him with, Pete. I don't believe it, any of it. Not about Gary."

Pete tried to redirect Marc's attention to work; but Marc wasn't hearing him.

"I've been going over and over it in my head, trying to think who might have done this. And I keep coming back to Teresa. I can't believe she'd…" He trailed off, shaking his head. "Not to Gary. She *adores* him! Why would she do a thing like this?"

"Maybe it wasn't Teresa," the program director suggested with a shrug.

"Then who? Who else worked so closely with him, Pete?"

***

Gary's arrest was the lead story on all the local TV stations' six- and eleven-o'clock news. By morning, details of the charges against him were plastered all over the newspaper. Morning jocks statewide – from Fairfield to Hartford, Norwich to Willimantic – picked up on the story, ripping into Gary as if he'd already been convicted.

Erin's friends tried to shield her from their classmates' cruel taunts. Her teachers did their best to quell the malicious comments in class, but they couldn't prevent the stinging barbs she had to endure between classes. Fortunately, it was a half day because of the Thanksgiving break.

Erin called home during study hall to beg Mom to pick her up; she couldn't bear to take the bus.

When the dismissal bell sounded, Erin bolted from the building and into Michaela's waiting car. "It was awful, Mom!" she sobbed. "You have no idea how mean they were!"

"I'm so sorry you have to go through this, honey," Micki soothed as Erin buckled her seatbelt. "But it'll be—"

"You don't *understand*!" the teenager wailed. "You don't know how it *feels*!"

Micki's throat tightened; she recalled how vicious her classmates had been, senior year, after a sensational murder in town… how Jennie Falmouth had taunted her about having been raped a month earlier by the man who murdered the Burnham woman. "I *do* know how it feels to be the target of humiliating remarks. But you're stronger than that. Maybe by

Monday, things will settle down and they'll have forgotten all about it." It wasn't likely; but Michaela had to say something to comfort Erin.

***

Thanksgiving morning, when Michael Conwaye arrived at his daughter's house, he brought the one thing Micki could truly feel thankful for.

"Blake Tierney's the best defense attorney I know," he assured her. "All three cases I lost this year, I lost to Blake; I respect him too much to let a few defeats in the courtroom taint my opinion of him. I've talked with him already, explained the situation. He's agreed to meet with Gary in the morning."

(November 28 – Friday)
In Middlebury, it seemed, they were awfully lenient with the "one phone call" rule.

"I miss you, baby," Gary said when Michaela answered the phone.

"When can you come home?" she asked, dissolving into tears.

"Not 'til Monday; but you can come visit." He tried to sound hopeful, although he knew what the extent of it would be. "I miss you so much… Please come."

"Of course," she whispered. "When?"

"They said this afternoon – two to two twenty. That's it. And no one under twelve."

Michaela drew in a ragged breath. "Okay. But Erin can come, right?"

Gary's heart soared. *Erin.* He'd get to see his daughter! At the same time, his hopes slammed into the iron bars of his jail cell: He couldn't see Amanda or Michael. Not 'til Monday… if then. He had no guarantee they'd even set bail. He didn't know when – or *if* – he'd get to go home. "Yeah," he murmured, a trace of a smile crossing his lips. "Please bring her." He ended the call before she could hear the cry in his voice.

***

Gary gazed at his wife and fifteen-year-old daughter. Staring back through the barrier separating them, Micki looked like she was about to cry.

For a long time, no one moved. Micki and Erin stood in the visitation area and watched him.

This didn't seem real. None of it seemed real. Sighing deeply, Gary lifted the receiver from its hook – his only link between freedom and captivity.

Finally, Erin sat in the hard wooden chair and picked up the wall-mounted receiver. "Daddy, I miss you," she said plaintively. "When can you come home?"

I don't know. He couldn't say that – even though it was the truth. And he'd taught her to always tell the truth. Her voice brought tears to his eyes. He fought them back with all his might. "Soon, punkin," he said, the sound of his lie echoing darkly in his heart. "Real soon." He sensed she wasn't buying it. He met her gaze as bravely as he knew how, and forced himself to drag their conversation back to the mundane. "How are things at school?"

Erin shrugged. "Oh, you know" – she lowered her eyes – "the same."

For years he'd been so closely linked to Pomperaug High – with the annual Holiday Bash and the all-night graduation party. He'd worked hard to foster a relationship between the school and the station. Now that was ruined. Worse, he knew how vindictive teenagers could be. He hated to see Erin caught in the middle of this, hated that the other kids were probably taunting her with cruel whispers, jeers and finger pointing… all because of him.

I'm sorry, sweetheart, he wanted to say. *I'm so sorry for putting you through this.* He forced a smile. "I know, punkin. Even at its best, high school sucks. But don't you worry; by the time you're thirty, it'll all be better. I promise."

Erin pasted on a smile. "I know. I love you, Daddy." She put a hand up against the barrier.

Gary pressed his to the other side. He looked at their hands, separated by shatterproof Plexiglas. So close and he couldn't hug her, couldn't even feel the slight pressure of her fingers against his! That quarter inch might as well have been a mile. "I love you, too, baby," he murmured into the receiver, his gaze meeting hers.

Each saw the tears in the other's eyes; their glances darted away.

Tears glistened in Micki's eyes, too. She wiped them away before he could notice them.

Erin got up and handed the receiver to her mother, who sank into the chair.

"Hi, honey," she greeted him, pressing the instrument to her ear.

Gary watched her lips move; as he did, he wished more than anything he could feel them against his now. "Hi, baby," he replied, touching the Plexiglas partition.

She touched back. "I miss you so much, Gary…" She started to cry.

He ached to hold her, to comfort her. He leaned toward the barrier, wanting desperately to reach out and wipe her tears. "Shh… baby, don't," he pleaded.

"I can't help it," she whimpered, swiping at her eyes with both fists. "I can't bear to see you like this!"

Erin gave her mother's shoulder a gentle squeeze.

At the touch of her daughter's hand, Micki's composure gave way. She dropped the receiver, lay her head against her arms on the countertop and wept. Erin hugged her.

Gary wanted to beg the officer to let him go to his wife — to comfort her and dry her tears. But as chummy as he and his staff had become, he knew better than to ask for that kind of favor.

Erin picked up the receiver and held it out to Michaela. "Go on, Mom. Talk to him."

With a trembling hand, Micki reached for the receiver. "I'm better now, really," she said, trying to poke fun at her breakdown. "You know me, always so emotional." Taking a deep breath, she made a valiant stab at small talk.

Gary made a similar effort.

They struggled through several minutes of idle chatter, trying not to acknowledge the Plexiglas forcing them to communicate through handsets as if they were miles apart… trying to ignore the fact Gary was sitting in a jail cell, awaiting arraignment on charges of raping a teenager.

"You woulda been so proud of me yesterday. I carved up that turkey like a regular bird surgeon! My dad said he'd never seen 'such an expertly dispatched poultry specimen.'"

"I'm sure it was marvelous. Hope someone took pictures to document the occasion." *Wish I'd been there to see it.*

Micki's eyes misted. She charged on with happy talk. "Amanda and Michael send kisses; they're over at Grandpa's. Mandy's got this peculiar idea you're away on business. I felt strange perpetuating a lie… but I could hardly tell her the truth. She's only six… she wouldn't understand." Her voice cracked. She sniffled. "*I* don't even understand!" Michaela fought hard, but her tears were gaining ground. Her lower lip trembled fiercely and the tears spilled over again.

Gary ached. He missed his wife, even though she sat right there before him; he missed his kids. He hated that she had to deal with his absence – and their three children – on her own. Not to mention all their questions and worries… also alone.

He hated that he'd missed spending Thanksgiving with his family. He missed his life. Three days ago, he'd awakened at five, spent half an hour making love with his beautiful wife, then got up to begin yet another perfectly normal day in his perfectly normal life… including perfectly normal pancakes with his wife and perfectly normal children. Then he'd kissed everyone goodbye and departed for his "screwy job in the wacky land of radio," as he often called it. And by noon, he was sitting in jail. It didn't make sense.

Gary missed Michaela. He missed everything about her – how her eyes would light up when they met his; the touch of her hand; the warmth of her embrace. He missed falling asleep beside her at night; her nudging him awake in the middle of the night to make sleepy but ardent love; awakening at daybreak with her wrapped about him, still asleep. He missed the sound of her laugh, the touch of her lips against his skin, the softness of her hair. He missed the distinct, warm and almost floral scent that was hers alone – the scent no perfume company could replicate. The one that told him she was near-by, or had been moments before. That aroma drove him wild. It was hers. And it was her.

He realized Michaela had begun speaking again. He loved her voice. And he'd missed it so, these past three days.

"My dad tried to get a judge to come in today to do the arraignment – so you didn't have to spend the weekend in… in here. But he said" – she lowered her voice and put a hand over the receiver – "no judge wants to appear compassionate toward an accused child sex offender." Her mouth contorted in pain at saying those words aloud in reference to her hus-band.

He nodded. "I kinda figured."

"He said he found you a lawyer…"

"Yeah – Blake Tierney. I met with him this morning. I hope he's as good as your dad says."

Awkward silence descended. Gary tried to come up with something – anything! – to say. He couldn't let their conver-sation end here. He hadn't heard nearly enough of her voice, hadn't told her how much he loved her. He wasn't ready. "The cops have been pretty good to me – so far," he said. "At least, they're not treating me like shit."

He was about to say more when Officer Jack Thompson laid a hand on his prisoner's shoulder. "Sorry, Gary. Time's up." It was after 2:30; he'd already given them almost fifteen extra minutes.

His shoulders drooped; his head sagged. "I'm sorry, ba-by," he murmured, gesturing with his free hand. "I gotta go."

Micki stifled a cry. She was silent for a long moment. "I love you, Gary."

He met her watery gaze. "I love you, too, Michaela. Give the kids kisses for me, huh?" He waved a little goodbye to Erin, who returned the wave before they turned to leave the visitation area.

"Oh, I always hate this part," the officer fretted as they turned away. He rapped urgently at the Plexiglas. "Go give her a hug," he instructed Gary.

Micki and Erin turned in surprise to find the policeman motioning them toward the door. As they approached, he opened it. "I hate these goodbyes. C'mon in. But just for a second. They'll have my job if they find out I let you in."

He held the door as they entered. "I'll be out here… give you some privacy," he mumbled as he pulled it shut behind him.

On his feet in an instant, Gary wrapped his arms around Micki, regretting every petty argument they'd ever had that kept them apart for even one precious second.

Noisy sobs raced out of Michaela unchecked, along with unintelligible babble. She broke from her husband's embrace and reached up to touch his face. "Oh, honey… I've missed you so much!"

Framing his wife's face with his hands, Gary kissed her mouth gently. "I've missed you, too, baby." Releasing her, he embraced Erin. "Punkin, I'm sorry this has been so awful for you. But I'll be home before you know it. It'll all be over soon. I promise." Drawing away, he forced a smile to try to convince her he believed what he was saying.

If Erin doubted him, she wasn't letting on. The fifteen-year-old came up to the middle of her dad's chest as she hugged him. "I love you, Daddy. Don't ever forget that. We all love you. And we all want you to come home soon – well, except the cats. They've been pooping in your slippers."

Bracing for a tearful goodbye, Gary laughed, grateful for her quirky humor. She could always disarm him, even when things seemed their grimmest. "Is that so?" He ran his hands over the glossy river that cascaded nearly to her waist. Gathering it into a loose ponytail, he gave it a playful tug. "Well, you give those little ingrates a message for me: My *next* pair of slippers is gonna be made outta *them!*"

Erin giggled. "Will do, Daddy. I love you." She squeezed him around the middle again. Stretching upward, on tiptoe, she pulled him down toward herself and gave him a peck on the cheek. "Behave yourself."

Gary grinned. "Hey! That's *my* line." He tweaked her nose affectionately. "*You* behave." Now he drew Michaela into the hug, too.

"Leave the porch light on," he murmured in his wife's ear as they parted.

Her fingers curled around his. "It already is."

Gary swallowed hard. He gave Micki a final kiss and nodded toward the door. "Okay, you better go – Officer Jack was good enough to let you scalawags in here; let's not get him in trouble." They each took one of his hands. "I love you both. See you soon." He smiled bravely, then turned away, unable to watch them leaving him.

Gary didn't turn around until he heard the door click shut.

Officer Thompson stood at the door. "Ready to go back?"

He shook his head. "No. But I know rules are rules. Speaking of which: Thanks for letting them in. It meant a lot to me. To them, too."

Jack patted Gary on the shoulder as he escorted the younger man back to his cell. The door creaked. The officer stood aside for the prisoner to enter.

"This whole thing's been such a nightmare," Gary admitted, slumping onto his cot as the steel-barred cell door clanged shut.

As it was a long weekend and there was no one else in the lockup, the officer on duty had little to do but keep an eye on his lone inmate. A small television kept boredom at bay. When nothing good was on – most of the time – they drank coffee, talked or played cards. After a while, Gary's only reminder he wasn't free to go was the barred cell surrounding him.

When Gary mentioned his fondness for the game, Officer Terry Bigelow, one of the evening staff, brought in a cribbage board to help pass the time.

While they chatted at length about a range of topics, Jack reminded Gary about the Miranda warning: If he commented on something related to the charges, "We can and will use it against you."

***

On Saturday, at Michaela's request, Father Dave went to see Gary after four-o'clock Mass.

Officer Bigelow escorted Gary to the visitation room.

"Hi, Gary," the priest greeted him cheerily as soon as the door closed. "How you holding up?"

"Three square meals a day; lumpy institutional cot; *terrific*" – he tugged at the shirt of his inmate garb – "outfit. Thank God I look good in blue. Bars all around but no bartender; and to top it all off, no conjugal visits. How'm I holding up, padre? You tell me."

"Sarcastic as ever, I see. I had a feeling you'd say something along those lines."

"So why bother asking?"

The priest shrugged. "Conversation starter."

"Well, you asked for it."

"That I did." Father Dave glanced about the pale-yellow room. It was a dreary place; he couldn't blame Gary for his acerbic rant. Sharpening his rapier wit against the iron bars was probably his only pastime.

"So," Gary said suddenly, sitting forward now and resting his elbows on his knees, "what brings you here?"

The priest raised an eyebrow. "Another conversation starter?"

He shrugged. "Something like that."

"It's last Saturday of the month. And you didn't show up at three…"

Gary had gone to Father Dave for reconciliation the second and last Saturdays of each month for years. "Right you are. So, you figured since Mohammed couldn't come to the mountain…"

"Something like that," the priest parroted, then glanced sideways at Gary. "Hey, that 'mountain' comment better not be a jab about my weight!" Father Dave patted his modest circumference, gratified at seeing Gary shake his head in amusement. "Actually, Michaela asked me to come."

"I love that woman," he admitted, smiling. "And I *am* happy to see you."

"I'm glad to hear you say that."

The two men were silent for a long moment. Then, his head bowed slightly, Gary made the sign of the cross and uttered a hesitant, "Forgive me, Father, for I have sinned. It's been three weeks since my last confession…"

Chapter 14

(10:57 a.m., December 1 – Monday)

"Case number 63-87547: People versus Gary Sheldon. Charges include first-degree sexual assault, first-degree…" The court officer droned on for nearly a minute, listing charges.

Gary stood beside Blake Tierney in silence. His eyes swept the front of the courtroom. This was not how he'd planned to spend his son's third birthday.

"Sounds like you've been busy, Mr. Sheldon. How do you plead?"

He didn't even flinch at the judge's remark. "Not guilty, Your Honor."

The judge eyed Gary over his glasses, then looked at the young assistant D.A. who was handling the preliminaries. "Bail recommendation, Ms Newell?"

"Defendant is a man of considerable wealth and means, Your Honor. We believe he constitutes a significant flight risk. The State requests he be held without bail."

"Are you out of your mind?" Blake shot back, glaring at the prosecutor. "Your Honor, my client is a well-respected citizen, a noted public figure with strong ties to this community. He's an outspoken advocate for children who's taught religion in his parish for fifteen years. We request bail in the amount of a hundred thousand dollars."

"I think you're both nuts," Judge Foster Wiggins remarked. "Bail is set at a half million dollars, cash or bond. The defendant is further ordered not to leave the state of Connecticut, and to surrender his passport."

"What're we going to do?" Michaela fretted as she and Gary sat facing his lawyer in a small room off the courtroom. "Half a million… Gary, do we even have access to that kind of money?"

Gary laid a reassuring hand on his wife's arm as Blake spoke. "You don't need to come up with all of it – just ten percent. A bail bondsman can front you the rest. Collateralized, of course."

Micki listened to the defense attorney, wide eyed. She turned to Gary. "Do we have fifty grand?"

"We can scrape that together. Sell some stock, or take it out of savings."

"What would we use for collateral? The house?"

Gary hesitated. "I'd rather not risk that… but I don't think we have a choice."

"It's only at risk if you jump bail," Blake reminded him. "I doubt you're planning to do that."

"Hardly. So how do I get out of here?"

(3:45 p.m.)

"Welcome home, Gary," Judy Cameron greeted her next-door neighbor with a hug when he came to retrieve his son. "It's good to see you back."

"Thanks, Judy; it's good to be home. And thanks for keeping an eye on the little guy for us."

"That's what neighbors are for. And he's such a joy to have around. We've been having ourselves a little birthday party. Join us. I've got a pot of coffee on; care for a cup?"

Gary smiled. "I'd like that."

"Michael, look who's here," Judy called as Gary followed her into the kitchen.

The little boy's eyes widened. "Daddy!" he exclaimed, chocolate-cake crumbs still clinging to the corners of his mouth. He scrambled to his feet.

Gary knelt to hug the pint-sized missile hurtling toward him. "Happy birthday, big guy!"

Dinner that night was a dual celebration: Michael's birthday and Daddy's homecoming. Instead of the usual extended-family dinner – with Grandpa Conwaye, Grandma Sheldon and all the aunts and uncles – they opted for just immediate family. Gary was relieved to see only five places set at the table. "I don't think I could've handled any more than that," he admitted later, as he and Micki cleared away the dinner dishes.

"I didn't think it'd be fair to you, having a houseful of people after all you've been through."

They worked in silence for a while. "I hope you like what I picked out as a birthday gift…"

Gary put an arm around his wife's slender waist and drew her to him. "I'm sure it'll be perfect," he told her, silencing her fretting with a kiss.

"Sheldon Arraigned on Sex Charges," "Millionaire Playboy Out on Bond," the morning headlines proclaimed. Michaela threw the newspaper, unread, into the trash.

She snapped off the radio when Gary came into the kitchen. Breezing over, she forced a smile and greeted him with a kiss. "Hi, honey. Did you sleep okay?"

He gave her a peck on the cheek, then turned away before she could hug him. "Not as lousy as the past few nights."

Unsure how to respond, Micki poured two glasses and a sippy cup of orange juice for the kids, and cranberry juice for herself and Gary. "What would you like for breakfast?"

Leaning against the counter, he shook his head. "I'm not hungry." Then, looking around, he asked, "Where's the paper?"

She decided the truth was best. "I threw it out. I didn't want the kids to see how they're smearing you."

"Oh." Gary turned and left the room.

A minute later, Micki heard his footsteps on the stairs. She turned back to the stove, her insides in tangles.

She ground pepper into the bowl of eggs she was beating, then turned the bacon in the skillet; it was just about done. Micki switched off the gas so it wouldn't burn.

Heating another pan, Michaela threw in a pat of butter. As she watched it melt and sizzle, tears filled her eyes. "God, please help me," she prayed. "I don't know what to do. Gary's so sad, so upset over this. I hate seeing him suffer… but I don't know how to help him."

She wiped away her tears and noticed the butter had started to burn. Shutting off the burner, she poured the scorched butter into the sink and wiped out the pan with a paper towel. Starting over, Micki melted the butter carefully this time, then scrambled the eggs.

Sliding the skillet into the oven, she started making toast. Before she knew it, the stack stood fourteen high. Cursing softly at her absentminded overzealousness, she tore up the extra slices and tossed them outside for the birds.

Just when she was about to go call the girls again, Micki heard two sets of sneakered feet charging down the stairs.

"Hi, Mommy!" both girls greeted her as they thundered into the kitchen. She kissed them, then shooed them over to the table.

"Where's Dad?" Erin asked as Mom plated up bacon, eggs and toast.

"Upstairs. I don't think he's feeling well," she replied. "You girls go ahead and eat; I've got to go get your brother up."

As she approached the stairs, Micki heard voices. And laughter. Looking up, she saw her husband and son at the top of the stairs, both dressed in jeans and t-shirts; Michael wore his favorite red sneakers.

"There you are," she called up the stairs, holding her arms out to the little boy as he made his way down, holding tight to Daddy's hand. "Good morning, little man. I was just about to come looking for you." Then she addressed her husband. "Thank you, honey, for getting him dressed."

Gary acknowledged her with a flicker of a smile and a nearly undetectable nod.

When they got downstairs, instead of going to his mom, Michael turned away from her; the little boy clasped his arms around Daddy's legs and hung on. He pressed his face against the faded denim as if clutching a beloved teddy bear.

"He really missed you," Micki said, kissing Gary. "We all did. I'm glad you're home." She patted his cheek, then headed back to the kitchen, where the girls were doing more fooling around than eating. "Girls, c'mon… settle down. Eat your breakfast."

Gary settled Michael into his booster seat, then went to sit at the table.

"Hi Daddy!" Amanda greeted him with a gap-toothed grin; she'd lost another tooth yesterday.

He reached out to stroke her cheek. "Hi, princess."

"Are you okay, Daddy?" Erin's eyes mirrored her concern. "Mommy said you didn't feel well…"

Gary cast a questioning glance at his wife, then gave a slight smile for his daughter's benefit. "I'm fine." He paused. "It's good to be home."

(December 20 – Saturday)
Gary skulked from room to room.

On his third arrival in the kitchen, Michaela looked up from chopping vegetables. "What'cha doing?"

He leaned against the counter. Reaching for a celery stick from her cutting board, he nibbled at it. "I dunno. Wandering, I guess."

Michaela reached for another cutting board. "Want to help me chop?"

After pondering this, Gary shook his head and pushed off from the counter. His voice was devoid of enthusiasm. "Nah. Not really." He watched her silently.

"I was gonna bake cookies, soon as I'm done here," she enticed. "What kind do you want?"

He shrugged. "Doesn't matter. Whatever you feel like."

Micki frowned. Gary always had a preference. "How about cinnamon-walnut?" Those were his favorite.

Not even a flicker of interest. "I don't care." Sighing softly, he headed for the living room.

She watched him go. As she returned her attention to the pile of vegetables waiting to be chopped, Michaela caught sight of the calendar. Of course: the Holiday Bash! No wonder Gary was so restless and moody! Since 1982, the benefit had raised more than $200,000 for area shelters, collected countless tons of nonperishable food items and tens of thousands of toys for needy children. It was, by far, the station's most successful community-outreach effort.

And now Gary, who'd instituted the Holiday Bash in his first year at Z97-3, as part of his final project for a Creative Marketing class at UConn, was excluded from it.

Michaela put down her knife and wiped her vegetable-y hands on her apron. In the living room, she found her husband slumped forward on the couch.

Sitting beside him, she laid a hand on his back. "Hey," she murmured.

He tensed at her touch.

"I'm worried about you, honey." As Michaela spoke, her fingers stroked his hair in a gesture of comfort. "I hate to see you so sad all the time. I wish I could help."

Within days of his arraignment, Gary exhibited signs of depression; Micki wanted to suggest he see a counselor, but she was afraid he'd accuse her of overreacting.

"You can't help," he mumbled from within his hands. "Nothing can help." He got up, keeping his face turned away from her as he plodded toward the stairs.

Sadness crushed Michaela's heart as she eyed Gary. She uttered a quiet, "God, please help him through this," as he trudged up to the bedroom.

Chapter 15

(23 December – Tuesday)

State's Attorney Michael Conwaye sat forward in his red leather chair. He frowned. There was no easy way to say this. "The A.D.A. who's got your case" – he shook his head – "real bulldog. In *and* out of court. They call her Godzilla. She's got a reputation for ripping defendants to shreds."

"But I didn't *do* it," Gary contended. "And anyway, my lawyer's good, too… right?"

"Of course he is. I just want you to be prepared, is all. It's gonna be an uphill battle."

The younger man paled. The small office in the Superior Court building kept feeling smaller. He was sure the walls would close in any second.

"If I thought for an instant they'd let me, I'd call Blake and offer to sit second chair."

"You'd do that? Even though you're on the other side?"

"I'm on *your* side, Gary. I believe you're innocent," Michael insisted. "But the state's attorney aiding the defense?" He shook his head. "They'd never go for it. I won't lie to you, Gar': It doesn't look good. Sabine wins more than eighty-five percent of her cases. And she *always* pushes for maximum sentences."

Gary felt like someone was crushing all the air out of his lungs.

That night, Gary voiced his concerns to his wife. "She got Sabine Delacourt," he moaned. "Do you know what that *means?*"

Micki shrugged. "It's something in French, but I dunno what…"

"*No*," he exclaimed impatiently. "Do you know what it means to my case?"

Worried, she drew her husband close. He looked scared. "What?"

His voice faltered. "It means I'm as good as screwed."

At Christmas, Michaela knew Gary was putting up a good front, for the kids' sake. And hers. He feigned enthusiasm as they unwrapped their gifts, and forced a smile when he opened his.

Marie and Marc stopped by in the afternoon; the twins, now three and a half, provided a nice diversion. The guys played with the kids and their new toys in the living room; the women chatted in the kitchen.

"I'm worried about Gary," Michaela confided, glancing into the living room.

"Oh?" Marie leaned forward; her slight head tilt was Micki's cue to continue.

"Ever since he found out who's prosecuting his case, he's been – I dunno… despondent. I mean, he's been worried all along; but lately, it seems like he's given up."

Marie laid a hand atop Michaela's. "It may help if he realizes you're aware of how it's affecting him; it might make him feel he's not quite so alone. Have you tried talking with him about this?"

"I want to… but I'm not sure how to approach him." She felt uneasy taking advantage of Marie's psychiatric expertise, but she had to ask. "Should I be concerned – I mean, given his history…?"

A look of worried confusion crossed her sister-in-law's face. "What history?"

"You know: the suicidal ideation… and this being Christmas."

Marie shook her head. "I don't understand. What's Christmas got to do with anything?"

Lowering her voice, Michaela fidgeted with her coffee cup. "I know he tried to kill himself years ago, on Christmas. The year your mom left."

Marie's eyes widened. "I had no idea; he never said anything to me. I always figured he could tell me everything… and I thought he *had*." She paused. "Maybe *I'd* better talk to him."

"I doubt he'd be receptive. He won't be too thrilled we're discussing this… especially since you didn't know about" – she gestured uncertainly – "you know."

Marie gave Micki a trusted colleague's card and urged her to get Gary to make an appointment.

"Umm… Gar'?" Micki said later that night, as they undressed for bed.

Gary looked up from unbuttoning his shirt. She had that tone in her voice: the one that said she was about to bring up something he didn't want to discuss. Instantly on the defensive, he gave his most disinterested-sounding reply. "Yeh?"

She approached him, arms out, for a hug. "I was talking with your sister today…"

Moving out of her reach, he tugged off his shirt and threw it into the hamper. He sat at the edge of the bed to take off the Christmas socks Micki gave him three years ago. "Their kids are awfully cute," he said, hoping to derail whatever she was about to say. "Did she tell you Fern's already started playing the piano?"

Michaela expelled a frustrated-sounding breath. "No. She'll be good at it; she's got a great sense of rhythm." She sat beside him on the bed. "But that's not what I wanted to talk to you about."

Gary got up, unzipped his jeans and shimmied out of them on his way to the bathroom.

She followed.

He opened the medicine cabinet, reached for the toothpaste. When he shut it again, Micki was watching him in the mirror, trying to make eye contact. He took an intense interest in the blue gel he was applying to his toothbrush. Screwing the cap back on, he replaced the tube.

"We were talking abo—"

Gary banged the cabinet shut. "Geez, Mick! Can this wait 'til I'm finished brushing my teeth?"

She snatched the toothbrush. "No!" she just about shouted. "It *can't* wait. 'Cause when you're done, I'll try to talk to you again, and it'll be, 'Can't this wait 'til I'm out of the bathroom?' or 'Can't it wait 'til tomorrow… or next week?' Well, it *can't* wait any longer!"

Crossing his arms, Gary heaved an exasperated sigh and leaned against the sink. "Well, if you're gonna get all flippy about it, go ahead." *I'm <u>obviously</u> not gonna get a moment's peace 'til you do.*

"I'm not getting *flippy.* I'm worried about you, Gary! I hate seeing you so… depressed and – and angry. I don't know how to help you… so I talked with Marie."

Gary reclaimed his toothbrush. Catching a glimpse of his reflection in the mirror, he noticed his features looked as if they'd been chiseled from granite. It felt like his face might crack off if he spoke. His cold gaze fixed on hers. His expression remained rigid. Only his lips moved. "About what?" Not really wanting to hear what Micki talked to his sister about, he began brushing.

"She gave me the name of a therapist who specializes in treating depression." She held out Dr. Scott Benson's card. "Please, Gary, give him a call. Set up an appointment. Talk to him."

Spitting into the sink, he shook his head. "No." Before she could expect him to say anything more, he continued brushing.

"Why not? Gary, what could it hurt? All I'm asking is that you talk to him. Just talk."

While she waited for him to finish, Michaela tucked the card into the waistband of Gary's boxers.

He pulled the card out, tore it to bits and flushed it down the toilet. "Forget it. Shrinks are for crazy people. I'm not crazy. If I *wasn't* concerned about this trial, you'd have cause to question my sanity." Stripping off the rest of his clothes, he flipped the bathroom light off and went to his bureau. "You have nothing to worry about, okay? I appreciate your concern. I don't need a shrink." He pulled on a pair of flannel pajama bottoms.

Pajamas. That meant there'd be no sex tonight. That was nothing new; there'd been no sex for over a month.

"Now, unless there's anything else you're dying to talk about, I'm going to bed." Gary plumped the pillows and crawled under the covers.

Micki knew he had to be plenty agitated; he'd forgotten to floss. Gary *never* forgot to floss. Turning out the light, she got into bed and cuddled close to him. He didn't respond.

She nuzzled his neck.

He drew away. "Leave me alone, Mick," he warned. "I'm not in the mood."

She rolled over and willed away the emptiness washing over her.

In the silence of their bed, she could tell her husband was fuming.

After several minutes, Gary turned over and unleashed his fury. "You had no right discussing my personal business with outsiders!"

"For goodness' sake, Gary – she's not an outsider; she's your *sister!*"

"All the more reason you shouldn'ta gone blabbing to her!" he snarled. "It's my life, Michaela! You've got no right interfering."

Sitting up, she reached for him. "I wasn't interfering, Gary; I'm trying to help."

He pulled away. "I don't remember asking for help. Next time, mind your own damn business!"

She masked her hurt with anger. "Fine! I'll do that. And another thing—" She was shouting now.

"What?" he shouted back, primed for confrontation.

"I love you, you ninny!" Michaela made no attempt to wipe away her tears, just sat there, hands flailing. "I love you, Gary! And it scares me to death to see you like this, especially knowing there's nothing I can do to make it better! I hate to see you so torn up" – she continued through heaving sobs – "and I'm afraid you'll try something stupid! And it's Christmas… and I know how hard Christmas is for you. It scares me to think you're so sad now you just might do it. I couldn't bear to lose you, Gary! I don't want to see you hurting and I love you so much it – it… it frightens me!"

Michaela was startled to find herself in Gary's arms. About midway through her rant, he'd drawn her to himself. Near the end, she beat one tired fist ineffectually against his arm.

"Shh," he soothed, rocking her back and forth, all resentment forgotten. "I'm sorry, baby." He stroked her cheek. "I don't suppose you've got another of that guy's cards?"

Even in the dark, Micki could tell he was smiling, making an attempt at lightening the mood. Amid her tears, she shook her head and smiled, suggesting, "I could get you a plunger… and some swim-fins."

Gary held her close and kissed the top of her head. "If it means that much to you, Mick, I'll call Dr. Caron to get a referral for a counselor. Maybe we could go together…"

Counselor. Not psychiatrist. Michaela sighed. At least it was something.

(January 4, 1998 – Sunday)
"I wanted to talk to you in private," the pastor said as they entered the parlor. "Please, sit down."

Already it didn't sound good. Gary watched expectantly as the priest shut the door.

"I'm sorry, Gary. I don't know a pleasant way to say this," Father Dave said. "I've had calls from several parents… parents of your students. They're uncomfortable with – well, with you. With these allegations. They don't feel safe leaving their children in your care."

Gary's blood simmered. "They're not comfortable?" he parroted. "They don't feel safe with me teaching their kids?"

"Some of them have said they'd feel better if someone else taught—"

"And what did you tell them?"

No reply from the priest.

"Father?" He waited.

Still no answer.

Gary sighed.

Father Dave gestured in futility.

"Father, most of those kids – I've taught their brothers and sisters. Their parents were thrilled to have them in my class. Suddenly I can't teach them? Because of some false accusations? That's absurd! Not to mention it makes me look guilty."

The priest still said nothing.

"Plus, that gives the impression *you* believe I'm guilty. I didn't do anything! Why punish me by taking away my class?"

"Gary, I'm sorry. I didn't have a choice."

"What do you mean? You're the pastor. You're in charge."

"But the parish council said they felt—"

"Now *they've* joined the witch hunt? They're an advisory board. You make the final decisions."

Father Dave gave a somber nod. "That's what I wanted to talk to you about, Gary. I've made my decision."

Pre-trial hearings began the following Tuesday; they were brutal. Blake assured Gary the trial "probably won't be any worse than this."

Probably. He took little consolation in that.

At the outset, the prosecutor announced her intent to file vicarious-liability charges.

"What's that mean?" Gary sounded worried.

"It means," Blake explained, "they've decided to bring charges against the radio station. As your employer, they're equally liable."

Gary paled. "Can they do that?"

The defense attorney's grim expression and cursory nod confirmed Gary's fears.

At the end of the second day, Gary was ordered to cease all contact with minors, including his own kids.

Next morning, he and Blake appealed the order.

Judge David Paterna promised to review their petition and render a verdict after the weekend.

(January 12 – Monday)

"Pending the outcome of this trial, I hereby order the defendant, Gary Sheldon, to abide by the order of this Court: namely, that he cease all contact with minors – including his own children. I further order he be removed from his primary residence at once."

"Your Honor, that's ludicrous," Blake asserted. "You can't take a father of three young children out of the family home on a whim. My client has lived in this area the past sixteen years; he's got roots here. He has a reputation as a community-minded public figure – and an advocate for children."

"That may be, Mr. Tierney, but he's also got first-degree sexual-assault charges pending, and it's my duty to protect children from accused predators."

"But these are his own children!"

"That doesn't leave them any less at risk. My order stands. Mr. Sheldon will vacate the domicile by six o'clock this evening."

At six, a uniformed officer stood at the front door of 18 Mayfair Lane, ready to usher Gary out.

By six fifteen, Gary was on the highway, headed toward the cottage.

And by eight, he was on his third scotch.

"We can fight this," Blake assured him by phone the next day. "I'm filing an appeal this morning."

Gary stared out the window at the snow falling on the beach. "What good will it do? It's hopeless, Blake. The judge has already sided against us. What could possibly change his mind?"

"Leave that to me, Gary. It may take a little time to get the wheels in motion, but leave everything to me." An instant later, he was gone.

Gary's first day alone at the cottage was misery; the second, anguish. Daily calls home couldn't stave off his emptiness. Neither could nightly doses of scotch. By the third day, Gary didn't think he'd ever felt more alone.

Michaela called at suppertime Thursday.

"I miss you, baby," Gary told her, already clutching his second drink.

During the few minutes their conversation lasted, he heard the strain in her upbeat tone. As they talked, he reheated last night's ziti.

After they hung up, he slumped into a kitchen chair and stabbed at the leftovers. He wasn't even hungry. With a heavy sigh, Gary threw his fork into the plate and shoved the whole thing aside. Burying his head in his arms on the table, he wept.

(9:17 a.m., January 18 – Sunday)
Gary awakened with the pounding headache that had plagued him for three days.

He couldn't recall the last time he'd felt this sick. Every muscle ached, and he felt so drained! Since Thursday, he'd trudged daily down the hall; only once did he manage to take the shower he longed for. Maybe today would be another good day. He reached in and turned on the water. While it heated, he gulped down two Tylenol.

He winced as the near-scalding water beat against his skin. For several minutes, he stood beneath the spray, drinking in its therapeutic heat. The water eased his sore muscles while the steam relaxed the tightness in his chest.

When he stepped onto the bathmat, Gary could almost breathe again. Filling his lungs with the vapor-drenched air, he launched into a coughing fit that doubled him over and left him grabbing at the wall for support. That's when he heard the phone.

Cursing it, he let it ring. *If it's important, they'll call back.*

It rang again as he dressed. He managed to croak a weak, "Hello," without coughing.

In reply, he heard his wife and children's voices singing a slightly off-key rendition of "Happy Birthday to You."

"Thank you," he said when they'd finished. He felt more like eighty than thirty-four.

"Happy birthday, sweetheart." Micki's tender voice filled his ear and made him sadder than ever.

Rivulets from his sopping hair streaked down Gary's face. Wiping them away, he forced a smile into his voice. "Thanks, baby."

"Did I wake you?"

"No, I was in the shower. I'm drip-drying in the bedroom." On his next breath he was coughing again. Deep shuddering coughs. The phone slid from his hand. Gary doubled over, certain a lung was about to come up.

"Gary! Are you okay?"

Even with the receiver on the floor, he recognized the alarm in Micki's voice. He tried to squelch the hacking. "Yeah, yeah – I'm fine. Just a bit of a cough." Gary didn't mention the all-over aches, the fever and the weakness that had gripped him since Thursday.

"Sounds like more than a bit. Gary, have you seen the doctor?"

He ran a hand through his hair. "I'll be fine. Really." More coughing punctuated his last words.

"Honey, I wish you'd go to the doctor."

"And have him say what? Take Tylenol, drink juice and get some rest? That's what I'm doing."

"I wish you weren't all alone there. Do you want me to come down?"

Gary knew she was only trying to help. "No. I'm fine." He paused. "On second thought… can you bring me some

Vampire Soup?" That was what he'd dubbed her garlic-rich chicken soup years ago; it always made the kids giggle.

"Of course." The worry in her voice was evident. "I'll be down later this afternoon."

His voice caught in his throat. "Can't you come now?"

"I gotta get the kids to church. But I'll be there as soon as I finish making that soup," Michaela assured him. Then she added, "You'll be home soon, honey."

"Yeah, right," Gary muttered, coughing again. He knew the separation was taking its toll on his wife and family. He hated being here without them.

By the time he stopped coughing, he felt worse than before his shower. All he wanted was sleep. He moved to the window. Low tide. Sunlight glinted off the icy water. Patches of snow clung to mounds of frozen grasses along the dunes. "I better let you go. Don't be late for Mass. Tell God I said hi, okay?"

When Gary dragged himself downstairs, he scarcely had sufficient energy to stumble to the couch. Crawling beneath a pile of quilts, he shivered himself into a restless sleep. Time after time, he dreamt of Micki, only to awaken disappointed at her absence.

It was nearly six when Michaela's car tires crunched over the gravel driveway.

Inside, a quick glance revealed evidence of Gary's worsening depression: Dirty plates and mugs lay strewn on the coffee table and mantel; old newspapers slouched on chairs. Discarded pizza boxes and takeout containers littered the floor. A stocky little scotch glass lay on the floor by the couch.

Finding him huddled beneath a heap of quilts, Micki knelt beside Gary. Pushing back his damp hair, she kissed his forehead. His skin was hot, perhaps from the quilts. But he was shivering. Not good. She tried to sound cheerful. "Hi, honey. I brought your soup. And birthday cards from the kids."

"You're here." Smiling, Gary strained upward to kiss her, but fell short and dropped back against the couch.

"C'mon, you," she said, helping him up. "Forget the soup; I'm taking you to the hospital."

"I don't need to go to the hospital…"

Micki would not be deterred. Stowing the soup pot in the fridge – the kitchen was in a worse state than the living room – she helped her husband navigate the slippery front-porch stairs.

The ER doctor quickly determined what had felled Gary was the flu. Dr. Mason had the nurse monitor Gary's temperature, pulse and blood pressure, then start him on IV fluids.

Weak from fever and dehydration, Gary's feeble protests proved no match for Velma, a beefy blonde who could have played linebacker for the Jets. She immobilized his arm against her sturdy body and found a suitable vein on her first try.

Despite her intimidating presence, the husky nurse was remarkably gentle, taking great care to ensure Gary was well cared for – even getting extra pillows to make him more comfortable.

"Now, you just lie back an' try to rest, darlin' – not that anyone ever gets any sleep in a hospital," Velma added with a kind smile as she patted his shoulder. "Can I get'cha anything else right now?"

Gary gave a weary headshake and flopped back against the pillows' cushy softness.

"Then you just lie quiet, ya hear?" The nurse turned to Micki. "He should go right to bed when he gets home. And stay there. *And* drink plenty of fluids."

A slight chattering made Velma turn back toward Gary; he was shivering. "It's the fever," she advised Michaela. "Be right back."

She returned with a folded blanket – fresh from the blanket heater up the hall. As she spread it over him, Gary let out a low "Mmm" of appreciation.

"There ya go, sweetie," Velma said, tucking it up under his chin. "That better?"

His shivering diminished. "Ohh… that feels nice," he replied weakly. "Thank you."

"Anything else you need, hon, you just holler, alright?" And she lumbered out.

Minutes later, despite Velma's predictions, Gary's eyelids drooped… then shut. Gradually, his breathing slowed and deepened.

Fraught with worry, Michaela watched him. He looked so pale, his cheeks so sunken! She knew being apart from his family had left him susceptible to this flu. She wanted to thumb her nose at the court order and care for Gary at home, but she didn't want to get him any deeper in trouble.

The sac hanging from the IV pole dripped fluid into her husband's left arm at a steady pace. She uttered a silent prayer for his speedy return to health – and to their home.

Unaware of her sitting beside him, Gary slept on.

Twenty minutes later, drenched in sweat, he was clawing away the blanket Velma had brought. His cycles of fever and chills repeated several times during his stay.

The next time Gary fell asleep, Michaela stepped into the hall to call home.

"Looks like I won't be home anytime soon," she told her sister-in-law. "Gary's got the flu; I had to drag him to the ER. Would you or Marc mind staying with the kids?"

"Overnight? No problem. Listen, Micki. You take care of Gary. If you want us to keep them for a few days while you stay with him, say the word."

"I don't want to impose…"

"It's no imposition," Marie insisted. "No doubt they're pumping him full of fluids; will they keep him overnight or send him home?"

"They haven't said, but I think they're leaning toward sending him home." She paused. "I kinda would like to stay for a few days – make sure he's getting enough rest, drinking fluids."

It was after midnight when Gary was discharged, and nearly one before Michaela got him back to the cottage. She helped him upstairs and into bed.

While the soup heated, she started cleaning the kitchen. Once it was warm, she brought Gary a bowl of soup and sat with him as he ate.

With its rich, hearty broth, chunks of tender vegetables and succulent morsels of chicken, Gary eagerly spooned up the garlicky soup.

When he finished, he leaned to give her a kiss. "Thank you. That was delicious."

Michaela reclaimed the bowl and swept back his hair with her free hand. "Glad you liked it." She kissed his cheek and drew the sheet up. "Try to get some rest, sweetheart. I'm right across the hall if you need anything."

In the lonely darkness of the blue room, Michaela prayed for Gary to feel better – both physically and emotionally. For a time, with silence from the rose room, she drifted off to sleep; but a round of hacking jolted her awake.

She recalled times they'd lain awake in there late into the night... for entirely different reasons. She missed his tender touch, his passionate kisses; she longed to feel him inside her again. It'd been months since they'd made love.

In the morning, Michaela brought Gary breakfast. After he showered and shaved, she herded him back to bed.

While he slept, Micki finished cleaning the kitchen, then tackled the living room. And the study. It wasn't quite so bad, but it still needed attention.

When she finished, she put on a kettle of water and invited Martha for tea.

"I'd love to, dear," the old woman said, and Micki could hear the wistful smile in her voice, "but I can't leave Sam. Why don't you come here?"

Micki turned off the kettle and went to check on Gary. Still asleep. She left a note at his bedside. With a kiss on his forehead, she disappeared downstairs and outside.

The women shared a companionable hour together.

Michaela asked how Sam was faring, and she delighted in the little triumphs Martha noted: He had recognized their son when he visited last week; and he still knew who she was most of the time.

"How's Gary doing?" Martha asked. "They're saying the most horrible things about him in the news lately…" She trailed off, shaking her head.

Micki gave a sad nod. "I think that's been the worst part. He's living down here now, because of that court order."

"What court order?"

She explained.

"Why, that's just mean!" Martha exclaimed. "How can they even think he'd pose a danger to any child – let alone his own! Can't he fight that?"

"Right now the only thing he's fighting is the flu. He ended up at the ER last night. I'm here to look after him. You're right. I think that judge is trying to make an example of him. It's an election year; everyone wants to look like they're tough on crime. But Gary's got a good lawyer; he's trying to get the order reversed."

By Tuesday, Gary felt markedly better; he even spent part of the day out of bed. And while he welcomed the return to relative health, he dreaded Michaela's leaving.

"Do you have to go?" he asked at the front door that night. He looked pleadingly into her face.

"I'm sorry, honey. I wish I could stay; but the kids need me at home."

But I need you here. Resignation filled his voice. "I know. It's gonna seem so lonely again without you."

She reached up to kiss his cheek. "You'll be home soon, too – you'll see."

"Soon" turned out to be another two weeks. And then some.

Chapter 16

(January 25 – Sunday)
"How's Gary doing?"

Everyone they knew had asked her that almost daily for the last two weeks; to avoid admitting the separation from his family had pushed him deeper into depression, she'd smile and say, "He's holding up. I'll tell him you were asking about him." But this time was different. Michaela told Marc the truth.

His hopeful expression eroded; his gaze darted away, as if eye contact physically hurt. "Should I go by to see him? You know, now and then?"

"I think he'd like that… only, don't let him think you're checking up on him."

(8:25 p.m., January 27 – Tuesday)
Marc found his brother-in-law on the back porch, nursing a substantial scotch. His third.

"Not much of a view this time of night."

Gary didn't even turn toward his voice. "Guess not." Taking a sip, he rattled the ice in his glass before setting it on the porch rail. "Beats the hell outta staring at four walls."

"Since you put it that way…" Marc leaned against the rail beside him. "But you're just getting over the flu; shouldn't you be inside?"

"What are you, my mother?" Gary swilled the rest of his scotch. "I just needed to get out."

A sudden gust made Marc shiver. "That wind's brutal. How can you stand it?"

"Won't be much longer."

When Gary's meaning registered, Marc laid hold of his arm. "You're not planning t—?"

Gary shook him off. "Oh, what do you care?" He tromped down the stairs and across the sand, toward the jetty.

Marc trailed after him. "I care *plenty*," he called out. "Your family loves you, Gary. Your wife and kids. Your sister. Your niece and nephew. And *me*. And I gotta tell you: I wouldn't be terribly inclined to forgive you if you kill yourself."

The younger man turned. "I don't need to hear this from you, okay?"

Marc caught up; he grasped his brother-in-law's arm. "Yeah, you do."

Gary shook free. "I don't need your forgiveness, Marc. I don't need your permission. And right now, I don't need you."

"Gary, I wasn't sayi—"

"Look, it's *my* life that's been ripped to shit, not yours. So don't go giving me this bullshit line that I'll leave behind a chain reaction of grief. Truth is, I don't care. And I don't need the fucking guilt trip." Turning away, Gary continued his seething trek toward the seawall. The wind buffeted them.

Marc fell into step beside him, teeth chattering. "I'm not trying to make you feel guilty, Gar'. All I'm saying is I—"

"You what? Know how I feel? Understand what I'm going through? Well, you don't!" he shouted into the wind. "You can't. You don't have a fucking *clue* what I'm going through – *or* how I feel!"

Marc shook his head. His voice was so soft now, Gary almost couldn't hear him. "You're usually pretty good at reading people… but, Gary, you're so far off here."

This time Gary didn't pull away from the hand on his arm.

"I *don't* understand what you're going through, but I can imagine how frightening it must be. And if you need someone to talk to, I'd hope you feel comfortable enough to come to me. I love you, Gar'. And I don't want to lose you… not if there's something I can do to help."

Some of the fire left Gary as he listened to his longtime friend's pleas.

"Promise me, Gary. If life ever… swallows you up and you want to end it all… promise you'll call me instead of' – his voice wavered – "instead of doing anything rash. Promise you'll let me help?"

Gary looked at his brother-in-law; he'd only ever seen Marc cry twice. Unnerved, he shook his head, continued walking. "I can't promise you that."

A strong gust whipped along the shore, hurling sand into a frenzy of tiny missiles that stung at their faces.

"Why?" The word came out as a wail.

"What'd you come here for?" Gary stalked along the sea-wall, his stride quick and purposeful.

Taken off guard, the other man made no reply.

Depression filled Gary with hollow suspicion. He turned back to his best friend. "Why'd you come here? And don't tell me you were just in the neighborhood and figured you'd stop in to say hello. Did Michaela tell you to come?"

Marc's eyes swam with tears. "She didn't tell me anything, alright? I came here, Gary, because I miss you – and I'm concerned about you. I asked if it was okay to come by and visit. She said she thought you'd appreciate that." Following Gary to the end of the jetty, Marc sucked in his breath as he saw how close Gary was to the edge.

Gary stared into the water that churned below. The rhythmic slap of the waves grew hypnotic. "You expect me to believe that?"

"Believe what you have to." Marc's subdued voice behind his brother-in-law's left ear contrasted with Gary's shouts. "But know this: If you jump, Gary, I'm going right in after you. I am *not* letting you check out without a fight."

The words sliced neatly through his haze of inebriation. An image of the day they met flashed through his mind: Marc had burst into the studio wearing a grey t-shirt with "Danbury

Y Lifeguard" emblazoned across its front. It occurred to Gary now – in a screwy kind of way – Marc was kind of like his own personal lifeguard. And, as comforted as he felt, that notion left him equally agitated.

Gary whipped around, intending to challenge Marc's assertion. His "Try and stop me" wasn't even out of his mouth when he felt himself being jerked forward.

Startled by his best friend's sudden movement, Marc grabbed Gary and hauled him away from the edge. With the element of surprise in his favor, he had no trouble wrestling Gary to the ground a safe distance away. Once he had him facedown on the cement, Marc positioned one knee against the base of Gary's spine.

"Let me up!" he bellowed, fighting to free himself.

"No!" For the first time, Marc raised his voice – startling Gary into silence. "Not until you listen to what I have to say."

Gary struggled for a moment more, then stilled.

Marc bent close so Gary could hear. "Are you listening?" His voice wavered. Gary thought it was from the cold.

"Yeah, I'm listening," he grumbled.

"I want you to repeat after me: My family loves me."

Nothing.

Marc applied a little pressure with his knee. "I don't hear you saying anything."

"Oww— alright, alright! My family loves me. Are you satisfied now?"

"No. Keep going. My friends love me…"

Grudgingly, he repeated it, and the rest of Marc's litany of affirmation. Finally, when he'd cried his way through, "I'm a precious and wonderful child of God and I promise not to kill myself," Marc let him up.

Sitting up, Gary rubbed away the hurt in his scraped knee; he glared at his brother-in-law. "Crazy bastard! What'd you go and do that for?"

Marc crouched beside him. " 'Cause I didn't do it twenty-one years ago… when my best friend in high school was suicidal."

Gary tried hard to focus on his words.

"Not a day goes by I don't miss Patrick... I spent years blaming myself for not noticing warning signs. I'm not gonna repeat that mistake with another best friend."

Gary felt suddenly grateful for Marc, who braved the bitter January cold – and his hostility – to remind him of all he had to live for. A moment later, gratitude yielded to remorse, and alcohol-induced tears; he crumpled forward, his cries drowned out by the wind and the waves.

Marc draped his coat over Gary's hunched and heaving shoulders. "I know it doesn't seem like it right now, Gar', but things *will* get better." He put an arm around his friend. "Of course, that scotch isn't really helping matters. Kinda hard to think straight when you're blotto."

Gary thought back twenty years, when Dad's drinking began spiraling out of control. Disgusted by his behavior, Gary swore he'd never fall into that pattern, never turn to alcohol to solve his problems, never be like that drunken jerk. For that matter, he'd never drink – period. But over time, promise after promise had fallen by the wayside.

Marc was still speaking. "I'm saying this because I love you, Gary, and I don't want to see you destroy yourself. I know you miss Michaela, and the kids. And I know you're worried about the trial. But that's all temporary stuff... and suicide is forever."

Gary's new deluge of tears had nothing to do with his brother-in-law's gentle tone or caring words. Or his hug.

Marc said nothing more for a long time.

Gary clung to him and sobbed.

"Please, don't ever feel that you're alone, Gary," Marc implored at last. "When things in your world seem blackest, don't turn away from the people who love you." He helped Gary back to his feet. "Come on," he coaxed. "Let's get you inside."

After guiding Gary unsteadily along the shore and back to the cottage, Marc brought him aspirin and a glass of water, then helped him upstairs.

"I can take it from here," Gary assured him, teetering at the bedroom door. "Really. Go on home to your family." His eyes welled with tears again at the word 'family.' He brushed them away. "And Marc? Thanks… for being here — and for knocking some sense into me."

"Any time." Marc gave him another hug. "I know I said some harsh words to you out there… but I did it because I love you, Gary; we all do. Don't ever forget that."

When Marc showed up the next night, Gary seemed in better spirits. And Marc noted with relief the absence of a scotch glass in his best friend's grip.

On Tuesday, he called Gary during the four-o'clock news. "Whaddaya say we go out and grab a pizza tonight?"

Marc was sure he heard caution — or was it suspicion? — in Gary's voice. "Sounds like fun."

By eight, the snow had begun accumulating; Marc called Marie when he turned off Route 1, to say he'd survived the highway crazies. He didn't tell his wife about the countless spinouts he'd seen — or about the cars littering the I-95 connector in Milford.

"If it's icy, stay there," Marie told him, sounding worried.

A few minutes later, Marc pulled to a stop in the driveway. The porch light's glow welcomed him.

Any other night, Angie's Pizza Barn would have been packed. It seemed no one wanted to brave the elements, except the trio of regulars perched at the bar.

When the door opened, the waitress looked up from wiping down a table. "Hey Gar'," she called to him. "Who's your cute friend?"

"He's not available," Gary called back. He'd been coming here for years; he liked the atmosphere and the good-natured ribbing the sociable waitresses doled out. They all knew about the upcoming trial, but still treated him like he belonged.

Cassie sidled over. Rag hand poised on her hip, she leaned against the counter. "Honey, *everyone's* available," the saucy waitress teased, winking at Marc. "There's just certain people you gotta go through first."

Marc looked rattled, like he wasn't sure how to respond to her shameless banter.

Gary took it in stride. "Ohh, I don't think you want to tangle with my sister."

The waitress flexed a bicep; it bulged obligingly. "Bet I could take her…"

He shook his head. "Unh-uh. You don't know my sister."

Cassie patted Marc's cheek. "Don't worry, hon; I'm only teasin'. Anyway, you think I'd go after anyone *he*" – nodding toward Gary – "brought in?" Returning her attention to Gary, she pointed across the empty room. "I think there's an open table way over there."

He squinted as if peering through a crowd. Pointed. "There? I think I see it. Thanks, Cass."

After the guys ordered a large sausage-and-mushroom pizza, Cassie suggested a pitcher of beer.

Before Gary could agree, Marc spoke up. "How 'bout a pitcher of Coke instead?"

She nodded. "Done."

Marc didn't even look over at Gary until after the waitress had retreated to the kitchen.

"I'm *not* an alcoholic," Gary muttered.

"I didn't say you were. I just thought, with the bad weather and all, beer probably wasn't the safest choice."

Gary's water glass was poised at his lips. "You're full of shit."

(4:57 p.m., February 1 – Sunday)

"Marc, he sounds awful," Micki lamented. "But the kids are so clingy when they don't feel well, so I can't get away. I hate to impose… Would you mind looking in on him?"

Marc reached for his car keys. "I'm on my way."

Bracing himself for the worst, Marc rang the doorbell and waited. He checked his watch: 5:49. He'd made good time, considering the road conditions. Getting no reply, he pounded at the door.

Now from inside, he heard fumbling and an indistinct shout that might have been, "Alright, alright. Keep your pants on!"

When the door opened at last, Gary eyed the interloper. Upon seeing his best friend, he slouched against the door-jamb, his hostility abating. "You keep showin' up an' people are gonna talk."

The scotch on Gary's breath overwhelmed Marc. "And if I *don't* keep showing up, *you're* gonna end up pickling your liver."

"Christ Almighty! Would'ja get off me about that? I'm not a fucking alcoholic. Alright?"

"Fine. Can I come in?"

"You gonna quit hounding me?" Gary waited for his friend's assurance, then stood aside to admit him. Shutting the door, he turned. "What brings you here?"

Marc ignored the question. "How much have you had to drink?"

"Fuck you." Gary turned and lurched toward the stairs.

"Denying it won't make it go away, Gary. And no, it won't make *me* go away either. I'd hoped this wouldn't get confrontational, but you seem insistent on it."

When Gary turned back, there were tears in his eyes. His question was a plea. "What do you want me to do?"

Marc kept his tone gentle, conciliatory. "I want you to admit – to yourself – there's a problem."

"I *told* you: I don't have a drinking problem."

"I *know* you've told me; and I'm telling you I don't believe you." Before Gary could protest, Marc rested a hand on his arm. "I know it's gotta be tough… the trial… being away from your family support system. But alcohol won't change any of that. It might make you feel better in the short term; but, Gary, look what it's doing to you. It's turning you into a numbed, uncaring zombie. Is that who you want to be? Because I'm telling you, that's who you're headed toward becoming if you keep this up. You're gonna drive away everyone who's important in your life. All that's gonna matter to you is where to get that next drink. And believe me, Gar', it's not pretty."

Gary trembled, helpless terror in his eyes, his empty bluster gone. "What do I do now?"

Marc put an arm around him. "I'm glad you asked. You don't need to go through this alone."

The double doors to St. Stephen's church hall were unlocked. Pulling one open, Marc stood aside for Gary to enter.

Shreds of conversation and laughter came from a meeting room down the hall. Gary took hold of Marc's sleeve and tugged him backward. "I can't do this."

"You can, Gary. I'll be right here with you."

"What if somebody recognizes my voice?"

"Don't worry; last thing anyone here wants to do is give someone away." Marc patted his arm. "You'll be fine. Now, c'mon… there's some people I want you to meet."

His suspicion surfaced. "Who?"

"Friends of mine."

Gary could feel eyes boring into him as they stepped into the room.

A 60ish man in a red-plaid shirt approached; he had a kind face with ruddy cheeks beneath wide-set blue eyes. He looked like he could've been somebody's favorite uncle. His name tag read simply, HENRY T.

"Hey, Marc… long time!" Henry's booming voice filled the room. The two men embraced briefly, thumping one another on the back. "You been okay?"

Marc nodded. "Fine. Busy – you know, family, work… the usual."

"What about school?"

"One more year to go."

Suddenly, the pieces all fell into place: Marc's worry about him, alternating with anger; his supportiveness about coming here; the fact he knew where and when to go; and now Henry

T's concern at not seeing Marc in a while. It never occurred to Gary his brother-in-law might have a drinking problem.

"I know this meeting's closed," Marc continued, sounding apologetic. He motioned toward Gary. "I hope it's okay I brought a friend. He's having a rough time and really needs some support."

"Of course." Henry turned to Gary. He smiled, stuck out his hand. "Welcome. We're glad you're here." Noting Gary's tenuous grip, he added, "First meeting's the hardest. Don't worry; it's enough that you're here. You don't have to say anything if you don't want to; it's okay just to listen. But I'm glad you came. Help yourself to some coffee; it's not half bad."

Just before seven, Henry asked the others to take their seats. Some hurried, others lingered at the coffee urn before meandering to rows of chairs. Gary followed Marc to a pair of seats on the center aisle in the fifth row. Marc leaned to whisper something to Gary, who mulled it over, then shook his head.

Gary listened as Marc's other circle of friends spoke, relating tales of triumph and difficulty. And he marveled at the applause that greeted each milestone – which tonight ranged from fifteen days to twenty-seven years.

When the discussion turned to challenges that threatened sobriety on a daily basis, several people spoke about family members and acquaintances who either didn't know or – worse – didn't care about their alcoholism and tried to push them into drinking.

Marc stood. "I play a friendly game of poker every month with coworkers – guys I've known ten, twelve years… or more. Every month, I have to decline their offers of beer or mixed drinks. Lately I've been showing up with a large coffee and, if anyone offers, I tell 'em I'm all set. So far it seems to be working. But I don't know what I'm gonna do come summer."

"Iced coffee?" suggested Chloe, the blonde sitting next to him.

"Maybe." He faltered. "The hell of it is, these are folks I consider my friends. But I can't tell 'em the truth. Even after all these years – all these meetings – I'm still too ashamed to say it: I'm an alcoholic. Three little words. It shouldn't be that hard to do, right? I just…" His words trailing away, Marc shook his head and sat, his shoulders sagging. "I can't bring myself to do it," he finished, his whisper directed toward the floor.

Jackson, a thin black man sitting one row back, patted him on the shoulder. "That's okay, man. You'll tell them when the time's right. And remember, there's nothing for you to be ashamed of."

Chloe slipped an arm around Marc and drew him into a sidelong hug.

Feeling powerless, Gary reached out to give his brother-in-law's shoulder a comforting pat.

In the awkward silence, Henry spoke. "Thanks, Marc, for sharing. I remember you mentioned that some time ago, and I wondered how it had turned out. I'm sorry you're still feeling bad about it."

Other people related similar experiences.

Taking a furtive glance at his watch after what he was sure could only be twenty minutes into the meeting, Gary was astonished at how quickly it had gotten to be 8:30.

(10:47 a.m., February 5 – Thursday)
"I've got good news and I've got *really* good news."

The corners of Gary's mouth twitched upward. "Okay, give me the good news."

"Judge Harriman reversed the ruling."

"Who's Judge Harriman?"

"As of this morning, she's your bona fide guardian angel," Blake reported with a triumphant smile. "She reversed Judge Paterna's ruling a few minutes ago."

Gary released his breath in an audible exhale. "What's the *really* good news?"

(11:50 a.m.)

In the laundry room, Michaela didn't hear Gary call out to her from the front door. She entered the living room just as Gary headed toward the kitchen to look for her.

"There you are."

Micki shrieked and dropped the laundry basket. Stacks of the kids' neatly folded play clothes tumbled to the floor.

Within moments, Gary had closed the space between them and enfolded her in a hug. "Hey," he cooed. "I'm sorry. Didn't mean to startle you."

Trembling, Micki clung to her husband, her heart pounding so hard she thought she might die.

He stroked her cheek. Gazing into her eyes, he smiled. "Hi, honey, I'm home." Framing her face in both hands, he kissed her. Michaela's warm, soft lips yielded eagerly to his.

Electricity sped through her. His mouth was inviting. It felt like their first kiss all over again.

Gary crushed her body to his and kissed her once more, long and fiery.

Michaela melted against him. Being in his arms again gave her a sweet rush of exhilaration, one she hadn't felt in far too long. When she'd been at the cottage those three days, he'd been too sick for her to entertain romantic thoughts; but now he was well again. And he was home; and she was in his arms. She wanted him badly; she could tell he wanted her, too. "Let's go upstairs," she breathed against his ear, pulling her mouth away for just an instant.

His mouth sought hers again, greedy with desire. As he kissed Michaela, he backed her toward the couch. "No," he said, his lips an inch from hers. "Right here." Lowering her onto it, he positioned himself over her. Swiftly undoing her jeans, he untucked his wife's turtleneck. Before sliding the clingy garment up over her head, Gary ran his hands along her body, skimming her taut midsection, his hands cupping the breasts he hadn't caressed in ages. He massaged them through the soft material; she pulsed with anticipation as he found and tweaked her nipples.

Arching her back, Micki let out a growl of desire. Oh, how she'd missed this! How she'd missed him! She reached upward and took possession of his mouth again.

Not only did Michaela welcome Gary's advances, she'd often initiated sex. She was a tigress. She made love with fire; biting and scratching… arousing passions in him he'd never realized were there. And she loved to tease him, bringing him right to the brink – then backing off, slowing her pace, tormenting him until he begged her for release.

Not this time. He was so aroused he doubted he'd be inside her for more than a minute before he came. He swept the blue top over her head in a single motion, flinging it across the room.

Struggling to free him from his sweater, Michaela raked her nails up his back.

Was it accidental? Intentional? It didn't matter. Searing lines of pain and pleasure scratched along his skin. Uttering a growl of his own, Gary reared back.

The sweater slipped from Micki's grasp. Pulled forward, it trapped his head and arms. Shaking himself free, he emerged, hair askew, arms ensnared in their green woolen straitjacket.

"Wait… wait." Micki's laughing voice cut through his haze of passion. She grabbed at his arms to get him to stop fighting her, and tried to tug the sweater off. After a brief tussle, she pulled it free and tossed it aside. She stretched toward Gary to kiss him, her mouth upturned in mirth.

He pulled away with a jerk. She was laughing.

Laughing.

At him.

With the onset of the panic attack, Gary's passion died. Even quicker than it had overtaken him, it was gone.

Michaela stopped mid chuckle and stared at her husband. "Gary?"

Muttering, he staggered off her and retrieved his cast-off sweater. Pulling it on again, he stared at her, sullen, stormy.

"Gary… what's the matter?"

"Nothing," he grumbled, turning away, his self-confidence shattered. "Forget it."

Micki scrambled to her feet. "No – I *won't* forget it. Honey, what just happened?"

His heart thumped; his breathing turned ragged and erratic. Glaring, he spun around, accusation in his eyes. "You *laugh* at me, then have the nerve to ask what happened? Geez, Mick – whaddaya do for an encore? Butter-knife castrations? I swear to God, I don't know wha—" A loud buzzing filled his head as everything went black.

He didn't hear her scream, didn't feel the impact as he hit the couch then tumbled to the floor.

Shaking, Micki knelt over Gary, trying to evoke her CPR training. Just before he collapsed, he'd looked so strange. His expression seemed odd, like he was angry and confused and about to cry at the same time. Rolling him onto his back, she touched his face. "Gary? Gary! Are you alright?"

When he failed to respond, she shouted his name. No response.

She checked for a pulse. Weak, but it was there. And he was breathing. Another good sign; rescue breathing wouldn't be necessary.

Never slap an unconscious person's face. The words loomed in her mind. *Use alternate stimuli.* Alternate stimuli. She tried to think. Her hand trembled as she reached out and gave his arm a pinch.

Gary recoiled. A moment later, he blinked, eyeing her reproachfully. "What'd you do that for?" He tried to sit up, but Michaela stopped him.

"Don't move," Micki commanded. *Ask simple questions to assess orientation.* "What day is it?"

"How should I know?" He floundered. "Thursday."

"What's your name?"

"Fred Rogers," he snapped. "Now would you let me up? My whole Neighborhood must be out searching for me. King Friday's probably beside himself."

She scowled. "I don't think you're funny at all, Gary!"

Gary struggled to sit up. "I'm fine," he insisted, still groggy. "I musta just blacked out, that's all."

She held a finger in front of his face. "Follow this with your eyes." Michaela moved it left and right, up and down, intending for him to track its motion.

Gary rolled his eyes, then crossed them. "Sorry, no can do. Nice try, though." He grasped her finger. "Don't go all Marcus Welby on me, huh? I get enough of that from Marie. But, hey" – with an appreciative leer, he snapped her bra strap – "nice getup. Wish Velma had worn something like that…"

She smacked him in the arm. "Why can't you take anything seriously?"

"Who says I don't? Just 'cause I'm not freaked out over this doesn't mean I don't take things seriously. I passed out for a minute. So what? It's not a big deal."

"It *is* a big deal! Passing out is not normal! You scared the hell out of me! I don't care what you say, Gary – I want you to go see your doctor. Today."

"Fine. I'll give him a call… but I doubt he'll be able to see me today."

(10:30 a.m., February 6 – Friday)
Gary told his physician about his three prior blackouts, during his weeks at the cottage.

Dr. Caron's mouth formed a tight line. He always looked like that when he fretted. "You should have called me sooner."

"Didn't think it was serious. I've been under a lotta pressure. I figured it was probably stress."

The doctor nodded. "Maybe so. How've you been sleeping?"

Gary smirked. "What's that?"

Dr. Caron jotted notes in Gary's file. "You know: when you lie in a dark room and engage in restorative subconsciousness for several hours at a time."

He's as much of a smartass as I am. "Not happening. Can't remember the last time I had a good night's sleep. *Any* real sleep, for that matter."

The doctor listened to Gary's heart. "How've you been feeling otherwise?"

"Had the flu last month. Spent half the night in the hospital hooked to IV fluids – and the rest of the night peeing it back out. It was loads of fun."

Dr. Caron checked Gary's lungs. "Deep breath. Good. Have you been eating regularly?"

"Now and then."

"Again – deep breath. One more… good. Define 'now and then.'"

"When I feel hungry."

"How often is that?"

Gary shrugged. "I dunno. Every few days."

The doctor frowned. "Get dressed, then come on into my office. Let's talk awhile."

***

Gary tried to ignore the whispering from the gaggle of sales secretaries.

"Was that *Gary?*"

"Yeah; he looks like hell!"

"He looks worse than that – looks like he's got AIDS."

"Gary's got AIDS?"

"I don't know… but it sure looks like it!"

Looking up when he heard the knock at his open door, Pete tried to disguise his shock. "Gary! How goes?"

"Not real good."

The program director motioned him into his office. "How do you feel?"

Gary slouched into a chair. "'Bout as awful as I look," he admitted.

"You've lost a lot of weight."

"Twenty-two pounds since December. I can't eat, can't sleep – my nerves are shot. I barely know what day it is. My kids look at me funny – they think I've lost my mind. Tell you the truth, I'm beginning to think they're right."

Gary's eyes were sadder than Pete could ever remember seeing them.

He went on, as if compelled to talk. "Their friends' parents won't let them come over anymore – especially Erin's friends. Now they've even taken away my CCD class. Folks complained they didn't want a child molester teaching their kids." Gary was silent a long time, head in his hands. "At least they finally let me come home."

Pete watched him in silence.

Gary looked up. "I didn't want there to be any surprises, so I may as well tell you… 'cause the way that lawyer of hers is digging, you'd probably find out eventually."

"Find out what?"

"I doubt it'll come up, but who knows what they'll establish as a precedent for me preying on unsuspecting female staff," Gary prefaced, his voice quavering. "Years ago, right after my grandfather died… Bren and I – we, uh, had a fling. Only lasted a couple months. But it was pretty intense."

"Oh." Pete tried not to look shocked. He knew Brenda had had a crush on Gary way back, and there'd been definite sexual tension between them. But, he had to admit, they'd concealed their tryst well.

***

On his way home, Gary stopped at the pharmacy to pick up the anti-anxiety meds Dr. Caron had prescribed.

"You might feel a bit queasy the first few days," the doctor had cautioned. "Just 'til your system gets acclimated to the medication."

"Anything's gotta be better than this," Gary had replied.

When he got home, he took one of the pills and went to bed.

(3:12 p.m., February 9 – Monday)
"Daddy?" Erin called, tapping at the locked door. "Daddy? Is that you?"

He hadn't expected anyone home already. Another convulsive surge assailed him as he was about to assure her he was fine.

"Dad!" the teen cried, knocking frantically now. "Daddy? Are you alright?"

The urgency in her voice wasn't helping. How could he convince her he was fine when he couldn't even control the panic-driven nausea that had seized him? Getting to his feet and leaning weakly against the bathroom door, Gary ran a sweaty palm across his face; it came away smeared with a dribble of puke. Dr. Caron wasn't kidding about those side effects! He wiped his hand against his jeans.

Erin pounded again at the door. "Da-ad!"

The insistent thumping vibrated against his back and he forced back the urge to hurl again. He managed a few breaths without puking on the exhales. "I'm fine, punkin," he croaked.

He must not have sounded convincing. She banged again. "I don't believe you, Daddy."

"I'm *fine*," he insisted. "I'm just—" A new rush of nausea interrupted.

"Yeah," she mocked. "You're *so* fine you're barfing your guts out."

Leave me alone. He hunched over the toilet. *Just leave me alone and let me die…*

When he was reasonably certain he could speak without throwing up, he addressed Erin again, his voice raspy. "Look, I'm just feeling a little queasy is all… and I can do without the audience, okay? No one's ever died from puking – and I don't intend to be the first. Just, please, Erin, leave me alone, alright? I'm fine."

Silence from the other side of the door made Gary think he'd been talking to himself. Then Erin spoke up. "You don't sound fine."

"Then call 911 if it makes you feel better. But won't *you* feel silly when all the EMTs do is give me a glass of ginger ale?" A guilty pang stabbed at him. *Asshole! She's concerned about you!* "I'm sorry, punkin. I know you're worried. And I appreciate that. But trust me: Some things in life you don't need your teenage daughter overhearing. Cut me some slack, huh?"

"But, Daddy…"

"I'm sure there are things you'd rather *I* didn't know about… right?"

No answer.

"Hey" – wondering if she was still listening – "I didn't go and bust up your little make-out session with Colin Desmond the other night. So you owe me, kiddo."

Silence.

"Didn't think I knew 'bout that, huh?"

"Uh…"

"I'll take that as a 'No.' And I'll have you know, Mom woulda killed you – *and* Colin – if she found out. Now, unless you wanna *continue* this discussion, punkin, scram."

Erin gulped. "Um… hope you feel better, Dad. I'll leave you a Coke on the counter."

Chapter 17

(4:15 p.m., February 10 – Tuesday)

"They've finished empaneling the jury. Initial buzz says you go to trial next Wednesday. Word from the D.A.'s office is Sabine's loaded for bear."

Gary's insides sank. "Thanks for the encouraging news," he muttered. "Did they make a decision about your helping defend me?"

He heard the gentle rush of air through the phone as his father-in-law sighed. "I'm sorry, Gary. As I expected, they felt it'd be prejudicial for a state's attorney to oppose one of our prosecutors. They said it would undermine the State's case against you."

"So, I'm pretty well screwed, six ways to Sunday." Gary's insides churned; bile burned at the back of his throat. "I may as well just give up now."

"Don't lose hope, Gary. Blake's an excellent defense attorney. If anyone can get you cleared, it's him. Just do whatever he tells you and you'll be fine."

By week's end, Gary's nausea abated. As the medication took effect, he started to feel almost "normal" again. His panicky spells eased and he no longer felt like his heart would explode.

Michaela noticed he was going to bed earlier and staying asleep longer. She wondered whether his meds contained a sleep agent. Awakening in the middle of the night to find her husband still asleep, she'd utter a silent prayer of thanksgiving for that small measure of peace.

(9:57 p.m., February 17 – Tuesday)

Gary couldn't find a comfortable position. The covers made him too hot. A minute later, he was cold. Then he was uncomfortable again; and he didn't want to tell Michaela her reading lamp was shining in his eyes. He turned the other way and tried to sleep. No use.

Micki, who'd been idly stroking his hair, leaned to kiss his earlobe. "Is the light bothering you?"

Not lifting it off the pillow, he shook his head.

The media had torn him apart again tonight. And tomorrow, day one of his trial, promised to be no better.

She laid her book aside. "D'you wanna talk about it?"

Another pillow-embedded headshake.

Still she stroked his hair. Gently. Gently. Laying a hand on his shoulder, she coaxed him toward herself. "C'mere, honey."

He let Michaela draw him closer.

"I know you're frightened, Gary." Her whisper was as soothing as her fingers through his hair.

She doesn't know the half of it.

"But it's okay," she continued. "Everything's gonna turn out fine."

If he tried to talk, he'd end up sobbing. So he lay curled beside his wife, listening to the sound of her voice.

"I'm gonna stand by you – no matter what," Micki continued. She traced a finger around the curve of his ear, then slid her fingers down to his neck to massage away the tension.

Now he *was* crying.

She turned out the light. In the dark, she murmured, "I love you, Gary. I know you didn't do any of those things. I'm sure the jury will believe that."

(3 a.m.)

Gary lay in a semi-fetal position, his head buried amid tear-drenched pillows, covers drawn over him. He hadn't slept. Desperate notions swam through his mind – despairing thoughts that both eased and frightened him.

He recalled Justin's words after Ellen's suicide: about how despair robs a person of clarity, clouds the ability to reason and limits culpability for certain actions… And that Christmas morning years ago – just weeks shy of his seventeenth birthday – when he nearly slit his wrists to end his misery.

He mulled over this whole sordid mess. The accusations. The humiliation. The devastation it had already caused his family. Gary thought about how much better off they'd be when it was all over.

The way he'd almost done it before was too messy. And what if one of the kids found him? No, it'd have to look like an accident.

Sitting up, Gary swung his legs over the edge of the bed. Pushing his hair out of his eyes, he took a deep breath, filling his lungs with resolve. Casting about in the dark, he knocked his keys off the dresser; they clattered to the floor.

Michaela stirred, rolled over… found her husband's side of the bed empty. "Gary?"

"Go back to sleep," he whispered in the calmest voice he could manage. With trembling hands, he groped for his keys. Found them. Pulled on jeans and a t-shirt.

"Where are you going?" she mumbled.

"I just need some air. Go back to sleep." Leaning over the bed, he kissed her. *Goodbye, Michaela. I love you. I'm so sorry to do this to you… Please forgive me.*

The roads would be deserted. He'd just have to slam into one of those big trees by the green. Oh, and figure out how to disable the airbag. Or maybe get on the highway, swerve in front of a semi and hit the brakes. *I could just get on 84 going the wrong way; I'm sure to hit oncoming traffic.* Gary smirked at his unintended pun.

Then you'd risk hurting someone else, he reasoned, heading downstairs.

So what? he countered. *Why go alone? Why not take someone along? You're goin' to hell anyway… why not _really_ make it worth your while?* he mocked himself.

Gary was almost to the back door when he heard it.

If you do this – what you're thinking of, my boy – you'll accomplish two things.

He instantly recognized the angry voice.

"And what would those be?" he challenged aloud, sweeping away the tears clouding his vision.

You'd leave your family with more grief and more questions, <u>and</u> you'll remove all doubt from everyone else's mind.

"All doubt about what?" he snapped defensively.

Whether you did it. They'll assume you did.

"But I *didn't!*" he insisted.

Ah, but <u>that</u> won't matter. In their minds, it'll be just the same as if you pleaded guilty and then carried out your own execution.

Gary's resolve wavered. He was listening to reason. "So, what do I *do?*"

What you should have done from the start: Stand up and fight like the man you are – not the meek little pushover they think they're dealing with!

"Easy for you to say… When was the last time *you* were charged with raping a teenage girl?!"

Something pulled Micki from her sleep. She stirred, listening in the dark. There it was again. She tugged her bathrobe on and went to investigate. Creeping down the hall, she stopped every few feet and strained to listen. Muffled sobs. A clinking glassy sound… silence. A long moan deteriorated into more sobs. Desperate, gasping sobs.

Before she reached the bottom of the stairs, she knew where the sounds were coming from. Taking a steadying breath, she tiptoed toward the kitchen. The cheery yellow room was dark; but by the moonlight streaming in through the windows, Micki could make out her husband's form hunched – no, slumped – over the kitchen table. His head rested against his right wrist; his left hand encircled a short, stocky glass.

Beside him was a bottle. Scotch. A cold stab pierced her. *Please, God, not him, too!* Her mom and Gary's dad had both been alcoholics. Taking a shaky breath, she neared the table.

She didn't want to be confrontational, but she wouldn't be an enabler again. Her bare foot kicked something. It scudded across the floor. Crumpled paper.

Michaela pulled out a chair and sat. Reaching out, she touched Gary's left hand.

It closed around the glass.

She whispered his name and tried to curl her fingers around his hand.

He only tightened his grip.

"Gary, please," she murmured. "I love you. Don't do this to yourself."

His voice snagged in his throat. One fist thumped weakly against something on the tabletop. "I – I can't… Micki, I can't do it. It's too hard."

Then she noticed the note; instinct told her what it was. A lump that felt about the size of an egg rose in her throat. Not wanting to alarm Gary by grabbing at it, she patted his hand and tried to sound comforting. "No, Gary, it's not too hard. It's *not*. We'll face this together, you and me. As long as we're together, we can face anything. *Anything.* I promise."

He turned his face toward her. Shook his head. "It's no good," he mumbled over and over, bringing the glass to his lips; ice clinked against the glass as he took a hefty gulp. Setting the glass down clumsily, Gary laid his head on the table again and wept. Deep, shuddering sobs.

What's no good? Panic seized Michaela. Her hand crept toward Gary's car keys and closed around them. She inched them out of his reach. "Gary, it's okay, honey. Everything's going to be fine. Just trust me. Please trust me…"

Back and forth they went. He'd say something incoherent about nothing being any use and she'd try to convince him otherwise.

Finally, tears streaming down his face, he gestured wildly toward the street. "I'da been out there by now! It'd all be over if it weren't for those voices."

"Voices?" *Is he having a psychotic episode? Dear God, please, don't let it be that!* She shook his arm. "Gary! What voices?"

His head wobbled, then dropped forward onto the table again. Out cold.

Trying not to panic, Micki checked for a pulse. She pulled the nearly empty bottle from him, then snatched the note; three pages. She folded it and secreted it into the pocket of her robe.

Keeping a wary eye on her husband, she poured the rest of the scotch down the drain, then dialed the phone.

Apologizing for the late hour, she tearfully explained why she was calling.

After she hung up, Micki jammed a fist into her mouth to stifle her frightened cries; she crumpled against the counter, trembling. Pulling herself together at last, she made her second call.

The call to Blake could wait until morning.

Standing by the door, Michaela unfolded the note and read it by the light of the gibbous moon.

When the car door slammed, she hastily stuffed the note in her pocket and swiped at her tears with the back of a fist. A moment later came footfalls on the front-porch stairs.

Micki pulled the door open before he could knock. "I'm sorry to bother you so late at night," she babbled, unable to keep the fear out of her voice.

"It's no bother," he assured her, his deep-brown eyes filled with concern. "Just wish I could've gotten here sooner. Besides" – he drew her into a comforting hug – "that's what family's for. Is he okay?"

Pulling away, she shrugged. "I dunno. He kept saying this really weird stuff; I was afraid he—" she broke off, not wanting to voice her fears. "I really don't know *what* to think." Jamming a hand into her pocket, Michaela felt for the note; she decided it was best not to mention it.

"Where is he now?"

"Passed out at the kitchen table. I got his keys away from him, didn't want to risk him driving like that. Marc – I'm so scared!"

He hugged his trembling sister-in-law again. "Shh… of course you're scared, Micki. But you did the right thing. And you called 911, right?"

Michaela nodded against his shoulder. A little cry escaped her. For the moment, she was thankful Marc didn't know exactly what she had in mind, and grateful for his reassuring embrace.

"So now we just sit tight."

Two minutes later, the ambulance pulled to a stop in the driveway, lights flashing.

Hazy from scotch and confused by the commotion, Gary railed against the EMTs' efforts to assess his condition; he flailed and shouted and fought them off.

Michaela tried to calm him, but couldn't.

One of Gary's attempts to repel her resulted in an inadvertent fist to her mouth.

An EMT made sure Micki wasn't seriously hurt. Then he returned his attention to Gary.

After a struggle, the paramedics subdued him. Maneuvering him onto a stretcher, they restrained Gary and wheeled him out to the waiting ambulance.

"Let me go!" he shouted, twisting and straining at the nylon webbing securing his arms and legs. "Damn it, leave me alone!"

Micki's eyes welled with tears as she watched the pitiful scene unfold. After conferring with the ambulance driver, she went to talk with Marc. "I don't know how long this is gonna take. Are you *sure* you'll be okay here?"

His eyes met hers. "Don't worry about me; you look after Gary."

Squelching a cry, she nodded. Micki ran upstairs to dress, then dashed away to Danbury Hospital.

"Mom?" Quiet footsteps sounded overhead. Erin appeared at the top of the stairs. "Mom? What's going on? I heard voi— Uncle Marc? Why're you here? Where's my mom? Where's Daddy? What's going on?"

Not prepared for questions at 4 a.m., he faltered. "Everything's gonna be fine, sweetheart."

Erin descended the stairs warily, stopping midway. "Where's my mom and dad?"

Marc went to meet her; putting an arm around the teen's shoulder, he led her to the couch. Before he could speak, she assailed him with questions.

"Why was Daddy yelling? And where'd they go? They didn't take him to jail again… did they?"

"Of course not, Erin. Nothing like that." Marc tried to think how to put this. "It's just… well, he hasn't been well; and your mom thought he should go to the hospital."

"What was all the yelling for?"

He drew his niece closer. "Your dad didn't think going to the hospital was such a good idea."

Worry darkened Erin's eyes; her lower lip quivered. Scenes from her grandparents' living room years earlier – when they told her Mommy was dead – scrambled through her mind like dizzy rats. Fear filled her. She wanted to throw up. "Is Daddy gonna die?"

Uncle Marc hugged her. "Of course not, honey. He's just not feeling well, is all. He'll be fine."

"Are you *sure?* Are you *sure* he's gonna be alright?" Her eyes pleaded with him to say yes.

He kissed Erin on the forehead. "I promise; he'll be fine. It'll just take time."

"How long?"

"That's hard to say. But don't you worry, sweetheart. I've known him a long time; if there's one thing I'm sure of, it's this: Your dad's a fighter. He'll get through this. We all will."

Reassured, Erin drooped in her uncle's arms.

After Marc soothed her fears and sent her back to bed, he returned to the kitchen, where more than a dozen discarded suicide notes lay crumpled on the floor. Gathering all he could find, he dumped the lot of them into the garbage, then tied up the bag and tossed it in the trash can outside.

(6:15 a.m.)
After he examined Gary and ordered a battery of tests, Dr. Sanjib talked with Michaela in the corridor. "Your husband appears to be suffering from extreme depression; but I'd like a second opinion. I paged a colleague, one of the best psychiatrists in Connecticut." The ER doctor laid a hand on her arm. "She's been cited for excellence the last three years; I have total confidence in her." Dr. Sanjib scribbled notes in Gary's file, then disappeared into another room.

Back in the room, Gary was feigning sleep. Michaela watched his eyelids flutter as she moved to the other side of the gurney. Reaching out a hand, she stroked his brow.

He turned away from her touch, his eyes squeezed tight against the tears.

(6:45 a.m.)
Her coat flapping, Doctor Lindemeyr dashed into the ER and stopped at the white patient-status board. To preserve confidentiality, it listed patients only by the intake number assigned during triage. She scanned the board until she found what she was looking for: 3087766; male, age 34. After checking his status, the doctor strode toward room seven.

"Wonder where *she's* going in such a hurry," mused one nurse, looking up from a stack of files.

"Hot on the trail of a new nutcase, no doubt," another replied.

Both women snickered.

The doctor turned. Her expression said she hadn't found their comments amusing. "First of all," she snipped, blue eyes fixing on one, then the other. "Show some respect, ladies. That better be the last time I hear either of you speak that way about a patient. *Any* patient. Is that understood?"

The nurses squirmed beneath her withering glare. "Yes, doctor," they mumbled in unison.

"And second, I shouldn't have to waste valuable time – time I *should* be spending with patients – to reprimand nurses for unprofessional behavior."

Not waiting to hear the nurses' stammered apologies, the psychiatrist walked briskly toward number seven again.

With a light rap at the open door, she stepped inside. "Good morning," she began cheerily, shutting the door. "I'm Doctor Lindemeyr. How ar—" She gasped. "Gary!"

Gary's eyes flew open. He looked straight into the face of his sister. Shame and worthlessness ganged up on him. He turned away to avoid her eyes.

"M-Marie!" Michaela stammered. "When the doctor said he'd called a top psychiatrist, I had no idea…" she shook her head, her eyes widening.

Marie gave her a swift hug. "It'll be okay," she whispered in her sister-in-law's ear, recalling bits of their Christmas-afternoon conversation.

At her brother's side, she took his hand. It was extraordinarily cold. "How are you, Gary? Do you want to talk?"

"Do I have a choice?" he asked the wall.

Marie figured she'd meet resistance; that was normal. But *this* was an unusual situation. "Of course," she said gently, drawing her hand away. "Of course you have a choice. But you've got to realize I can't discharge you until I'm sure you don't pose a threat to yourself… or anyone else."

"What's that supposed to mean?"

Marie leveled with him. "It means whatever I need it to mean."

"How do you know whether I pose a threat?"

His challenging tone was a good sign. It meant there was still some fight there. Either that, or alcohol just made him belligerent.

"We can't determine that until after we finish your evaluation." She paused. "I shouldn't do it myself, but there's no one else on call 'til after noon. And honestly, I don't think this can wait."

He grimaced. "Which means I'd better talk to you." He was still touchy, still addressing the wall.

"That's a good place to start. After the initial workup, I'll refer you to another doctor."

"I'll be outside." Michaela's voice startled Gary. Going to his side, she took his hand and leaned to give him a kiss.

He turned sad eyes toward his wife, then quickly looked away.

Michaela squeezed his hand. "I love you, Gary," she whispered.

He barely squeezed back.

When they were alone, Marie spoke. "Guess I don't need to ask the standard identifying questions…"

Gary said nothing.

"Or if you'd rather pretend we don't know each other, I could ask you that stuff anyway—"

"Why don't you can the doctor shit and go the fuck away?"

"If I did that, there'd be little chance of you getting out of here. Now, why don't *you* dial back the hostility and answer a few questions for me, okay?" Realizing she was acting more like his big sister than a medical professional, she abandoned her condescending tone. Marie laid a hand on his shoulder. "I'm sorry; that was inappropriate. Look, Gar', just tell me what I need to know. Then I can set you up with someone who'll help you get to the root of wha—"

"I don't need your psychiatric bullshit, okay?" Gary whipped around to face her, struggling at his restraints. She leapt back in alarm. Fury surged through his eyes and erupted in his voice. "Just leave me the fuck alone!"

"Hey," Marie began softly. "I know this" – she tugged at the lapel of her white coat – "says cold, clinical doctor. But in here" – releasing the coat, she pressed her hand to her heart – "I'm your sister first, and I hate to see you hurting. Above all, I don't want to lose you. So please… work with me here, huh?"

His silence told Marie she was starting to get through to him. "We have to do this, Gary. I realize it's awkward for you… but I promise: Nothing you say will leave this room. Not a word. It won't get back to Michaela. Or the kids. Or

Mom." Marie paused to let him absorb her words. "Or even Marc."

A flicker of worry and not-quite-belief crossed her brother's face. His lower lip trembled slightly.

"*Especially* not Marc," she stressed.

Some of the fire seemed to leave Gary; his face relaxed a bit and he unclenched his fists.

"And I swear to you" – she took his hand; he didn't pull away – "no matter what you tell me, Gary, you'll always be my little brother… and I'll always love you."

Now his fingers curled around hers; he turned moist eyes toward her. "You mean that?" he said barely aloud.

Marie nodded. "Of course I do."

With his relieved sigh came tears. They rolled silently down his face. Ashamed, he turned away.

His sister hugged him.

The restraints on his wrists prevented Gary from hugging back. Or wiping at his tears. "I feel so… so *worthless*…" he mumbled into her shoulder.

Marie settled into a chair beside him. "Why don't you tell me about it," she prompted.

"It's like my whole world changed, the day I was arrested. I mean, he was nice enough and all, that cop… he's a friend of Pete's; but it was so *humiliating!* Sitting there in the kitchen with my wife and my boss while a police officer read this list of charges. And they're all *lies*" – he stopped as a new torrent of tears started. He tried to wipe them away; the restraints tugged at his wrists. He shook his head. "And then, being marched out of my home in handcuffs – in front of all my neighbors…"

Marie listened, nodding her understanding. "Tell me how that made you feel."

"It made me feel like scum. Like a criminal!" Words poured out of Gary now like water from an open hydrant. "And I didn't do it – I *know* I didn't… but being arrested – and interrogated in that little room with those cops sneering at me… and – and – not even listening to what I was telling them! It made me feel like no one believed me and it didn't *matter* I was innocent!" He paused. "Then, after awhile I started to wonder if I had it wrong. Maybe I really *was* this beast who'd done that awful thing. You can't know, Marie. You don't know what it's like to – to hate yourself so much… to feel so despicable!"

She tilted her head. "But you didn't do it…"

"No one believed me. And then the media started in" – he sniffled, tried again to wipe at his tears – "and when you hear the same shit, day after day…" Gary shook his head, fell silent.

"Go on," Marie prompted, laying a hand on his arm.

He looked away. "I dunno; just hearing those lies over and over… I started to doubt myself – like maybe I was remembering wrong? I began feeling like there was some truth to what they were saying about me…"

Experience had taught Marie to expect a reply like that. But hearing her brother express such deep self-doubt chilled her. She wiped at the tears that sprang to her eyes, wishing she could allay his fears, as she'd often done when they were kids. "Have you shared this with Michaela?"

Gary looked surprised to see her eyes glistening. He gestured feebly. "How can I?"

"Just talk to her. Tell her what you've told me."

He shook his head. A shock of dark hair fell across his eyes.

Marie pushed it away. "You don't always have to be the strong one," she reminded him. "It might help if you opened up to her some." Her hand rested against his cheek.

Her touch chipped away at Gary's resistance. "I can't tell her something like this," he protested, his voice choked with emotion.

"I don't see why not," she countered. "She's your wife. Would it be so awful to let her in?"

"Letting her in is one thing," he mumbled, sniffling. "I don't want her to see my… failings. I can't let her see me as a fuck-up."

Marie nodded in pensive acknowledgement.

"So you agree I'm a fuck-up?"

"Of course not. I was just acknowledging what you were saying. I didn't want to interrupt." *Especially since you were getting to some important stuff.* She laid a hand atop his. "You encourage her to talk with you when she's feeling bad… right?"

"Yeah."

"How is this different?"

He didn't answer.

"Do you feel like you should be able to control your emotions and not have to lean on her?"

Gary shrugged. "I guess."

"And you don't want her to see you as weak?"

He nodded.

"There's nothing wrong with admitting you're afraid."

"I'm supposed to take care of my family," he lamented, "not the other way around…"

Now we're getting down to his insecurity. Time to poke the bear. "What were you planning to do when Michaela found you?"

"I didn't plan for her to find me," Gary replied testily, then mumbled, "at least… not alive."

Marie shuddered. "When she found you and stopped you, what had you been planning to do?"

"What do you *think?*" he snapped.

"What *I* think isn't important, Gary. I need you to say, out loud, what you were planning to do."

He looked away, his voice steeped in shame and disappointment. "Kill myself."

"Why would you do that?"

Gary sighed. "Grandpa asked me the same thing."

Marie's heart skipped a beat. *He __what__? Back in high school or now?* Her eyebrows shot up. "Oh?"

"Yeah." His glare reflected contempt. "See? I *knew* you'd think I was nuts. Then again, you're paid to think that."

Big sister edged out psychiatrist again. "That's not fair."

"Come off it, Marie. As much as this little brother-sister chat is s'posed to make me feel all warm and fuzzy, we *both* know it's all gonna be in your final nutcase report. So, yeah, you may as well know: I hear my dead grandfather's voice in my head. I have for years" – his eyes narrowed in confrontation – "Go ahead, doc. Write *that* in your evaluation; then they'll *never* let me outta here."

Marie pondered this. "So, you don't *want* to get out?" she baited her brother. " 'Cause that's what I'm hearing…"

"Oh, blow me," Gary muttered. He rolled onto his side, toward the wall, as much as his restraints would permit. "Just go away. I've got nothing else to say to you."

Marie stood. She bent to kiss his cheek. "I love you, Gary. I won't let you twist in the wind. I'll be back later to check on you." She gave his shoulder a pat before going to open the door. She turned back to offer a parting comment. "Just so you know: I hear him talking to me sometimes, too."

A moment later, the door clicked shut.

Hands jammed into the pockets of her coat, Marie stood before the slender Indian doctor. "I can't treat this patient, Naresh."

Dr. Sanjib looked up from the patient file he was studying. His dark eyes scanned her face. "You mean the guy in number seven? He's quite difficult, yes," he said with a nod.

Marie nodded. "He is. But that's not what I meant. I can't treat him because he's my brother."

The doctor's thin lips rounded into a silent O. "I see. That does pose a problem, yes it does."

"It's only a problem in that *I* can't treat him. And I definitely believe he needs more-specialized care than he'd get here."

"I don't think it's in your husband's best interest to allow him to return home," Dr. Sanjib told Michaela a little before eight. They were in one of the small consultation rooms near the ER. "At least not yet, no. Not until he's had a proper psychiatric evaluation."

Marie nodded. "That would be my recommendation."

Michaela looked from one of them to the other. "What do you mean: a *proper* evaluation?"

"First we'd transfer him to an appropriate facility" – the ER doctor backpedaled – "not that this isn't a perfectly good hospital; it is, yes! But we want to ensure his particular needs can be addressed adequately. So, with your permission, we would admit him to a facility that specializes in treating certain psychiatric conditions."

Michaela's tone was flat. "You mean commit him." It was more statement than question.

He hedged. "We try not to call it that, no."

"But that's what you mean… right?" she asked, pressing him for clarification.

Marie touched Micki on the arm and gave a slight nod. "At this point, we think that's best."

"For how long?"

Dr. Sanjib deferred to his colleague.

Dr. Lindemeyr was silent for several seconds. "Ten days. Two weeks. Hard to say. It all depends on how Gary responds and progresses."

"Responds to what?" Micki's mind conjured images of makeshift electroshock-therapy gadgets: overturned metal colanders with coils of brightly colored wires and electrodes attached; liquids of uncertain origin dripping into steaming, bubbling beakers over Bunsen burners; cackling, wild-haired men in white coats hunched over unsuspecting victims in dungeon labs – straight out of an old mad-scientist movie.

"A combination of therapy and medication."

Marie's voice refocused Michaela's thoughts. A psychiatric hospital. It's what she'd had in mind all along, even before she dialed 911. Faced with the reality of it now, a chilling fright took hold. "Could he be treated locally?"

"Of course." Marie nodded. "There are several fine facilities nearby."

"Is there one you can recommend?"

"The Wainwright Center in Darien has excellent doctors. The Carmichael Center for Wellness in New Haven, also a fine facility. Crestview in Wilton. And Foxbridge. It's close by, it's a smaller facility."

Micki felt tears welling.

Marie put a hand on her arm. "I know it's not something you want to think about – let alone have to decide," she said kindly. "But it really *is* the best way for Gary to get the help he needs." When her sister-in-law's first tears fell, Marie continued. "If it was my decision, I'd go this route."

Michaela dabbed at her eyes. "Okay," she agreed. "What do I have to do?"

***

(9:27 a.m.)

Blake glanced at his watch, then assessed Judge Paterna's deepening scowl. "Your Honor, I'm sure something must have happened. My client fully realizes the implications of failing to appear. I simply haven't been able to reach him."

"If he's not here in five minutes, Mr. Tierney, he forfeits bail. And I'm holding him in contempt. He may be a minor celebrity, but that doesn't give him the right to saunter into my courtroom whenever he feels like it."

"Yes, Your Honor. I'll be sure to convey that to him."

Blake darted from the courtroom, cell phone in hand. He punched in Gary's home number. On the third ring, a male voice he didn't recognize answered.

The attorney identified himself and asked to speak to Gary.

A chill seeped through Marc as he wiped grape juice and oatmeal from Michael's face. "Didn't Michaela call you?"

The ringing in Michaela's pocket startled her. She fished the phone out, conscious of the other people in the waiting room. "Hello?"

"Is there somebody you forgot to call this morning?"

Michaela scrambled to place the voice. "Blake! I'm so sorry! I totally forgot. Is Gary in trouble?"

"He's about to be. What the hell happened? Where is he?"

"He's in the hospital. He" – she lowered her voice, then turned away from the others and mumbled into the phone.

Blake stifled a gasp; his heart lurched. "He what?" He paused, recovered quickly. "Never mind – I'll get the details later. Right now I've got to make nice with the judge before he revokes Gary's bail. Call you back," he shouted, racing back toward the courtroom.

Sabine Delacourt's beige shoe dangled from a stockinged toe at the end of her shapely right leg – a leg that bobbed in time with the fingers she drummed on the table before her. She sighed aloud as the door banged open. "Have you found him, Mr. Tierney?" Her scornful tone matched her withering look. "Can we get on with this now?"

"May I approach, Your Honor?"

The judge waved the two attorneys forward.

"Your Honor, I just spoke with my client's wife. He can't be here today; he's been hospitalized."

"Well, isn't that convenient." Sabine's tone oozed sarcasm.

The judge looked as if he agreed with the prosecutor's observation. "I see. What dire reason did he give for suddenly needing to be in the hospital?"

Blake glanced nervously at the other attorney. "I don't know the details yet, Your Honor, but his wife said it may have been a suicide attempt."

"Oh, that's just beautiful!"

"Ms Delacourt, please!" the judge sputtered. He eyed Blake. "When can we expect Mr. Sheldon to be released?"

"I don't really know, Your Honor. I didn't get that much information. I wanted to get back within your time limit. I said I'd call her back for details."

The judge's lips tightened. He glanced from one attorney to the other, then picked up his gavel. "Very well. Step back, please."

He waited for them to return to their respective tables before addressing the Court. "Ladies and gentlemen of the jury, I'm afraid there's been an unavoidable delay. We'll have to recess indefinitely, until a new date can be scheduled. I apologize for any inconvenience this may have caused you. Meanwhile, I'll remind you not to discuss this case with any-one. I'll likewise ask the attorneys not to discuss specifics of the delay with any member of the media. Or the public." He banged his gavel. "Court stands in recess."

Chapter 18

(10 a.m., February 19 – Thursday)

"Good morning, Gary. I'm Dr. Benson."

Gary barely acknowledged the psychiatrist at the door. *Benson.* He was the doctor Micki tried to get him to see at Christmastime. The one whose card he'd torn up and flushed.

Dr. Benson entered the room, unfazed by Gary's ignoring him. "How do you feel this morning?"

Gary eyed him resentfully, refusing to believe he could learn anything from this *teenager!* All that was missing was the raging acne and the keys to Daddy's Buick. He didn't look at all like a doctor. Sure, he had on a white coat... but even Attila's vet wore one of those!

"I understand you've had kind of a rough time of it lately. Want to tell me about it?"

It was like addressing a cinderblock.

"It might help if you'd talk," the doctor suggested, closing the door. "That's one of the best ways to get through a difficult time."

"Well, maybe I don't feel like talking," Gary grumbled irritably.

Dr. Benson nodded. "Okay, what do you feel like? See if you can describe it."

"You think you know so much!" His anger flared. "You don't know shit about me."

"Then tell me. What's the single most important thing I should know?"

Glaring, Gary spoke through gritted teeth. "I don't need a fucking shrink."

"Maybe you don't… but you're here, aren't you? Let's talk about why you're here."

"You mean here on earth? 'Cause it's God's idea of a big fucking joke."

"Are you angry with God?"

"No. With my wife." Hostility spewed from his lips like blood from a knife wound. "She got me locked up. I dunno why she bothered. Why didn't she just leave me alone and let me die?"

The therapist settled into a chair at the foot of Gary's bed. "This is helpful. Why do you think she interfered?"

Gary formed a mental picture of her smiling face. His voice got quiet. "Because she loves me?"

"Are you asking me or telling me?"

"I dunno. Telling you."

"Okay, she loves you. How do you feel about that?"

"Just terrific," he scoffed. He fell silent for a long, bitter moment. "She thinks I'm nuts."

"Why do you say that?"

"She had me committed. What else should I think?"

"Some would say it sounds like she wants you to be well."

"Yeah? Well some would say you're fulla shit!" he mocked the psychiatrist. "You don't get it, do you, doc? It's her fault I'm still alive. It should all have been over by now."

"What should have been over?"

Gary stared at the wall. "My whole miserable life," he mumbled.

Dr. Benson was silent for a moment. "That's pretty all-inclusive. Can you think of even one time your life wasn't miserable?"

An image of his kids nudged at Gary's brain; he shoved it away. "No. I just wanted to end it."

"You were planning to kill yourself?"

His eyes misted; he gave a slight nod.

"Did you see suicide as the answer to your problems?"

No answer.

"Was it the only way out?"

Gary felt a sudden squeezing in his chest, as if someone had wrapped steel mesh around him and was tightening it little by little. It frightened him; he was sure he was having a heart attack. He made no reply.

There were no answers the rest of the hour, either. He just glared at the psychiatrist and picked at the hospital-issued plastic bracelet around his right wrist with the tips of the fingers that could reach it.

(3:45 p.m., February 20 – Friday)
Marie settled onto the couch in her office beside Micki. Dr. Benson sat in a chair off to one side.

"I talked with Gary this afternoon," Marie said.

After a day's observation in the hospital's psychiatric ward, Gary had been transferred yesterday to the Foxbridge Institute, a 42-bed private facility in Newtown where his sister was chief of psychiatry.

"He finally cooperated enough to let Dr. Benson do a full work-up this morning."

"Oh?" Michaela turned toward the other psychiatrist.

"Yes," Dr. Benson spoke up. "The good news is: I don't think we're dealing with psychosis."

Micki's body went limp, as if her skeleton had been made entirely of fear. Her relief came as an audible exhale. Seconds later, worry crept into her eyes again. "What's the bad news?"

"It's nothing worse than I expected," he said. "I've made a dual diagnosis of depression coupled with moderate alcohol dependency. Naturally, we're weaning him off it. But since it hadn't progressed to full-blown dependency, I doubt his withdrawal will be too traumatic. I also started him on anti-depressants, but it'll take time to get the dosage regulated."

Micki listened intently. None of this seemed real.

"Gary's depression has quite a grip on him; he said he feels like he's drowning. But with the right combination of therapy and medication, we can get to its root... and he should start to surface."

"How long will that take?"

Marie replied. "Depends how quickly he responds to the meds. And the therapy. Dr. Benson will work with him daily in individual and group sessions. I'll touch base with him now and then – informally. He's been resistant, but I think he's beginning to trust me."

"Why wouldn't he? You're his *sister.*"

"That can cause more problems than it solves. That's why it's not recommended, treating a sibling" – she shook her head – "too many family issues, for starters. Harder to make headway."

Michaela's brow furrowed. "So, why did you…?"

"It was an emergency situation," Marie explained, "one I've handled before. Many times. I didn't want to alarm you that first night, because you'd already been through so much; but it was critical we got him proper care right away."

"What was so critical?"

"Between the anti-anxiety meds and all the alcohol, he was pretty messed up. If you hadn't found him when you did" – she gave a headshake – "there's a good chance he wouldn't have needed to go out looking for a way to kill himself. One more drink could have done it."

A chill raced through Michaela; she recalled the note still in her bathrobe pocket and pretended they hadn't had that conversation at Christmas. "What makes you think he really wanted to kill himself?"

Marie glanced at Dr. Benson. She couldn't say Gary freely admitted plotting his demise. Or told her this morning he was "pretty sure" he'd written a suicide note. Honoring Micki's denial, she shrugged. "It's my job to think these things."

"What if I told you he wasn't? That he was just sad… and frightened?"

Marie pierced her with a gaze that said, as plainly as if she'd spoken, *You're not fooling anybody.* "I'd say you're trying really hard to convince yourself. I'm sorry to be so blunt, but I know the classic signs of suicidal behavior. And he was exhibiting a whole flock of 'em. All the denial in the world won't erase that fact. You're a counselor yourself, Michaela; you know this. If you want to help Gary, I need you to tell us what you know."

Michaela met Dr. Benson's gaze. "What do you need to know?"

The therapist turned to a clean page in his notepad. "Can you tell me what's been going on with your husband lately?"

The look Michaela gave him said, *You must be joking.* "You have to *ask*?"

Marie patted her hand. "Actually, in order for him to do this evaluation, he *does* need to ask. Because you can provide information from your perspective Gary might not have mentioned… or Dr. Benson might not notice from observing him."

"I'm sorry to put you through this, Mrs. Sheldon," Dr. Benson continued, "but I need your help. Your husband needs your help. Could you tell me about any changes you've noticed in Gary's attitude, behavior or mood these last several weeks?"

Micki put a hand to her mouth to suppress an involuntary cry. With her other hand, she dabbed at her eyes with a wadded-up tissue. "It's like he's not even in there anymore. I'm watching him disappear before my eyes. Every day there's less of him there."

Dr. Benson leaned forward slightly. "How do you mean?"

"It's like" – she hesitated, thought of how to say this – "a hermit crab. Like some awful creature found the empty shell of my beautiful, loving husband and crawled into it. And took over. It's like I don't even *know* him anymore."

***

Gary awakened with a jolt; his heart raced. That dream again! It seemed so… real! Drenched in sweat and semen, he cried out in alarm and struggled against his restraints.

Hearing the commotion, a nurse went to check on him. Entering the semi-darkened room, Allie approached the bed with caution as Gary fought to free himself. "Please don't do that," she said in a reassuring tone. "You don't want to hurt yourself. Please," she repeated, laying a hand on his tethered wrist as he let out a bellow of frustration.

Gary fought a moment longer. Then, conceding defeat, he abandoned his effort. Allie's voice soothed him. All he wanted to do was curl up and sleep, listening to her voice. That would be heaven, he decided.

She changed the sweat-soaked sheets, bathed Gary with a warm washcloth and helped him into fresh pajamas. Bidding him goodnight, she left the room.

Again and again, the nightmare tormented him. Afraid to go back to sleep, Gary lay awake in the dark, horrified by the twisted sexual images his brain had conjured.

The next morning, the day-shift nurse greeted Gary cheerfully when she brought his medication. Yesterday, he'd almost taken it; she'd gotten the pills in his mouth, but he spat them across the room.

Now, for the second day in a row, he refused his meds. She cajoled. He resisted, convinced they were causing his nightmares.

She finally got him to agree to take the three little pills. But he refused to drink his orange juice through a straw. With permission from the head nurse, she briefly undid one of the wrist restraints, so he could hold the juice cup.

Putting the pills in his mouth, he took a long, slow drink. He handed the cup back with a little juice still left. When urged to finish it, he insisted he'd had enough.

After her rounds, when Dawn emptied the cup into the sink, she noticed the residue at the bottom.

That night, Gary stayed up as late as he could, to stave off the nightmare. Almost as soon as he drifted off to sleep, it tormented him. Over and over. Each time, he awakened in a panic. And each time, he tried to stay awake afterward, so it wouldn't happen again.

Next night, the same thing. Gary willed himself to stay awake, but succumbed to sleep around 2:30 – only to be beset by the same nightmare.

By Monday, Gary was exhausted. So exhausted he didn't resist taking his medication. He even drank all his juice.

(8:47 p.m., February 23 – Monday)
Eager to get home after a long day, Dr. Lindemeyr stopped at Gary's room on impulse.

Approaching the bed, something about his expression made her ask, "Is everything okay?"

He looked away.

Marie tried again. "Gary?" She rested a hand on his shoulder. "What's the matter?"

Still no answer.

"Are you in pain?"

He shook his head.

"Are you uncomfortable? Do you need the nurse? Do you have to use the bathroom?"

To every question, he kept shaking his head, refusing to look at her.

"Do you want to talk with Dr. Benson?"

After yet another headshake, her patience was beginning to thin.

"Then *what?*" she asked a little too harshly. Immediately regretting it, Marie softened her tone. "I can't help you if you won't tell me what's wrong."

When Gary turned to look at her, the psychiatrist saw hopelessness and despair in his eyes.

"She thinks I'm nuts," he lamented.

Dr. Lindemeyr perched on her brother's bed. "Who?"

"Michaela. She thinks I'm crazy. That's why she had me locked up here."

"She doesn't think you're crazy, Gary; she knew you needed help." Marie laid a comforting hand on his shoulder. "There's nothing wrong with admitting you can't fix things yourself."

His expression told her he didn't quite believe her.

She reached out, stroked his hair. "Trust me, Gary. I wouldn't lie to you."

At her assurance, some of the anxiety left his face.

She studied him carefully. "Is something else bothering you?"

"Those," Gary muttered, nodding toward the restraints binding his wrists.

Marie shook her head. "I'm sorry. Since you won't cooperate, I can't have them removed. It's for your own safety." Her expression eased at the thought of Marc and the twins waiting at home. She stood. "It's been a long day. Why don't you try to get some rest?" She checked his chart, then added a notation. "Becky'll be right in with something to help you sleep."

At her words, Gary tensed.

An insistent wind tugged at his shirt; it whipped his hair into his eyes and churned the seawater into an angry froth. Turning in to the wind, Gary felt it buffeting his face. Still he walked.

The jetty's cement surface felt cool against his bare feet. It was nighttime; the sky was clear and filled with stars. Moonbeams spilled in front of him, lighting his way.

After what seemed like his longest-ever walk on the jetty, Gary reached the end of the seawall; waves crashed against the rocks at its base. Glancing back, he couldn't see the shore. He looked down at the water. It was high tide; moonlight glinted on the waves that surged far below.

Gary breathed deeply, taking in lungfuls of salt air. Holding his arms out from his sides, he tipped his head back to let the cool midnight air caress his face; he forced himself not to dwell on all he was leaving behind.

He looked back toward shore again; he saw a light in an upstairs bedroom in the beach house… and someone in the window, waving. Waving goodbye. The wind dried the single tear that slid down his cheek. Facing forward again, Gary stretched upward onto his toes, bounced for a moment on the balls of his feet… and plummeted headfirst over the edge.

An instant before his skull smashed against the rocks, Gary awakened with a start. Crying out in fright at the too-real nightmare, he jerked at his restraints, endeavoring to break free. At the realization he was lying secure in his hospital bed and not hurtling to a horrid death, he began to shake.

A moment later, his sobs bubbled to the surface. "I don't want to die," Gary cried aloud. "I don't want to die!"

Trembling, he tried to wrap his arms around himself. Comfort eluded him. His desperate cries rang through the otherwise-silent ward.

Lynnette switched on one small light and approached the bed. Bad dreams and tears weren't uncommon here, especially during a new patient's first few nights. "Shh. It's okay," the nurse soothed, clasping Gary's hand. She patted it with her other hand. "It was only a dream."

He tried to speak, but only blustery sobs came out. His only consolation was at least it was a different nightmare.

Offering a running stream of calming words, the night-shift nurse helped him sit up. She poured a cup of cool water and held it for Gary while he drank. Then she fluffed his pillows and eased him back against them. "There… try to rest now. There's nothing to be afraid of." Her words were as comforting as the hand stroking his brow. "Okay?"

His breathing slowed as the panicky feeling slipped away. He was still trembling, and his skin still felt hot, so Lynnette wiped his face with a cool washcloth. "There you go, hon… how's that?"

Gary drew in a ragged breath. "Better," he acknowledged with a nod. "Thank you."

"No more bad dreams, now," she told him gently, patting his shoulder. "Ya hear?"

✳✳✳

Gary clung to stubborn silence, despite Dr. Benson's most creative efforts.

"We can keep doing this, Gary, as long as you want to," the psychiatrist told him one afternoon, "but you won't get better until you start expressing your feelings and examining them."

Gary rolled his eyes. "Can't I just wait for the drugs to kick in?"

The doctor shook his fluffy hair. "That's not how therapy works. You've got to give voice to your emotions. Once you do, they cease to have power over you."

He slumped in his chair. "I doubt that."

"Trust me. By naming what's bothering you, you break its hold. *You* become the master, not some pack of out-of-control feelings."

(February 25 – Wednesday)
Gary slouched onto the hunter-green couch.

Dr. Benson settled into the matching wing chair and picked up his notepad.

Gary glanced around the office, then looked at Dr. Benson; he still didn't speak.

Neither did the psychiatrist; his clock's second hand made three trips around and started on a fourth.

Gary picked at his plastic ID bracelet. Fidgeted with his wedding ring. Scratched at his stubbled chin. Uncomfortable with the lingering silence, he spoke. "I hate this; I can't take any more."

"Can't take what, Gary?"

He raked his hands through his hair. "It's all so bleak… like this nightmare's never going to end."

"Which nightmare?"

Sitting forward, he rested his elbows on his knees; his head drooped into his hands. "My life. This isn't how it was supposed to turn out."

"How was it supposed to be?"

"Not like this, that's for sure!"

Dr. Benson was quiet for a moment. "Why do you presume any control over what happens to you? Fact is, we make our own choices and deal with the reality surrounding them."

While Gary stared at him, half a minute ticked away. His gesturing was nearly as feeble as his voice. "Do you have any idea of the shame I've brought on my family? My wife… my kids. My mom?"

"Why do you feel you've shamed them?"

"Don't you read the headlines, doc? Or watch the news?" Gary stood, paced.

Dr. Benson nodded. "Of course. And they say terrible things that aren't true all the time. You can't control how other people treat you, Gary. You can only control how you respond to them."

Gary's left eyebrow dipped slightly. It frequently did that when he was perplexed. "What?"

"These things happen. Newscasters air inaccurate stories; shock jocks rip people to shreds in the name of entertainment… and there'll no doubt be more lies told about you before this is all over."

"What do I do about that?"

"You can't do anything about these indignities, Gary. Just decide how you'll behave in light of them. You make dozens – no, *hundreds* – of decisions a day. Big and small ones. Which shirt goes with these pants… what to eat for breakfast… which route to take to avoid a traffic jam. It's all choices. You have to choose your path. No one else can do that for you."

Gary was silent, taking this in.

"You can choose to be driven underground by vicious comments, or ignore them. How you respond is up to you. The question is: What do you want?"

Gary's shoulders sagged. "I want to not be harangued by reporters camped outside my home. I want to not be torn apart in the media." Then he mumbled, "I just want my life back."

"So, take it back. I'm not saying it'll be easy, putting up with the media hype, the snide comments, whispers in the grocery store. But it's up to you how to respond. You can handle it with grace, or you can let it destroy you. The choice is yours, Gary."

Shifting in his seat, Gary squinted at the bookshelves across the room. He'd done it often enough the psychiatrist must certainly know he'd lost interest.

"Focus on what your body's telling you; how do you feel right now?"

Rubbing his throbbing temples, he shrugged off the question.

"Still having those headaches?"

"Some."

"Have they lessened since we tweaked your meds?"

Mention of the medication agitated Gary. His jaw tightened; his fists clenched.

"Is there a problem with the medication?"

He exhaled audibly.

"Gary? Is there a problem with your meds?"

"Yeah," he hissed. "I hate having to take that shit."

"We've talked about tha—"

"Yeah, and I'm sick of talking about it. That's all we ever do — talk-talk-talk-talk-talk. It doesn't do any good. Doesn't help. I don't want to talk anymore. I don't care."

"Don't care about what?"

Gary eyed the doctor with disdain, then let his head drop back into his hands. "Can't you shut up?" he implored wearily. "Just shut up. I'm so tired of your yammering."

"Fine. It's your session. We can do whatever you want."

"There you go again! Can't I just get a moment's peace? Geez!" He wiped his hands down his face, then looked at the therapist again, as if daring him to speak. "Before you say it — don't!"

Dr. Benson held up his hands in capitulation.

Gary glanced about the room. Seconds ticked by. Then a minute. Two minutes. He looked around again… at the shelves of books, low tables with groupings of odd little sculptures, a stodgy-looking floor lamp beside the therapist's chair.

Still the doctor said nothing, just watched Gary take stock of his surroundings.

Gary stared him down. "You think I'm a real asshole, don't you?" he challenged.

"Why do you say that?"

His eyes narrowed. "You think I'm a lousy little prick who should rot in jail for raping that girl."

The psychiatrist jotted something in his notepad. "Is that how you see yourself?"

That placid tone made Gary want to crash the lamp over Dr. Benson's head. "Fuck you!" he spat out, his hostility spilling over. "You self-righteous little fuckwad. Think you're so fucking perfect, so much better than me" – he sneered – "you make me sick!"

After a silent minute, the doctor straightened in his chair. "You never answered the question, Gary: Is that how you see yourself? Or… is it how you think others perceive you?"

"Fuck you!" Gary stalked to the door, trying to ignore the uncomfortable tightness in his chest. "I'm outta here."

"That's fine… if you want to continue avoiding your problems," the psychiatrist baited him.

He turned. A scowl darkened his face. "What did you say?" he challenged.

"I said go ahead and leave. Keep running away from your problems instead of facing them."

"How dare you! You don't have the slightest idea how I—" he sputtered. His hand slipped away from the door-knob. "You got some nerve, doc, accusing me of avoidance. I've dealt with shit that'd make you crawl under that chair and whimper like a little girl!"

Despite Gary's shouting, the psychiatrist's voice remained gentle. "I'm sure you have, Gary. Why don't you come on back and sit down," he invited. "Then we can talk some more… about whatever it is you want to discuss."

Gary didn't move.

Dr. Benson motioned toward the couch. "C'mon. Come sit down."

Gary's fury ebbed; the tightness in his chest eased. He returned to the couch and drooped onto it.

The therapist watched in patient stillness.

Gary took a deep breath… then another. Before he knew what was happening, he'd started crying. His breath came harsh and ragged; his shoulders shook with silent sobs.

The scratch of Dr. Benson's pen was the only sound in the room. He glanced at his watch, glad he'd scheduled an extended session for Gary this morning. Dr. Benson looked up when he heard a sob.

Gary's skin was pallid. The expression on his face begged for comfort, for help. "I can't stand it," he whispered. "I just can't…"

Dr. Benson planted his feet on the floor and sat forward; he rested his elbows on the arms of his chair. "Can't stand what, Gary?"

He spoke slowly, struggling for composure with each breath, each word. "I can't bear that – for the rest of my life – people will see me as some kind of pervert… a sexual predator… a – a – a criminal."

"That's certainly a disturbing notion," the doctor conceded. "But Gary, let's try to break this down and look at it one bit at a time, okay?"

"How?" Something akin to fear surfaced in his watery eyes.

"The other day, Gary… What were the two things we decided it didn't make sense to stress over?"

Gary rubbed away tears. "The past… and stuff that might never happen."

The therapist nodded, a slight smile hitching the corners of his mouth upward. "Why?"

He sniffled. " 'Cause there's nothing I can do about either of 'em."

"Exactly," Dr. Benson replied. "Let's take that one step further: Even if people *do* think badly of you, Gary, does that change who you really are?"

"I guess not. But I'm a public figure – and my image and reputation are such a big part of who I am… And it's so demoralizing!"

Dr. Benson was silent for several seconds. "I can understand that. Now, let's look at the next piece: You said you were concerned this is how people would see you 'for the rest of my life.' Would it really be the rest of your life, Gary? Realistically?"

He shrugged. "Wouldn't it?"

The psychiatrist leaned forward. "In my experience, people easily forget what they're up in arms about. There's bound to be a handful of people who'll dog you; but by and large, within six months' time, most of them will be buzzing about the latest Hollywood scandal."

Gary looked minimally reassured.

"Besides, no one said you have to stay put. It's a wide world, a free country. You could move out of state; pack up your family and go. You've got options, Gary."

"You call running away an option? No way, doc. I'm not running" – he gave the doctor a defiant glare – "That'd make it look like I've got something to be ashamed of."

"And you don't."

"Of course not." He sounded exhausted.

The doctor let the silence stretch out before giving Gary something to ponder. "You say running away isn't an option. Wouldn't killing yourself have been the ultimate act of running away?"

Gary rubbed his temples. After a brief silence, he looked up at the therapist. "That was almost a week ago," he acknowledged.

"Yes, it was," the doctor agreed. "What's changed?"

"I dunno… guess I'm thinking clearly now."

"I'll buy that." He glanced at the clock on his bookshelf. "Our time's up for this morning, but I want you to think some more about coping skills and ways to put the whole 'deciding to deal with this' into action. Maybe next time we can explore some of the other issues weighing on you."

By Thursday, the local news media had caught wind of Gary's hospitalization, and the morning-drive jocks were merciless. One station was asking listeners to call in with their favorite "Crazy" songs; another morning team played snippets of the Napoleon XIV novelty song, "They're Coming to Take Me Away, Ha-Haaa," and Donnie Iris' "Shock Treatment," interspersed with slickly produced audio of Blake Tierney at the pre-trial hearings telling reporters, "No comment. We have no comment"; and a Foxbridge spokesman saying, "We can neither confirm nor deny."

The door slammed.

"Hey Stef," Brenda hailed the usually cheerful midday announcer. "What's the matter?"

The feisty strawberry blonde scowled. "Have you heard what they're saying about Gary?"

Before Brenda could reply, Steffi stomped off toward the DJ prep room, muttering.

"Five minutes past ten on Z97-3. I'm Steffi Kinkead and I've had enough of those morning-show boneheads at those other stations – not that anyone should ever *listen* to 'em; but the things they've been saying about our own Gary Sheldon – they're getting out of hand. It's just… well, it's ludicrous, is what it is!" she fumed. "In solidarity, it's time to play this, from Billy Joel: 'An Innocent Man.' Z97-3."

Three minutes later, Pete stood at the door, his expression grimmer than Steffi had ever seen it. In one hand was a set of headphones; in the other, a sheet of paper. Stepping inside, he shut the door.

"Sorry, Stef," the program director began. "I'm gonna have to ask you to pack up your things."

The midday announcer's eyes widened. "Are you firing me?"

"I'm afraid so." The program director held out the paper with Steffi's signature at the bottom. "Remember this?"

It was the form they'd signed the day Gary was arrested.

Steffi mounted the only defense she would offer. "I could see if I'd said something negative. But, Pete – I was sticking up for him."

"I know. And I agree with every word you said. But Tom makes the rules. I just see to it they get enforced."

Steffi stared at him.

"I'm no happier about this than you are. In fact, this is the part of my job I hate."

Without further protest, she unplugged her headphones and picked up the stack of 'topical tidbits' she'd planned to use. About to sweep the lot into the trash barrel, she handed Pete the clippings. "Help yourself. I doubt you've had a chance to do any show prep."

"Thanks." He gestured in futility. "I'm sorry, Steffi." He plugged in his headphones, then paused for a long, awkward moment. "Feel free to use me as a reference, okay?"

Steffi nodded. Angry tears filled her eyes; she turned away.

Pete settled his headphones over his ears and pulled the mic close. "Ten minutes past ten, Z97-3. Good morning, I'm Pete Donovan along with you this Thursday morning; thanks for joining me. That was Billy Joel, 'An Innocent Man,' going back to eighty-three, title track from that album. Coming up this hour, we'll hear from Elton John, Sugar Ray and Smashmouth. And we'll take a look at your morning forecast in about 'One Week' – here's the Barenaked Ladies on Z97-3."

After helping Steffi collect her things, Pete walked her down the hall to Tom's office. Long faces prevailed as she was issued her final paycheck and escorted out.

When the staff learned of her termination, the atmosphere in the station turned as dismal as if there'd been a death in the family.

That could've been me… ran through each of the announcers' minds.

Late that afternoon, Tom met with Pete about the on-air lineup. For sake of continuity, he didn't want to move Marc or Rob to middays. "I hate to take you away from programming, Pete," Tom told his program director, "but I don't have much of a choice."

Pete nodded his understanding. With any luck, it would only be for a few months.

***

Within a few days, Gary had become more cooperative about taking his meds and participating in therapy, and Dr. Benson felt comfortable enough with his progress to allow the nurses to remove his restraints.

Moreover, Gary's nightmares had subsided and he acknowledged the drugs weren't to blame.

Friday night, almost giddy with the freedom to sleep in whatever position he wished, he went to bed before eight. He fluffed his own pillows and punched them into just the right shape. Within minutes of being wished a pleasant night's sleep by one of the second-shift nurses, he was on his way to making that wish reality.

When Marie stopped in just before nine, her brother was already deep into a REM cycle.

Saturday morning, Gary awakened refreshed – and with a smidgen of hope. Maybe he'd gotten past those nightmares; perhaps now he could sleep.

That night he went to bed at nine, reveling in the prospect of a second night's undisturbed sleep. The respite hardly seemed worth it, as the nightmare returned Sunday. Gary considered mentioning it in therapy the next morning. After all, this shrink was supposed to be picking him apart and rearranging his brain; he might as well give the guy a challenge.

He didn't mention it. And the dream continued to torment him.

(March 3 – Wednesday)
"Good morning, Mr. Sheldon," Dina chirped, bustling into the room.

Gary wanted to clobber her with his breakfast tray. He eyed her silently, clutching at the blankets drawn up to his chin. He gripped them so fiercely it sent a twinge through the tendon in his elbow. He winced but did not let go.

"How are you feeling this morning?"

He ignored the perky day-shift nurse, focusing instead on a spot high up on the wall, above and to the left of the crayon pictures Amanda and Michael had colored for him.

No matter; she kept up a running stream of chatter as she drew back the curtains to let in the sunlight. She told him what the weather was like, how cold it had gotten overnight and how much snow the weatherman was predicting for the rest of the week.

Still he declined to answer.

Dina brought his morning meds. With cranberry juice. His wife said he preferred it to orange or apple. And she knew the little things sometimes made all the difference.

As she approached, Gary turned away.

It was shaping up to be another difficult morning of refused medication. Perhaps she could persuade him without resorting to paging the doctor. Dina hated to do that. Besides, she figured Dr. Benson had bigger concerns than monitoring patients' med schedules. She tried a gentle approach. "If you take them, you'll feel better and you can go home that much sooner. You want that, don't you?"

Suddenly, he couldn't see the point in fighting. Worn out from trying to stave off his recurrent nightmare, every bit of opposition drained away. Gary accepted the three little pills Dina poured into his cupped palm. Docile now, he swallowed his meds and let her take away the empty plastic cup.

"When we stopped last time, we'd just touched on your internalized anger. Can you tell me some more about that?" Dr. Benson prompted.

In an unaccustomed spirit of receptiveness, Gary asked, "What do you want to know?"

"What's it like, trying to hold in all that anger?"

He released his breath in a weary sigh. His eyes flickered. "Like trying to hold a beach ball under water." The steel bands loosened; he took a deep breath. "The more force I use to press down against it, to keep it hidden, the more it wants to surface… and the harder it is to keep down."

"That's an excellent way to describe it. But why do you want to keep your anger in?"

He looked away. "I can't talk about that right now."

It was a reply the therapist had taught Gary to give in lieu of stony silence. It at least gave him an inkling Gary had heard – and understood – the question. "Why not?"

The familiar tightness in his chest resumed. "I don't wanna talk anymore."

"Not at all? We just started."

"We can discuss the weather if you want. I hear it's gonna snow."

"But your anger's off limits?"

He nodded.

"Why?"

Gary's brow furrowed; his fists clenched. "I don't want to talk about it."

"Whatever's bothering you, it might help if you opened up a—"

An image from last night's dream flashed in his head. "I said I don't want to talk about it."

"Gary, we're making real progress; don't sabotage it. I realize it's frightening, getting so close to the pain… but there's no other way. The only way through is through."

"That doesn't make any sense."

"Sure it does. Let's go back to your beach-ball analogy. You're in the middle of the ocean with that ball. You've been at it all day, keeping it under. Now it's getting dark – and you're tired. You can't tread water all night. You've got to get back to shore… but how?"

He waited for Dr. Benson to continue. When he didn't, Gary shrugged. "Guess I gotta swim."

"Precisely. You've got to swim. There's no other way. You can't say, 'I'll just float here a while,' because the sharks'll get you. So you swim. It's hard, because you've still got that beach ball to stuff down. It's sapping all your strength. You can't get to shore if you're focused on that ball."

He started to bounce one foot; shifting in his seat and crossing his legs, Gary folded his arms over his chest. Through it all, he watched Dr. Benson in silence.

"And somewhere along the line, it happens: You realize it's more important to reach the shore than to keep that ball submerged." Dr. Benson paused. "Let go of the anger, Gary, and swim to shore. Trust me. It's time to swim."

(March 6 – Friday)
"How are the kids?"

"They're fine. They send their love, and hugs and kisses." Michaela glanced around the cheery solarium. "Look: I think that plant's about to bloom." She feigned interest in the swollen buds on the shiny-leafed exotic plant near where they sat. "What kind of flower is that?"

"I dunno," Gary mumbled, disinterested. "Who cares?"

She patted his hand, then charged ahead with a story about something she knew he didn't care a whit about… and neither did she.

Each week, she did her best to present a positive image. She didn't want Gary having to focus on anything other than getting well and coming home. Not the mortgage payment; not the funny noise her car was making. Nothing. So, whenever he asked about the kids, her answer was always the same. Then she'd change the subject.

How could she tell him Erin had suddenly turned sullen and aloof? Except when anybody mentioned Daddy. Then she became volatile. That started a few days after her dad's hospitalization. One day she was concerned about his well being; the next, it was as if she believed he was Satan himself. She didn't want to hear about him, didn't want to talk about him, even refused to include him in her nightly prayers.

While Erin's disturbing behavior baffled her, Micki was determined to figure out what was wrong – without having to worry Gary.

She'd tried repeatedly to talk to the girl, but Erin shut her out every time.

"And don't try your counseling crap on me, either," Erin had warned earlier that week, before slamming her bedroom door. "Just leave me the hell alone!"

(10:57 p.m. March 8 – Sunday)
Gary was playing poker with Steven Tyler, Ann Landers, St. Joseph and God. Ann had six tall piles of chips in front of her. No one else had more than four tiny stacks. Gary had seven chips left.

The singer elbowed him. "I think God's letting her win." He rasped out a laugh. "I hear He's got a soft spot for good advice."

St. Joseph chuckled good naturedly. "I thought I had a pretty good in with Him… guess not." He tossed in his cards. "I fold."

"Well, if he's screwed, then you know I'm pretty well doomed myself," Steven conceded.

Gary looked at Steven's hand: three aces – all with little Aerosmith-logo wings instead of suits. "I guess the Big Guy's a fan," he mused.

"Nah. These ain't real." Steven tapped the cards in his hand; they shimmered and disappeared. In their place were the two of hearts, three of spades and seven of clubs. "See? Just a little trick He likes to play on me sometimes."

Gary's smirk was rueful. "Yeah, I'm learning all about His tricks."

St. Joseph fired a warning look at him.

God eyed Gary but said nothing.

"Thought I had it pretty good… then He went and tossed a big ol' monkey wrench into my life," Gary muttered.

Ann Landers reached down and picked up the biggest hand tool Gary had ever seen. It had to be four feet long. He wondered how she'd lifted it one handed. "You mean this one?" She tossed it onto the table. It landed with a crash, toppling her neatly stacked chips.

With a hesitant glance at God, Gary nodded. "Y-yeah… that's the one."

"That's a hell of a tool," Steven observed with a filthy laugh. "Man, wish I had a tool like that."

"You do," Ann replied. And when he stared at her in shock, she quipped, "What? You think just 'cause I'm an old lady I don't notice these things?"

She turned back to Gary, snapping her gum. "So, as I was sayin', dearie: Use the tools God gives you. And if he gives you a monkey wrench, well… go find a monkey to loosen with it." She paused, reconsidered. "Or tighten."

St. Joseph scratched his head. He leaned over and nudged Aerosmith's lead singer. "Hey, buddy! That make any sense?"

Steven leapt onto the table. "Weeeeell, babyyyyy, that makes no sense to meeeee," he wailed.

"Oh, get off the table, Stevie; you're messing up my chips," Ann chided.

"Sorry." He climbed off the table and sat back down. "And don't call me Stevie," he grumbled.

Meanwhile, God was still watching Gary.

Gary looked back at Him. "What?"

Steven gave Gary a poke. "Uh oh… looks like you're in trouble now, kiddo."

"Monkey wrenches are so subjective."

For an instant, Gary didn't know where the voice had come from. "E-excuse me?"

"It was meant to be an opportunity. I'm sorry you didn't see it for what it was. But that doesn't make it any less a gift. But I'll tell you what I'm gonna do" – God laid down his cards: four aces and the two of spades – "since I'm so fond of you, I'll give you a chance to redeem yourself for that 'monkey wrench' crack. Fair enough?"

"Y-yeah, sure thing, chief," Gary stammered, hardly believing he'd spoken so casually to the Supreme Deity. "What do I have to do?"

"Just this," God said. "Honor Me with faithfulness, and I will bless you twofold."

Steven snickered behind his cards. "Twofold. Other guys get a hundredfold, even tenfold. You get twofold. Good luck with that one, sucker."

St. Joseph took off his Mets cap and whapped the singer in the head with it. "I thought I told you to put a sock in it."

"You never said anything of the sort."

"Well, I'm tellin' you now: Shut up."

"Hey, listen you… if you're not careful, I'm gonna bury you upside down in my neighbors' lawn and sell the place."

"That doesn't actually work," Ann piped up. "It's a story cooked up by some real-estate agent. Probably ran a religious-goods shop and had too many St. Joseph statues in stock."

Distracted by their chatter, Gary turned back to God. "Wh-what was that again?"

God's voice sounded to Gary like a rumble of distant thunder. "Honor Me with faithfulness, and I will bless you twofold."

Slowly Gary took it in. Suddenly he was sitting in a tiny chair – like one of the first-graders' seats in his CCD class-room – and God was enormous and far away. The others had receded into the shadows, as if they'd been images on an old TV screen that had just been shut off.

"God?" His voice echoed in the cavernous room. "Are you still there?"

No answer. Gary felt empty and chilled, like his insides were made up of bitter winter winds that whipped through him, howling in forsaken pain.

"God?" he heard himself scream, panicked. "Where are you?"

A familiar warmth filled the lonely space; birds sang again and it felt and smelled like springtime after a rain shower.

"I'm right here."

"Where'd you go?" He sounded as frightened as a small child left alone in a department store.

"I stepped out for a second. I wanted you to know firsthand how it feels to be apart from Me. Doesn't feel so good, does it, Gary?"

God's use of his name chilled Gary. But of course He'd know his name. Of course He would. "No," he admitted, shaking his head, shivering at the memory of it. "No… It felt awful."

Tears filled Gary's eyes; God dried them with a tuft of cloud. "I will never leave you again," He promised. His hug felt like being wrapped in the world's coziest blanket. "No matter what."

(10 a.m., March 9 – Monday)
Dr. Benson welcomed Gary. He didn't say anything about Gary's missing their last two sessions.

"I had a really fucked-up dream last night."

"Oh?" The psychiatrist sat forward. "Tell me about it."

Gary described the dream in detail – right down to the color of Ann Landers' dress.

"Interesting," Dr. Benson said when Gary finished. "What do you think it means… for you?"

"Well, the last part's pretty obvious. I mean, from a faith standpoint. But the first part of it's got me a little confused. I mean, why would I be playing poker with St. Joseph, Steven Tyler and God?"

"Why indeed?"

Gary hated when he said that. He gritted his teeth but said nothing.

"What do you think it means?" the psychiatrist asked, gesturing toward him.

He thought for a long time. "Well… I've depicted myself betting – with my life, apparently – and down to my last few chips. That can't be good. Yet I've surrounded myself with things I take comfort in on different levels: my favorite saint, my favorite singer, my faith."

Dr. Benson shrugged. "But why Ann Landers? Where's she fit into your dream?"

"Someone's got to give me advice I'm gonna listen to… right?"

"I suppose. And it's not going to be me, is it?"

Gary smiled at the therapist's teasing. "Guess not."

In the silence that followed, he wondered whether to mention that other dream… the recurrent sexual one that had disturbed him so terribly. Before he could decide, the therapist spoke.

"When we left off last time, we'd been discussing your anger; but you didn't want to talk about it." He flipped back a page in Gary's file; the nurse noted he'd been docile – even amiable – about taking his meds this morning. "What do you suppose is causing all that anger?"

Gary's shrug was automatic. But then he gave the query some thought. "Knowing I've got no control… over anything."

Dr. Benson gave a pensive "Hmm" and nodded. "So you thought you'd take back control by determining how and when your life would end?"

Another shrug. That sounded about right. "I guess."

"Hell of a way to get back control, don't you think?" When Gary didn't reply, the psychiatrist tried a different approach. "You told me at our first session you were angry with your wife. Why?"

"She wouldn't let me—" he broke off.

The doctor's pen paused an inch over his notebook. His head tilted. "Wouldn't let you what?"

Gary eyed Dr. Benson. Shook his head. Remained silent.

"I need you to say it, Gary," he prompted. "Wouldn't let you what?"

The two words hurt like hell. "Kill myself."

"I see. Why do you suppose she wouldn't let you do a thing like that?"

Gary spoke as though addressing an idiot. "Because she doesn't understand."

"Do you doubt her intelligence?"

"Not understanding something doesn't make you stupid. It means you don't understand."

"Why do you feel she doesn't understand?"

"I dunno."

The therapist's calmness unnerved him. "Why do you *really* think she stopped you?"

Gary's tone was steeped in self-pity. "Because she's a fucking sadist; she wanted to see me suffer."

"I don't think you believe *that*, either. Why wouldn't Michaela let you kill yourself?"

"Beca—" his voice caught in his throat. "Because she—" he stopped.

Dr. Benson nodded his encouragement. "Go on, Gary… you can say it."

"Because she loves me?"

"What do you think?"

He nodded.

"How does that make you feel?"

Gary scrunched into a tight little ball on the couch. Arms around knees; chin to chest. "Worthless – no… *Unworthy.*"

The psychiatrist waited for him to go on.

"And guilty."

"Those are two extremely powerful feelings. Either one alone would be painful, but both? What do you do with all that pain?"

His voice wavered. "I dunno." His head was down, his eyes brimming with tears.

Dr. Benson pressed further. "How do you deal with the pain? It's got to be excruciating, all that hurt. All that guilt… that overwhelming sense of shame. How do you live with it?"

"I didn't *want* to live with it!" Tears poured in a torrent down Gary's face. "I never meant to live with it. It was supposed to be over! Don't you get it? I wanted it all to be over…" His face contorted in anguish; he drew a huge, gasping breath.

"That's why I ignored the voice. Don't you see? I had to: I didn't deserve for her to love me as much as she does. I'm not good enough—" his breath came in short gasps. "I'm not worthy of her – never have been…" His words trailed to whimpers, punctuated by sniffles.

"You mentioned the voice again," Dr. Benson pressed,

his tone as comforting as flannel sheets on a February night. "That was your grandfather's voice you heard, yes?"

Gary nodded as he tried to compose himself.

"What about your grandfather's voice?"

"What about it?" he replied testily.

"He was always the voice of reason for you. What made you turn your back on him this time?"

Gary wiped stray tears from his eyes. He shook his head. "It's just a stupid voice."

"Is it? You've described him as your 'guide through troubling times.' Do you remember that?"

"Yeah – while he was alive!"

"What about now? Is he any less real to you now?"

Anger flickered in Gary's eyes; his voice rose to a shout. "He's dead! And so should I have been!"

"Do you honestly believe that?"

He turned away, ashamed and crying.

Dr. Benson waited. The room was quiet except for Gary's wrenching sobs.

Grinding away tears with his fists, he spoke. "I didn't want to die; I just wanted the pain to stop."

"Can you tell me about that?"

Gary shook his head.

"Why not, Gary?" Dr. Benson coaxed. "Why can't you tell me about it?"

"It hurts."

"Sometimes therapy hurts," he acknowledged, "but that doesn't mean it isn't helping. Whatever's inside – whatever pain or anger or guilt you're hanging onto – it's got to come out before any real healing can happen."

Gary quieted just enough to listen to the psychiatrist's calming voice.

"It's time to let go of that beach ball and swim. You're so close! I know it hurts, Gary, but don't stop now. Don't let the pain win. Once you release it, it'll be better."

Wiping away a flood of tears, Gary eyed Dr. Benson, wanting to believe him – aching to take the next step – but desperately afraid. "I… I can't," he murmured, drawing his knees in to his chest and clutching his arms around them.

The doctor's words cut through his haze of fear and insecurity. "You can, Gary."

"I'm afraid."

"It's okay to be afraid. All you have to do is take that first step and confront the pain."

His confident tone reassured Gary, made him want to do this. Steeling himself against the pain, he summoned his courage and met the therapist's gaze. "Alright. What do I have to do?"

Dr. Benson offered an encouraging smile. "You just need to say what you truly feel. Out loud."

Gary wanted to shut out the directive, wanted that more than anything right now. But he didn't. The steel bands surrounded his heart again. Squeezing. Squeezing. Ignoring them, he spoke as evenly as he could. "I feel like I don't have any say in what's going on in my life."

"Okay." Dr. Benson nodded. "Stay with that a minute. How does that make you feel?"

He was silent for a moment. "Helpless."

"Why?"

"Everything's happening *to* me. Like I'm a marionette or something. Someone pulls this string and I do this; another string and I do something else. I don't have any control. Over anything. First it was the police. Then my pastor. Then the courts. Everyone else is running my life. Everyone but *me*."

"How does that make you feel?"

His breath came rapid and shallow. "Trapped. Like a skunk in a garbage can. Like there's no way out."

"What was the one way you thought you could regain control?"

Fighting for composure, Gary took several ragged breaths. "Killing myself," came out in a whisper ahead of a sob.

"Why?"

"I was gonna be convicted of something I didn't do!"

"What made you so sure you'd be convicted?"

"That prosecutor – she's relentless. She wins all the time! And what kind of chance did I have?"

"What chance indeed?"

Gary glared at the therapist, instantly defensive. "What's that supposed to mean?"

"It means, I can't believe you were just going to roll over and – quite literally – die."

"What else was I going to do?"

Dr. Benson gave a slight shrug. "Oh, I don't know. You could have tried what your grandfather suggested: fight."

"Yeah – and what if I lost anyway?"

"Suppose you did. What's the worst that could happen?"

"I'd spend the next twenty-five years in prison."

"Okay, that *is* pretty grim," he acquiesced. "But you figured killing yourself was a better option?"

A tear trickled down his cheek. "At the time? Yeah."

"Why?"

"I told you – it was hopeless!" Gary's head sagged. "*I was hopeless,*" he whispered.

"What got in your way?"

"That damn voice."

"Your grandfather."

His fists clenched. "It was a *voice!*"

"Okay, a voice," Dr. Benson placated Gary. "But the voice of someone you loved dearly – and trusted."

No reply.

"Gary?" he prompted. "What's going on in there?"

When he finally spoke, the therapist had to strain to hear him. "I feel guilty, alright?"

"About what?"

"Trying to deny he still mattered to me."

He jotted something in his notepad. "Go on. Why do you feel guilty about that?"

"All my life, Grandpa was the voice of reason. And compassion. I could always count on him. And trust him."

"I see. So why deny him now?"

"I had to convince myself he wasn't real – so I could take back some control over my life… if only long enough to kill myself. Does that make sense?"

Dr. Benson nodded. "Mm-hmm. Tell me more."

"He was trying to talk me out of it, and I kept arguing. But he kept making sense. So I had to shut him out – deny he was there – so I could go ahead and off myself."

Dr. Benson tilted his head. "This is important. What would make you deny what you've known – all your life – to be true?"

"Fear?" he guessed. "Fear that he didn't exist… and I really was crazy?"

"Possibly. What else?"

"I don't *know!*" Gary slammed a fist against his leg in frustration.

"I think you do," the doctor replied calmly. "What else, Gary? What would make you deny a truth you've held your whole life?"

A notion popped into Gary's head. It made no sense, but he said it. "Anger? Anger because he wasn't there to rescue me?"

"Go on."

"I wanted him to stop me. But none of his arguments for living was convincing enough… so I – I guess I had to test him."

"Interesting. You say you 'had to test him.' Let's go back to your poker dream. Might you actually have been testing your faith?"

That question stopped Gary cold. He stared at the doctor, blinked, and then stared some more.

"Wasn't that what you were doing at the poker game?"

"You mean, testing God?"

"Calling his bluff; challenging Him. People do that when they're in crisis. They see no way out, so they challenge God to get them out of it. Except, you called on God in a more familiar form."

"My grandfather?" Things were starting to make sense.

"Isn't it plausible? And when he couldn't stop you, Michaela did. Someone else you love. So there you were, all set to kill yourself… and she foiled your plans. How did *that* make you feel?"

Gary's jaw stiffened. "Angry."

"Just angry?"

He couldn't feel his lips move. "And guilty."

"Ah, the terrible twosome. Anger and guilt. Why?"

This one was a toughie. The answer hurt. But he said it anyway. "Because I was being selfish. I wanted out. I'd turned my back on the people who love me most… my wife and kids. My kids would grow up believing their dad abandoned them…" *Just like I believed I'd been abandoned.*

Gary realized the enormity of what he'd done. As the truth sank in, he doubled over in anguish; his tears started again in earnest. He struggled to speak through them. "It's like I was saying, 'Screw you; I don't need you, don't need your love. You don't mean that much to me. I can get along without you.' " He shuddered, recalling the brief but terrible emptiness from his dream last night. Blinding pain shot from his midsection, radiating through his body. "Oh God!" he cried aloud.

In agony, he crumpled to the floor. Drooping against the couch, he thumped its cushions with a fist. He gasped for air, unable to speak. His sobs were coming too hard and too fast.

Look at you… crying. You're not a man. You're a pathetic little crybaby! What's the matter with you?! The voice taunted Gary as his pain intensified.

It didn't sound like Grandpa. And, surprisingly, it wasn't Dad, either.

You're nothing but a coward. A miserable, selfish coward.

That voice! Of course he recognized it. How could he not? It was his own!

You're nothing of the sort, Gary. Don't you pay any attention to that voice, Grandpa's calm voice countered.

Gary sobbed harder, convinced he truly was losing his mind. Scrunching into a ball, he rocked back and forth.

Listen to me, Gary. Tears do not equal weakness. Fear does not make you a coward. And just because someone says something about you does not make it so — even if you're the one saying it.

Drawing several ragged breaths, Gary tried to calm himself. He stopped rocking, and listened to the voice that had always offered solace.

You've experienced a huge amount of stress these past few weeks; even so, Gary, you aren't crazy. The next few weeks will be even more stressful, but you've got the fortitude to get through them. Just remember, your faith and your family will sustain you through even the most difficult trials... if only you trust in them.

Chapter 19

High tide. The wind howled, tossing Gary's hair into his eyes as he stepped onto the jetty. Rain pelted his face like spitballs. He winced, continuing to walk into the midnight storm. At last he reached the end of the seawall. He couldn't see the waves crashing on the craggy rocks below; but he heard them. The wind whipped through his hair and rain-soaked clothes. He wished he'd worn something warm.

Behind him came footsteps. Not just one set. Two. Slow and steady. Like a gentle heartbeat.

"See? I told you we'd find him out here."

That voice! Gary turned. There in the dark, on the seawall, stood Grandpa Sheldon. Beside him was Grandma Jo! His heart launched into frantic overdrive.

The short, grey-haired woman spoke. "Here, put this on, love. Don't want you to catch cold."

Tears filled Gary's eyes as he accepted the sweater she offered. Slipping it over his head, he felt an immediate warmth.

He also noticed the rain had stopped. At least where they stood. All around them, it was still pouring. Gary wondered why.

"Love is a powerful force, my boy," Edward Sheldon said, patting his grandson on the shoulder. "The most powerful force there is; more powerful than hate, or fear... or lies. It wraps you up – nice and warm – like that cozy sweater, and it keeps you safe."

Gary listened to the comforting resonance of his granddad's voice.

"No matter what goes on around you, Gary, where there's love, there's protection. And with that protection, you can get through anything." Edward drew his grandson into a strong hug. "Anything."

For the longest time, Gary said nothing, just delighted in the comfort of his granddad's embrace. It was thirteen years since he'd felt one of Grandpa's hugs.

When the old man released him, Gary looked at Grandma Jo. She didn't look a day older than he remembered her. Tears of shame filled his eyes as he recalled his vicious final words to her.

Somehow, she knew what he was thinking. "Don't cry, sweetheart," she consoled him. "You're not still feeling guilty over that, are you?"

Her hug triggered his breakdown. When he nodded against her shoulder, weeping, she patted his back like she used to when he was a small child in need of comfort.

"That was so long ago, precious," Grandma Jo cooed. "A child's angry words. I know you didn't mean it. I know how sorry you are… and I know how much you love me. I always knew."

"You did?"

Josephine smiled. "Of course." Regarding her grandson closely, she caressed his cheek. "You've been afraid to let me into your dreams all this time because of *that*?" she chided lovingly.

He realized she was right. Ashamed, Gary nodded.

"Silly goose." She tweaked his nose. "Don't you give it another thought, okay?"

He nodded, a little uneasy.

"Guess you need to say it anyway, huh?" Grandma Jo surmised. "Well, go ahead, then."

"I love you, Gamma Jo," he said, addressing her the way he had as a child. "I'm sorry I ever said I hated you – and I'm sorry I never got to tell you that… or to say goodbye."

Reaching up, she kissed his cheek loudly. "I forgive you, Gary. And there'll never be a need to say goodbye – not as long as you have memories, and dreams." She wrapped him in another hug. "You're *still* the apple of my eye." He felt all warm, like the insides of the marshmallows they would toast in the fire pit. "Look at you – all grown up. With children of your own. I remember the day you were born."

Her eyes shone with a brightness Gary had never seen.

"It was a snowy, snowy day. We were minding your sister," she recalled. "Marie kept saying she couldn't wait for the baby to come home – because she 'wanted to name it.'"

"*It?* What did she want to name it?"

"Huckleberry. She insisted your mom and dad name it Huckleberry."

He heard his granddad chuckling softly.

"I'm glad she didn't get her wish. I'da been beaten up on the playground every day."

Grandma Jo smiled. "I remember the first time I held you. My first grandson. Your mama placed you in my arms and said, 'Marie will be furious, but we decided not to call him Huckleberry. Mom, this is Gary.' You were sweet and perfect" – she held her arms in front of her as if holding an infant and gazed down, entranced – "and so alert! You looked up at me with those huge round eyes, those beautiful grey eyes… and I was hooked."

Gary felt content, as if he were right then being cradled in her arms. He realized the rain had changed. Instead of drops of water, tiny red hearts – like red-hot candies – accumulated along the surface of the jetty in fragrant cinnamon puddles.

"So, you see, Gary… time and distance can't change love. I still love you every bit as much as I did that first instant I laid eyes on you."

"That's right, Gary." This was Grandpa. He bent down, scooped up a handful of the fallen hearts and poured a drizzle of them into his grandson's open palm. "We're still here and we want you to know how much we love you."

Grandma Jo stroked his cheek. "Just because you don't see us, doesn't mean we're not still right here with you." Her caress was tender, comforting.

"C'mon, let's walk," Edward suggested. He took his wife's hand, slipped his other arm around his grandson's shoulder and headed back toward the cottage.

"It's so good to see you guys again," Gary told them as they neared the shore end of the jetty. "I've missed you so much."

Grandpa's merry blue eyes twinkled. "Well, my boy" – he thumped Gary's shoulder affectionately – "maybe you should spend more time at target practice; then you won't miss us anymore."

Grandpa's deep, hearty chortle overshadowed Grandma Jo's gentle twitter. Gary grinned; he surmised his granddad didn't want their time together to turn maudlin.

He stopped walking. Glancing backward, he saw only his footprints amid millions of red hearts scattered along the wet sand.

Gary scanned the darkened room. No wind, no rain. No millions of tiny red hearts. No Grandma Jo or Grandpa, either; but he detected a faint hint of cinnamon. They'd been here.

With a contented sigh, he drew the covers up and settled back to sleep.

Next morning, Gary woke up happy. Happy. He couldn't recall feeling just plain happy in ages! When the nurse came in, he was already up and dressed, committing his dream to the crisp pages of the journal Dr. Benson had provided. He met the nurse with a cheery, "Good morning, Elise."

His smile and blithe greeting alerted her something was different; but when Gary asked for his medication, she knew he must have had some kind of breakthrough.

He was smiling when he arrived for his 10 a.m. session. "Hi, doc," he greeted the psychiatrist and sank into a corner of the green couch, journal in hand.

Dr. Benson checked the most recent sheet in Gary's file, opened to a clean page in his notepad and scribbled a quick notation. "Looks like *your* day started off well. It's good to see you smiling."

Gary nodded in assent. "It feels pretty good to be able to smile again."

"*Pretty* good?"

"Alright, it feels awesome!"

Dr. Benson smiled. "That's better. To what do we owe this terrific mood?"

He slid off his shoes, folded his legs beneath him and opened his journal. "I had this dream…" Briefly, he described the poignant reunion with his grandmother, then spoke at greater length about the dream's reassuring, albeit surreal, nature.

The psychiatrist listened as Gary related the details, his expressive voice unfettered by either anger or tears.

"So… whaddaya think, doc?" His eyes were bright, his manner animated; he'd shifted position and now sat cross-legged on the couch, leaning forward slightly.

"I think it's interesting; but I'd like to know what *you* think," he said. "What do you make of it?"

Gary sat back. "I think it's a good sign. I mean, I have no delusions this trial's gonna go away and everything's gonna be rosy the rest of my life; but I *do* think, no matter what happens… I guess it means what's not important is just not important. What *is* important is I know my family loves me and believes me – and believes in me. And what anyone else thinks just doesn't – or shouldn't – matter."

"How does that make you feel?"

His smile broadened. "Reaffirmed. Like I can withstand whatever those bastards throw at me."

"Even prison?" The therapist braced himself for a hostile – even volatile – outburst.

Gary's smile decayed, but didn't disappear entirely; he gave a slow nod. "Even prison."

There was a peace about him Dr. Benson had never seen in Gary. The psychiatrist consulted his calendar. Gary had been here just under three weeks. This turnaround was a good sign. He jotted a note to consult with Dr. Lindemeyr.

***

"Good morning," the nurse greeted Gary with customary perkiness early the next morning. "How did you sleep?"

"Lousy," he mumbled.

Instead of replying, 'That's nice,' and scurrying to open the drapes before giving him his meds and dashing off, Dina's kind face puckered in concern. "Ohh. I'm sorry."

She sat at the edge of the bed. Her hand lingered on his wrist for a moment after she checked his pulse. There was an intensity of emotions here, she noted. The highs were higher, the lows much deeper. And today, her favorite patient wasn't merely sad; he seemed *tremendously* sad, almost mourning. She had a soft spot for Gary, because of his vulnerability and his tenuous emotional state.

"Still having those nightmares?"

"Yeah."

"I'm sorry to hear that." The nurse gave him his pills. "I know you'll get through it soon."

Dina went out of her way to be extra kind to Gary – not that she neglected or mistreated any of her patients. She'd just taken a particular shine to him; he always had this little-boy lost look about him that made her want to hold him and comfort him.

She gave Gary's hand a compassionate squeeze as she reclaimed the empty juice cup, pretending not to notice the tears in his eyes. She'd heard doctors Lindemeyr and Benson in the hallway yesterday; they'd said he was ready to be released. And now this. Whatever had made him so sad, Dina hoped it was only temporary and he'd be able to go home on schedule.

Gary picked disinterestedly at his French toast, then shoved it away and retreated under the covers.

When Dr. Lindemeyr arrived minutes later, he was asleep. Or pretending to be. She approached the bed and spoke his name quietly.

No reply. She tried again, a bit louder.

This time Gary opened his eyes.

Marie shook her head. "So hard to tell when you're faking."

He smirked. "Ya know, I only let you get away with that 'cause you're my sister."

"I appreciate that." She nodded toward the abandoned tray. "Not hungry this morning?"

He shook his head.

Taking hold of his wrist, she consulted the clock. "Pulse is fine," she murmured, letting go again. "How'd you sleep?"

Gary shrugged.

"What's that mean?"

"Didn't they teach you to interpret nonverbal cues in shrink school?"

"Of course. But I'm an auditory learner. Indulge me. How'd you sleep?"

He looked away. *Had that dream again… but I'm not about to tell you about it.* "Not bad."

"Why didn't you say so in the first place?"

Gary gritted his teeth; he knew she was baiting him. " 'Cause I didn't feel like it, okay?"

Marie watched her brother for a moment, then moved toward the doorway. "C'mon."

"Where?"

"It's a nice day. Let's take a walk."

"Yeah, right," he scoffed. "Where're we gonna go? It's a locked ward. Or had you forgotten?"

"It's okay. You'll be accompanied by a physician." He still didn't look convinced. "It's fine, Gary. Really. C'mon, get dressed. I'll wait for you in the solarium."

"What's it like out?"

"You'll want a coat, but it's quite pleasant for March."

"See? I told you it was nice out."

Gary stepped onto the courtyard's cobbled walkway, treading carefully around patches of ice glimmering in the sunlight. It was the first time he'd set foot outside in three weeks.

"How's it feel?"

Turning, he squinted into the brightness of the morning sky. "How's what feel?"

Marie gestured outward with her arms. "This. Everything. Being outside. Breathing fresh air." *Being alive,* she wanted to add.

He shrugged. "Okay, I guess."

"Just okay?" she pressed. "How does it make you feel?"

Gary exhaled audibly. "Makes me sad." He turned away. "I wanna go home. I miss my kids; I miss my *world*" – his voice grew quieter, wistful – "I miss feeling *normal.*"

The siblings walked in silence past the still-dormant lilacs, toward a bench at the center of the courtyard.

"D'you know what today is?" Gary asked as they sat.

Marie thought for a moment, then shook her head. "No. What?"

"Thirteen years since Grandpa died."

The sadness in his voice told her the pain felt particularly fresh. Her good news would have to wait. "That's right." She entwined her fingers with his. "Some pain never really goes away, huh?"

He shook his head. After a long silence, Gary looked at his sister. "Lemme ask you something."

She met his gaze. "Shoot."

"When Mom was pregnant with me, and Dad took her to the hospital, Grandma and Grandpa took care of you, right?"

"Yeah." Marie wondered where this was leading.

"Did you tell Grandma you wanted to name it Huckleberry?"

"Who told you that?"

He ignored her question. "Did you?"

"W-well, yes… but how— Gary, how did you know about that? Who told you?"

"You're gonna think I'm crazy…"

Marie grinned lopsidedly and elbowed her brother in the ribs. "I *already* think that, ya goofball." Instantly, she regretted it. "I didn't mean it like that, Gar'. I'm sorry! I meant—"

She was surprised to see him smiling. "I know." Gary paused. "Grandma told me the other night."

Marie's mouth dropped open; she stared at her brother.

Gary explained about the dream. And his ideas about its significance. "I think it's a good sign," he concluded. "I think it means I'm getting better."

"I'd say you're right." She took his hand again. "What would you say, Gary, if I said you could go home tomorrow?"

He turned toward his sister; his hand closed tight around hers, so tight she winced. "Are you just messing with me?"

She shook her head. Her "No" was mouthed, her gaze steady.

"I can go home?"

"Dr. Benson thinks you're well enough. He said you've made great progress, remarkable strides. But – and this is important, Gary; it's a condition of your release: You've got to stay on your meds. I don't care how stable you feel, how emotionally balanced. You need to keep taking them, because they're what's keeping you on an even keel. You're not strong enough yet to do it on your own." She paused. "Will you do it, then? Will you stay on your medication?"

Gary looked away; his sigh was deep, resigned. "Yes. I'll stay on my meds."

"For as long as Dr. Benson says you have to?"

"If it means I can go home."

Their eyes met. Marie gave a slight nod.

An instant later, Gary had his sister wrapped in a mighty hug.

Gary phoned Michaela from Doctor Lindemeyr's office as soon as they returned inside.

Michaela declared it wonderful news, she could hardly wait for him to be home. Then she asked to speak to Marie.

"Are you sure he's ready?" she fretted, twirling the phone cord around her finger. "I mean, I *want* him to come home, but is he… *ready?*"

"I consulted with Dr. Benson yesterday; we both think the timing's right. It's something he wants enough to work for," Marie assured her quietly. "I don't anticipate any problems."

"She still thinks I'm nuts," Gary lamented when Marie finally hung up.

"No she doesn't," she scolded lovingly. "Why would you say a thing like that?"

"Oh, come on! I heard her voice. She's afraid of me. Like I'm some sort of freak or – or monster or something."

"Not true." Marie met his gaze. "She just wants to be sure you're" – her voice softened – "Look, it's a big adjustment, re-entering the world after even a few weeks. She knows that; she wants to be sure she's prepared to meet whatever needs you may have."

"Like what?"

She gestured with one hand. "Withdrawal issues, fear… coping skills. The kinds of things you've worked on this past week with Dr. Benson."

Gary hated to think she and his shrink had been comparing notes about him.

"But Gary, I think the most important thing for you to remember is it's a process. Don't expect things to be the same as they were when you left; they'll be different. We *want* them different. We want to see a change.

"Now, your kids might be a little apprehensive around you the first few days," Marie cautioned. "That's normal. And Michaela might hover too much; that's normal, too. She's just looking out for you, because she loves you. And yeah, it'll seem awkward. And frustrating. But, Gary, it's all part of the process."

***

Gary jolted awake. He could hear the angry edge in Dad's voice – even over the thump of his heart. He reassured himself it was a dream; but as soon as he fell back to sleep, the nightmare returned.

"Don't you know how to answer his questions, boy?" Jeremy berated him between swipes with his heavy leather belt. "Can't you get anything right?"

All the while, Dr. Benson remained silent in his green armchair, jotting notes.

"You've always been a colossal fuck-up," Dad taunted as Gary cowered in a corner of the dream. "I figured you'd get yourself into trouble like this one day. Why don't you just go ahead and admit what you've done? Go on, tell the truth, boy: Tell him you fucked that girl. Enjoyed it, too, I'll bet. You lousy little shit!"

When he sank into the cushions of the familiar hunter-green couch for his final therapy session the next morning, Gary felt like he hadn't slept more than fifteen minutes.

"How are you feeling this morning?"

He raked a hand through his hair. "I gotta tell ya, doc: I'm just relieved to be going home."

Dr. Benson smiled. "You worked hard, Gary. I'm proud of you – and of the progress you've made. Any last things you want to talk about?"

"Actually, there is. I had a really disturbing dream last night."

"Tell me about it."

Unlike the other times, today Gary welcomed that invitation.

"Huh… What do you make of that?" the psychiatrist asked when Gary had finished.

"I was hoping you'd tell me."

Dr. Benson shook his head. "I don't have answers, Gary; you know that. I'm here to help you figure out the truth." He gestured with one hand. "What does it mean to you?"

"I guess," he began, uncertainty in his voice, "I don't think my dad is necessarily him; I think he represents every-one who's been beating me down" – scratching his right cheek absently – "or beating me up. But I can't understand why you didn't stop him from hitting me."

"How's that make you feel?"

"Betrayed," Gary replied distractedly, his mind grasping for another meaning. "How can you do that? You're s'posed to be helping me, not letting me get beat up…" He struggled for understanding.

Suddenly, his eyes widened. "I know what it means! My dad's not my dad. Not here. He's *me*. *I'm* the one beating me up. Of course you wouldn't try to stop him from hurting me! There was no one else there. You were watching me beat myself up – like I've been doing all along."

"Okay. What about all those things he was saying?"

"Addressing me as 'boy' and swearing at me: Those were real things he did. But the rest of it? I think it's just me doing a number on myself, emotionally."

The doctor nodded. "Nice job interpreting that dream. How do you feel about it?"

Gary gave it some thought. "Now I know what it means, I guess I'm okay with it."

As their session time dwindled, Gary grew visibly uneasy; he stood. "I guess this is it…"

The psychiatrist walked him toward the door. "How's it feel?"

Halfway there, Gary stopped. "Honestly? Kinda strange," he fretted, running a hand through his hair. That seemed to take forever; he wasn't used to it being this long. "Don't get me wrong, I'm glad to be going home… but it's almost hard to let go. Scary. Does that make sense?"

"It's normal to feel apprehensive, Gary," Dr. Benson reassured him. "I'm sure you'll do fine once you're in familiar surroundings again."

He looked unconvinced.

"Still, I don't want you to feel like we're cutting you loose entirely," the therapist went on. "If you feel it's necessary, I can continue seeing you on an outpatient basis."

Trembling slightly and shifting foot to foot, Gary nodded.

The psychiatrist patted Gary's shoulder. "For now, let's focus on the positives" – steering him the rest of the way to the door – "You've worked through your anger and guilt issues… and survived. You're going home."

Gary still looked uncomfortable. He gestured feebly. "I'm sorry I was such a jerk to you."

Dr. Benson gave him an understanding smile. "No apology necessary. It's part of the process."

"I was a major asshole."

The psychiatrist shrugged it off. "You were in pain. It's not uncommon. Anyway, I didn't take it personally. You did good work, Gary. It was hard, but you did it."

Michaela arrived a little past noon; she said the children were at her dad's. "Didn't want to hit you with too much reality all at once," she explained, gesturing awkwardly as her car keys jangled in her hand.

For the first time since his committal, Gary noticed how tiny and frightened his wife looked. He managed a grateful smile, but he'd really looked forward to the kids' joyful mayhem. He gave her a long hug. "It's so good to see you," he murmured against the softness of her hair.

Chapter 20

(9:57 a.m., March 16 – Monday)

"Gary?"

He couldn't place the voice. "Yes?"

"It's Jackie DeMay. From Pomperaug High. Is this a bad time?"

"Not at all, Jackie. What's up?"

"Something's come up at school, concerning Erin." The guidance counselor paused. "Could you come in this morning?"

Only home from the hospital a few days, Gary was still wary of venturing out; he hadn't even gone to Mass yesterday. "Is this something you could discuss with Michaela?"

"No, Gary. It needs to be you."

He'd need to shave and shower; he looked at the clock. "Can it wait 'til this afternoon?"

"I'd rather do this sooner than later." Her voice held a worried edge.

What difference could a few hours make? "I can probably make it there by noon. Will that work?"

He heard pages rustling as Jackie consulted her date book. "That'll be fine."

The school secretary asked Gary to wait in the outer office.

Minutes later, Ms DeMay emerged from the guidance department. "Gary, it's good to see you." He recognized the alarm in her voice. And why not? He knew he looked pale and gaunt. "Thank you for coming in," she continued, hurrying him along the corridor.

Behind closed doors in her office, she motioned toward a row of chairs. "Have a seat."

Wary, Gary lowered himself into the chair nearest her desk. "Jackie, what's this about?"

"Maybe it'd be best if we waited for Erin to get here."

He'd never seen her look so ill-at-ease. They'd worked together on functions for years; she'd never been evasive. "No, Jackie." His voice was crisp, no-nonsense. "I'd like you to tell me what's going on. *Now*, please. What's with all the secrecy?"

Put on the spot, Jackie asked whether he'd noticed unusual changes in Erin's behavior.

He gave the vaguest answer he thought he could get away with. "She's been kinda touchy the last couple days. Why?"

"Erin's been behaving rather… strangely lately." Jackie seemed reluctant to continue.

"Jackie, what are you trying to tell me?"

"You honestly haven't noticed anything odd this past month?"

This was no time for vagaries and dancing around. "No, and I'll tell you why. I've been away the last three weeks — in the hospital. I came home Thursday. I did notice she seemed hostile; but my doctor said that'd be a normal sort of reaction, given the circumstances, so I didn't worry about it. What kind of behavior did you mean?"

"Acting out in class. She nearly came to blows with other students in the cafeteria. At its worst, it got as far as shoving. We had to call Michaela in a few times."

"I… wasn't aware of that." *Micki probably figured I didn't need any more imbalance in my life.*

"That's all settled. What I called you in for today, Gary, goes way beyond lunchroom squabbles. Erin's made some serious allegations I thought we should bring to your attention immediately."

Allegations? Suspicion prickled through him. "About what?"

"Well…" the guidance counselor hedged. "About you."

"Excuse me?" Gary felt ill.

"Erin had an English paper due Friday. The assignment was to address something significant, something she felt strongly about. She turned in a poem. A most disturbing – alarming – poem. It rattled Mrs. Sweeney so much she called me at home Saturday night to tell me about it."

Gary looked confused. "I've read some of her poetry, Jackie. It's good – I mean, for a teenager. How bad could this be?"

"It's pretty damning. First thing this morning, Mrs. Sweeney gave it to me. Her concern was not unwarranted. I talked with Erin during first period. She was defensive and hostile. For some reason, she believes you're guilty; she said you admitted it – and claims she has proof."

"*Admitted* it? Where'd she dream that up?"

"I haven't the slightest idea. But she was adamant about it." Jackie faltered. "I hate to pry – and I'm sorry, but I don't even know a delicate way to ask you this…"

He had a feeling his discomfort quotient was about to rise dramatically. "Ask me what?"

"Please understand: I'm only asking because of something she wrote." Her voice dropped to just above a whisper. "Was there a… recent suicide attempt on your part?"

Gary's stomach dropped into his shoes. He felt nauseated and ashamed. "Why?"

"Again, I don't mean to pry. It's just" – she reached for something on her desk – "Maybe you'd better read this."

His hand trembled as he opened the folded paper; his heart clamored to escape his chest. When his eyes could focus on Erin's neatly printed words, marching across the paper on near-perfect iambic feet, Gary started to read.

I can't believe I trusted you
When you told me that you loved me
And family meant everything…
Were you just trying to bluff me?

You told me, "Always tell the truth,"
'Cause my integrity's at stake.
How can I trust a thing you say
When your whole world is fake?

Were you honest when you told me that
You like the guy I'm dating?
Or was it yet another lie
And the truth is still left waiting?

Can I believe a thing you say?
Can you, my dad, be trusted?
Or are you a lying, sicko creep
Who finally got busted?

You wanted us to trust in you,
But your words gave you away.
I wish you'd killed yourself that night
And not dragged it out this way.

You lied to Mandy and to Michael,
To Mom and me as well.
I hope they find you guilty and
You rot in jail - then Hell!

Each stanza brought a deeper expression of torture to his face. Midway through, he was shaking and his insides felt like ice. By the time he reached the last line, Gary was fighting tears.

Jackie sat beside the devastated dad. "I realized how difficult this would be for you. I wanted you and Erin to talk it through here – in a neutral environment."

"How could she do this? Why would she write these lies?" Dr. Benson's words about discounting strangers' remarks blared in his head. *This isn't some stranger. It's my own daughter!* The paper trembled in his hand. A searing tear slid down his cheek.

"Had you written a note?" Jackie's quiet tone forced him to focus on her words.

He nodded, ashamed. "Micki has it hidden away. But even if Erin saw it" – he spoke through shuddering breaths – "I never would've admitted to something I didn't do."

"She mentioned having proof, but she refused to show it to me this morning."

Gary looked frightened. "How can she have proof of something that never happened?"

"She said it was—"

A knock at the door interrupted.

"Just a moment," Jackie called out. After making sure Gary was ready to face his daughter, she opened the door.

"I dunno why I had to come back to talk to you again. There's noth—" Tensing, Erin backed away, shaking her head. "Unh-uh, Miss – I'm not staying in here with *him!*"

Jackie draped an arm around her shoulder. "C'mon, Erin. Let's sit down and talk."

"No way! I've got nothing to say to that child molester!"

Gary winced, as if she'd struck him.

"Maybe not," she said gently. "But let's curb the name calling and listen to what he's got to say."

"No! I hate him! He's a sick bastard who fucks teenage girls!"

"Watch your mouth, little girl!" Gary warned, his mortification over her poem replaced by anger.

"Erin, you know better than to use that language in here. Do it again and you'll serve detention this afternoon" – Jackie indicated a chair along the wall opposite Gary – "now please, sit down."

Folding her arms across her chest, Erin jutted her chin forward. Her gaze flickered toward her dad, gauging his reaction. "Why?"

Gary hadn't seen such hatred in Erin's eyes since she'd learned he was her father.

"So we can discuss the English assignment you handed in Friday."

"Oh. *That.*" She dropped abruptly into a chair. Slumping low, Erin crossed her legs and kicked the top one back and forth. The hem of her jeans was shredded; she wore a pair of torn, ink-scribbled sneakers her dad would normally never have let her out of the house wearing. "One of my better efforts, don'cha think?" she asked the room, her defiance flourishing.

"Actually, no," the counselor replied. "It was angry and mean. And hurtful."

"So? What about what *he* did? I'd say *that* was more hurtful than anything *I* coulda written."

"Okay, Erin. Enough. You'll get a chance to talk; for now, I need you to listen." Jackie gestured to Gary. "I asked your dad to come in because you made some serious allegations – allegations every bit as serious as the ones already leveled against him. No matter how angry you may be, you can't go making accusations about people without some basis for them."

"Oh, I've got proof," Erin interjected. "I've got proof he's a lying, cheating son-of-a-bitch." She directed her steely gaze across the office, challenging Dad either to reprimand her or deny his guilt.

Father and daughter eyed each other.

Jackie watched them. Silent seconds ticked by; then half a minute. "I've known your dad all your life, Erin" – she held up the poem – "and I simply cannot believe he'd do this. You said you have proof to back up these claims, but refuse to provide any. I'm inclined to dismiss this as—"

"You want proof?" Erin shrieked. She jammed a hand into her pocket. With a flick of her wrist, she flung a wadded-up paper across the room. "*Here's* your fucking proof!"

Stunned into silence, Jackie cast an uncertain glance at Gary before retrieving and uncrumpling the paper. Words sloped across the page, defying the ruled lines.

I'm sorry to leave you this way, Michaela... but there's no other way out. I'm so sorry for all the ways I've failed you over the years... I regret every harsh word, every time I was unkind to you in any way. But most of all, Michaela, I'm sorry for being unfaithful to you. That was the biggest mistake of my life and I

The drunken parade of ink stopped.

Jackie looked up, her face pale; her hand trembled as she handed the crumpled paper to Gary.

As he read the fragmented note, he forced back nausea. He tried to recall gauzy remnants of that desperate February night. This must have been one of a dozen or more notes he'd started before he wrote the one Micki described as "three pages of anguished rambling." But where'd she find this? God, it sounded damning! He understood how she'd have gotten the wrong idea.

Erin scowled like she wished him dead.

Jackie's expression showed worried disbelief.

Gary hated the idea of anyone having seen this – let alone his teenage daughter and her guidance counselor! "This is *not* what it seems like."

"Oh no?" Erin challenged. "I suppose next you're gonna try to convince me the earth is flat."

He withered a little inside. "This isn't an admission of guilt. It's an apology – for something I did years ago… something I'll regret the rest of my life."

The teenager folded her arms. "You're lying."

"If you don't believe me, ask Mom."

"Yeah, right. Like that'll prove anything. By the time I get home, you'll already have gotten to her. She'll just repeat whatever you tell her to say."

"Then call her now." He turned to Jackie. "May we use your phone?"

"Of course."

Gary punched in the number and waited. Michaela's "Hello" was music to his tormented soul.

"Hi, it's me. I'm at school with Erin, in Ms DeMay's office. I'm gonna put you on speaker phone" – he pressed the speaker button and replaced the handset – "Are you there?"

"I'm here."

"Good. Micki, I need you to do something. It's gonna sound crazy, and you're not going to want to; but just do it, okay?"

"Gary, what's going on?"

"Erin's got a few questions; they're not going to be easy, but I need you to tell her the truth."

"What kind of questions? Gary, are you alright? You don't sound so good…"

"Just – please – answer whatever she asks you, alright?"

"Alright…"

"Go ahead, Erin," Gary prompted.

"Hi, Mommy."

"Hi, sweetheart." Gary heard the tender smile in Micki's voice. "Daddy said you had something to ask me…"

"Yeah. Mommy" – she eyed her father with contempt – "when did he cheat on you?"

She gasped. "What?"

"Answer the question, honey," Gary murmured, one hand shielding his eyes from Erin's icy glare.

"Years ago. Right after your grandpa died." She hesitated. "It was one time. That's all."

"What about that girl at the radio station?"

Her tone held a prickly edge. "Those charges are false. Your dad didn't do any of those things."

"He cheated on you before," Erin protested. "What's to stop him from doing it again?"

"That was ages ago, Erin. It happened once and I forgave him."

"So, who was this slut he was fucking?"

"Erin!" Gary rebuked. Then, softer, "You don't have to answer that, baby. I'll tell her." *I dunno how… but I'll tell her.*

"No, Gary – please," Micki implored, her voice wavering. "She doesn't need to know *that*."

"Why?" Erin taunted, smirking. "Was it a guy?"

"Erin!" This was Michaela.

Wounded, Gary turned mournful eyes toward his daughter. From her expression, he knew she had no such suspicion, but it was the most shocking thing she could think of. His voice was hollow and cold. And equally mean. "It was your mother." He barely heard Michaela's gasp.

When the words sank in, Erin leapt at her father with a screech, fists flying. "You asshole! You lousy, two-timing sack of shit! You – you lying son-of-a-bitch! I hate you!"

"Stop it, Erin!" Jackie tugged the slender teenager away. "Sit down."

Erin fought the counselor off. Bitter tears streaked down her cheeks. "I hate you," she raged at her father, eyes dark with fury. "I hate you!" A moment before Jackie yanked Erin away, the girl's nails caught Gary just below his left eye.

Father and daughter eyed each other in tension-drenched silence. No one noticed Michaela had hung up until the dial tone's buzz filled the room.

Jackie silenced it. She looked from Gary to Erin, wondering how to bring father and daughter around to speak to each other. The girl had reason to be upset, and Gary must be drowning in shame. Finally, her sensible voice slit the hostility. "I need both of you to take a step back now and listen."

Two sets of eyes turned toward Jackie – the deep-brown set narrowing in defiant suspicion; the slate-grey ones damp and not quite able to meet her gaze.

"Erin, I don't know whether you realize what your dad did just now."

"Sure I do. He admitted he's a lying, cheating jerk."

"Erin, you need to stop with the personal attacks."

Scowling, the teen grumbled a terse apology.

"It's not me you should be apologizing to."

"Well, I'm sure as hell not gonna apologize to *him*." Folding her arms, she glared at her father.

Jackie gave Gary a helpless look. He shook his head. "Let it go," he murmured.

"As I was saying, Erin," she continued, "it takes a big man to do what your father just did: admit his personal failings to his own child. Not to mention to an outsider as well."

Erin sneered. "Well goody for him. Give him a gold star."

After a long silence, Gary crouched before his daughter. Taking her hands, he looked into her face. "Erin, I know you're angry at me. And I accept that," he said quietly. "But do you believe me now – that I didn't do those things?"

Eyes riveted on her father, she didn't reply.

Silence enveloped them; neither heard Jackie shut the door behind her.

"Punkin, I need to know you trust me about that. I never intended for you to find out about what I did with your mom. But don't you see how much more important it is that you know the truth about *this*? Erin, you now know the worst thing about me. The absolute worst thing there is to know about your dad. As ashamed as I am to admit that, I gladly offer it up to prove what you read is not an admission of guilt to those charges. It's a deeply personal, heartfelt apology – to the woman I love – for something horrible I did to her long ago." A tear slid down his face; it landed on his jean-clad leg.

"Why did you do it?"

Dad looked up, stymied. He had no answer for her.

"Why'd you do it?" Erin repeated fiercely. "Why'd you cheat on Mommy… and with my mom!"

He sniffled. "Because, punkin, I was stupid and" – he shook his head – "well, it doesn't matter. What matters is I'm sorry. Mommy forgave me and we've put it behind us. And that's the last I'm going to say about it."

Erin watched him for a long time, her eyes welling with tears. A dozen questions swirled in her head; her hands trembled in her lap as she asked the only one that mattered. "You weren't really gonna kill yourself… were you?"

He looked downward, then nodded. "Yeah," he admitted in a whisper. "I was."

Her tears spilled over as a rush of emotion overwhelmed her. "Why, Daddy?" she implored. "How could you do that to me?"

He hugged her. "I wasn't doing it to *you*. I hate to say this, honey, but I wasn't thinking about you. I was hurting and I wanted it to stop. I couldn't stand all those things they were saying – and yes, I hated what it was doing to Mommy and you kids… and in part, I wanted to spare you that shame and misery. But mostly, I just wanted the pain to go away."

A hideous moan fell from Erin's lips as great sobs wracked her petite frame.

Dad held her close, to still her shaking. "I'm sorry, punkin," he murmured, smoothing her long dark hair. "I'm so, so sorry."

Erin's tears came faster and harder as he tried to console her. She recalled vividly how devastated and empty she felt when Mom died. She couldn't bear it if Daddy killed himself! The emptiness was too horrible to think about. Dead. Gone. Forever. She couldn't imagine how she'd ever go on if Daddy were dead – instead of here, hugging her and comforting her.

"I love you, Daddy," Erin mumbled against his neck. "I'm so sorry I wrote those horrible things, and called you those awful names. I'm sorry, Daddy…" Her remaining words were lost amid sobs.

Through his own tears, Gary shushed his daughter and assured her everything was fine.

When Erin's tears tapered off, he loosened his embrace and sat in the chair beside her. Pushing her hair out of her eyes, he asked, "Are we okay?"

She nodded, her voice too shaky to be trusted.

"Good." He leaned in to kiss her on the forehead. "I love you. I gotta go, and you've got a class to get back to. I'll pick you up at four."

Wiping away her tears, Erin looked at him strangely. "I love you, too, Daddy. But I get out at two fifteen."

"Not today." He touched the end of his daughter's nose. "Detention. Remember?"

Erin sighed. "Oh, yeah. Right." She hugged him. "See you at four."

Chapter 21

(March 24 – Tuesday)

"Please state your full name."

"Gary Joseph Sheldon."

"What is your occupation?"

"Provided I still have a job? Afternoon-drive announcer and music director at Z97-3."

The machine's arm darted back and forth across the page.

"What is your birth date?"

"January eighteenth."

"What year?"

Gary eyed the test administrator, refusing to make this easy for them. "Every year."

The man scowled. "I meant, What year were you born?"

"Then why didn't you say so?"

"Answer the question."

"Nineteen sixty-four."

"What is your marital status?"

"Married. To Michaela Conwaye Sheldon."

The test administrator scribbled something on the pad before him. Gary couldn't tell what it was. Too hard to read upside down.

"Do you have children?"

Gary shifted position in his chair. "Yes."

"Please don't move around," the administrator intoned. "Answer again: Do you have children?"

"Yes."

"How many?"

Gary's eyes bored holes through the other man. "Three."

"Are they all your wife's children?"

His reply was frosty, edgy. "They are now."

More scribbling. "What do you mean by that?"

"I mean she adopted Erin, my older daughter."

"Did you make improper advances toward Jolene Cunningham?"

That was abrupt. "No, I did not."

The polygraph's arm swept furiously, like a seismograph recording a major earthquake.

"Did you have sexual relations with her?"

Gary's insides clenched and rattled. "No, I did not," he repeated. Slowly and distinctly.

More scribbling. From both the machine and the man with the notepad.

"Did you coerce Jolene Cunningham into a sexual relationship?"

"No. I did not."

The machine's arm swept broad strokes across the page. The test administrator glanced at his assistant monitoring the machine. *Is he lying?* his expression seemed to ask.

The assistant arched an eyebrow in silent reply.

"Did you offer Jolene Cunningham drugs in exchange for sexual favors?"

"No, I did not."

Did you rape Jolene Cunningham?"

He clenched his teeth. "No. I did not."

"Do you find Jolene Cunningham attractive, Mr. Sheldon?"

Gary exhaled loudly. He glared at the interrogator, who repeated the question. Still no answer.

"Mr. Sheldon – I asked a question. Do you find Jolene Cunningham attractive?"

It became a sparring match. "Define attractive."

"Just answer the question."

Gary jerked his head, tossing his longer-than-usual hair out of his eyes. "Define attractive."

"Answer the question!"

"She's a teenager, for Christ's sake – I'm twice her age, God damn it! Of course not!"

Micki greeted Gary at the door, little Michael tugging at her skirt. "How did it go?"

He bent and lifted the child in his arms. "Hi there! How's my big boy?" Kissing him on the cheek, Gary set his son on his shoulders, then leaned to kiss his wife. "Hi, baby. It went fine."

His eyes told her it hadn't gone well at all.

(3:20 p.m., March 27 – Friday)

"At least polygraphs aren't admissible in court." Blake sounded furious.

"That bad?"

"I told you this wasn't a good idea, Gary."

"So, what are you upset about? You just said they're not admissible."

"The tests themselves, no. But they can say a test was administered and they got the results they expected." He paused. "Things don't look especially rosy right now. Look, don't do anything… stupid, huh?"

More than anything, Gary hated to be scolded. "What's that supposed to mean?"

"Stay under their radar," the defense attorney said in an impatient staccato. "Don't do anything to draw attention to yourself. And while you're at it, Gary, get a haircut."

"Ya know what, Blake? Don't fuckin' tell me what to do, alright?" He thumped the wall phone into its cradle.

Turning around, he spied six-year-old Amanda staring at him.

"Daddy!" Aghast, the child ran to the refrigerator to pull down her copy of The Rules – the code of behavior for Gary's CCD students, in and out of class. She ran back to him, pointing at Rule 7. "No bad words, Daddy."

Embarrassed at the girl's innocent reprimand, Gary stooped and stroked her silken hair. "You're right. I'm sorry, sweetie. I'll be more careful." Drawing Amanda close, he kissed her forehead. "Will you forgive me?"

"Okay, but don't let me catch you doing it again," she solemnly parroted her dad's admonition to first-time Rule breakers. Then she put her arms around him and snuggled close. "I love you, Daddy."

"I took this case as a favor to you, Michael," Blake groused. "Innocent or not, the guy's a loose cannon. I can't represent him if he won't take direction."

Michael removed his glasses and rubbed the sore spot at the bridge of his nose. This wasn't how he'd envisioned this call going when Claudia buzzed to announce Blake Tierney on line one. "I know he can be hot-headed someti—"

"Hot-headed! Is that what you call it? Do you know what that little punk said to me just now?"

Michael listened as the defense attorney reeled off a litany of Gary's unsatisfactory behaviors over the past four months, beginning with his reaction to Blake's mention of a haircut minutes earlier.

"I understand your frustration," he said when Blake had finished. "But before you do anything drastic, let me have a chat with Gary. If I can talk some sense into him, will you stay on?"

"Hi Grandpa," Erin said when she heard Michael's voice. "You wanna talk to Mommy?"

"Actually, I'm looking for your dad. Is he home?"

Erin ran off to find him, in full teenage yell. "Da-ad! Telephone! It's Grandpa."

A minute later, Gary picked up the phone in the kitchen. "Hey, Michael, what's up?"

"Let's can the small talk. We've got a problem that needs to be addressed – right away."

Determined to hold his temper, Gary leaned against the counter and watched a gang of robins peck at the ground in the back yard. "Go ahead."

"I don't how to say this tactfully, but we can't afford to dance around it. Blake's just fed up with your prima-donna behavior and he's ready to walk."

Gary started to say something, but Michael stopped him.

"If he drops your case, Gary, you're screwed. I said I'd have a talk with you, but whether he stays is on you. I strongly advise you to watch every word that comes out of your mouth. I'm not denying you've been through the wringer. But Blake Tierney is *not* someone to piss off. I don't want to seem like I'm telling you what to do, but maybe you should see a therapist, develop some coping skills – *something*, Gary. Don't jeopardize your case by driving Blake away. This is too important."

"Can I say something here?"

"Of course."

"I'm sorry. I didn't mean to go off on him. I just find myself losing patience all the time." Gary raked a hand through his hair. *Shit, I <u>do</u> need a haircut!* "You're right, Michael. I screwed up. I'll give Blake a call now and see if I can smooth things over."

(4 p.m.)

"Sorry I missed your call. What can I do for you?"

Gary's heart hammered in his chest. "I want to apologize, Blake. I've behaved horribly and I treated you..." he searched for the right words.

"Like crap," the attorney finished for him.

"Exactly," he admitted. "I'm sorry, Blake. Please stay on. I'm screwed without you... Please."

The defense attorney considered his options. He could drop the case; but then Gary – whom he truly believed to be innocent – would likely end up serving a sentence that would have him leaving prison a very old man. But he didn't want to continue being the guy's verbal punching bag.

Gary went on, filling the silence. "I know it's no excuse, Blake, but this whole thing's been such a nightmare. I'm snapping at people for no reason. The other day, I reamed out a cashier at the pharmacy. That's not like me. I'm sorry for treating you the way I did. I know I can behave better. Just don't drop the case – please?"

"If I stay on – and at this point it could go either way – but if I stay on, you're going to do *what* I tell you, *when* I tell you and *how* I tell you. Is that clear?"

"Perfectly."

"I expect you not to second-guess or challenge me – about anything regarding the legal aspects of your case. If I tell you to jump, you jump. And you don't ask 'how high?' I'll tell you when you need to know how high."

"Got it."

"And if I tell you to do something, I do not expect you to swear at me and hang up."

"My six-year-old daughter already scolded me for that," Gary said sheepishly.

Blake chuckled, surprising himself. "Good. I'm glad someone can get through to you. And about that haircut…"

"I've already got an appointment – tomorrow at nine."

(9:17 a.m., March 30 – Monday)
"Have you eaten *anything* in the last eight weeks? You're down ten more pounds since February."

"Maybe I've got a tapeworm."

Dr. Caron wasn't amused. "This is no laughing matter, Gary. Are you still experiencing nausea? Or is it you're not hungry?"

"I don't feel like eating. Nothing tastes good. I can't see the point of eating something that has no flavor."

"How long has this been happening? Maybe your medication's suppressing your appetite."

"I dunno; I just don't find joy in anything anymore."

"That may be, but if you don't reverse this weight loss soon, Gary, you could be in for some serious problems."

"You mean worse than twenty-five years in the slammer? 'Cause a little weight loss I can deal with; it's the three-hundred-pound boyfriend named Bubba that scares me."

Dr. Caron nodded. "Have you begun seeing that counselor I referred you to?"

Gary shook his head. "I'm thinking of going back to see Dr. Benson."

"That's an excellent idea," the physician said. "When you see him, be sure to mention the weight loss. It might not be the medication at all."

He jotted a note in Gary's file. "So… aside from the not eating, how are you feeling otherwise? Sleeping okay?"

"I'm falling asleep fine; it's what happens *while* I'm asleep that bothers me."

"Sleepwalking?"

"Nah, nothing like that. Just this really wacked dream – the same one, over and over." Filled with trepidation, Gary described the nightmare.

Partway through, Dr. Caron held up his hands. "Whoa! This is *way* beyond my area of expertise. Dr. Benson can probably help you figure out what's going on there – at least, better than me. I'd suggest you talk this over with him."

"I wanted to… I didn't mention it the first few days I was in the hospital because I" – he paused, flustered – "well, I didn't know if I could trust him. And then, after I was having it for awhile—"

"Wait – wait a minute. You've had this same dream for six weeks, and this is the first you've said anything about it?"

"It's not like it's all that easy to talk about…"

Dr. Caron faltered. "Granted. But, Gary, Dr. Benson's a professional. Talk to him. Soon."

When he got home, Gary called the psychiatrist.

With 4 p.m. Friday penciled in on the calendar, he was sure he'd have no trouble sleeping.

Twice that night he awakened in a panic.

Both times, Michaela asked what was wrong.

Both times he lied and assured her it was nothing.

The next night, angst kept him awake until well after two. And when he fell asleep, the nightmare haunted him anyway.

Wednesday, Gary was so jittery he was popping anti-anxiety meds like M&Ms.

That night, he crawled into bed around ten, determined to get a good night's sleep.

(3:23 a.m., April 2 – Thursday)

Gary stirred. His body was tangled in the bedclothes. The sheets slid down past his torso; cool night air chilled his skin.

Then, suddenly, warmth.

Her kisses were electrifying. His skin burned where her lips brushed against it. He felt her hot breath as she kissed her way along his body. Her long hair tickled as it skimmed his bare chest, along his midsection… and lower. He lay against the pillow and sighed aloud. She wrapped herself around him and soon he was floating on the delicious wave of passion that swept over him.

She raised her head for a moment, breathless with excitement, her heart pounding. Licking her lips and purring with anticipation, her mouth engulfed him again.

Gary shuddered. Through half-closed eyes, he watched her sleek dark hair glint in the moonlight as her head bobbed rhythmically. He wanted her. Badly. Now.

Growling with passion, he pulled her away and struggled to sit up; they wrestled for nearly a minute – until he maneuvered on top of her. She lay, panting, amid the rumpled bed clothes, arms askew, hands lying palm-up beside her head.

Pinning her wrists, he swiftly mounted and entered her.

Squealing, she bucked beneath him, arousing him further.

He released her wrists, braced his hands against the bed. His kisses were hard, urgent.

Clamping her legs around his hips, she raked her nails savagely across Gary's back, leaving little bloody trails along his skin. He arched backward, groaning in exhilaration and pain. With a low growl, he lowered his mouth to her throat and sucked mightily at her tender flesh.

Reaching slender arms upward, she stroked his face, his hair… then pulled him close for a kiss.

He kissed her mouth. She tasted warm and delicious…just like he remembered from years ago. *Years ago? Wait a minute! Something's not right.* Dismissing the thought, Gary raised himself on his hands again and bent to kiss her breasts, nudging her long, nearly black hair out of his way.

Nearly black? This isn't Micki. It's Ellen! That can't be right! She's dead… so who, then? As he pondered this, he thrust vigorously into the squealing young woman.

"Ohh," she sighed in breathless delight. "Yes! Harder…"

He obliged willingly. On the verge of a powerful orgasm, a familiar voice sliced through his haze of passion and befuddlement. "Ohh, that's soo good!" the voice purred ecstatically. "Mmm – ohh, yes… Mom always said you were great in bed – but I thought she meant you didn't snore or hog the covers. Oh, Daddy! You fuck like a machine!"

Gary recoiled from the curvaceous teenager writhing lasciviously beneath him. This was one of those horrible times when he *knew* he was dreaming but couldn't bring himself out of it. Looking again, he saw her hair was blonde… and her face had changed.

"C'mon, Gary. Finish the job. If you're man enough," Jolene taunted now, viciously pinching his nipples. "Fuck me. You know you want to."

With a horrified gasp, he pulled away. Jolted awake, Gary sat up. His erection withered; his heart raced. He tried to will himself into composure. His head was pounding almost as hard as his heart. And, inexplicably, his nipples hurt like hell!

Michaela stirred. "Gary?" she whispered to the darkness. "Honey?"

He took the hand she reached toward him. "Right here, baby."

At the tremor in his voice, she turned toward him. "What's wrong?"

Her hand felt comfortable in his. Soothing. "Nothing's wrong, baby. Go back to sleep."

"You had that dream again, didn't you?" Her tone held a hint of accusation. But mostly concern.

Lying about it was futile. "Yeah."

He'd never say what the nightmare was about, said he didn't want to worry her with silly dreams.

Michaela flicked on the bedside lamp. "How many times is that now?"

Forty-two. Or three, if you just meant tonight. "I dunno."

"Gary, you can't go on like this… you're not getting any sleep" – she slid her arms around him; his heart was still thumping like crazy – "C'mon, honey, why won't you tell me about it?"

He pulled away, dropped his head into his hands. "I can't."

"Why not?"

"It's too—" He bit back the word *graphic*. "No; it'd just hurt you… and I don't want to hurt y—"

"I *am* hurt! I'm hurt you don't trust me enough to confide in me. Gary, I'm *worried* about you. You've barely slept since you came home! Please, tell me what's tormenting you."

Gary hated to hear Michaela doubt his trust. Her words about feeling hurt cut him deeply. He'd wanted to protect her. But she was right: He *should* be able to confide in her. Especially when things were so rough. He raked a hand through his hair, then, haltingly, he told her.

It always started the same: He'd awaken in bed with a woman giving him a blowjob. In the midst of rough sex, he'd recognize it wasn't Micki. At first it was Ellen; then she became Erin, full breasted and sensuous – nothing like the sweet, modestly developed girl she actually was – making lewd remarks about her dad's sexual prowess. Just as he realized he was screwing his teenage daughter, she'd morph into Jolene. But once, she became Terri, which really threw him!

Michaela listened in silence.

By the time he finished, Gary was blushing deeply, embarrassed at having told his wife about this devastating – yet highly erotic – dream. He expected her to make a wry comment about his "nocturnal escapades," with an underlying kernel of hurt. After all, it was nearly four months since they'd made love. Any time she tried to initiate sex, he pulled away and told her – without apology – he wasn't in the mood.

He'd been so unwilling to touch her in bed, Michaela had wondered whether something was physically wrong with Gary. But he'd admitted the dream, while disturbing, had aroused him sexually. It always did. So it was beyond physical. While she understood the huge role emotions played in sexual response, it didn't help her at all as a wife feeling rejected by her husband. And as much as Gary may have needed her reassurance from a counseling standpoint, what he craved more was her understanding and support as his wife.

She did her best to offer that compassion, but addressing the overt sexual nature of his dream would embarrass him. "Thank you for sharing that. I know how" – she avoided using the word 'hard' – "difficult it must've been to talk about, but I couldn't stand to watch it keep tormenting you."

"I'm glad I told you," he admitted.

Micki cuddled against his chest. *I knew you would be.* When she tipped her head upward, Gary bent forward. His mouth found hers. Tentatively at first.

Her parted lips yielded to his, as they were accustomed to doing. She heard a low, rumbly growl from her husband's throat as their kisses re-ignited his passion.

A sense of relief swept through her. When she let out an involuntary "mmm" of delight, Micki leaned into Gary. She felt the strength of his arms supporting her.

Bit by bit, he inched her nightgown up, over her hips, across her midsection – and higher, freeing her breasts… finally off altogether. He cast the filmy garment aside as his mouth descended, devouring his wife with fervent kisses – the kind she hadn't felt in far too long!

Gary turned out the light and eased Michaela against the pillows.

She groaned in pleasure and relief as he entered her. Craving his touch, she wrapped her arms around him and rocked gently beneath him.

When Gary kissed her face, it was wet. "What's wrong?" he asked, his voice rough with passion.

Trembling at his touch, Michaela forced back tears. "Nothing," she whispered, overcome with emotion as she pulled him close for another kiss. "I'm fine. It's just… I've missed making love with you, Gary. I missed you so much."

Gary caressed his wife's face, shushing her with tender murmurings and kissing away her tears.

Michaela did her best to calm down, but his nearness felt overwhelming and all she succeeded in doing was bawling like a baby and drooling on his arm. She couldn't bear that something might really have been wrong, and she didn't want to burden him with those worries. All she wanted was to feel him inside her, filling her, and to feel him coming deep within her. "Please," she managed to choke out at last, "make love to me, Gary… I've missed you so much!"

"I missed you, too, baby," he murmured against her throat. Now he was moving inside her again.

Sighing softly, she settled back against the pillow. Her lower lip trembled when Gary kissed her.

Afterward, when they'd snuggled awhile and were drifting off to sleep, Micki was awake enough to roll onto her back, knees bent and legs shut tight. She prayed this lovemaking would be the start of a new baby. She knew Gary wanted another child. And as much as she wanted more kids, mostly she wanted something good to come of this whole awful mess. She looked at the glowing red numbers on the clock radio: 4:37. Still plenty of time to sleep.

For some minutes she lay awake in the dark, praying for a baby and listening to the peaceful sound of Gary's breathing as he lay curled up beside her. She prayed he would find respite in sleep.

And when he slept, Gary's dream did not return.

Lying still in the barely light room, Michaela listened to the erratic scribbling sound coming from across the room. She noticed Gary in a chair by the window, hunched over the journal Dr. Benson had given him in the hospital. His hair was mussed, his expression intense – like he couldn't write fast enough to keep up with his thoughts.

Not wanting to disrupt him, she waited until he stopped. "Good morning."

Running a hand through his hair, he looked up, smiling as their eyes met. "Hi, baby."

"You're up early. Doing some dream journaling?"

Gary shook his head, set down the book. "Not this morning" – he came back to bed – "I had an idea… haven't got it all fleshed out yet, but I think it could work."

Michaela snuggled close as he slid beneath the covers. "What is it?" As he explained, she listened intently, loving the rumble of his voice in her ear pressed to his chest. These last several months, she missed the closeness they'd always had. As much as she'd ached for the kind of passion they shared last night, she'd mourned the loss of simple tender moments – moments like these – even more. Safe now in his embrace, and secure in his love, she drifted back to sleep.

The foot of snow that fell overnight meant there'd be no school; no kids to wake up. Suddenly drowsy again, Gary pulled the covers up, drew Micki closer and fell asleep, too.

When they awakened, Michaela made breakfast while Gary shoveled the front walk.

As he cleared a path for the mailman, his mind raced. Sorting out details, he thought about how best to implement the ideas coming as fast as the heavy, wet snowflakes.

After breakfast, Erin helped the kids build a snow fort. Gary refilled his and Micki's coffee and rummaged for the cinnamon; he sprinkled a smidge in each mug, then went to the window to watch the kids playing in the yard.

Just as Micki was about to comment on the quiet, Gary spoke. "I'm gonna call Paul, see what he thinks."

She looked up from her coffee. Paul had been his boss back in Jersey. "About your idea?"

He turned to look at her. "Yeah. He always had a good head for that kind of thing. He's been in radio forever." It sounded like he was trying to convince himself of the idea's merit. "If anyone knows what I need to do next, it's him. Plus, he'll tell me the truth. If it's a lousy idea, he'll say so."

***

Paul Ramsey smiled. "There's only one way to go on this, Gary: Call Steve Reynolds."

Gary's voice teemed with anxiety. "I dunno; that's not a well I think I oughta visit too often."

"Too often?" Paul echoed. "When was the last time?"

"When he recommended me for the job at 'ZBX."

"Geez, Gar', that was a hundred years ago! Hardly 'too often.' Anyway, that's a great idea you've got. I'm sure Steve'll love it. In fact, if you need studio space in the City, I bet he'd be happy to set you up."

With all the skittishness of the teen he'd been last time they'd spoken, Gary punched in the number Paul gave him.

When the media mogul answered his private line, Gary faltered through introducing himself.

"Of course I remember you, Gary! What can I do for you?"

Gary looked over his notes from their conversation. And smiled. Possibly the most important indie media giant in New York City had asked in on a project he – a nobody from a small radio station in Connecticut! – had initiated.

Steve seemed hesitant after he'd invited Gary to come to New York, and Gary had to admit he wasn't permitted to leave the state. Once he allayed the other man's concerns by assuring him (with manufactured certainty) the bogus charges would be dismissed, Steve agreed to meet "whenever you're available," even offering to come to Connecticut.

Steve's private jet landed at Tweed-New Haven at 11:10 the next morning. Gary took him to lunch at Aspirante, over-looking the green. Between the Caprese salad and Tuscan chicken, Gary outlined his preliminary plans for the project.

Steve offered recommendations and ideas for implementing them.

Over espresso, Gary flipped through the eight pages of notes he'd taken. There was so much to do before they could get this off the ground!

"You look a little overwhelmed," Steve observed with a grin, reaching for an almond biscotti.

Gary gave a slow headshake. *Only a little?* "I had no idea it would be this complex."

Steve dipped the biscotti into his espresso. "It only seems complex. You've got it extremely well outlined; it'll be a breeze to put into action. As far as marketing goes, I think your idea of going with two separate programs is brilliant! You've doubled your chance of success right there, targeting two distinct market segments.

"I really think it'll take off. You've got my full backing and support, Gary. If you're ready, I'll have my lawyer draw up a partnership agreement and send it to your lawyer next week. Meantime, you can start doing your homework, researching stations in markets you want to hit."

Gary made it back in plenty of time.

The conversation flowed easily today. Gary was warm and affable – the opposite of who he'd been at Foxbridge.

"I started working on a new project."

"You mean like a home-repair project?"

Gary laughed. "Hell, no! I'm like the anti-Bob Vila."

Dr. Benson smiled.

"It's kind of a work thing, but a whole new direction. It's got nothing to do with the station. It's a syndicated show. I've got a backer in New York excited about it. And it's done wonders for my outlook."

The therapist nodded his understanding. "Still…"

He held up a hand, forestalling the doctor's admonition. "I know what you're gonna say, doc: I shouldn't depend on others to bolster my self-image, shouldn't rely on them to make me feel good about myself. I'm not. It's just *encouraging* that someone who took a chance on me sixteen years ago is enthusiastic about pursuing one of my ideas now. It's reaffirming – professionally, as well as personally." He paused. "What if – okay, maybe Freud would be stretching it… but what if one of the giants in the field of psychiatry told you a theory you'd devised was the greatest concept he'd ever heard?"

The psychiatrist laughed aloud. "I'd say he needs to have his head examined."

Gary grinned. "C'mon, doc. I thought *I* was the wise-ass here."

"You are. I guess I've been treating you too long." They shared an easy laugh. "But seriously," Dr. Benson continued. "I do understand what you mean, Gary. Something like that, it's quite a validation. And you're right; that *is* something to be proud of. Good job."

Michaela noticed the change immediately. It was as if this idea had given Gary a new sense of purpose. He was up early every morning now. Sometimes he'd nudge her awake, too; and the sex was almost as dynamic as when they were newlyweds!

Right after breakfast, he'd pour a second cup of coffee, head to his study and spend the morning tackling logistics: jotting notes; instant messaging distant colleagues; emailing record-company execs with whom he'd fostered relationships the past dozen years; placing countless long-distance calls; tracking down referral after referral.

On the days he wasn't seeing Dr. Benson, Gary cooked supper.

Micki recognized this was as therapeutic for him as the journaling. She welcomed the break from kitchen detail. Besides, Gary was a phenomenal cook. What's more, his appetite had returned.

She would come home from running errands to find him prepping vegetables and looking as close to happy as she could remember seeing him in months. There'd be wonderful aromas emanating from the kitchen… often a pot of broth bubbling on the stove and – almost without fail – Aerosmith, Led Zeppelin or AC/DC blaring from the countertop CD player.

She often wondered whether it was this new project, his medication or twice-weekly sessions with Dr. Benson that was responsible for the change. She decided it didn't matter; all that mattered was Gary was feeling better. Michaela sent up a silent prayer of thanksgiving.

(April 14 – Tuesday)

"How's life treating you?"

"It's not treating me at all; it's making me pay my own way," Gary teased, his grey eyes full of play. "Okay, I guess."

"But…?" Dr. Benson prompted.

He sighed. "How much longer do I have to stay on this medication?"

A direct question – no dancing around. The therapist knew it was only a matter of time before that topic came up. "Hard to say. There haven't been any problems, have there?"

Gary shook his head. "No. It's just… well, I've made progress; I know I have! I haven't exhibited a single symptom of depression in—"

"Likely due in large part to the medication," Dr. Benson interjected quietly. "It'd be premature to stop now, especially so close to the start of your trial. I don't want you coming unglued right when it's most important for you to be in control of your emotions."

Gary glanced away, scowling, then looked back at the therapist. "Before you say it, here's how it makes me feel: Inadequate, alright? I understand what you're saying and I kind of agree. But I still feel like I ought to be able to keep my emotions in check on my own – without having to resort to popping pills."

Dr. Benson nodded. "I can appreciate that. Thank you for being so forthright. I know how hard it can be to admit how we're feeling, or even acknowledge we *have* feelings sometimes.

"There's nothing wrong with admitting you can't do everything on your own. When was the last time you repaired your own car? Or your leaky water heater? You wouldn't. You'd turn to a professional, someone with the right tools to fix what's wrong. You turned to me for help when something in your life needed realigning. One of my tools is therapy; another is the medication you're on." He paused. "Don't think I haven't noticed the progress you've made. It's the result of a lot of hard work on your part. But I know there's still a ways to go. I know I can't force you to stay on your meds, Gary, but I'm asking you to be patient a little while longer. I can't promise a positive turnout with this trial, but I know — whatever the outcome — it'll be easier to deal with *on* your medication than *off* it."

Gary sat silent for most of a minute, absorbing Dr. Benson's words. "Okay," he acquiesced. "I've come this far. Guess I can stick with it a few more weeks" — he looked at the doctor — "or longer."

(2:17 a.m., April 20 – Monday)

Despite the busy-ness of the weekend, sleep eluded Gary. After lying awake in bed for over an hour, he slipped downstairs. Putting the radio on low for background noise, he sat in his study, intending to work.

Distracted by a seemingly endless stream of commercials, he fiddled with the tuning knob until he hit a station whose signal came in strong. He didn't recognize the frequency, but the soothing voice emanating from the speaker put him at ease.

"… wasting so much precious time and energy holding onto grudges," the man was saying. "Perhaps there's some unrest in your life, some issue weighing heavy on you that needs resolving."

One of those late-night preachers whose messages of love invariably worked around to 'Send in your money.' And that turned him off. As Gary was about to flip stations, the minister asked, "Is there someone who needs your forgiveness? A relative, coworker… maybe a close friend who hurt you?"

Gary's hand stopped an inch from the knob.

"Everybody knows someone who needs to hear those precious words, 'I forgive you.' It's time to let go. Yes, I'm talking to you. Let go of that grudge. Whatever hurt you're nursing, is it really worth the sleepless nights, the angst, the tears? Release the hurt. Set it free. Give yourself permission to let it go."

An image entered Gary's brain. He felt his heart thump, heard his steady, rhythmic breathing. Looking down, he watched two pairs of running shoes moving in tandem.

In that instant, he realized why he gave up his daily run. Not because he was so busy at work — nor that he'd gotten involved with the business of life and fatherhood. It wasn't that at all. Not if he was honest with himself. He didn't want to be reminded of what used to be… and how it had all ended.

"You may be saying, 'But you don't know what he did to me…' Doesn't matter. Let it go," the preacher's voice urged. "It may not be easy, but remember: No one ever lost sleep forgiving someone."

Thump. Thump. Thump. Two sets of feet pounded along pavement, rustling crunchy autumn leaves with each step. Neither strove to outrun the other; they ran side by side, as companions. Equals. Friends.

As their feet flew along the three-mile course, snippets of conversation mingled with easy laughter. Sometimes silence. They'd been the closest of friends once; they'd talked about everything. Everything. Good and bad. Even the most painful things. Except that last painful thing.

Gary flinched. *That* they hadn't been able to talk about.

"Holding grudges is like lugging around a steamer trunk. Envision yourself dragging that thing everywhere: to work, to church, out with friends… even to bed," the preacher continued. "It gets heavier all the time, because you keep stowing more stuff inside. And that's all it is: useless stuff. Old, worn-out, moth-eaten *stuff*. Yet you cling to your emotional baggage. Why? It's familiar. It's been hanging around so long you've gotten used to it.

"It's taking up space in your life – space that could be better filled with experiences and people who bring you joy. Valuable space that could be filled with love and happiness – and forgiveness. Instead, you choose to hang onto that musty old trunk full of long-ago hurts and wounded feelings."

Gary thought back to their last conversation: that horrid, contentious one. If he was hones with himself, it wasn't so much a conversation as a venomous tirade. Gary hadn't let his once-dearest friend say anything. He'd simply stated his position and demanded immediate compliance… or else. No room for compromise. Not on this.

"Why not do some spring cleaning?" the minister suggested. "Throw open that heavy old lid and discard what's lurking there. Maybe thirty years ago Aunt Sue called you fat. Is that why you didn't invite her and Uncle Theo to your wedding? Or maybe your sister inherited Mom's silver tea set and the good china, and all you got was those silver-plated butter spreaders. Is that why you cut yourself off from your nieces and nephews?"

This isn't like that. Gary wrapped himself in self-righteous ire. *This isn't a silly misunderstanding. This is real. This is huge. This is unforgivable.*

"Or maybe a dear friend did something monumentally awful to cause a major rift between you."

Gary inhaled sharply. He hadn't listened to Greg's pleas for mercy or forgiveness. How *could* he? What he'd done was the worst sort of betrayal. Bigger than 'monumentally awful.' He'd really crossed the line! But still… they'd been through so much together, shared so much. Maybe he was right, this minister guy. Maybe it was time to release the hurt; maybe it *was* possible to forgive.

Gary listened as the man went on, as if he were addressing him personally. "Aren't the bonds of friendship stronger than human weakness? Would you really cast aside one who means so much to you just because you're feeling offended or hard done by? Our Lord would never do that. He's always ready to forgive, no matter what we've done. So how can we withhold forgiveness from someone we've loved? Or deny ourselves the forgiveness He freely gives — over and over again?"

Weary of fighting his emotions, Gary made no attempt to stifle them. Regret washed over him as he mourned the lost friendship, the years wasted hating his first friend in Connecticut, who'd reached out to him when he was a stranger, made him feel welcome, then led him to understand what it meant to be a good friend, a loving husband. Over the years, they'd laughed and cried, shared triumphs and burdens; discussed everything from theology to women to sex. They'd supported each other amid boundless joy and unspeakable suffering. Greg had even officiated at Gary and Michaela's wedding!

And yet, all it had taken was one act of betrayal to shatter everything. Gary reminded himself his own faithless act had set the ball in motion; but still, that didn't give Greg free rein to destroy his world, jeopardize his marriage and ruin their friendship. Gary's emotions swirled madly within him.

"Pull out those old grudges you've nursed. They've grown bigger and heavier with each passing year, haven't they?" he heard the preacher say. "It's tempting, but don't even take a final look at them. Just throw them on the trash heap. Discard them. There's no better time than now to forgive."

Gary's cries of distress sounded big and loud in the cozy little study. He'd clung to his hostility so long! Hunching forward, he crumpled against his desk. He begged God for strength to forgive. He wept in bitterness for the damage done, and in fear his reaching out might be spurned. What if too much time had passed and Greg was content to let the leprosied friendship die? What if he still harbored hostilities of his own? After all, Gary *had* gotten him fired.

When Gary's relentless sobs stilled at last, the preacher's soothing voice filtered through his haze of pain and guilt.

"While you're at it, forgive yourself. Sometimes we focus so much on forgiving others, we forget *we* need forgiveness, too. Next time you go by a mirror, stop and take a good long look. Look yourself in the eye and say, 'I forgive you.' And really mean it…"

With an unsteady finger, Gary poked the OFF button. The preacher's words of encouragement stopped and the room was silent, except for an occasional sniffle.

On his way back to bed, he stopped in the front hall and peered into the mirror. His eyes were red and swollen, his face blotchy. *Yuck.* He looked exactly like he felt! Gary stared at his image for several seconds before deciding self-forgiveness was too much effort right now. He turned away from his forlorn reflection and trudged upstairs.

Gary was still in bed when Micki was leaving to bring Michael to his play group. "Are you feeling okay?" she asked, peeling back the covers from her husband's face.

He gathered them back around himself. "Just leave me alone."

Eventually, he plodded into the bathroom. After he showered and shaved, Gary cast a furtive glance at the mirror. Guilty eyes looked back. He retreated in haste to the bedroom.

Micki returned home almost three hours later; she fed and played with Michael for a while, then put him down for his nap.

She entered their bedroom and sat beside Gary's crumpled body. "Honey? Are you hungry? I made you some soup."

"Please go away."

"Do you feel sick? Do you want some Tylenol?"

Now he didn't even answer, just retreated further under the covers.

"Is there anything I can get you?"

"A big glass of hemlock."

Michaela tried excavating him from beneath layers of bedclothes. "I'm *serious*, Gary."

"So'm I," came the disheartened reply. He fought to re-embed himself.

"But, sweetheart… you've been doing so *well*. What happened?"

Gary looked up at his wife, his beloved. For a moment, his eyes met hers.

In that instant she thought she saw a flicker of hope. As quickly as it appeared, his eyes turned vacant and disinterested again.

The anguish on his face spoke clearer than any words he could have uttered. She sensed he ached to let her in, but – even after all these years together – he didn't know how.

"Can you tell me what's wrong?"

He shook his head and buried his face in the pillow.

"Is it something physical? Emotional?"

No reply.

"Should I call Dr. Benson?"

Again, no response.

Michaela's tone sharpened slightly. "Okay, this is getting nowhere. You want me to go?"

The covers shuddered.

She waited for him to say – or do – something. Gary remained ensconced. Unresponsive. After almost a full minute, she let out a sigh of resignation and got to her feet. "Have it your way," she mumbled, patting his shoulder.

As his wife turned to leave, he snaked a hand out from beneath the covers and closed it around her wrist. She came back toward the bed.

His hand was shaking. He peeked out from beneath the covers, his eyes beseeching. Slowly, Gary drew Michaela's hand to his lips and kissed it, then pressed her palm against his cheek.

Within moments, she heard his erratic breathing slow. Feeling tears spring to her eyes, she blinked them away. He was connecting the only way he could. She crouched by the bed. The covers rose and fell more evenly as his breathing steadied and deepened.

"I wish you'd talk to me, sweetheart," she whispered, smoothing his hair with her free hand.

Withdrawing like a threatened turtle, Gary drew in his breath audibly and retreated beneath the covers; he released Micki's hand.

A cry of frustration caught in her throat. "You keep shutting me out, Gary. I won't let you just lie here – *marinating* in your self-pity. Talk to me, damn it!" She drew the bedclothes away from his face. He pulled them back.

Micki tried again; this time he held them fast.

Hot tears slid down her cheeks. She swiped them away with both hands. "Alright, fine; you don't want to talk. I get that. But we're on the same team. You think I like to see you hurting?" she warbled in desperation. "It scares me, Gary, when you're like this. I don't know what's going on and it makes me feel useless. I can't help you if you won't let me in."

Her sneakers squeaked against the hardwood floor. At the door, she turned back. Gary had moved the covers just enough to see out around them. He looked away when her watery gaze fell on him.

A moment later Michaela clicked the door shut behind her.

After the kids were in bed, Gary ventured downstairs, looking more haggard than Michaela had seen him in a while.

"Are you hungry?" she asked as he slumped past.

He grunted what sounded like "no" and kept going.

As she heard the study door shut, Michaela wiped away a mist of tears and headed up to bed. Worried he might have gone off his meds, she counted the pills in the bottles in the medicine chest – but the appropriately diminished quantities reassured her he was still taking them.

It was after three thirty when Gary returned upstairs.

Next day, Gary remained cocooned amid the covers, emerging only to use the bathroom and – at Michaela's urging – to get something to eat.

Leaving most of his bowl of Raisin Bran untouched, he went back to bed.

Micki watched him go, wondering how to reach him. She prayed for answers, for insight, for help.

That night, back in the study, Gary turned on the radio, hoping to catch the call sign of the station where he'd heard that preacher the other night – or hear what he had to say tonight.

Nothing but static. Same as last night. He switched off the radio and checked an online listing of AM stations; that frequency wasn't assigned to any 24-hour station northeast of Kentucky.

Gary returned to bed with chills.

The bedside light came on. It was almost three. "Gary, please," Micki begged, sitting up. "Talk to me. What can I do to help?"

For two days, Greg had occupied every thought, every moment. Gary couldn't dispel him. Not even in sleep. He grasped Michaela's hands, struggling with how to word his query. "Do you" – it took a long time to get the rest of the question out – "ever think about Greg?"

Micki's breath came in a sharp gasp; she felt like he'd slapped her. Her eyes filled with tears, her heart with shame. Neither of them had spoken that name in seven years.

"Of course not!" She tugged her hands free. "Is *that* what you've been— How can you even ask that?"

Gary backpedaled. "I'm not trying to make you feel guilty. I've thought about this for days and there's no way to ask that doesn't make it sound horrible. But that's not how I meant it, Mick. Please don't take it the wrong way. Okay?"

Despite his assurances, humiliation consumed Michaela. Unwelcome images of their short-lived affair saturated her memory. Deeply ashamed, she pulled away from Gary, sat at the edge of the bed and wept.

Regret pressed on Gary's heart. This was *not* how he'd envisioned their talk going. He drew her back into his arms, cuddling her close.

Amid sobs, Michaela assured Gary she had never once looked back on her infidelity with anything but profound sorrow and remorse – and no, she'd never given Greg another thought.

Gary's words were so quiet Micki wasn't sure she'd heard correctly.

She stared at him, her eyes streaming with tears. "What?"

"I said '*I* do.' These past few days, I've done nothing but think about Greg."

He ached to tell her about the preacher on that phantom station. "I mean Greg, our *friend*," he clarified, "not—"

Micki put her trembling fingers over his mouth to hush the words that would shame her further.

"I miss him," Gary lamented. "I miss his wisdom… his humor. And his friendship. I keep feeling like a piece of me is gone. The piece where Greg should be."

Big salty tears poured down Micki's face. Guilt and regret stung her heart. "What do you want to do?"

Gary's voice was hesitant, plaintive. "I think I want to forgive him."

In the morning, Gary didn't stir when Micki got up to make the kids' lunches.

It took him until midmorning to summon the courage to reach for the phone. He withered a little when the folks at the archdiocesan chancery said they had no information about particular deacons' whereabouts and suggested he call the diaconate office in Bloomfield.

After a fair bit of sleuthing, the lady at the second office found the information Gary sought. "But he's been laicized," she informed him.

"What's that mean?"

"Mr. Andrews is no longer functioning as a deacon. He's been returned to lay status."

"Oh." Gary felt numb; he couldn't help feeling partly responsible.

"I believe he still works at St. Gerard's in West Hartford," she added helpfully. "You could try him at this number…"

Gary listened as the connection went through; it rang and rang. As he was about to hang up, he heard a click.

"Hi, you've reached the religious-education office at St. Gerard's. I'm sorry I can't take your call just now; but if you leave your name, number and a message, I'll get back to you soon. Thanks for calling and have a bles—"

Gary's hand shook as he hung up. *It's just as well. Dunno what I woulda said to him anyway.*

Minutes later, the phone rang. Gary leapt. *What if it's him? What if he's got Caller ID and knows it's me? I can't talk to him – I don't know what to say…*

The insistent ringing continued. He stared at the phone. On the fifth ring, he answered. "Hello?"

"Gary?"

Panic seized him. "Greg…?"

"Gary, it's Pete."

"Oh!" His heart clattered against his ribcage, trying to get out. "Hi, chief. What's up?"

"You don't sound so good. You okay?"

"I'm fine. What's goin' on?"

"You've got a bunch of mail piling up over here," his boss said. "Can I bring it over?"

"Nah – no sense you going out of your way. It's probably junk, anyway."

"Most of it's marked 'personal.' Figured you'd want to see it. Besides, I was kinda hoping you'd be up for a visit this afternoon."

Gary managed a wan smile. "I could probably do with a visit. C'mon over."

"Hi Gar'," Pete greeted him when Gary answered the door. "You're looking better."

Gary smirked. "Yeah, well, it's hard to look worse. It's good to see you. C'mon in." He nodded toward the cardboard tube the other man was carrying. "What'cha got there?"

"Just a little something we made," he replied as Gary motioned him toward the living room. "Go on, open it."

Sliding the contents from the tube, Gary unrolled it on the coffee table. "We Miss You, Gary!" the oversized poster proclaimed. It was signed by the entire staff. Many had included personal messages or little doodles. He scanned it, then looked up at Pete, grinning. "You guys are the best!" After a more careful look, he smirked. "Guess I shouldn't be surprised Steffi didn't bother to sign it; we've always been like oil and water."

Pete shook his head. "Steffi's gone. She violated Tom's edict about not mentioning you on air."

Gary snorted. "I can just imagine what she had to say."

"It wasn't like that at all. She came in one day loaded for bear and railed about how sick she was of hearing other stations' morning teams trash you. I was so proud of her… which made it particularly hard to go in and fire her. But I had my orders: No mentioning you on air except for news coverage."

Cold numbness seeped into Gary's insides. His lips felt sluggish, heavy. "Where'd she end up?"

Pete shrugged. "Don't know. That was almost two months ago. I told her she could use me as a reference, but I haven't heard a word from or about her since."

The coldness worked its way up into his chest. "I feel kind of responsible – I mean, she got fired because of me."

"No, she got herself fired. But I know what you mean."

Pete pulled a bulging envelope from his overcoat pocket. "Here's your mail – and this is just the personal stuff. Jenna came back to take care of the business end of things."

"That's nice of her."

Jenna Glesson had been Gary's predecessor as music director; she'd left years ago to care for her ailing son. Now

Aiden was well again and back in school, so she had more free time.

He opened the overstuffed parcel. Dozens of letters and cards tumbled onto the coffee table. "This is just the non-business stuff? Who're all these from?" A few return-address labels looked familiar.

"Some from record-company reps, others from local businesses," Pete replied. "Plenty I don't recognize. Maybe listeners?"

Gary looked up from the imposing jumble of mail. "This is unreal." He shook his head at the outpouring of support, then shoved the pile aside. "I'll read these later. What's up with you?"

After Pete left, Gary turned his attention to the heap of mail before him. He neatened it into a teetering stack. One letter caught his attention: a cream-colored envelope of heavy stock, postmarked Hartford. The return address was unfamiliar, but Gary recognized the handwriting. His breath snagged in his throat. Hands shaking, he stuck it at the bottom.

When he'd gone through everything and could avoid it no longer, he picked up the remaining envelope and retreated into the study. He sat at his desk, agonizing over whether to open it. It felt rich, substantial. Its surface felt like linen. Finally, he inserted the tip of the letter opener. With a deep breath, he slid the chrome blade the length of the sealed flap. His hands trembled as he pulled the one-page letter free.

Gary's insides clenched and fluttered as he unfolded the sheet of stationery to read the handwritten message within.

He stopped reading partway through. He crumpled the letter. His talk with Michaela early that morning clamored through his head. The way she sobbed in shame made him profoundly regret having dredged up that pain and humiliation for his wife.

After listening to that radio preacher, he'd felt called to forgive his longtime friend. But what about restoring their friendship? Gary groaned with the weight of indecision. He supposed he could manage the first without necessarily allowing the second. He smoothed the wrinkled paper, re-folded it and shoved it back in its envelope. His left eye twitched. It did that lately, whenever his stress level spiked.

Gary studied the postmark. It had been mailed the day before he'd heard that preacher. *What are the chances?* He didn't believe in coincidences. He slid the envelope into his desk drawer.

Gary shut the door on his way out, needing an extra physical barrier against Greg's letter.

***

That night, Gary went to bed uncharacteristically early.

He awoke before dawn. Careful not to disturb Micki's sleep, he got dressed and went for a run.

When he got back, Gary packed the girls' lunches and started breakfast. He made coffee and brought a mug up to Michaela, just how she liked it: with plenty of milk and a hint of cinnamon.

Setting the mug on her nightstand, he leaned to kiss her awake. "Good morning, baby."

Her eyelids fluttered. As her gaze focused on his face, her smile bloomed. "Good morning." She sat up and met his kiss. "You're up early."

Now she looked him over. "And already dressed."

Gary sat beside her on the bed. "Been out for a run, too." He handed her the coffee mug. "Thought you'd like a little something to get you going."

"Thank you." Michaela smiled and took a sip. "Mmm... perfect! I'd better get moving – gotta make lunches."

"Already done. Breakfast is in the oven, too. It should be ready in" – he checked his watch – "about twenty-five minutes."

"Ooh, ya don't say? Guess that gives us plenty of time." She gave him a warm kiss.

"Actually, I'm pretty gross. I was about to go take a shower..."

"How about we take one together?" she suggested, an impish grin darting across her face.

Over breakfast, Gary offered to drive the girls to school. Twenty minutes later, as he herded them out of the house, he told Michaela, "Got some errands to run. I've got my phone if you need me." After a long, slow kiss, he headed out to the car.

An hour and a half later, Gary pulled into the parking lot beside the building whose address he'd scribbled on the sheet of paper in his hand.

Getting out, he looked up at the imposing three-story Greek Revival structure. It wasn't at all what he'd expected. Then again, nothing these days was as he expected it to be. Taking a deep breath to steady his nerves, he made his way up the sidewalk to the grand entryway.

The receptionist welcomed him and asked how she could be of assistance.

He told her why he'd come and listened carefully to her reply. He thanked her and headed in the direction she indicated.

Gary stopped in front of the third office on the right. The wooden door was ajar, but not open wide enough for him to see inside. After a nervous few seconds, he gave a slight tap at the door.

"Come in."

With a hard swallow, Gary nudged the door; it swung inward on silent hinges. He glanced around. The office was smaller than he would have envisioned, given the building's overall structure. Bookshelves lined two walls and a hulking gunmetal-grey desk stood guard over the windows along the third wall. Two chairs sat opposite the circa-'70s metal desk.

"Hello?" The greeting, which emanated from behind the door, startled Gary.

Hastily shutting the door, he came face to face with

Greg Andrews, standing by yet another bookcase behind the door.

"How can I hel—" The question died on his lips. "Gary." The man took a stumbling step backward. His jaw slackened and his face paled.

"Hi." Gary didn't quite know what else to say.

'It's been a long time.' 'You're looking well.' 'Nice to see you not with my wife.' None of them would have seemed quite appropriate.

Visibly uncomfortable, Greg motioned toward the guest chairs. "Please, sit." Retreating, he sat in the creaky wooden swivel chair behind his desk.

Gary sat. He drummed his fingers on the chair's slim wooden arms. Painful silence swirled through the room. Finally, he spoke. "I got your letter."

Greg responded with a slow nod.

"Thank you for the prayers. It means a lot to me. More than you know. These past several months… it's been horrible."

"I can only imagine how awful that must be, Gary. Like I said in the letter, I—"

"I didn't read the whole thing," he admitted. "Just the first paragraph and part of the second. I appreciate the prayers," he reiterated.

The other man nodded. "I'm glad you opened it at all."

Gary hedged. "Had it arrived at any other time, I might not have."

Leaning forward slightly, Greg tilted his head. "Why?"

Briefly, Gary explained about the radio preacher's exhortation about forgiveness. "Honestly, I've done nothing but think about you all week," he admitted. "How we could talk about anything… and how much I've missed your presence in my life."

Greg opened his mouth to say something, but stopped.

Gary leaned back in his chair. "You were my first friend in Connecticut. You welcomed me when I didn't know anyone. You taught me so much – whether you realized it or not. And for that, Greg, I'm truly grateful." Now he sat forward again, leaning his elbows hard against the arms of the chair. "That's why this is so hard for me to say."

Greg's expression changed from openness to worry. "That doesn't sound good."

Gary shook his head. "No, it doesn't." He glanced down. "You always counseled me to err on the side of kindness, on the side of forgiveness. I know that what destroyed our friendship was, at its root, as much my doing as yours. I'm still working on forgiving myself. I came here today because I want you to know I forgive you."

Greg nodded. "But?"

Gary gave a slow, sad headshake. "I've given this a lot of thought, Greg, and I've prayed about it even more – constantly, in fact. I don't want to rebuild our friendship."

Seeing the other man about to protest, Gary held up a hand. "Let me explain. I've missed our friendship. Missed running with you and our talks about everything from faith issues to movies. I can't count the times I've wanted to call to tell you about some silly thing at work, or something cute one of the kids said. But I think this is where it has to end."

"Why do you say that?"

Gary grappled for words to convey his feelings without assigning blame. "These past several years, I've worked hard to mend damaged relationships, but if we repaired this one, I'd always feel like I couldn't tell Michaela I'd fixed things with you. It would seem too deceitful. I also wouldn't feel comfortable sharing information about her. Micki's the priority in my life. Let's leave it at this: I forgive you, Greg. And I apologize for my part in derailing our friendship. But I can't in good faith rebuild that relation-ship."

Greg folded his hands on the desk before him; he gave a slow, deliberate nod. "I understand, Gary. That saddens me, but I respect your decision."

After a long silence, Greg spoke again. "I appreciate your coming here to talk, face to face. It can't have been an easy thing to do. Frankly, if things had been reversed, I might not have been able to do what you've done."

Gary nodded. "I won't take up any more of your time. Thanks for not making this harder than it already was. Goodbye, Greg." Standing, he extended his hand toward the other man.

Greg clasped it. "It was good to see you, Gary. I'd like it if you came back again sometime."

Gary shook his head. "It'd feel too much like cheating on Michaela. I promised her I'd never do that again." He offered a melancholy smile. "Bye, Greg."

Chapter 22

(April 27 – Monday)

Jolene's voice trembled as she spoke of the degradation she endured from Z97-3's music director all those months ago; she wept into the tissue wadded in her fist. Several times, the teen covered her face with her hands and blubbered as she recounted the "beastly" acts the defendant coerced her into.

Each time, the assistant D.A. patted her arm. "I know how painful this must be for you, Jolene… especially with *him*" – she motioned vaguely toward Gary – "sitting right over there."

"Objection."

"Sustained."

Sabine continued as if there'd been no objection. "But I need for you to tell the Court about the things he did to you."

Gary jotted notes on a lined pad, occasionally turning it for Blake to read; and once, he leaned to whisper something to his attorney.

For the most part, while he paid close attention to everything being heaped against him, Gary resisted showing any outward reaction.

Before the trial started this morning, Michael Conwaye advised his son-in-law to remain calm during the prosecution witnesses' testimony. "You'll get your turn to set the record straight. Anything glaring, Blake will object. If someone testifies to something you know is a lie, make note of it, so he can question them about it on cross. Just don't lose your cool."

He wanted to protest; but Gary figured Michael – with thirty-plus years' courtroom experience – knew better than he did what went on here. He promised he'd keep his temper in check.

"He'd come up behind me in the break room when no one else was there and rub up against me. And he'd whisper these suggestive things… things he wanted to do to me. I thought it was sexy at first. But then he forced me to *do* those things with him in the production room."

She dabbed at her eyes with a tissue. "The first time, he um — seduced me. I kind of didn't mind at first, 'cause he was this older, sophisticated guy who'd taken an interest in me. I mean, who wouldn't feel flattered? And he started out real gentle… said I was 'nice and tight,' just like his daughter, but—"

"You're a fucking liar!" Gary sputtered, scrambling to his feet. Blake had to restrain him from rushing the witness stand.

"Sit down!" Judge Paterna pounded his gavel, then pointed it at the defendant. "We'll have some decorum in here. And let's get this straight right now, Mr. Sheldon: I will not tolerate profanity in my courtroom. One more outburst like that and I'm holding you in contempt. Is that clear?"

"Yes, Your Honor." Gary straightened his suit jacket as Blake pulled him back into his seat.

"And perhaps, Mr. Tierney, you should advise your client to act like a civilized human being in my presence — or you can clue him in as to what awaits if he continues to behave otherwise."

"Yes, Your Honor," Blake said, firing a warning look at Gary. "I'm sure there won't be any further disruptions."

"There'd better not be." Giving Gary a disapproving glower, the judge turned to Jolene. "Please continue, dear."

Big tears pooled in the teen's eyes. She wiped them away. "Like I said, he started out gentle — but then he got rough and I was scared, so I told him to stop. But he wouldn't. He hurt me. He said as much as he wanted to, he shouldn't get me pregnant — 'cause his 'stupid cow of a wife' wouldn't understand — so he always used a condom. I think he just didn't want to leave any evidence."

"Objection, Your Honor," Blake spoke up. "Is the witness an expert in divining what other people are thinking?"

"Sustained. The jury will disregard the last portion of the witness' statement."

Sabine picked up an evidence bag. "Your Honor, I'd like this entered into evidence as People's Exhibit Three. Jolene, are these the condom packages Gary provided?"

Jolene nodded. "Yes."

"You said he 'always' used condoms. How many times did Gary force you to have sex with him?"

The girl's voice wavered. "Twice."

Sabine counted. "But I see four condom packages here…"

Jolene looked at Gary, her eyes glinting with vicious triumph. "That's because he couldn't always… you know — *perform*."

A snicker ran through the courtroom. Judge Paterna banged his gavel to restore order.

The prosecutor turned toward the jury, then back at Jolene. "Okay, defendant's… er, *prowess* notwithstanding: What did he do with the condoms?"

"Whenever he took one out of his pocket, he'd wipe it off on his shirttail, then drop it onto the countertop."

"Which explains why, when the packets were examined, there was no trace of Gary's fingerprints on them," Sabine pointed out. "Then what happened?"

"He made me open the condom and put it on him."

"And did you?"

"What choice did I have? He threatened me. He said if I didn't, he'd have my supervisor write a bad review. And he'd make sure I never got a job in radio."

"He had the power to do that?"

"Of course he did. He's like a god over there."

"Objection, Your Honor. Witness has no knowledge of the defendant's supposed deity status."

"Sustained. And Mr. Tierney, tone down the cuteness."

"It's like he can do no wrong – they all listen to him," Jolene turned toward the judge and charged onward. "Of course they're gonna believe his word over mine."

Judge Paterna banged his gavel. "I said, the objection is sustained. Ms Delacourt, please instruct your witness to stick to the facts and stop running on at the mouth."

"But I'm telling you the truth," the girl insisted, her eyes wide and tearful. "Gary raped me in the production studio."

Blake stood. "Miss Cunningham, a moment ago, when Ms Delacourt asked whether you put the condoms in question on my client, you asked, 'What choice did I have?' What choice, indeed? Couldn't you have said 'No'?"

She shrugged, sniffled. "I – I guess so… maybe."

"Couldn't you have, oh… run from the room? After all, you testified there were still other people around – surely someone could have saved you from this beast."

"He would have chased after me."

"With all those other people around? I mean, if Gary was—" he paused, paced for a moment. "How can I put this delicately? If Gary was in the" – he gestured with one hand – "*compromised* position you described, and expecting you to put a condom on him, let's face it: He'd have been at a distinct disadvantage. You could have been clear out of the building before he got his pants back up. Excuse my bluntness, Your Honor, but I can't imagine that stuffing a full-fledged ere—"

"Mr. Tierney," Judge Paterna cautioned. "Stop right there. I'll ask you to watch your wording."

"Yes, Your Honor." He hesitated, figuring how best to rephrase this. He tried again. "I can't see how maneuvering such… obvious arousal back into his pants *and* zipping them up would exactly be an easy endeavor. Not to mention trying to run after her in that condition."

A few jurors stifled snickers.

"Well, it wasn't all *that* big," Jolene interjected viciously, eliciting more laughter.

Judge Paterna forced his lips into a tight line, stifling a chuckle of his own. He debated whether to caution Blake again about his use of creative imagery. He realized the defense attorney was trying to make a point while preserving a degree of respectability. Provided Blake didn't start acting out the events he was describing, he would allow some latitude.

Unfazed by the girl's comment, Blake continued. "Alleged size notwithstanding, Your Honor, with other people still there, Gary would not have risked running out of the studio with his pants around his knees."

Now he addressed Jolene again. "And you know as well as I do, there's no way he would have chased after you with others around."

"Objection. Is there a question here or is the defense jumping right to his closing argument?"

"Sustained. Save it, Counselor."

Blake paced for several seconds. He stopped in front of the witness stand. "Miss Cunningham, when Mr. Sheldon first started *allegedly* coming on to you in the break room, did you ask him to stop?"

"Uhh… no."

"Did you tell anyone?"

"No."

"Why not?"

"Well, like I said, at first I kind of liked it. It wasn't 'til he had me alone in production that things got scary."

"But what you contend he was doing – isn't that sexual harassment?"

"I guess."

"So why didn't you report him to his superiors? Or at least tell your supervisor at the station – or someone from your school?"

"I told you…"

"Oh, that's right. It was flattering at first. Now, you're certain it was the production studio where you were alone on the night of November seventeenth?"

"Yes."

"Which one?"

"Excuse me?"

"The station has two production studios. Which one were you in?"

"Uhh… I – I don't remember."

"Either time?"

She shrugged. "I don't know."

"I see. So you and Gary were alone in a production studio. And suddenly, out of the clear blue, he attacked you. At least that's what you testified to earlier. Is that correct?"

"Y-yes."

"And then, according to your testimony, he assaulted you again on the twentieth. Is that what you'd like us to believe?"

"Yes! Gary raped me." Sniffling, Jolene wiped her eyes with an already-soggy tissue.

Blake strode to the defense table. Snatching a squat little box of tissues off the table, he returned to the witness stand. The protruding tissue made a little *ffffpp!* sound as Blake tugged it from the box. His expression hovering between boredom and impatience, he held it out to Jolene.

With a wary glance at the defense attorney, she accepted the tissue. She looked around for a wastebasket. Finding none, Jolene wadded the used tissue in her hand, Sniffling, she dabbed at her eyes and blew her nose.

Still holding the tissue box, Blake drummed the fingers of his other hand on the witness stand. "So, where is the physical evidence?"

"What?"

"The physical evidence of rape, Miss Cunningham. Where is it?"

"I told you, he used condoms!"

"That's right; you did," Blake leaned against the witness stand. "So, tell me: Where are these used condoms?"

"Objection, Your Honor. Badgering."

"Overruled. Please answer the question, Miss."

"I-I don't know," Jolene stammered. "He – he must have taken them with him."

Blake turned toward the jury and shook his head, then faced the witness stand again. "You just testified when he was finished, Gary removed the condom, threw it away and left you, alone and crying, in the production studio. Now, if your rapist had just tossed a discarded condom into the trash — a condom with both his DNA *and* yours present on it — why wouldn't you have taken it from the trash as evidence? And gone directly to the police?"

The girl sat there, mouth open. "I – I – I guess I was too upset to think straight." Jolene's lower lip quivered. Her eyes welled with fresh tears, which spilled down her round pink cheeks.

With a melodramatic sigh, Blake tugged a second tissue from the box and held it out to her. When she sogged that one up, he pulled forth another.

Casting about for some place to put them and finding none, she shoved the three sodden tissues into her pocket. Then she accepted a fourth fresh one from Blake. "Thank you," Jolene murmured, her pouty lips trembling.

He gave a slight nod in reply, then waited while she blew her nose heartily before continuing his line of questioning. "You had the presence of mind to save the condom wrappers you claim Gary discarded. Why not the used contents, too? Maybe you didn't want to get your fingers gooey. Is that it? Or it could be simply because you're lying!" He thumped the top of the witness stand and stared down at her. "Isn't it true, Miss Cunningham, none of this ever happened at all and this whole story is a hoax?"

"Objection! Your Honor, he's intimidating the witness."

"Watch your step, Mr. Tierney," Judge Paterna cautioned. "You know better than that."

Several jurors frowned.

"Your Honor, she claims my client used condoms the two times he allegedly forced her to have sex with him, then disposed of them in the trash. It's a reasonable assumption she would have retrieved them as proof of the assault." Blake turned once more to Jolene and gave her an indulgent smile.

"Perhaps you misspoke in your earlier testimony. I'm willing to give you the benefit of the doubt. But where *did* those pesky condoms go? Did Gary throw them in the trash at all? Did he wrap them up and stuff them into his pocket instead? Was he a magician performing sleight of hand and tricked you into thinking he'd thrown them away? Or did they simply vanish into thin air?"

"Objection!"

"Withdrawn. But didn't you testify that, after my client had his way with you – twice – you saw him remove the used condoms afterward?"

"Y-yeah." Jolene wiped at her eyes with the last dry corner of her tissue.

Blake pulled out another for her. "Then what did he do with them?"

Jolene took the tissue, stuffed the used one in her pocket. She wiped her eyes again, said nothing.

Blake handed the girl another tissue, watching her take it and stuff the used one in her pocket with the others. He let her squirm in silence for several seconds before trying a new tack.

"Mysteriously missing condoms aside, did you tell anyone the first time Gary supposedly coerced you into having sex with him?"

"No."

"Why not?"

"I was afraid."

"What about the second time?"

"No, because that time he threatened me."

"That's an awfully convenient set of circumstances. Isn't it true you fabricated this entire elaborate scenario just to get Gary Sheldon into trouble because he wouldn't respond to your advances?"

"No!"

"Then how do you explain the lack of physical evidence?"

"I don't know!" she wailed.

"And I'll ask you again: You're certain it was the production studio where Gary allegedly attacked you just after seven on the evenings of November seventeenth and November twentieth?"

Jolene nodded. "Yes. Right after he got off the air."

Returning to the defense table, Blake reached for two sheets of paper, which he handed to the judge. "Defense Exhibits One and Two, Your Honor. These are the production studio sign-up sheets for WZBX-FM for the two nights in question."

When the judge handed the papers back, Blake gave them to Jolene. "Would you please read the highlighted information on the page marked Studio One?"

The girl glanced at the papers in her trembling hands, then up at the defense attorney. When she opened her mouth to speak, nothing came out.

Coming around to the side of the witness stand, Blake pointed to the middle of one page. "Right here. Start reading here. Date. Name. Time in. Time out."

Jolene swallowed hard. "November seventeenth. Randy Lear. Six thirty to eight fifteen. November twentieth. Bill McLaughlin – WZBX-AM program feed. Six to eight p.m."

"That wasn't so hard," Blake intoned cuttingly. "Let's try the next one. Studio Two. Please read the highlighted portions: Date. Name. Time in. Time out."

"November seventeenth, Marc Lindsay. Six to seven. Bill McLaughlin – WZBX-AM program feed. Seven to eight thirty. November twentieth. Barbara Dwyer. Five thirty to seven thirty. Randy Lear. Seven thirty to nine p.m."

Fidgeting, Jolene handed back both sheets.

After setting the papers on the defense table, Blake returned to the witness stand. Instead of addressing the witness, he leaned an elbow on the stand and surveyed the jury. "As it turns out, both production studios were occupied during the very times my client's accuser claims he was assaulting her in one of them. It's quite an interesting revelation" – he turned to face Jolene – "wouldn't you agree, Miss Cunningham?"

She opened her mouth to speak, but, not sure what to say, closed it again.

Blake returned his attention to the jury. "*I* contend the witness is either confused or mistaken. Either that, or she's flat-out lying."

Sabine stood. "Objection. Move to strike, Your Honor."

"Sustained. Defense's entire previous statement is stricken. I've told you once, Counselor: Save it for summation."

"Yes, Your Honor." Blake turned back toward Jolene, as though entertaining an afterthought. "Oh – one last thing, Miss Cunningham: What did you do with those used tissues you were holding?"

She looked at the defense attorney in confusion. "Wh-what?" she stammered. "I – I put them in my pocket."

Blake gave a pensive nod. "In your pocket. Interesting. So you've got no aversion to putting *some* soggy, discarded items in your pockets. Nothing further, Your Honor."

Chapter 23

Having survived the first day of the trial, all Gary wanted to do was go home and sleep. But the local TV news crews crowded around the courthouse steps.

"Gary!" shouted one reporter, shoving a microphone in his face. "The testimony sounded pretty damning today. Do you think you'll get convicted?"

"What kind of chance do you think you've got?"

"Gary, do you think you're getting a fair trial?"

"One question, Mr. Sheldon: Did you do it?"

Gary, Michaela and Blake kept walking down the steps, ignoring the microphones and reporters.

"Mrs. Sheldon, is your husband into rough sex at home, too?"

"Does he make you dress up like a school girl?"

"What other fetishes does he have, Mrs. Sheldon?"

"Gary – how many other girls have you raped?"

"Do you like young boys, too?"

Gary stopped.

Smelling blood, the reporters surged closer, hungry for any response.

His head held high, Gary looked directly into the camera facing him. His voice was clear and steady. "No comment." Now he kept on walking.

Months ago, at his arraignment, Blake said not to duck reporters or shrink from prying cameras and intrusive questions. "You've done nothing wrong; you don't need to hide." But he'd advised his client to answer every question exactly as he just had.

"You mean I can't tell them to go fuck themselves?"

"Of course not! That's precisely what we're trying to avoid."

Gary decided all those years of law school must have stunted Blake's sense of humor. But he was an excellent lawyer; and Gary was grateful for his expertise.

(April 28 – Tuesday)
When he and Michaela arrived with Blake, Gary recognized the dark-suited figure waiting outside the courtroom.

"Man, am I glad to see you! It'll be nice to have some support in there."

Troubled, Pete clasped Gary's hand. "Wish I could say that's why I'm here... but I'm testifying this morning – as a prosecution witness."

"What?"

"They asked me to testify against you. When I refused, they subpoenaed me."

Gary felt like he'd been kicked in the stomach. He turned to Blake. "Can they do that?"

"Unfortunately, yes. They're going to do everything they can to make you look bad."

Pete gestured toward his longtime employee and friend. "I'm sorry, Gary. I consulted our corporate attorney. Like it or not, I have to do this. We're on the hook, too."

Sabine stood, approached the stand. "Mr. Donovan, you've been acquainted with Mr. Sheldon how long?"

"I've known Gary since the middle of nineteen eighty-two."

"In what capacity have you known the defendant?"

"When he first came to work for me at WZBX-FM, Gary was my afternoon-drive announcer; he was also later promoted to music director. And over the years, we've become friends."

"And is it your friendship that made you reluctant to testify here today?"

"In part, but mostly because I know he's innocent."

"Your Honor, permission to have the witness' last comment stricken?"

Judge Paterna looked over his glasses at the D.A. "He's your witness, Ms Delacourt."

"Permission to treat as hostile?"

He nodded. "Fair enough. But his comment stays."

With a final glare at the judge, the prosecuting attorney returned her attention to Pete. "To your knowledge, has the defendant ever been involved with a coworker?"

"Absolutely. Gary's involved with nearly everybody at the station. He's one of the most involved employees I've got. He instituted two major annual charity events; plays on the station softball team – horribly, but he plays; takes part in the student-mentoring program. Oh, he's involved."

"You know that's not what I meant. Has he ever been sexually involved with a coworker?"

"If that's what you meant, why didn't you say that in the first place?"

Laughter rippled through the courtroom.

Judge Paterna even stifled a chuckle; he disguised it as a cough and banged his gavel. "Okay, people, settle down. Mr. Donovan, please answer the question: Has Mr. Sheldon ever been sexually involved with a coworker?"

Pete fired an apologetic look at Gary. "Just one."

"That you're aware of," Sabine prodded.

"Just one. Period," Pete reiterated. "Back in eighty-five."

"What was the nature of their involvement?"

"I really don't know. You'd have to ask Gary."

"I'm asking you."

Pete gave the prosecutor the scornful look Gary knew all too well. "You seem like an intelligent woman. Exactly what part of 'I really don't know' did you have trouble grasping?"

"So you don't know anything about their involvement?"

He whistled. "Man, you're the sharp one today."

"Please answer the question. You're saying you knew nothing about the nature of their involvement?"

Pete drummed his fingers on the arm of the chair. "Well, gee… let me think. They might have been playing Parcheesi. Or cribbage – that's always fun. But if I had to venture a guess, I'd say they were probably having sex. Is that helpful?"

Gary tried not to laugh aloud.

Judge Paterna fought to stifle laughter as he banged his gavel. "No, Mr. Donovan, it's not especially helpful. Let's try to keep the sarcasm to a minimum, shall we?"

"Will do, Your Honor. But I think that falls under the 'Ask a stupid question' category. She asked me something I said I didn't know the answer to; yet she insisted on asking twice more. I don't see the sense in that."

"He makes a valid point, Ms Delacourt. Move on."

Sabine glared at Pete. "Okay, Mr. Donovan, how *did* you find out about their involvement?"

"If you mean, 'Was there any slap-and-tickle going on in the radio station?' obviously, the answer is no. Their involvement was strictly after hours. Outside the office. And totally discreet. I never knew about it 'til Gary mentioned it to me earlier this year."

"Boasting of his conquests?"

"Objection!"

Before the judge could bark, "Sustained," Sabine put up her hands in a gesture of false resignation. "Withdrawn. I have nothing further for this witness," she said crisply.

"Your Honor, I'd like to answer her question."

Startled but agreeable, Judge Paterna gave Pete the go-ahead.

"Gary's not the type to seek out conquests. That relationship was something he told me about a few months ago — because he was concerned it'd come up here. He didn't want me to be caught off guard and he didn't want the woman to be hounded."

"Very well." The judge nodded toward Blake. "Your witness, Mr. Tierney."

Blake approached the witness stand. "Mr. Donovan, you testified you've known Gary nearly sixteen years. In that time, have you ever seen him show disregard for a female coworker or subordinate?"

Pete shook his head. "No, I've never seen Gary show disregard for anyone – male or female."

"Ever heard him make disparaging remarks about female coworkers or subordinates?"

"No, I've never heard him do that."

"To your knowledge, has Gary Sheldon ever made any off-color or suggestive comments to female coworkers or subordinates?"

"Never."

"Has he ever made such comments to you, about female coworkers or subordinates?"

"Never."

"And Mr. Donovan, have you ever known Gary Sheldon to take drugs?"

"No!" he replied vehemently.

"Sell drugs?"

"Of course not."

"Push drugs on teenagers?"

Pete was incredulous. "Never. He's got a teenage daughter himself, for crying out loud!"

"Offer anyone drugs in exchange for sex?"

"No!"

"As his boss, you're in a position to monitor and evaluate Gary's professional behavior, yes?"

"That's correct."

"Over the past nearly sixteen years, how would you rate Gary Sheldon's conduct, overall?"

"He was a bit mischievous early on, but he was also a teenager. Overall, I would have to say I'd classify Gary as practically a model employee."

"Thank you. Nothing further, Your Honor."

Sabine stood. "Re-direct, Your Honor?"

The judge motioned for her to go ahead.

Her heels clicked on the marble floor as she approached the witness stand. "Mr. Donovan, you say Gary was 'a bit mischievous early on.' Tell me, what did his 'mischievous' behavior entail?"

Pete ran a hand through his hair. "Nothing serious, just a few harmless pranks. He filled the sales manager's desk with packing peanuts once, glued the guy's letter opener to his desk – that kind of thing."

"So, there's never been anything more serious than childish pranks? The whole time he's worked for you?"

Pete looked a little uneasy. "Well, he was reprimanded once."

"I wondered when you'd get around to that," she said smugly, carrying a file folder to the witness stand. "People's Exhibit Six. Would you tell me, please, what this is?"

Pete looked through the folder the prosecutor handed him. "It's a copy of Gary's personnel file."

"Would you be so kind as to identify the item labeled Exhibit Six-A?"

"It's an official-reprimand document."

"An official reprimand?" Sabine acted surprised. "Why, that doesn't sound like something you'd find in the personnel file of your 'model employee,' does it?"

"We're all human. Everyone makes mistakes."

"Even model employees?"

Pete leaned forward slightly to speak directly into the microphone. "Even model employees."

"And would you tell the Court what the defendant was cited for in this official reprimand?"

"Violation of station policy."

Sabine turned toward the jury. "And who issued him this reprimand?"

"As his immediate supervisor, I did."

"Would you read the highlighted portion, please?"

Pete exhaled softly. He hesitated.

"The first sentence, Mr. Donovan," she prompted, tapping the page with a red-lacquered talon. "If you please."

Unwillingly, Pete read. "I am issuing you this Official Reprimand for your negligent behavior and your blatant disregard for official written station policies concerning staff interactions with interns, and directives that prohibit WZBX staff members' 'consorting with minors.'"

The prosecutor reclaimed the file. "'Consorting with minors.' Doesn't sound much like behavior I would ascribe to a 'model employee.' What – specifically – did he do?"

"He escorted a student intern off station property."

"When was this?"

"October thirteenth of last year."

"Hmm… just weeks before Mr. Sheldon was charged with raping yet another student intern. It seems your model employee's upstanding comportment went careening downhill late last year, wouldn't you agree?"

"It was an isolated incident. Gary wa—"

Sabine held up a hand to silence him. "Or maybe he just likes little girls."

"Objection!" Blake leapt to his feet.

"Sustained. The jury will disregard that last comment. Watch it, Ms Delacourt. You're treading on dangerous ground."

Next, Sabine called Alice Curtis from Glenmede.

"We already know Mr. Sheldon was disciplined for an incident involving one of your students. In your own words, what was the nature of the trouble with Mr. Sheldon?"

"I wouldn't exactly call it trouble. Truthfully, I wouldn't even have known about it if it hadn't been for Gary's letter."

Sabine handed the witness a sheet of paper from the file. "People's Exhibit Six-B. You mean this letter?"

Mrs. Curtis examined it. "Yes, that's the one."

"Let the record show the witness has identified a letter signed by the defendant. Mrs. Curtis, would you tell the Court, to your knowledge, what happened on the afternoon of October thirteenth, nineteen ninety-seven?"

"As I understand it, Gary took one of our students – an intern he was supervising – to lunch, to discuss a project he wanted her to work on."

"Is that standard procedure for the intern program?"

"This was our pilot year, so there were no guidelines in place regarding that sort of thing."

"I see. If the intern program with WZBX is continued, would that behavior be condoned?"

"Objection, Your Honor. The witness has no knowledge of what is permitted at my client's place of business."

"Overruled. The witness' school knowingly entered into a contractual arrangement with the defendant's employer. As such, it was her duty to find out whether things of this nature were permitted. I'll allow it."

"I don't believe so," Mrs. Curtis replied.

The prosecutor held up another document from Gary's personnel file. "People's Exhibit Six-C. Is this the letter you sent in response?"

Mrs. Curtis examined the document the prosecutor handed her. "It is."

"Let the record show Mrs. Curtis has identified a letter she wrote to the defendant. What action, if any, was taken against Mr. Sheldon?"

"In my letter, I had requested they show leniency toward Gary – because I've found him to be someone of outstanding character and integrity. And this was clearly an isolated incident. Beyond the official reprimand, I'm unaware of further punitive action taken against Mr. Sheldon by his superiors. You'll have to ask them."

"Thank you. No more questions, Your Honor."

Blake stood. "Mrs. Curtis, you discussed the lunch incident at length with the dean, as well as with the music intern in question. And what was the outcome of these discussions?"

"From what the student told me, I'm satisfied Gary meant her no harm. She said he acted like a gentleman at all times, she felt safe in his company and had not even the most fleeting concerns about his behavior or intentions."

"And what is your opinion of Mr. Sheldon?" Blake asked.

"Objection! Witness' opinion doesn't matter. We're dealing with facts."

"Her opinion goes directly to her assessment of the student's claims, Your Honor," he explained.

Judge Paterna shook his head at the prosecutor. "Overruled, Ms Delacourt. I'll allow it."

Alice smiled broadly. "I've found Gary Sheldon to be a goodhearted, decent, upstanding man. He's a professional and, as my students have said, a real gentleman. I'd trust him with my own daughters."

Chapter 24

"What is your relationship to the defendant?" Sabine's voice was brittle.

"Gary was under my care at Foxbridge."

"And what exactly is Foxbridge?"

"It's a private psychiatric facility in Newtown."

"For how long did you observe the defendant?"

"I treated Gary during his three weeks there; I've continued to work with him privately, since his discharge from the facility."

"Three weeks. Is that an average length of stay at your institution?"

"It was appropriate for Gary; it gave me ample time to assess his state of mind."

"Tell me, doctor: Is he a sexual predator?"

"Even if we had discussed that, I couldn't divulge that kind of information. What I *can* tell you is this: The kinds of things Gary expressed guilt and remorse over are in no way consistent with the profile of a man who could have perpetrated the crimes he's accused of."

"But it is still *possible* he's capable of having coerced the girl into a sexual relationship? Even capable of rape?"

"Gary?" Dr. Benson frowned. "Physically, yes. I'll grant you that. He's an adult male, six feet tall, fairly muscular build; he's certainly *capable* of physically overpowering a teenage girl. But is he *disposed* toward doing it — either psychologically or emotionally? There, I'd have to strongly disagree."

"But it is *possible*," she prodded.

"Perhaps. But not plausible."

Sabine returned to her seat with a dismissive sniff. "Your witness," she told Blake.

Blake ambled to the witness stand. "Dr. Benson, why do people consult psychiatrists?"

"People seek psychiatric care for all sorts of reasons."

"For instance… someone who's been under excessive emotional stress?"

Dr. Benson leaned closer to the microphone. "Yes, that's often the case."

"Or perhaps someone who's been held up to public scorn and ridicule… dragged through the mud by the news media?"

"That's correct."

"Even if that person is innocent?"

"Especially then. People are so quick to judge, so ready to believe the worst about others."

"So it's not just people who are trying to repress guilty feelings who seek psychiatric care?"

Sabine stood. "Objection, Your Honor. He's leading the witness."

Judge Paterna shook his head. "Sorry, Counselor. This is cross; he's entitled. Overruled. Proceed, Mr. Tierney."

"Thank you, Your Honor. So, Dr. Benson, you're saying people who've been wrongly accused of terrible things will sometimes consult psychiatrists to resolve particular… issues surrounding these false accusations. Is that correct?"

"That's exactly right."

"In your opinion, doctor, is that the case with my client?"

"Yes. I believe Gary Sheldon is simply not capable of the behavior he's charged with. I've found Gary to be deeply committed to his family and his faith. In fact, the two are so intrinsically linked, I don't see how he could commit an act of such treachery to all he holds dear."

"Thank you, doctor. Nothing further, Your Honor."

"Please state your name," Sabine instructed with crisp precision.

The witness gave a discreet tug at the sleeves of his grey suit. He pushed his black glasses up to the top of his nose. "Dr. Hamilton Forsythe."

"And Dr. Forsythe, what are your credentials?"

"I'm a licensed, board-certified forensic psychiatrist working for the State of Connecticut."

"And exactly how long have you been employed in this capacity?"

"I've worked for the State since nineteen eighty-five and practiced psychiatry in Connecticut since nineteen seventy-two."

"I see. You've heard the testimony offered by Dr. Benson regarding the defendant. In your expert opinion, is his assessment accurate?"

Dr. Forsythe crossed his legs, leaned back in his chair. "Based on my experience, I'd have to say no. I believe the defendant is likely not only to have been *capable* of committing the crimes of which he's accused – but in fact, it is my opinion he probably *did* commit them."

A murmur ran through the courtroom. Some jurors nodded; a few others shook their heads. Most sat expressionless. Gary's fist tightened around the rosary in his pocket.

Sabine strolled toward the jury box, turned and faced the witness stand. "And what, doctor, leads you to that conclusion?"

He pushed his slipping glasses back up his nose. "Years of experience, for one thing. I've been a practicing psychiatrist in this state for twenty-five years – since Dr. Benson here was in diapers."

A chortle ran through the room.

Judge Paterna frowned his disapproval and the laughter decayed to nervous silence.

Sabine continued as if her witness' answer hadn't been interrupted. "Anything else?"

"Yes. From reading his pre-trial depositions, I'm quite sure Mr. Sheldon is convinced of his own superiority over the rest of society, and an errant belief the law and its consequences don't apply to him. Furthermore, his arrogant posture gives him away."

"How so?"

"I can tell, simply from interpreting body language, when someone is lying. Look at him: the rigid shoulders, the cocky set of his jaw, the hand in his pocket – he's hiding something. But he's not doing an adequate job hiding it from me."

"Thank you, Dr. Forsythe." Sabine's heels clicked sharply on the floor as she returned to her seat.

Blake didn't step away from the defense table. "Dr. Forsythe, you're being paid to offer testimony as an expert witness for the prosecution, are you not?"

"That's correct."

"And you're being paid a rather handsome sum, am I correct?"

Forsythe's mouth twisted unpleasantly. "You could say that."

"Would you say that?"

"Well… yes. Yes, I suppose."

Slowly, Blake approached the witness stand. "I'm not clear on something: Were you retained as an expert in psychiatry or in body language?"

"Psychiatry, of course," he replied gruffly.

"See, that's what I thought," he replied genially. "So let's leave your contrived assessment of my client's body language out of the equation, shall we?"

The psychiatrist shifted awkwardly. A few snickers broke the silence in the courtroom.

"Mr. Tierney, there's no need to be smug," Judge Paterna reminded him quietly.

"Sorry, Your Honor. Now, Dr. Forsythe, other than reading depositions and observing him from thirty feet away these past few minutes, have you taken time to personally evaluate my client?"

He tugged at his sleeves. "That wasn't part of what I was asked to do."

"I see. But you reviewed his medical files… right?"

"Certainly not. Doctor-patient privilege prohibits that."

"So, his psychiatric files would have been off limits, too."

"Naturally."

"Well, then, you surely must have at least conferred with Dr. Benson at some point… yes?"

Dr. Forsythe tugged at his sleeves again. "Well… no."

"Have you, in fact, ever even *met* or spoken to my client?"

"No, I have not."

Blake paced across the marble floor. "Let me get this straight. You have no firsthand experience with my client. You have neither directly evaluated him nor reviewed his medical or psychiatric files. And you haven't spoken with his treating psychiatrist." He came to a full stop before the witness stand, hands raised in a gesture of perplexity. "How can you sit there and claim to be an expert? You may be an expert in some area of psychiatry, Dr. Forsythe, but you're clearly no expert regarding Gary Sheldon. If anything, where my client is concerned, you're nothing but a hack."

"Objection – badgering."

"Your Honor, I'm merely establishing the witness has no direct knowledge of my client. How can his so-called *expert* testimony – regarding someone he knows nothing about – be considered valid?"

"He does make a reasonable point, Ms Delacourt. The objection is overruled."

Dr. Forsythe uncrossed his legs and drew himself up as tall as he could in his chair. "I've based my evaluation on years of case studies of other criminals," he intoned, his ears reddening. "I'm here offering expert testimony regarding the likelihood of a specific behavior from a particular type of individual."

"Oh. What *type* of individual would that be?" Blake subtly mimicked the witness' snooty tone.

Dr. Forsythe eyed Gary with contempt. "The type that's rich and powerful. And spoiled. The type that thinks the law doesn't apply to him."

"You admit you've formed an opinion of my client based on case studies instead of direct observation. I can't see how the jury can place much stock in anything you say."

"Objection!"

"Sustained. Mr. Tierney, save the editorializing for summation."

Blake shot a disgusted look at the psychiatrist. He shook his head. "Nothing further." Turning, he stalked back to his seat.

When the prosecutor called her next witness, Gary felt as if a kangaroo had taken up residence in his colon.

"Would you state your name and your relevance to these proceedings, please?" Sabine asked.

"My name is James Farley; I'm president of the parish council at St. John of the Cross Church in Middlebury."

"And how are you acquainted with the defendant?"

He eyed Gary with revulsion. "Let's just say his reputation precedes him. And we, as a council, decided he had to go."

"Had to go? In what sense?"

"He was teaching our youngest kids. Teaching them *religion*. We couldn't have that kind of thing going on – someone of questionable character alone with classrooms full of little children…" He shook his head, frowning. "That's not right. It's just not right." Mr. Farley thumped a fist against his knee.

"So what action did you take?"

"We did the only right thing to do: We called a special meeting and demanded that Father Williams get rid of him. People like him" – sneering, he pointed at Gary – "we don't need. Especially teaching our kids."

"And who is Father Williams?"

"He's the pastor."

"What did he do when you told him of the decision you'd reached?"

"Didn't have much choice. We told him we wanted that creep gone; he had to do what we said. It doesn't look good –

you know, having a child molester teaching kids. We have to protect them."

Blake stood. "Objection. The defendant hasn't been convicted of anything."

"Sustained. Mr. Farley, I'll ask you to preface any such labels with 'accused' from here on in."

"Right. *Accused* child molester. But we all know he did it."

"Objection!" Blake roared. "We know nothing of the sort. Move to strike."

Sabine didn't wait for the judge's decision. "Thank you, Mr. Farley. Nothing further."

Blake approached the witness stand. "Mr. Farley, in your testimony a moment ago, you referred to my client as 'someone of questionable character.' How well do you know Mr. Sheldon?"

"I don't," the witness replied. "Except from seeing him at church. And his picture on that billboard on the highway — only, they had the good sense to take it down. Decent people don't need pictures of rapists forced on us."

"*Accused* rapists," Blake corrected. "So, you admit you've never met Gary Sheldon personally?"

"No," he scoffed. "What do I need with a child molester?"

Gary hoped Blake would object. Now it felt as though the kangaroo was tap dancing.

"*Accused* child molester," Judge Paterna intoned, frowning at the witness.

"And yet, Mr. Farley, you feel hearsay is sufficient to make a character judgment?" Blake asked.

The witness nodded toward the defense table, scowling. "About him? Yeah."

"Would it surprise you to learn Mr. Sheldon has been a leader in the community in child advocacy?"

The witness shrugged.

"Please respond verbally, Mr. Farley. The court reporter can't interpret your shrug. Would it surprise you to learn my client has been a leader in his community with regard to child advocacy?"

He scowled at the attorney. "Actually? Yes."

"Why?"

"Because he's a pedophi— an *accused* pedophile," he corrected himself before the judge could say anything.

"Would it surprise you to learn the man you've so quickly written off as a child molester and 'someone of questionable character' has helped raise hundreds of thousands of dollars over the past fifteen years, to benefit countless women and children living in homeless shelters?" – Blake ticked off items on his fingers – "has been a foster father to a pregnant and homeless teenager? and has worked consistently to provide area high-school students a safe, alcohol-free celebration on graduation night?"

Mr. Farley squirmed a little in his seat. "I – I wasn't aware of any of those things, no."

"So you agree your initial assessment of Mr. Sheldon isn't necessarily accurate? And maybe a bit hasty?"

"Well… perhaps. But still – doesn't mean he didn't do those things to that girl." Flustered, the man glanced at the prosecutor. Then his jaw tightened as his self-righteousness resurfaced. "And we were well within our rights to demand he be removed."

Gary groaned inaudibly. He watched with a sense of deepening betrayal as the man approached the witness stand to be sworn in.

"Please state your full name – and your position."

"Reverend David P. Williams, pastor of St. John of the Cross Parish in Middlebury."

"How do you know the defendant, Reverend Williams?"

"Gary's a parishioner of mine."

"What else?"

"He's been a first-grade CCD teacher for the past fifteen years."

"CCD – that's religious education?"

"That's right. Confraternity of Christian Doctrine."

"Is he teaching now?"

"No, he isn't," Father Williams said softly.

"Why?"

"I asked him to step down."

"You asked him to step down. Tell me, Father: Why would you do that?"

The priest looked uncomfortable. "Because of this… because of these charges."

Sabine turned. "Thank you. No more questions."

Blake stood, approached the witness stand. "Now, Father Williams, I can understand your reluctance to be here today, having one of your religious-education teachers on trial. It must be awfully difficult to have to testify against him."

"It's never easy to testify against someone you believe to be innocent."

"Objection!"

"Overruled."

"I know the seal of the confessional is absolute; and even if you were at liberty to say whether my client had in fact gone to you for confession, you couldn't reveal what – if anything – he said within the protection of that sacrament. Even if you wanted to—"

Sabine stood. "Objection. Is there a question here?"

"Mr. Tierney? A question?"

"Yes, Your Honor. I was establishing a basis for that question."

"Very well. The objection is overruled. Proceed."

"Thank you, Your Honor. Now, Father, even if you had wanted to speak in Gary's defense – based on something you may have been privy to in confession – you couldn't. Isn't that right?"

"That's correct."

"So the decision to remove Mr. Sheldon from teaching his CCD class was not one you were happy about?"

"Obviously I wasn't happy about removing someone so dedicated from a class he had taught for so many years – especially someone as well loved as Gary. But several parents expressed concern; and those concerns could not go ignored. I had no choice but to relieve Gary of his teaching duties. That was not a decision I came to lightly – or without serious prayer and deliberation. It pained me deeply because, based on everything I've come to know about Gary, I believe he's innocent."

Gary turned away when the priest gave him an apologetic look.

"It's my duty to protect children. Given allegations of wrongdoing, even if they go against all I know to be true, I have a legal and moral obligation to remove the accused from contact with children – for his own protection as well as the safety of the parish as a whole – until such time as the matter can be investigated and resolved. And – as much as I regret having to take this action against Gary – I had to act within the constraints of archdiocesan regulations."

Chapter 25

It was mid-afternoon before Gary was called to testify. Sabine asked him his name, age, occupation and town of residence. As she fired off questions, the prosecuting attorney paced before the witness stand, her heels clicking like a metronome.

Eyeing her warily, Gary answered each question without hesitation.

"Would you tell us, Mr. Sheldon, what happened on the night of November seventeenth?"

"That's the night I stayed to listen to Jolene's demo tape in the news studio."

"*That's* what you call it, eh?" Sabine muttered, earning a severe look from the judge. "Tell me, Mr. Sheldon, was there anyone around the radio station at the time who can corroborate your story?"

"Yes, ma'am. There were several people there: One of the AM guys was taping program feeds; our production director was working in the other production studio; some sales staff were around. And our nighttime guy, Marc Lindsay, saw us from the on-air studio. We weren't in there more than ten minutes – and we were fully visible to him the whole time."

"Would that be the same Marc Lindsay who was best man at your wedding? And you at his?"

Gary nodded. "That's correct."

"Isn't he also married to your sister?"

"He is."

"So, he's not *just* a coworker, is he? He's a close personal friend and now a family member, too."

"True. But that changes nothing."

"But that isn't how you represented him just now. You identified him simply as a coworker, when in fact, he's your brother-in-law. And being so close, he'd be inclined to cover for you, wouldn't he?"

Gary's skin prickled with animosity. He turned toward the bench. "I object."

"You're the defendant, Mr. Sheldon; you don't get to object," Judge Paterna reminded him drily. "You get to answer the question and leave the objections to your attorney. Please continue, Ms Delacourt."

"Wouldn't Mr. Lindsay be inclined to cover for you, Mr. Sheldon?"

"Objection, Your Honor. Calls for speculation."

"Thank you for finally weighing in, Mr. Tierney. Unfortunately, your objection is overruled."

"Wouldn't he be inclined to cover for you, Mr. Sheldon?" Sabine asked, pointedly, a third time.

He mimicked her snotty tone. "Why not add him to your witness list and ask him yourself?"

Judge Paterna banged his gavel. "Mr. Sheldon, cut out the hostility and answer the question."

Gary glanced at the judge, then at Blake, who was shaking his head in warning. "Yes, Your Honor. No. Marc wouldn't be inclined to 'cover for me'; he'd tell the truth. And he'd swear I never laid a hand on the girl. On the contrary: She was the aggressor."

Sabine smirked. Her tone was condescending. "Mr. Sheldon, do you really expect us to believe this girl – this *child* – was the one who initiated the sexual encounter?"

"She was the aggressor. But there was no so-called sexual encounter. Not like she described."

"Why don't you tell us, then, what *did* happen?"

"We were in the news studio. I asked her to start the tape. She said there was plenty of time for that later… and didn't I find her attractive? I thought it was wholly inappropriate, and told her so. I said if she wasn't going to play the demo, I was leaving. She begged me to stay and started the tape."

"What happened then?"

"About a minute in, I stopped it to critique her delivery. I could tell she wasn't paying attention to what I was saying. I figured I was wasting my breath, so I restarted the tape."

"Then what happened?"

"She stopped it."

"To discuss your critique?"

"Not exactly."

"What then?"

"She started unbuttoning her blouse. She had her back to the on-air studio; from where he was, Marc couldn't see what Jolene was doing. It was evident she wasn't wearing a bra. She started rubbing up against me and making suggestions – the likes of which I'd never heard come out of the mouth of a sixteen-year-old girl before."

"For instance?" Sabine prompted.

Gary looked uneasy. "She offered… well, she offered me oral sex."

"Sounds pretty tame – even for a teenager."

He shook his head. "Not the way she said it."

She folded her arms. "How did she say it, Mr. Sheldon?"

Gary turned toward Judge Paterna. "Do I really have to say this? In front of all these people?"

He nodded. "I'm afraid so, Mr. Sheldon. For the record. Please tell us what she said."

"She offered to – and I'm quoting – 'wrap my sweet Southern lips around your thick Yankee cock and blow you into ecstatic oblivion.' "

"Those were her exact words?"

Gary could feel his cheeks burning. "Yes, ma'am. Those were her exact words."

Sabine's tone was scathing. "You remembered her exact words? Even five months later? Must've been quite a turn-on, Mr. Sheldon."

"Some things, ma'am, you just don't forget," he replied, trying to squelch both his nausea and his South Jersey accent. "And trust me: A proposition like that from some little tart who's just a year older than your daughter is one of 'em." Gary paused. "For the record: It was no turn-on."

"So you contend Jolene's the one who came on to you."

"That's exactly what I'm saying. Because that's what happened."

"And what did you say when she offered you, um… that?"

"I told her, 'Little girl, I got concert T-shirts older than you.' "

A snicker ran through the courtroom. Sabine frowned. Judge Paterna glared at the snickerers.

"What, if anything, happened then?"

"I called a cab and put her in it, paid the driver and told him to take her back to the school. Then I went home."

"Hmm. Let me see if I've got this straight: You turned down an offer – an *alleged* offer – of earthshaking oral sex from this" – she gestured toward Jolene – "supposed nubile blonde sexpot and went home to your wife and children – as though nothing had happened?"

Gary bristled. He didn't like what she was insinuating. "That's right."

"I admire your fortitude, Mr. Sheldon," Sabine mocked. "You must have a really terrific marriage, then."

A glance at Michaela, seated in the gallery, steadied him. "I like to think so," he replied guardedly.

Smiling sweetly, Sabine stood before the witness stand. Resting a hand on its wooden rail, she fixed her gaze on the defendant. Her smile reminded Gary of a serpent; he envisioned a brown forked tongue darting from between scaly green lips. Her words would have been a hiss. "So… tell me, Mr. Sheldon: Within that really terrific marriage of yours, have you ever been unfaithful to your wife?"

Gary paled; he looked at Blake, whom he expected would object. When no objection came, he gritted his teeth. "I don't see what bearing that has on this trial."

"Your Honor, please instruct the defendant to answer," the prosecutor intoned blandly.

Judge Paterna turned toward the witness stand. "Mr. Sheldon, please answer the question."

"I will not. How dare you even ask!"

The judge's harsh warning to Gary, about being held in contempt if he addressed the Court in that tone again, was interrupted by Sabine's perfunctory observation.

"I guess we don't need it answered after all; it seems Mr. Sheldon's refusal has told us all we need to know. If he'd been faithful, he would've automatically answered, *No*. But by insisting on not responding, he's removed all doubt."

"Your Honor, I object!"

"Sustained." The judge banged his gavel. "The jury will disregard that last bit of commentary by the prosecution."

Blake stood. "Approach, Your Honor?"

Judge Paterna waved both attorneys forward.

"Your Honor, would you instruct her to leave her saccharine remarks for summation?"

"Ms Delacourt, do try to restrain yourself."

"And, Your Honor," Blake continued, "may I have ten minutes to confer with my client?"

The judge waved them back. "Ten-minute recess." He banged his gavel and left the courtroom.

Blake swept over to the witness stand, where Gary still sat, bewildered and numb. "C'mon," he said softly. "We need to talk." He steered Gary into an adjacent consultation room.

"You've got to answer the question, Gary. Even if the answer is yes." He paused. "*Is* it yes?"

Ashamed, he looked away. And nodded.

"Christ," the attorney muttered. "You coulda given me a heads-up before we went to trial."

Gary looked at him helplessly.

"Well, what's done is done. But you've got to be upfront about it."

"But it had nothing to do with—"

"Doesn't matter. She's trying to undermine your credibility and paint you as an opportunistic predator. You need to maintain your composure and defuse her grenade."

"How do I do that?"

"By answering as forthrightly as you can. And while I'm thinking of it: Watch your tone." He held a thumb and forefinger less than an inch apart. "Paterna's this close to slapping you with a contempt charge. And next time, he won't just scold you in open court. There'll be a hefty fine – and I mean *hefty*. As in, I hope you can liquidate a bunch of stock in a big hurry."

Gary looked down at the floor.

Blake sighed. "Okay, tell me what happened."

He hedged.

"Gary. We've only got eight minutes left. I need you to tell me – *now* – what happened, so we can manage this before it gets any more out of hand."

"Alright. It was seven years ago…" Quickly, he recounted his dalliance with Ellen. "I don't see what that has to do with this trial," Gary concluded, his cheeks tinged pink.

"It has everything to do with it," Blake countered. "She needs to establish a pattern of behavior. I know it'll be embarrassing for you, and for Michaela" – a sickening thought occurred to him – "Michaela *does* know, doesn't she?"

"Yes," he mumbled, ashamed. "I told her right after it happened. We split up fo—" he rephrased his sentence. "She threw me out. But we got past it and she took me back."

Blake nodded. "Okay. What you're going to do, Gary, is this: When she asks, 'Have you ever been unfaithful to your wife?' your answer will not be, 'Yes.' It's going to be, 'Once; years ago.'"

"You want me to admit it – just like that?"

"You're under oath. You've got to admit it. But, by answering this way, you're not letting her stop you after a simple 'yes.' And since you're not being evasive, Gary, since you're answering the question, the judge is more likely to let your answer stand." The attorney looked him over. "Fix your tie."

Recalled to the stand, Gary was reminded he was still under oath.

"You may resume questioning," Judge Paterna told the prosecuting attorney.

"Alright, Mr. Sheldon, let's go over this again, shall we?" Sabine's tone was degrading and smug. "I'll keep it simple for you. Yes or no: Have you ever been unfaithful to your wife?"

One hand in his pocket fingering his rosary beads, Gary replied as Blake instructed.

"That's not the answer I asked for, Mr. Sheldon."

Indignation flashed in his eyes. He kept his tone light, offhand. "Well, it's the one I'm giving."

Sabine turned to the judge. "Your Honor, please direct the defendant to respond," she droned as the courtroom door opened.

Michael Conwaye slipped inside and took a seat beside his daughter. "Sorry. Couldn't get away before now," he whispered.

Michaela squeezed his hand. Her grim expression told him it wasn't going well.

"Objection! Asked and answered, Your Honor," Blake insisted.

"Non-responsive," Sabine bit back.

The judge banged his gavel once as a warning to them both; he turned to the prosecutor. "Ms Delacourt, it sounds to me like the defendant answered the question, but how would you expect him to respond?"

"I would like a yes or no answer," came her retort. "For the record."

The judge turned to face Gary once more. "Mr. Sheldon, please answer the question. With a yes or a no."

"Your Honor, I object! The question has been asked and answered. Why is she being permitted to badger my client?"

But Gary'd had enough. "Yes," he hissed. "I cheated on my wife. Alright? Is that what you want to hear? Christ! It was seven years ago. And it happened *once*" – he pointed at Jolene as his voice rose to a shout – "but not with *her!*"

A gasp tore through the gallery. Reporters jotted in notebooks. Sketch artists scurried to capture the fury in Gary's face as he pounded the arm of his chair, scrambled to depict the contortion of his features in chalk before it dissipated.

Blake's head drooped.

Michaela covered her face with her hand.

Michael Conwaye gaped at his son-in-law.

Judge Paterna banged his gavel as the murmur in the courtroom swelled to a buzz. "Order," he called. "Order in this court. Settle down."

As the commotion subsided, Blake stood. Buttoning his jacket, he approached Gary and started to pace. "Gary, please describe what happened at the radio station just after seven on November seventeenth."

"Jolene had asked me the previous week if I'd be willing to critique her demo tape one evening. I didn't have any production work to finish that night and I had a few minutes to spare; so when I got off the air at seven, I called my wife to let her know I'd be a little late getting home."

"And where did you go to listen to her demo?"

"The news studio."

"Are you certain? Because Miss Cunningham testified you'd gone into the production studio."

"It was the news studio," Gary asserted. "Jolene *wanted* to go into a production room, but they were both in use."

"Can you think why she might have wanted to go into one of those studios?"

"Yeah. No windows. And they're soundproof. Frankly, I was glad both studios were tied up."

"Why?"

"After the incident a month before, I'd been careful not to get into situations where I'd be alone with any of the girls; that's why the news booth was perfect: It has a big window into the on-air studio – and Marc could see us the whole time."

"Did there come a time when you started to believe this wasn't simply an innocent request on her part, having you listen to her tape?"

"You mean, like I was being set up? Yeah. After she asked whether I found her attractive, I knew she was up to something. When I critiqued her delivery, I thought it was odd she'd gone to the trouble of asking for my input, yet when I made suggestions, she stood there with a blank look on her face – like nothing was getting through to her."

"What happened then?"

"That's when she started undoing her blouse. And she made those – suggestions."

"What did she say when you turned her down?"

"She told me I'd be sorry."

"She threatened you?"

Gary nodded. "Yes. But I never considered she might be serious. I know how melodramatic teenagers can be."

"What, if anything, happened then?"

"That's when I called for the taxi. When Jolene left in the cab, I went home."

Chapter 26

While Micki was putting the little ones to bed, Gary retreated to the study, ostensibly to research the syndication process. Instead he immersed himself in an online search for information on the appeals process. He didn't realize Instant Messenger was running until a message popped onto his screen.

Tabby714: *Gary? Are you there?*

Caught off guard, Gary wondered who it was – then he recognized the screen name.

EBSpike118: Terri?
Tabby714: *Yeah. Need to talk - urgent!*
EBSpike118: I'm not supposed to have contact with you – or any of the interns.
Tabby714: *I know, but this is important!*

He was about to close out of the IM conversation window when Terri's next message appeared.

Tabby714: *New information - it'll clear you.*
EBSpike118: What?!?
Tabby714: *Yeah - I have to talk to you. Have your lawyer get a search warrant for Jolene's room.*

Gary didn't want this in writing.

EBSpike118: Hold everything, Terri. **Don't type anything else**. Give me a call.

He swiftly typed in his cell-phone number.

Two minutes later, Gary's phone rang. He answered on the first ring. "Terri?"

"Yeah."

"What did you mean, you have new information?"

"It's good to have a computer geek in the family." Terri explained she'd cut class that day and her brother walked her through every step on the phone – even how to crack Jolene's password. "Plus, I've got everything c-copied to disk. E-even if she deletes it all, I've still got proof."

Gary paled as she told him what she'd uncovered. "You could get into huge trouble, Terri."

"If it means clearing you of s-s-something I know you didn't do, it's worth it. Besides, who'd ever think t-to connect *me* with something s-so underhanded?"

She's got a point. "If they ask how I came to learn about it, I've got to tell them the truth."

"W-we'll deal with that if and when it happens."

Gary's heart was pounding. "Terri… thank you. If this pans out, I owe you – big time."

(April 29 – Wednesday)
The morning headlines were crushing: "Sheldon: Yes, I cheated on my wife." And "Radio star admits infidelity."

Bolstered by the information from Teresa, Gary didn't let the headlines unnerve him. First thing in the morning, he called Blake, careful not to reveal how he'd learned of the new evidence. And Blake knew better than to ask.

"Can we get the trial stopped 'til we find what we need?"

"I don't know. The judge will want probable cause before issuing a warrant."

Because Judge Harriman knew Blake Tierney, she knew he wasn't the type to waste the Court's time with frivolous requests.

And because they had secured a warrant, Judge Paterna granted a 48-hour delay, pending discovery of new evidence covered by the just-issued warrant.

(2:37 p.m.)
Jolene was returning from classes when a cadre of officers arrived. Informing her they were there to search the premises for evidence, they showed her the warrant.

"You can't do this!" Jolene insisted. "This is illegal – this is an outrage! I'm calling my lawyer."

"You do that, miss," one of the officers placated her. "I assure you, it's quite legal."

"*I'm* the victim here," she raged. "But you're treating me like some kind of criminal! Why don't you go search *his* house? Go tear up his things and look for evidence. This is insane!"

Jolene perched atop her CPU and wouldn't let the police officers near it. When they tried, she screeched and kicked and flung things – books, CDs, mugs, anything within reach. She made such a fuss, the house mother had to summon Dean Myers to the dormitories.

"Jolene, please. Don't make this more difficult than it already is," the dean said, steering the girl into the corridor.

"But Dean Myers, that's all my homework! And my computer. I've got term papers on there— hey, you can't take that!" she insisted as an officer walked past with her dismantled computer. "Put that down, you stupid asshole. That's my stuff!"

"Miss Cunningham," the dean chided, "this isn't helping matters. Now leave the officers alone and let them do their work."

After a thorough inspection, all pertinent documents and equipment in the room were seized. Officers carried several boxes, labeled as evidence, out to their cars. Jolene could only stand by and watch.

Police investigators pored through the confiscated materials; a computer-forensics team cracked her password and accessed her email files.

"We hit the motherlode," one of them told Blake late Thursday.

"Great. Can you get me printouts of everything?"

"I'll send 'em over by courier first thing tomorrow – and copies for the prosecution. How'd you know to look for this stuff anyway?"

"Anonymous tip."

(9:23 a.m., May 1 – Friday)
"The defense calls Kenneth Felton."

A tall, thin black man stepped forward and took his place on the witness stand to be sworn in.

"Mr. Felton, on the evening of November seventeenth, were you dispatched to an address in Middlebury?"

"Yes, sir. To the radio station – WZBX."

"What time did you receive the call?"

"My service record for that date shows the call came in to dispatch at seven twelve. I arrived at seven twenty-one."

"And do you see here today the individual who met you at the station?"

He pointed. "Yes, sir. That's him, right there."

"Let the record show the witness has indicated the defendant. What happened that night, Mr. Felton?"

"When I arrived, he came outside with" – pointing over at Jolene – "that girl, over there. He asked me to drive her back to school. He gave me the address and said to make sure she got inside safely. I remember he was real polite. He said it was very important I not take her anywhere but directly back to her school."

"Did he say anything else?"

"He asked how much for the cab ride. I said it'd be about eight bucks."

"What happened next?"

"He gave me fifteen, told me to keep the change. I gave him a receipt for the fare, he thanked me and told the girl goodbye."

"How did she seem to you?"

"Objection, Your Honor. This witness isn't qualified to determine the victim's state of mind."

"Overruled. Counsel is asking for the witness' opinion, which he's adequately qualified to give." Judge Paterna turned to the cabbie. "You may answer the question."

"She didn't want to go. Kept trying to talk him out of sending her away. At first I thought she mighta been a daughter – but he didn't look old enough to be her father. Then I thought maybe she was his sister; but the way she kept trying to touch him seemed awfully – you know… sexual."

"Touch him? How?"

"Funny like. Touching him on the arm. Trying to cozy up, sweet talk him into letting her stay. That kind of thing."

"Did you notice anything else?"

He nodded. "Whenever she got too close, he'd move away. He was trying to talk to me about getting her home, and all she wanted to do was make me go away. Every time she tried to get too close, he'd shrug her off or step back. I could tell he didn't want to scold her in front of me, but he sure didn't want anything to do with her advances."

"Did it seem to you like he tried to force himself on her?"

"No, sir. Just the opposite: He was trying his best to keep her at bay."

"When she finally got into your cab, did she say anything on the ride back?"

"She muttered something like, 'I'll teach him' and 'Nobody makes a fool of me.' Something like that. I don't recall the precise words."

"Thank you, Mr. Felton. Nothing further, Your Honor."

Sabine approached the stand. "Mr. Felton, you say you don't remember her exact words. After all, it was quite some time ago."

"That's right."

"For all you know, she could've been saying, 'I can't believe that lousy bastard raped me.' Right?"

He shook his head. "No, ma'am. I might not recall her exact words – it was over five months ago. But I know the gist of what she said. I got an ex-wife; I know vindictive muttering when I hear it."

Chapter 27

"Has the defense rested?"

"No, Your Honor. I wish to recall a prior witness."

"Very well."

"I call the defendant, Gary Sheldon."

Gary took a deep, slow breath and stood. His knees wobbled almost imperceptibly as he stepped forward.

"Mr. Sheldon, I'll remind you you're still under oath," the judge cautioned.

"Yes, Your Honor."

Blake Tierney sidled over. "Gary, when were you last in Georgia?"

He gave his attorney a perplexed look. Blake had prepped him for every other bit of testimony offered during the trial. Why wouldn't he have gone over this? Still, he trusted his attorney not to steer him wrong.

"I was in Atlanta April of ninety-two."

"That was the last time?"

"It was the only time."

"You're certain?"

He wondered where this was going. "Positive."

"You haven't been there… oh, say, within the last nine months?"

"I was in Atlanta six years ago. For a music directors' convention. I haven't been back since."

"I see." Blake returned to his table. Picking up a bag entered into evidence earlier, he brought it to Gary. "People's Three, Your Honor. Gary, would you mind telling me what this is?"

"It's a bunch of torn condom packets."

"Correct." Now he turned back toward the bench. "Your Honor, let the record indicate the defendant has identified the condom wrappers previously admitted into evidence as People's Exhibit Three. Let the record also indicate the wrappers are printed with easily identifiable lot and serial numbers."

Blake showed the evidence to Judge Paterna.

The judge examined the wrappers, nodded and handed the bag back to the attorney – who in turn handed it to the jury foreman to pass among the rest of the panel.

"Yes, Mr. Tierney. Now, what is the point of this line of questioning?"

"Well, Your Honor" – reaching for a document on the defense table, Blake turned to face the jury; then, deliberately, toward Jolene – "perhaps this will help. Defense Exhibit Three."

Turning again, his gaze rested on the jury foreman. "It's a notarized statement by the condom manufacturer's vice president of merchandising and distribution. He verified this brand, type, size and color of condom – with this particular lot number – was distributed for sale exclusively to Dollar Plus stores in Georgia. After July first, last year. Further, this document authenticates delivery records for every condom package bearing the lot number in question."

Jolene blanched. She leaned and whispered something to Sabine Delacourt.

Sabine frowned.

Meanwhile, Blake turned away from the jury and gave Gary a brief, triumphant smile.

"Further, the defendant has sworn under oath he hasn't been to Georgia in six years; and it'd be highly unusual, unlikely and implausible for Mr. Sheldon to have mail-ordered condoms from a Dollar Plus store in Atlanta when he could get them at any local drugstore."

The judge gave a slight nod. Several jurors did likewise.

"Objection!" Sabine snapped. "Does Mr. Tierney have a question, Your Honor?"

"Overruled. Please sit down, Ms Delacourt."

"Coincidentally, Miss Cunningham" – Blake motioned toward the prosecution table – "comes from Atlanta herself. I contend she purchased the condoms in question – and then made up the story about my client in order to frame him for a crime he didn't commit. A crime which, in fact, never took place at all. And – if I may be so bold, Your Honor – the only crime is the one being perpetrated against my client and his employer. Therefore, I submit he's being prosecuted under false pretenses and I urge the Court to dismiss all charges against him."

A murmur ran through the courtroom.

"Further" – he returned to the defense table for a passel of papers – "I submit Defense exhibits Four through Thirty-seven: printouts of evidence taken from Jolene Cunningham's computer. Messages she emailed to friends in New York, Georgia and California – gloating about how she was about to, and I quote, 'take down the music director of the radio station I'm interning at.' That, and dozens like it, that detail the manner in which she planned to" – he read first from one page, then from another – " 'set this sucker up' and 'make him pay' for spurning her advances."

Aware every eye in the court was on her, Jolene shook her head. "No – no, it's not true. It's not true! You're making it up." She turned to Sabine. "Don't you see? They're trying to set me up. They planted those things in my computer after they took it!"

Judge Paterna banged his gavel to call for order. "Miss Cunningham, that's quite enough out of you. Ms Delacourt, kindly control her. Mr. Tierney, let me see those documents, please."

Blake brought the stack of emails to the bench. "These were made available to us this morning, Your Honor. The prosecutor's office has been provided copies as well."

Judge Paterna reviewed each of the messages, pausing to read a passage here or there. Looking up, he wore a grave expression. "Mr. Sheldon, please step down."

Gary returned to his seat, his face lined with worry, his grey eyes dark with anxiety.

"Approach," Judge Paterna commanded the two attorneys. They scurried forward. After nearly two full minutes of consultations, the judge dismissed them, waving them back to their respective tables.

"Will the defendant please rise," he intoned solemnly.

Giving Blake an anxious glance, Gary stood. Releasing his black-onyx rosary beads, he took his hand from his pocket. A slight tremor unsteadied his knees. The five seconds before Judge Paterna spoke dragged out interminably.

"Based on this new evidence, I'm convinced Miss Cunningham fabricated her entire story in an effort to discredit Mr. Sheldon and besmirch his name and reputation in this community." He turned to Jolene, his frown deepening.

Sabine stood, nudging the girl to her feet.

"Shame on you, Miss Cunningham," the judge went on, "for your reprehensible actions, and for wasting my time — not to mention countless police and judicial resources — on this foolishness. This is no trivial matter. Nor will I treat it as such. Miss Cunningham, you have sullied your reputation and that of an innocent man. You've also perjured yourself and destroyed any credibility you may have had. I would not be inclined to dissuade the accused parties from bringing civil or criminal charges against you. In fact, I'm ordering you be held, pending trial, for perjury, filing a false report and attempting to pervert the course of justice. I'll also leave the door open for reparations to be made to those you victimized by your hateful and malicious behavior, should they desire to pursue such avenues."

The teen's mouth fell open. Her eyes widened as an excited buzz filled the courtroom.

The judge banged his gavel. "Further I am vacating the indictment against the defendant. All charges against Gary J. Sheldon are hereby dismissed — as are all charges pending against WZBX-FM and its management. Mr. Sheldon, you're free to go, with our apologies. This Court stands adjourned."

Gary felt as if a steamroller had pressed all the air out of his lungs. His knees trembled; he wasn't sure he could trust them to support him much longer.

"Oh, thank God!" Michaela leaned across the partition between the gallery and the defense table and embraced her husband. "I knew you'd be cleared, sweetheart!"

Gary held her as if for the first time. It was over. The nightmare was finally over.

At opposite sides of the room, two sketch artists captured the tenderness of the Sheldons' kiss. One detailed Gary's fingers caressing Micki's porcelain-fine cheek; the other depicted the relief on his careworn face, marked by a lone tear.

After they parted, Gary bear-hugged Blake. "Thank you," he told his attorney, his voice shaky, "for sticking with me. I never coulda done it without you."

Friends and family members swarmed the defense table, all hugging and congratulating Gary.

Across the courtroom, Jolene Cunningham stood, alone and stunned, as the bailiff handcuffed her. A moment later, she was on the other side of the heavy wooden doors, being led to a holding cell, pending arraignment. Gary stared after her as the doors swung shut again.

On the courthouse steps, reporters teemed around Gary, pressing him for a statement. With Blake's approval, he consented to an impromptu press conference.

"Gary, how do you feel?" someone shouted.

"I'm relieved," he admitted. "The Court just validated what I've maintained all along. I'm grateful for the family and friends who've stood by me, and I'm glad this is finally over."

"What do you feel was the most significant factor in the Court finding in your favor?"

"Actually," Blake clarified, "they didn't find in his favor. They dismissed the charges. Big difference."

"Good point," Gary said. "But certainly the evidence was there – particularly the emails. Of course, there's this: I didn't do anything. But the most *significant* factor? I'd have to say it was my faith God wouldn't let me be unjustly convicted." Removing the ever-present rosary from his pocket, he held it aloft. "Prayer is a *mighty* weapon."

"What are you going to do, now you've been exonerated?"

He turned to Micki and smiled, holding fast to her hand. "I'm looking forward to some quality time with my family. Beyond that" – he shrugged – "it's anyone's guess."

"Are you going to press charges against your accuser?"

The crowd surged closer, eyeing him carefully, awaiting his reply – but none as intently as Micki.

Gary hesitated. "I don't have an answer yet. I need to give it some thought. And pray about it."

"Will you go back to work? And if so, when?"

"I'm sure I will; the bills aren't gonna pay themselves. As for when, I'll discuss that with my boss. I'm hoping soon – certainly within the next couple of weeks."

"Gary, how has this experience changed you?"

Gary looked at the woman holding the mic bearing the blue Z97-3 mic flag. Making eye contact, he smiled at the news director. "That's an excellent question, Barb. It's tested and strengthened my faith, and made me more appreciative of those who've stood by me – including some whose support I never expected. Or deserved."

"Like who?" Barb Dwyer asked.

Gary shook his head. "I'm going to respect their privacy. They know who they are. Suffice to say several individuals may be assured of my lifelong gratitude."

"You've mentioned gratitude and appreciation several times," another woman pointed out. "You're a religious man, Gary. Do you forgive your accuser?"

"I don't know," he replied thoughtfully. "I *do* know what my faith calls me to do… but I'm not entirely sure whether I can do that just yet. I don't know."

"Are you bitter? Or angry?"

"Good question. Part of me is tremendously angry at this girl. Another part – I think the wiser part – is saying, 'It's over; get on with living.' So I think that's probably what I'm going to do."

"Some folks would say you've been harshly treated in the press."

Gary's burst of caustic laughter interrupted the questioner. "Just some?"

"What would you like to say to the media who've covered your trial?"

"As part of the media myself, this is kind of a tough call. I understand you've just been doing your job; at the same time, I wish that job didn't involve being so invasive. I guess the one thing I'd say is, 'You've trampled my front lawn into mud and I'll expect you all there at eight a.m. tomorrow to re-seed the darn thing.'"

He paused as the reporters laughed. "Seriously? I doubt it'll happen, but I hope you'll devote as much time to reporting the news of my exoneration as you did to trashing me early on. That goes for broadcast *and* print media."

Gary looked around at the sea of reporters and cameramen. "Now please, no more questions. I've been as forthright as I can with you this morning, but from here on in, I'd appreciate your respecting my privacy and that of my family. I'm sure the station will be releasing a statement shortly. I just want to put this behind me and move on with my life. That's all I've got to say for now. Thank you."

As they made their way to Blake's Saab, the attorney nodded his approval. "You handled yourself well, Gary. Your unusual mix of sincerity and humor should go far. You seem to have won them over."

"I didn't do it to win them over. I want them to leave me alone. I figured the best way was to let them have their little vulture fest right up front and get it over with," Gary told him. "Maybe now they won't pester me – well, at least, not as much."

Taking a roundabout route to his office, to ensure they'd shaken the most tenacious of the media hounds, Blake dropped the Sheldons at their car.

"I take it you'll have a bill for me?" Gary asked before getting out of the slate-grey sedan.

Blake waved off the question. "It'll keep. For now, savor your victory."

Chapter 28

Holding Michael, Diane was waiting out on the front porch when Gary's car pulled up. She set the child down and, as soon as his parents emerged, he hurtled down the driveway. "Mommy! Mommy! Mommy! Daddy was on the TV! We saw Daddy on the TV!"

Michaela bent to scoop the child into her arms. "You did? What was he doing on TV?"

She listened with delight as Michael chattered about the morning's excitement.

Diane followed her grandson at a more dignified pace. Gary's face looked weary, but relieved. Her own face aglow, she wrapped her son in a hug. "I'm so happy for you, sweetheart. It's finally over."

Since his mom had already planned to watch the kids for the day, she told Gary and Michaela she'd keep her scheduled activities with them and bring them home around 5:30. "That way, you two can have some quiet time to yourselves."

His fingers entwined with Micki's, Gary smiled. "Thanks, Mom. Why don't you come out with us tonight? We're going out to celebrate. Just family – us, the kids, you and Micki's dad."

Amid all the excitement, Michaela nearly forgot the 1 p.m. doctor's appointment she'd scheduled months earlier. When she returned, she hung her keys in the kitchen and went to find Gary. He was in the living room, slouched in a chair, talking on the phone. His voice had lost the underlying tension that had been constant since his arrest. Moreover, he looked more at ease than she'd seen him in ages! In fact, he was laughing. She could scarcely remember the last time she'd heard her husband laugh.

Not wanting to interrupt, Michaela leaned over the chair and gave him a quick kiss on the side of the throat, to let him know she was home. "See you upstairs," she whispered. As she drew back, she caressed his cheek.

Gary nodded in reply, then watched Michaela go, taking particular delight in the sight of her shapely legs and pert, short-skirted backside as she retreated up the stairs. A smile crept across his face as he watched her – accompanied by another appreciative response somewhere considerably south.

"Hey, lemme get going," he told Marc. "Something's – um, come up I gotta take care of, okay? Give Marie and the kids hugs and kisses for me. We'll see you this weekend."

When he'd ended the call, he scampered upstairs.

Nudging open the bedroom door, Gary saw Michaela beside the dresser, her back to him. Arms raised, she worked to unfasten her necklace. Her skirt hitched up a few inches.

Latching the door, he watched her in silence for several seconds, his longing for her intensifying. Coming up behind Micki, Gary slipped his arms around his wife's slender waist. As he drew her gently against himself, he bent to kiss the side of her throat.

Still raised behind her head, Michaela's fingers abandoned the clasp of her necklace and reached to stroke Gary's hair.

A moment later, his hands skimmed upward across the taut expanse of his wife's midriff to cup her breasts. His mouth remained at her throat, kissing and tasting. With a low growl of desire, he pressed himself against Michaela more firmly, with a deepening sense of urgency.

She turned within his arms, her lips seeking his. They kissed with hunger, mouths yearning for each other, hands stroking, touching, groping as their passion flared.

A moment later, they dived for the bed, shoving each other's clothing aside and quivering with electrified anticipation.

Michaela clawed at the fly of Gary's jeans, then yanked them to his knees. He slid her skirt up over her hips and around her waist; tugging her panties down, he pulled her down on top of him. Trembling with pleasure, she let out a moan as she felt Gary enter her. Consumed with longing, their writhing bodies twined together, rolling and tussling on the bed.

Grunting and groaning, their passion built to a frenzied crescendo. Gary reared upward in tortured ecstasy as Micki raked her nails across his back. Bucking frantically beneath him and uttering a loud cry, she clenched against him and fell limp against the bed, panting. Moments later, Gary shuddered with a staggering climax.

Spent and sweating, he lay atop Micki, delighting in the heat of her body beneath his. Raising himself on his elbows, he sought her mouth; his kiss was slow, languid against her parted lips, carrying none of the animal passion they'd just shared. Gary stroked his wife's soft cheek, still flushed with desire. Nuzzling her throat, he inhaled her scent deeply; he loved the smell of her after sex. It was intoxicating.

Usually, after making love, he felt like he could snuggle with Micki for hours… but not now. Not with all these clothes bunched up between them – her blouse half off, skirt gathered around her waist; his jeans and briefs around his knees. Nope, it just wasn't comfortable. He tried to get up.

"Where d'you think you're going?" Grinning fiendishly, Michaela clamped her legs around Gary's hips and tousled his sweat-dampened hair.

"Just getting rid of these clothes."

"Okay, as long as you come right back. Because I'm not finished with you yet."

After kicking off his jeans, Gary returned to the bed and helped her wriggle out of her blouse. When she rolled over so he could undo the zipper on her skirt, he gave her bottom a sharp little spank.

"Ow!" she cried out in surprise, rolling back to face him. "What was that for?"

"That," he replied, leaning to give Michaela a smoldering kiss, "was for looking so damn hot when you came home that I couldn't help myself." Grinning devilishly, he kissed her again and maneuvered her skirt over her head and off. "Don't do it again," he scolded with mock sternness.

Challenge danced in Michaela's eyes. "Oh yeah?" she retorted saucily. "And what if I do?"

Gary rolled his squirming wife over and gave her three quick spanks as she squealed, struggled and did her playful best to get away. "Then there's more where that came from," he warned, lying beside her again and pulling her into his arms. "Impertinent wench!"

Micki snuggled against him, resting her head against his chest. Relaxing in Gary's embrace, she felt warm all over — especially her bottom, which kind of stung, actually… in a sexy sort of way.

"Gee," she mused, rubbing at her smarting behind. "If this is what I get for something that innocent, I wonder what you'd do to me if I came home pregnant." Craning her neck, she turned to look at Gary.

When she saw the look of recognition in his eyes, she couldn't repress the joy that bubbled up within her. Michaela turned in his arms so they lay face to face, and let out a chirp of delight.

Speechless with excitement, he gave her an exuberant kiss and hugged her close. When he found his words again, he asked, "When did you find out?"

"This afternoon. They did a test." She held her thumb and forefinger a fraction of an inch apart. "I'm about this pregnant. I was a couple weeks late, but I thought it was just, you know, stress about the start of the trial." A puckish smile crinkled her whole face. "I'm so glad it wasn't just stress!"

Gary framed her face in his hands. His kiss was warm, tender. "Same here." He kissed her again. "This is the best news I've had in ages. Including the news this morning." Slipping one hand behind her head, he drew her close and kissed her again.

Michaela's lips parted beneath the slight pressure of his. She melted against him, delighting in his touch as he stroked her cheek with the fingers of his other hand.

They lay together, kissing, loving and reveling in their shared secret, until footsteps pounding up the stairs told them the kids were back from Grandma's.

Gary nudged his wife, who'd begun drowsing in his arms. "Troops are home."

"Guess we'd better get out there, then, huh?" Michaela stretched, then curled up again. "Mmm… you're comfy. I could just stay here all night…" She rested her head against his arm.

"Oh, no you don't, lady. You have to take a shower – we both do – and then we're going out to celebrate." Reaching over, he pretended he was about to give her another swat to get her moving.

Michaela looked at him with feigned indignance. "You wouldn't dare hit a pregnant lady!"

Gary grinned. "Probably not, but don't push your luck" – he winked – "and don't tempt me."

Chapter 29

(May 3 – Saturday)

For the first time in weeks, Michaela didn't have to hide the newspaper.

"Cleared!" "Exonerated! Sheldon Innocent," the morning headlines proclaimed. And "Intern Fabricates Story."

Micki smiled. *Innocent.* What a relief. She'd known it all along… and now the public knew it, too.

When Gary came downstairs, he smiled at seeing the folded newspaper lying by his place at the table. Opening it, he scanned the headlines, then went to greet Michaela, at the stove, preparing breakfast.

"Nice to be able to read the paper again, huh?" she asked, turning to give him a kiss.

"Sure is." He caressed her cheek, leaned to kiss her, then wrapped his arms around her. "Even nicer to see you not looking worried."

While Gary and Michaela waited for the kids to come downstairs, they enjoyed large mugs of coffee from rocking chairs on the back porch.

"What are your plans for the day?" Gary asked, reaching for his wife's hand.

She loved how their hands fit so nicely together. "I have to take Mandy to CCD class, then go grocery shopping. After that, laundry and tidying up the living room. Why? What're you up to?"

"I was thinking we drop the kids at my mom's, go grocery shopping together – like old times… and enjoy some quiet time."

"Does it have to be quiet?" Micki's slow wink and the brush of her thumb against his told him she approved of his plan. "And if we ask nicely, I bet she'd be open to keeping them for a sleepover."

Father Dave phoned late that morning to inform Gary he was being reinstated as the parish's first-grade CCD teacher.

"That is, if you still want to," he added.

"Of course I still want to," Gary replied. "Why wouldn't I?"

The priest hedged. "After the way we removed you, I wasn't sure you'd want to come back."

The memory of his abrupt and degrading ouster still stung. He shoved it aside. "Father, if there's one thing this whole experience has taught me, it's humility. This is *so* not about me. It's all about the kids. Of course I want to come back. How soon can I start?"

"I'd like to get an announcement in the parish bulletin first. Is the seventeenth soon enough?"

(9:37 a.m., May 19 – Monday)

As Gary entered the radio station, Brenda rushed over to hug him. "Gary! Welcome home. It's so good to have you back!"

"Thanks, Bren. I'm glad to be home."

Returning to her desk, she handed Gary his phone messages. "Pete and Tom want to see you. I think they've got paperwork for you to sign."

"There's always paperwork. I'll go see 'em now. Thanks." He started down the hall toward Pete's office.

"Uh, no… Gary" – Brenda pointed the other way – "they're in the conference room."

He gave the receptionist a perplexed look. A strange flutter began in his insides. "Must be a hell of a lot of paperwork." He headed back in the other direction.

The door was shut. Gary gave it a cautious tap.

"Come in," came from inside. Pete's voice.

When he opened the door, Gary saw the program director and the operations manager seated at the near end of the conference table.

"You wanted to see me?" The fluttering intensified, accompanied by slight nausea.

"Yes, Gary. C'mon in." Tom motioned him into the room.

Aware of movement at the far end of the room, Gary looked around and saw practically the entire staff watching him.

"Welcome back!" A surge of coworkers surrounded him, all smiling and offering hugs, high fives and pats on the back.

Gary fought back a swell of emotion. "Aww, you guys! You're the best. And here I thought I was just going to be filling out a ton of paperwork."

"We don't want to disappoint you, Gar'," Tom said, "so we've got plenty of that." He patted a stack of papers on the conference table. "But it'll keep. For now, let's celebrate!"

One of the account execs opened a bottle of champagne and poured it into plastic cups. When he handed one to the guest of honor, Gary shook his head.

"Thanks, Tim, but my drinking days are over."

"Aw, go on," the sales guy urged. "One won't hurt."

Gary put up a hand. "One *would* hurt. I'm three months and a day sober. And I've come too far to go back to those days. So, thanks, but no."

"Proud of you, bro," Marc murmured.

Tim blanched. "Sorry. I didn't know. That's cool. Good for you, Gary." He offered the bubbly to the next-nearest person, who happened to be Marc.

"Thanks, but like this guy" – he clapped a hand on Gary's shoulder – "I don't drink anymore either. I'm closing in on nineteen years sober." Gary heard the self-assurance in his brother-in-law's voice. "But don't let us stop you from raising a glass. Have at it."

Setting the unclaimed champagne on the table, Tim initiated a round of applause for his colleagues. "Excellent! Three months, and nineteen years. Good for you, guys – that's fantastic!"

Amid the applause, Gary slid an arm around Marc. "That wasn't so hard, was it?"

Marc's relieved expression gave Gary his answer.

Staff floated in and out as breaks and job responsibilities dictated. Ken Coffey and Barb Dwyer had their morning show to finish, but when they returned just after ten, Pete rounded up the rest of the staff for an announcement.

He draped an arm around his returning afternoon-drive announcer. "On behalf of the entire Z97-3 family, let me say we're thrilled to have you back, Spike! And we know how protective you are of the music library, but while you were gone, we took it upon ourselves to yank a few things, because we all decided they were kind of inappropriate, given the circumstances. But now you're home again, you can have them back. And, because we're not above a little bad taste around here – hell, we're not above a *lot* of bad taste – your first task is to go through these songs and decide which ones you want to put back into rotation."

Gary looked perplexed… then worried. As he looked through the pile of old 45-rpm singles his boss handed him, he began to chuckle. They hadn't used 45s in years.

"So… what are they?" someone asked as quiet snickers circulated the room. Clearly, curation of the stack of vinyl had been a group effort.

After he read off their titles, Gary flipped each record, Frisbee-style, around the room toward his coworkers. "Gary Puckett, 'Young Girl.' Mac Davis, 'Baby, Don't Get Hooked On Me' – you guys are terrible! Chuck Berry, 'Sweet Little Sixteen'; Ringo Starr, 'You're Sixteen'; KISS, 'Christine Sixteen'; Dr. Hook, 'Only Sixteen.' I'm beginning to sense a theme here. Jethro Tull, 'Aqualung.' "

Gary's hand flew to his mouth. He laughed so hard he had trouble catching his breath. He wiped away tears before going on.

"Donny Osmond, 'Go Away, Little Girl.' Billy Idol, 'Cradle of Love.' Dolly Parton, 'Jolene' " – shuddering, Gary snapped this one in half, then in fourths, and tossed the bits into the trash – "Billy Joel, 'Only the Good Die Young.' Neil Diamond, 'Girl, You'll Be a Woman Soon.' "

Another burst of laughter interrupted Gary's recitation of song titles.

"Nick Gilder, 'Hot Child in the City.' Marcy Playground, 'Sex & Candy.' Oh geez, you guys are goin' straight to hell. Stray Cats, 'Sexy & Seventeen.' Benny Mardones, 'Into the Night.' Police, 'Don't Stand So Close To Me.' Hall and Oates, 'Family Man' – and last but certainly not least, Stevie Nicks, 'Edge of Seventeen.' You guys are awful!"

Toward the end of the three-o'clock news, Gary settled at the control board and donned his headphones. He took a deep breath, adjusted the microphone on its boom arm and flipped the mic switch.

"You're up to date, I'm Lauren Fisher with Z97-3 News, and I've waited six long months to say this: Welcome home, Gary Sheldon. It's great to see you back behind the mic."

He slid the volume control up midway. "Thanks, Lauren, for the warm welcome. It is *fantastic* to be back. Five minutes past three, Z97-3. I'm Gary Sheldon and – oh, *man*, it's great to be back! I appreciate your joining me today. I gotta thank Rob Tyler and Marc Lindsay for keepin' my chair warm." He pressed the remote-start button for his upper-left CD player and adjusted the volume so the music came up beneath his voice. "And thank you for stickin' with me, and for all the calls and cards and letters during my absence. Much appreciated… more than you could possibly know. Now, I wouldn't normally do this, because, frankly, it's called 'blowing format' and it's really frowned upon. Under ordinary circumstances, I could get in a whole heap of trouble for it… but I think they'll let it slide today. Because I just had to do it. Here's the first track from Aerosmith's *Rocks* LP, released in seventy-seven. And as they're about to tell you…"

Just on cue, Gary flipped the mic button off and punched the air as Steven Tyler screeched, "I'm baaaack! I'm back in the saddle again…"

Exhausted after his first day back at work, Gary declined the supper Micki had prepared. Instead, he ate a bowl of cereal and went right to bed. Asleep before eight thirty, he didn't wake up 'til almost seven the following morning.

Gary's sessions with Dr. Benson and resumption of a regular routine eased his transition back into "real life." His sleep patterns normalized and eventually he settled into a schedule that included a return to running three days a week, an hour of daily research for his syndicated shows and full days of work at the radio station… dinner, then homework, play time and prayers with the kids before bedtime stories… followed by some treasured private time with Michaela.

Toward the end of her first trimester, the rush of pregnancy hormones gave Micki a voracious sexual appetite. Occasionally she'd haul Gary away to the bedroom the instant he came home from work, and be eager for more at bedtime.

One such night, momentarily sated, Michaela stroked the arm Gary draped around her. "I had an ultrasound today," she informed him drowsily.

"Oh yeah? How'd that go?"

"Fine." She snuggled closer. "Say, Gar', what d'you think about the name Christopher James?"

He nudged aside Micki's hair and nuzzled her throat. "I like it." Suddenly Gary recalled God's promise from his poker dream at Foxbridge: *Honor Me with faithfulness and I will bless you twofold.* He sat up. Turning on the bedside lamp, he saw Michaela gazing at him expectantly. "You're having twins."

Her excitement yielded to bewilderment. She thumped a fist against his chest. "How do you *know* these things? How do you *always know*? First you knew I was having a girl before

I ever said I was pregnant with Amanda – and now you know we're having twins. Do you have Dr. Quill's office bugged or something?"

Pulling his flummoxed wife close, Gary kissed her forehead. "Nothing like that. Just a dream."

"It was a dream last time, too, as I recall. Those are some pretty dead-on prophetic dreams, pal!"

He shrugged. "I can't help it if I've got connections."

As he winked at Michaela, her smile decayed.

He slid one hand over his wife's barely protruding belly. "What's the matter?"

"I'm a little worried," she admitted. "Two babies at once. We're gonna have our hands full."

He kissed her. "We've faced tougher situations. I've got a feeling everything's going to turn out fine."

"You've said that before," Michaela reminded him.

"And was I wrong?"

From within his embrace, she shook her head. "No."

Gary stroked her hair. "Then will you quit worrying and trust me?"